"Where the hell are you?"

He knew he sounded pathetic. She probably wouldn't call back. "I gave you the damn phone and you never answer."

She did it on purpose. To torture him. She hadn't wanted him here tonight and this was payback.

But he'd find her. He always did. *All part of the game.*

He drank down the Vox and clawed at the bow tie choking him. He wondered what good might come out of Daniel bringing that woman here. Nothing good.

But suddenly he smiled, shoving the bow tie in his pocket, mulling it over. Then again...

For the last twelve years they'd all been clocking time, waiting for this moment. Finally, finally, the waiting was over.

"Tick tock," he said. "Time's up."

"A terrific writer who knows how to keep the reader turning the pages."
—Jayne Ann Krentz

Shattered

OLGA BICOS

MIRA® BOOKS

*MIRA is a registered trademark of Harlequin Enterprises Limited,
used under licence.*

*First published in Great Britain 2004 by
MIRA Books, Eton House, 18-24 Paradise Road,
Richmond, Surrey, TW9 1SR*

© Olga Gonzalez-Bicos 2003

ISBN 1 55166 732 0

58-0304

*Printed and bound in Spain
by Litografia Rosés S.A., Barcelona*

For Andrew, Leila and Jonathan,
my reasons for everything.

And for my mother and father,
whose continued faith is always a revelation.

ACKNOWLEDGMENTS

I am incredibly thankful to my three fairy godmothers at MIRA Books, Dianne Moggy, Amy Moore-Benson and Martha Keenan, for all their faith and hard work on my behalf. In particular, I would like to thank Martha, my editor, for making this book possible.

Every once in a while, an author gets lucky. My agent, Dominick Abel, is a big part of any luck that comes my way. Thank you, Dominick, for making it all seem so effortless. We high-strung folk appreciate the calm.

I could never have brought *Shattered* to life without the expertise of Ciji Ware and Lisa Sawyer. Thanks, guys, for taking all my calls and e-mails. The mistakes, of course, are all mine.

Inspiration comes from many sources; here are a few of mine. My plot group—Meryl Sawyer, Lou Kaku, Jill Marie Landis, Lori Herter and Suzanne Forster. You all keep me going. My muses—Jill Hunter and Barbara Benedict. I couldn't do this career without you. I wouldn't even want to try. To the chief operating officer at Club Bicos, Lu Campos, thanks for keeping our heads above water. And to the ladies who opened the door, Debbie Macomber and Stella Cameron, I am eternally grateful!

Finally, I want to thank my guides to the vine, John Hustlebee of Thorton Winery, Elizabeth Campbell of Callaway Coastal Winery and Mike Calabro of Wilson Creek, and acknowledge the beautiful book, *Sparkling Harvest: the Seasons of the Vine*, by Jamie and Jack Davies of Shramsberg Vineyards, that brought Napa Valley to my doorstep and gave insights into one family's experience introducing sparkling wines to California. But most of all, I am grateful to Don Frangiapani of Churon Winery, winemaker extraordinaire, who inspired each and every scene about his craft.

_____ Prologue _____

"Did you kill her?"

The voice from the tape recorder crackled and popped in the overheated room, the words almost lost in static. Two men and a woman sat bellied up to a table long enough to crowd the cracker-box space. The youngest, a lanky nineteen-year-old seated at the corner—black hair, shocking blue eyes—studied the Rorschach test of coffee stains and cigarette burns as he listened, the tips of his fingers reading the tabletop like Braille.

"No, of course not." On the table, the recorded voice sounded a galaxy away. "Jesus. I can't believe this is happening." The taped voice dropped an octave. "I can't believe she's gone."

"But it's your fault, right? That she's dead?"

"Yeah...maybe."

The woman, a homicide inspector with salt-and-pepper hair and a young face, punched off the tape. Last night at the hospital, struggling with shock, the suspect couldn't stop talking, his words coming just shy of a confession. Now, with counsel at his side, mum was the word.

Just goes to show what a little legal advice could do for a guy. They had zero on the kid, and even the wet-behind-the-ears attorney sitting next to him could pass along that bit of good cheer.

Sergeant Amy Garten shuffled the papers in front of her, wondering how hard to push. "Things happen, Ryan. We can lose control of a situation. It's not what we mean or want to happen." She gave a sympathetic lift of her shoulders. "If we could take it back, just press Rewind... But a man steps up. Takes responsibility."

"As in confession is good for the soul?" The look the kid gave her wasn't exactly cocky, but he wasn't scared anymore, either.

The attorney placed a hand on his arm. "Do you want to get to the point, Sergeant?"

"I thought that was obvious." God, she hated defense attorneys. "A woman is dead."

"My client has been more than cooperative. There is absolutely no evidence that his—" the attorney stumbled over the words, a verbal hit-and-run "—fiancée's death was anything other than a tragic accident." The guy sounded fresh out of law school, all passion and no finesse. "Do you have any idea how difficult this is for Ryan?"

"And he's being a peach, coming in, answering questions. Really."

The kid said he'd been tailing the girl's Mercedes in his convertible when the victim lost control and plunged to her death. He'd called 911.

He admitted they'd been drinking. With a little prompting, it came out they'd had a fight. They'd ended up in separate cars, him chasing her. But not to hurt her. No way.

The problem was, she'd died at the hospital. Suddenly, he gets vague about the details of their argument. Intelligent minds might think he had something to hide.

On tape, he'd practically admitted he'd wanted the girl dead, he'd been in such a rage.

Amy saw it all the time. Young men of privilege getting away with just about anything. The family turned a blind eye to the bad seed they'd spawned until the situation flared like kudzu. Drugs, date rape—even murder. Only, by the time it all went bad, the clan was used to circling the wagons, making excuses about how Johnny really wasn't such a bad kid. He deserved a fair shake—and the best lawyers money could buy.

Which is where the Cutty case fell off that well-beaten path…no helpful Mommy and Daddy. Strangely, the opposite. Just when Amy thought there was no way she was getting her hands on San Francisco royalty, the suspect's own father gives a jingle to point the finger at his flesh and blood. *There were problems… I overheard a fight.* Earlier that morning, there'd been an anonymous phone call to the police, a husky woman's voice saying, "Ryan ran her off the road. He killed her."

The attorney who showed up this morning didn't seem much older than his client, but more like some friend's older brother doing a favor. And certainly nowhere near what the Cutty money could pull in.

She glanced across the table at Ryan. Good looks and a pedigree. He could easily fit the bill of sinner or saint. *The kind of man who just might get away with murder…*

Only, she wasn't so sure.

Which almost made the point. These guys, the Kennedy clones, they could fool you.

"That's your voice on the tape, Ryan, admitting that last night you thought this was all your fault." Dead debutantes, suspicious fathers, anonymous tips. Despite pressure from the brass to wind things up—the autopsy results sure to confirm the victim's intoxicated state—Sergeant Garten thought a case like this was worth a little persistence. "Why don't we talk about that?"

"Forget it, Sergeant. Unless you're ready to arrest Ryan, I'm pulling the plug on this fishing expedition of yours." His attorney stood, ready to jet out before she could see him sweat. "I'm sure that, with proper perspective, you'll come to understand my client did nothing wrong."

But the kid took a moment to lean in close over the table. She could see he had something to say, that finally she'd triggered a reaction.

"Ryan," the attorney warned.

"You think I'm getting away with something," he told her, ignoring his attorney, zooming in with those too-blue eyes. There was a rough quality to his voice. Maybe emotion. "But I'll be paying for this the rest of my life."

"A guilty conscience can do that."

For the first time he smiled. But before he could say anything else, his attorney had him by the arm, giving a tug.

"If you have anything you want to add to your statement—" she slid her card across the desk "—you give me a call."

Oh, yeah, Amy Garten thought, watching Cutty leave the room. There was something there, something that made him almost sympathetic. A hardness that could hide the deepest sort of loss.

Just goes to show, Sergeant Garten told herself, shutting the case file that most likely would remain unsolved. Even a seasoned professional could be fooled.

GRAND DESIGN

1

Never jam something in to try and make it fit…finesse, not force. Holly Fairfield considered these words to live by.

Which made the next three hours an interesting proposition.

Armored in designer clothes, torture-me shoes and enough hairpins for satellite reception, her appearance tonight felt all veneer. She, the proverbial square peg, loomed over the round hole of the evening's society gala, waiting for the sledgehammer to drive her home. In the world of the bejeweled, the moneyed, the nipped and the tucked, Holly Fairfield didn't exactly blend.

But she was the guest of honor.

"Stop fidgeting. You're acting like a twelve-year-old."

"Easy for you to say, Mr. Tall, Dark and Self-confident," she told her brother, standing beside her in the foyer of Cutty House. The Beaux Arts building lay nestled near the pinnacle of San Francisco's Nob Hill and had already been christened by her brother as Holly's personal Moby Dick.

Harris preened. "I do look good in Armani."

"Everybody looks good in Armani. Just remember, you turn into a pumpkin at twelve. And don't spill on the tux."

Though she'd stick ten thousand needles in her eye before she'd admit it, her brother did have a certain panache. It startled people, how those same dark, masculine features could somehow transform into her own sweet looks. But Holly had come to see their resemblance as nothing more than a variation on a theme. In architecture, context was everything.

She caught herself tapping her finger against the crystal flute, a nervous woodpecker. She tried to remind herself that tonight was a high point and that high points came with a price, schmoozing being a very small one. For a moment, she actually missed Drew, wishing she could channel some of that radioactive ego that defined her ex-husband, ex-business partner and ex-traordinary pain in the butt. *That's the past, Holly. Forgive…*

Drew would never have hidden behind a Corinthian column where she stood planted like an anemic fern. He'd be working the money crowd, a game-show host of personality, ingratiating himself to all until he became the inevitable center of attention.

Of course, those same qualities had resulted in the crash and burn of their marriage three years ago when she'd walked in on him and the caterer at the opening of what was to be their first and final new building together. The bankruptcy of their architecture firm soon followed, a loss she felt even more deeply than the divorce. She'd always suspected that, romantically, Drew had the attention span of a Tic Tac.

Her brother trapped her fingers against the glass. "Stop thinking about Drew," Harris finished with his weird we're-not-twins-but-I-can-read-your-mind way. "You don't need him, Hol. Never did. Besides, you have me, right? And unlike Drew, you won't find me banging some Betty in the hall closet come dawn."

"You have no idea what I'm thinking, Spiderman," she said, taking a drink of champagne as she tried valiantly not to catch anyone's eyes. *I'm not here...I am invisible.*

"Tell you what. Let's practice one of those affirmation exercises you were talking about last week. Close your eyes and visualize The Druid back in Seattle, pondering how on earth he is going to get a piece of this job. But, oh darn—" he tsked softly "—those nasty divorce papers, all final-like," he said in a mock-Drew voice.

That made her smile, a silver lining to braving the crowd. "Maybe."

The Druid was her brother's nickname for Drew Manticore, the man who'd coaxed Holly, a rising star, to leave her berth at one of Seattle's top architecture firms where he'd been a partner. Together they were going to set the architecture world on fire. And they did for a while. Until it all went up in flames.

Drew Manticore—the man-lion-scorpion beast thing. Like heaven had flashed this neon marquee of warning. Maybe that's what happened when you broke the rules, she thought. Marrying her business partner might have been like breaking some law of physics. The mushroom cloud of divorce and bankruptcy was sure to ensue, in her case, devastating everything she'd worked for for the last ten years.

Only, tonight, she was all about breaking the rules. Even the shiny sacred ones she'd clung to through the disaster of divorce and financial ruin.

"I can't believe you're not just a little amped by all of this," her brother insisted.

"Do the words 'painfully shy' ring a bell?"

Harris gestured at the mingling beautiful people of

San Francisco. "Come on. They're all here for you, Princess Leia."

"Let me just toss back this champagne and throw the Waterford at the hearth. Give a big shout, *Opa!*"

"Damn straight," he said, taking her arm. "Come on. Let's get something to eat before the clock strikes and I turn into a pumpkin or a rat or something."

Cinderella was a little too close to the truth. This night of glitz and glamour came courtesy of a fairy godmother of sorts. And she, once dubbed Seattle's designer to the dotcom world, was infinitely more comfortable behind a drafting table. Tonight, she felt out of her league. The last time she'd drunk champagne and eaten caviar...well, that was the point. What last time?

Holly navigated through the sea of the opera set, tugging nervously at her sleeves. She had donned the black Donna Karan suit and paired it with Jimmy Choo heels because she'd heard some style magazine fashion czar declare that Jimmy Choo heels were practically a cliché, everyone wore them. Tonight, she wanted to be the cliché.

"Holly."

Hearing her name, she turned and smiled at the man who had, in just a few short months, changed her life. She'd come to think of Daniel East by all those corny titles: a prince among men; her knight in shining armor...

"The guy who saved your cookies from the fire makes an appearance." Harris didn't bother to lower his voice. "Has he hit on you yet?"

She gave him a look. "Lest you forget, my cookies and yours, Spiderman."

Daniel East was an intrinsically beautiful man, reminding Holly of a piece of art. Brown hair with blond highlights that didn't even pretend to be natural. Tall, with a quarterback's physique. Tonight, funky eyeglasses complemented his dark eyes. Like Cutty House, he was a work in progress. Whatever was new, edgy, impossible, Daniel East already had three pairs. His sense of style did nothing to diminish his masculinity, and he looked sleek in an indigo tuxedo that would have made Robert Downey Jr. proud.

"Don't be frightened, little one." Taking her arm, he guided her toward the crowd ahead. "It's time to come out and play. You don't mind, do you, Harris?"

She telegraphed a silent, *please, please, please!* But Harris wasn't up for the rescue, lifting his glass in salute as Daniel pressed a hand at the small of her back.

With a tight smile, she sallied forth as passersby paid homage. *Daniel, so wonderful to have Cutty House back...when do you think you'll open? Is this your secret weapon, then? She's delightful.*

Slipping into the main dining hall alongside Daniel, she held tight to her drink and her nerve as the sound of Blondie pulsed off the walls. Tables crowded the room, their pale tablecloths cloaked in bloodred rose petals and candles flickering from votive candleholders. Martinis in a rainbow of colors sprouted from the hands of young tight bodies wearing still tighter clothes.

But even in the gypsy's den of light, she found herself searching out the damage—missing floorboards that opened like a wound, the shadow of a medallion where a chandelier once hung. Cutty House was a treasure trove of work to be done.

As Daniel entertained, she remained the silent sentinel, knowing she'd hit the jackpot with this job. Certainly nothing in her résumé warranted Daniel's faith.

She'd had only a few published pieces, the latest one in *Architectural Digest*, for a Japanese restaurant in Seattle that had been critiqued by the local paper as "overblown modernism."

And then there was the write-up in *Fortune* magazine last fall, showcasing the unseen victims of the dotcom bomb. The article featured a rather soulful photograph of Holly sitting on moving boxes outside her defunct architectural office, several plans lying at her feet like the Dead Sea scrolls.

Just as the photographs of Enron employees had given a handful their fifteen minutes for all the wrong reasons, Holly had felt the glare of failure's first light. A few weeks later, Daniel, her own Wizard of Oz, had come knocking on her door.

"What do you think of the place?" Daniel asked.

She woke up, realizing an audience awaited her comments. She'd been hired to fix a botched remodel, fulfilling Daniel's dream of updating the family business. She glanced at the stripped molding, wondering what had been plundered there. The low ceiling—no doubt accommodating the more modern conveniences of heating ducts and air-conditioning—made the dining hall claustrophobic. The shape of the windows seemed all wrong.

Her only other renovation had involved revamping a warehouse into funky office space. Cutty House felt like Versailles in comparison, the task ahead exciting and just a bit daunting.

"She has nice bones," she offered.

Daniel laughed. "Bones? Well, the place needs a face-lift, all right. It's what Holly does," he said to his audience. "She makes things over. Like staring at a fresh piece of marble or a blank canvas, she sees the possibilities here."

Holly forced a smile. "I don't think you'll be disappointed," she said, forcing the obligatory bravado. Oh, she could get good at this.

"No," he said, turning to her. "I don't imagine I will be."

Daniel East had a way of looking at you. Suddenly, the crowd vanished as the white-hot spotlight of his interest centered on Holly. Not for the first time, she had to remind herself to breathe.

In the beginning, everything about Cutty House and Daniel had seemed too grand, mildly terrifying. Or perhaps, as Harris contended, failure had taken its toll. *You've lost your mojo, Hol.* But she told herself she couldn't allow dark doubts to interfere with the necessary brilliance she'd once found so effortless. It was time to wake up from the fog of the past, time to pull out all the stops.

And right now, with Daniel's faith to buoy her, Holly felt as if she could do just about anything....

"Excuse us," he said, taking her hand, his eyes never leaving hers. "Our patron saint, Vanessa, needs to meet you."

Holly followed, knowing full well that Daniel East and his five-star financing had earned her undying loyalty. Her creditors had been marching into the nearly deserted offices, carting away whatever wasn't nailed down like ants at a picnic when Daniel appeared, handing her a get-out-of-jail-free card. Whatever lay ahead, he would get her best.

Strangely enough, from the get-go Daniel had acted as if *Holly* had come to *his* rescue when she'd agreed to leave Seattle and update the San Francisco icon that, in its heyday, had drawn U.S. presidents and South American dictators alike. Daniel wanted to dust off the Nob Hill attraction's traditional format and transform it into the new place-to-be-seen. Renamed the East Side Café, the restaurant would feature an innovative grazing menu and a bar that could rival any celebrity trap, wooing a famed roster of guests to its dining room, art gallery and dance club.

For Holly, this chance was beyond a lifesaver tossed into the tsunami that had become her life. As if divorce and bankruptcy weren't enough to earn her a scarlet R.I.P. across her breast, Harris had shown up on her doorstep, canned from his corporate America job. For the first time in his life, her brother needed her, and Holly didn't plan on dropping the ball.

Entering one of the smaller dining parlors, she took in the subdued flock roosting in the relative quiet of a string quartet, the beat of the Cosmopolitan crowd contained in the larger hall behind them. Here, the occupants appeared adorned in the same old-fashioned wealth as Cutty House itself, the tuxes and elegant black gowns making Daniel look like some exotic bird come to pay a visit.

"Thanks for the tip on the clothes," she said, mentioning the boutique Daniel had recommended.

"The hair's great. But the suit is much too conservative. I'll have to talk to Sonia—I'm deeply disappointed. The shoes are divine." His smile took the sting out of his critique. "You need a makeover as much as this wretched old place."

"I think I've just been insulted."

He touched her hand. "Don't hide the flame under a bush, I always say."

She had to remind herself that he was a client. His charm, at times, was a little hard to resist. And tossed in with the whole saved-my-skin thing…hey, she was only human. Luckily, she'd already gone a round with the forbidden fruit of mixing business and pleasure. Once burned...

"There they are," Daniel said.

As the sea of glitterati parted, Daniel steered her toward one of the scariest women she had ever seen.

There was something not real about her skin, it was so smooth, looking like alabaster. Her black hair was styled into an elaborate French twist, making her appear even more ageless. Holly clocked her in at fifty, but she could have been twenty years older, preserved by expensive treatments and creams, or maybe a Dorian Gray portrait hanging on one of the gallery walls upstairs.

Holly knew immediately that this woman owned the place. No one else could carry off that air of possession.

At a gesture from Drew, the woman trained her gaze on Holly. Instantly, she felt like Snow White caught in the sights of the Evil Queen. *Bring me her heart....*

The moment passed with the woman's smile. She stepped forward, taking Holly's hand in both of hers.

"You must be the fabulous Holly Fairfield. Daniel speaks of nothing else. You've come to save our palace from ruin." She glanced at Daniel. "And make all of Daniel's dreams come true."

"Rescue us from this fucking nightmare, will you, darling?"

Both Daniel and the woman appeared struck dumb by the words coming from behind them. As Holly stared, nonplussed, a white-haired gentleman shouldered past the two. He took her hand in his and granted a lingering kiss.

"Now, be nice and give that back, Uncle Samuel," Daniel said, stepping between them to retrieve her hand from the man. "Holly, this is my uncle and aunt—my silent partners—Vanessa and Samuel Cutty."

The man retreated into the background just as clumsily as he'd taken center stage. His eyes glazed over as he focused inward and began humming to himself in an odd, distracted manner. Daniel again tried to gloss over the awkward moment by angling Holly to face Vanessa Cutty.

Holly half listened as Daniel waxed poetic about her curriculum vitae, fighting the urge to glance back at Samuel Cutty. *He's drunk.*

"Emma," Daniel called out, motioning someone toward them. "Join the gang. I want you to meet our heavenly Holly."

A beautiful woman, right off the pages of *Vogue,* eased in beside them. Strawberry-blond hair complemented green catlike eyes. She wore a sheath of a dress, backless and in a nude tone that left little to the imagination—entirely appropriate for someone who had the body of a goddess. What Holly thought was a beauty mark was, in fact, a pierced stud right above her full mouth. Interestingly enough, she seemed about as comfortable in the gown as Holly did in her Donna Karan. A fish out of water.

"Holly, this is Emma Wright. She's our most talented and fabulous chef."

Holly watched the woman's eyes glance around the room, her small hands fluttering at her side.

"Emma is the one who convinced me that a Boba bar by the gallery was all wrong. Too many cheaper versions around these days. But she's come up with the newest thing, a bar specializing in foods that are aphrodisiacs. I've learned all sorts of things from our Emma. Did you know kiwi is a natural vasodilator?

She's made up a beautiful hors d'oeuvre featuring the new gold one. What do they call them, Ems?''

"Zespri."

"That's right. We'll be all the rage thanks to Emma."

Emma Wright, who looked to be in her early twenties, didn't once acknowledge Daniel's homage. She appeared ready to jump out of her skin, a child playing dress-up in the sexy gown and strappy heels.

Sensing a kindred spirit, Holly stepped forward, her hand outstretched. "I think the marriage of décor and food is a must. I'd love to hear any ideas you might have about the kitchen and dining room."

The chef gave Holly a brutal stare. "Sorry. You'll have to do your own work."

Daniel laughed. "Don't mind Emma. She's a bit of a misanthrope, but she'll have them lined up around the block. Trust me."

"I have to get back. Help the caterers," Emma said, abruptly turning.

But she hadn't taken a step before she did an about-face. There was no mistaking the smile she gave Daniel, though Holly wasn't quite sure about her whispered words.

She thought she heard Emma say, "He's here."

A stillness fell over the group as Daniel stepped in front of Holly, his stance almost protective. Holly braced herself, unable to imagine what could set the easygoing Daniel on edge.

She peeked around his shoulder to see a tall man in his early thirties walking toward the group as if targeting them. The candlelight allowed only the merest sense of dark hair and dark eyes, but she didn't need the whispers that followed in his wake to set off an alarm. Despite the tiny smile of relief she'd seen on Emma's face, Daniel appeared far from pleased.

The man was dressed casually. Holly thought the button-down shirt, leather jacket and chinos made a point, but the nonchalance didn't quite reach his eyes. They appeared lit up from the inside, his expression too tense as he held out his hand to Daniel, who again shifted to stand in front of Holly.

The tableau that followed struck her as almost surreal. Everyone froze, suddenly carved out of ice. Only the man in the chinos had color or life. And Emma, holding on to her secret smile.

Vanessa moved first, stepping out as if to block the man's path. But Daniel intervened, steering her back in place.

"Ryan." For the first time, Daniel took the man's outstretched hand in a quick, almost hostile shake.

"Everyone can holster their guns. I only came by to wish you luck," Ryan said.

"That's a little difficult to believe, under the circumstances."

A wealth of emotion passed through the man's dark eyes. She could tell this wasn't easy for him.

"Think what you want, Dan. I came with a clear conscience."

"I'd like to believe that, Ryan. Really, I would."

Almost as if he were parting a curtain, Daniel stepped back, revealing for the first time Holly's presence. She felt distinctly out of place, a stranger among them. She had no idea what to expect.

So, of course, the last thing she expected happened.

The man named Ryan turned to her, his eyes drawn to her by the motion of Daniel moving aside. For an instant, his expression showed a startled recognition before a shadow fell across his face.

He stepped forward, forcing her to step back. Daniel interceded, once again taking her arm to guide her behind him.

Daniel whispered, ''Don't.''

Okay. She wasn't Miss America, but she wasn't one of America's Most Wanted, either. Nothing about her had ever, or should ever, produce the emotion she had seen on the man's face. Or the quiet that fell over the group.

She felt suddenly out of the loop, not in on some joke. She wanted to tap Daniel on the back, ask with a smile, ''Okay. I'll bite. What gives?''

Or maybe she should slide over to Emma, the one person she felt sure would tell her the truth. Because from the reaction of those around her, Holly was certain the news wasn't good.

The man never took his eyes off her.

''What the hell are you doing?''

His words came out hushed. She couldn't decide if he was speaking to her or Daniel.

In the end, it didn't matter. The question was clearly rhetorical. He wasn't waiting for an answer in any case.

Watching him walk away, she felt all out of breath, as if she'd just run a 10K race. Maybe it was the champagne—or more likely fear. Up until tonight, she'd held her head high, telling herself she could handle the Cutty project, no matter what. But somehow the man who had just left, the man they'd called Ryan, had shaken that faith.

''Don't look so worried. He's just the black sheep come to pay a visit,'' Daniel whispered in her ear. ''Family business. It doesn't concern you.''

So why had the man been staring at only her?

''Here's Harris,'' Daniel said, turning her toward

her approaching brother. Trust Spiderman to come to the rescue…two minutes too late, of course.

But when she turned to say as much to Daniel, liking her attempt at levity, she found him gone.

Daniel was, at that moment, in a heated discussion with Vanessa Cutty. Samuel Cutty waited beside Emma, who appeared no longer in a rush to fend for her caterers.

"Hey, Cinderella," Harris told her, sensing all was not well. "Do I hear the stroke of midnight?"

"I'm not sure." But there was a distinct chill in the air.

"Should I call a cab?" he asked.

"No," she said.

She'd turned tail and run once before, after the fiasco with Drew. She'd let him destroy their business while she recovered from her broken heart. But in the last year she'd found reserves she'd never before tapped.

And courage. She wasn't about to let a complete stranger take that away.

"You go ahead," she told Harris. "This isn't exactly your scene." She scanned the crowd, seeing that, indeed, the mysterious Ryan had exited stage left.

But Harris turned her around to look at him, his hands on her shoulders. "Are you sure?"

The way he spoke, he wasn't talking about just making an early night of it. He was talking about the whole deal. Her coming here, taking on this Goliath project.

A long time ago, Harris alone had slain the dragons for them. It was Harris who had taken over for Dad, putting Holly through school, later paying off Dad's medical bills. She'd never had to worry about a thing. *Just get good grades and a good job, Hol.* Her big brother had taken care of the rest. Neither of them was quite used to their reversed roles.

"Hey," she said with her newfound bravado, "read my mind."

She looked up into eyes the same dark brown as her own.

"Okay," he said. "But try to have some fun. And if you need me…"

"I know. That's why God created cell phones."

"Absolutely."

But he wasn't smiling. And she could feel his eyes on her as she made her way across the room.

With guardian Harris on the job, she knew she should feel some sense of relief. Only, the last five minutes made everything teeter-totter in her head. She could hear that ugly little voice of fear telling her, *You failed in the past. You could fail again.* And renovating what amounted to a local monument…

"Stop it," she said out loud.

She picked up her second glass of champagne of the night from a passing waiter and drank, too fast. She wasn't much for drinking, but she thought tonight might call for a toast or two.

Halfway through the glass, she thought she'd hit the right pitch, not woozy, but certainly loose. She overheard some gossip about an insanely expensive interior decorator for yachts and smiled. The rich were different.

It was a strange new world she'd entered, inhabited by people with multiple homes and great big boats, men and women for whom new experiences were to die for. An aphrodisiac bar?

Just visiting, thank you.

With Daniel still missing in action, she headed down the hall to explore the other rooms. She and

Harris had barely unpacked their bags before Daniel
had insisted on her "coming out" party. She hadn't
had a chance to go over Cutty House, though she'd
seen the as-built plans drafted by the previous architect. Tomorrow, with Harris at the other end of a tape
measure, she planned to begin her own measurements.

"Eenie, meenie, minie, moe," she said, coming to
a crossroads, choosing right.

As the music receded, she reached the end of the
carpeted runner. She bent down to look at what appeared to be exotic colored marble.

"So that's what's hiding here," she said, wondering
if the foyer were covered with the same marble. There
was a lot of damage, which accounted for the carpet.
It would cost a small fortune to restore the treasure of
it.

Not that it would ever happen. Daniel had a different vision for Cutty House. *We need to drag ourselves
into the new millennium.* He'd talked about "shock
value," about how important it was in this world to
create a scandal if you wanted to gather a crowd.

Dusting off her hands, Holly stared ahead to a velvet rope strung across the hallway, obviously to keep
party-goers at bay.

"Which doesn't include me."

She told herself to be careful. The house was old;
it might not be safe beyond the rope. And then there
were the Jimmy Choos to consider. But after a couple
of steps in the heels, she thought she heard something.

A man calling her name? Just ahead.

She stepped closer, climbing over the rope, heading
toward the arched doorway.

"Hello?"

She heard it again. Definitely a man's voice calling
out a name. But not hers.

Nina?

* * *

He needed a drink.

Samuel Cutty handed his glass to the waiter. When the damn fool tried to foist champagne on him, he nearly growled, ''Martini, Vox. Dirty, with two olives,'' sending the boy on his way for a proper drink.

He watched quietly as Daniel plied Vanessa with excuses. It was a risky business, what his nephew was doing. He wouldn't have believed it of Daniel. The boy had always wanted things easy and fast.

Don't we all.

But the architect... What had he called her? Holly? Samuel stared out over the crowd, his eyes focusing on some distant spot. From now on, nothing would be easy with that one around. Certainly not for Ryan.

Samuel hadn't looked at his son's face. He hadn't dared.

Grabbing the glass from the waiter, he pushed past, leaving Vanessa in Daniel's very capable hands. He stumbled on the carpet where it wasn't taped down. The place was falling apart. God, he hated coming here.

Sometimes he'd have these dreams. The phantoms of the past would find him and chase him around the labyrinth halls of Cutty House. He'd wake up covered in sweat, scared that somehow he'd died and now must pay for his crimes in the next world.

Maybe he'd died already. Maybe he was just a ghost.

''Nina,'' he whispered to those same moldering walls.

He needed air, before he passed out. He headed for the courtyard. Dammit, he couldn't breathe.

Outside, the cold mist seemed too thick. He told himself nobody this drunk could have a heart attack.

He grabbed his cell phone, managed on the second try to get the number right.

She didn't pick up.

"Where the hell are you?" He knew he sounded pathetic. She probably wouldn't call back. "I gave you the damn phone and you never answer."

She did it on purpose. To torture him. She hadn't wanted him here tonight and this was payback.

But he'd find her. He always did. *All part of the game.*

He drank down the Vox and clawed at the bow tie choking him. He wondered what might come of Daniel bringing that woman here. Nothing good.

But suddenly he smiled, shoving the bow tie in his pocket, mulling it over. Then again…

For the last twelve years they'd all been clocking time, waiting impatiently for this moment. Finally, finally, the waiting was over.

"Tick tock," he said. "Time's up."

2

"Anybody here?"

She'd entered a cave of a room, barrel-vaulted, receding into darkness—*the ballroom, then*—feeling half foolish as she listened to her words bounce off the walls. She could have sworn the man's voice had come from somewhere inside.

"Olly olly oxen free." But she only whispered, trying to rid the shadows of their *Scream III* peek-through-your-fingers vibes.

She remembered the room from the plans. This was the center of Cutty House, its heart. Here, there was nothing ripped or torn out, no signs of the blundered renovation at all. Just the ravages of age and the faint smell of mold.

City lights filtered through windows, bleeding in to merge with the fingers of light from the hall behind her. Pillars and Versailles-like mirrors surrounded a dance floor the size and shape of a small roller rink. Straight boards of light and dark wood ran the length of the floor, while elegant moldings decorated the walls and ceiling like a wedding cake. She imagined gas lights glittering from chandeliers, could almost hear the illegal gambling and drinking of Prohibition.

"I've fallen down the rabbit hole."

Into another place and time.

There was a presence here, the spirit of Cutty

House. The warehouse renovation had been merely a functional space for which she'd planned a new purpose. Progress. But this room had a life of its own.

From the outset, Daniel East had made his intentions clear. Gut the ballroom, transform the space into a dance club. *Make the past disappear, Holly.* Every room had to be updated. He wanted Holly to take a house in desperate need of repair and reconstruction of lost architectural elements and just hang a disco ball. That simple.

"Oh, Holly," she asked out loud, allowing the disappointment to settle in. "What have you gotten yourself into?"

"A little late to be asking that question," came the reply.

She managed not to scream, but she did perform a rather nice clutch of her chest accompanied by a B-movie gasp. Turning toward the voice, she watched a man emerge from the music shell, an alcove built into the wall to her left.

Ryan stepped into the weak light pooling front and center. The shadows seemed to cast him in the role of villain. She tried to convince herself the effect was so much smoke and mirrors, fears brought on by a tense night of new beginnings. Before her stood a perfectly ordinary man, really—if someone with heart-stopping good looks could be ordinary. No need to make a scene. The party crowd was just down the hall; help was within easy reach.

Don't bolt—don't be silly.

Then again, she remembered a book she'd read about women and their fears, and how you weren't suppose to rationalize a dangerous situation. You were suppose to listen to that gut feeling telling you to run for your life.

"Hi," she said instead.

He didn't answer, but he did laugh, as if it was just too much, that tiny salute in the face of his looming presence. Visually, he was the opposite of Daniel's manicured good looks. Tall, with dark hair cut short and combed in an absentminded manner, wearing clothes that spoke of nothing but comfort. And he needed a shave.

She could see the true color of his eyes now, dark blue made a near black by his dilated pupils.

"You were the one calling, weren't you?" she asked. "I heard you say Nina or Tina or something?"

He circled closer. She tried not to be obvious as she inched back toward the exit.

"We weren't exactly introduced. My name's Holly. Holly Fairfield." She had a nervous habit of filling in the silence. *Stop it. Stop now.* "I mean, maybe you have a problem with my getting this job?" she guessed, trying to slap a label on his aggressive advance.

"Were you the architect here before?" she asked, thinking of the foul-up with the remodel. "You know, maybe we could work something out— No," she said, stopping herself. She was always trying to appease. She wasn't going to do that now, even in this dark room, a little frightened and wondering what he wanted.

Shoulders back, she told him, "I can't offer you a job because, quite frankly, I think what you've done…well, I shouldn't be so quick to judge. I don't know the whole situation and Daniel can be very adamant—"

"Be quiet," he said. "I want to look at you."

Okay. That was different.

"That's why they brought you here, isn't it?" he

continued, speaking in an angry hush that still managed to fill the room. "For me to look? Then, let me. Just be very quiet. You ruin the effect when you talk."

It was the most extraordinary thing anyone had ever said to her…and garnered the desired effect. She couldn't find the breath to speak.

Maybe that's what happened to those poor people on the six-o'clock news, she thought. Maybe it wasn't like in the movies, where you could scream.

He stopped inches from her, so close they could have shared a dance. She told herself she was being stubborn, holding her ground, even when she thought he might just reach out and touch her…which would have made her jump right out of her skin. But he didn't, retreating instead with a strange sort of smile.

"Very nice," he said, now studying her from the dark. "Very well done."

Somewhere in the distance, a clock struck midnight.

Holly spun toward the sound, wound too tight by the events of the night. When she turned back, the man named Ryan was gone.

Letting out the breath she'd been holding, she whispered the only word that seemed to express it all.

"Wow."

Emma stared at the checkerboard of hors d'oeuvres, each a work of art, made with precious ingredients like Tobiko caviar and white truffle oil. Daniel had insisted on classical French. Empty Cristal bottles lined the counter like good soldiers.

It should all feel better than this.

She looked around at the new defunct kitchen, watching the staff of five she and Beth had hired pack up. Nothing in the cavernous kitchen functioned since the remodel, but ice chests and sterno had done the job.

She knew Daniel would be pleased. And Ryan showing up like that had been the crowning touch.

So why did she feel so empty?

"Tada!" Beth came up behind her, her hands resting on Emma's shoulders as she whispered, "As always, the dream team of culinary magic comes through with the impossible."

"We did good." Emma managed a smile as she gave her partner a high five.

Beth had dressed for the occasion, adding Day-Glo pink evening gloves in vinyl and combat boots to her 1950s waitress outfit. She'd tied her improbable orange hair in pigtails, and with her pierced eyebrow and black lipstick, she looked like the punk version of Pippi Longstocking. But of the two, Emma knew it was she who felt silly in her gown and heels.

"I think that does it for me." Beth gave Emma a quick hug. "Catch you at home?"

"Yeah. And thanks," she told her catering partner. "You were awesome."

Beth wrinkled her nose. "I should have sabotaged the whole deal. Then he wouldn't have given you the job and I'd still have you."

"You don't need me. And if you do, I'm here."

Beth managed a look of forgiveness. "Yeah, I know. It's cool. I want this for you, Emma. It's a great gig. Hey, if I thought Daniel would give me a shot, I might just elbow you aside...."

"Liar."

"You never know."

They shared a moment, each knowing what the other was thinking, both filled with regret. Beth blew a kiss, and Emma watched her ex-partner and roommate shepherd out the troops. She and Beth had met at culinary school during the time in her life Emma liked to call "The Great Escape." In those days, everything had seemed possible—leaving Cutty House, starting her own business.

She sighed, wondering why tonight felt like a death rather than a beginning.

She heard the pop of a champagne bottle, turned in time to see Daniel step inside the now abandoned kitchen. Her heart started to beat faster.

He poured the Cristal, extravagant as he allowed the expensive champagne to bubble over, spilling everywhere. Daniel needed extreme. He liked a good show.

He forced a sip of the Cristal to her lips. "You embody perfection in that dress, my love."

She turned her face away from the glass, not liking the alcohol. "I feel like an idiot."

He took a drink and laughed. "Now see? I said you were a bad judge."

"I've been permanently crippled by these heels." She tried to catch her breath as he lifted her onto the old countertop. He settled between her opened legs, inching the hem of the gown to her knees.

"I hope you're pleased by my great sacrifice," she told him.

"Always." He bent down and stroked her bare calf, making her shiver. "Heels make a woman's legs look beautiful."

He slipped the silly shoes off her feet, letting them drop to the floor. She wrapped her legs around him, pulling him to her.

He pushed the dress slowly up her thighs to her hips. "But there was one thing I would have liked even better," he whispered into her ear.

"Okay," she said, bracing herself. With Daniel, there was always a catch.

He bit down on her earlobe. "You have to learn to be nice."

"I don't want to be nice. I don't like her."

"You'll learn to like her." And then more seriously, "For me."

She wanted to protest. Hadn't she done enough? Things she wasn't proud of? And now, she was even leaving Beth in a lurch. She almost asked him then and there why it was never enough?

But she knew it was just the dumb party and not Daniel that had her so wound up. *Too many weird memories.* Her anger surprised her. It seemed a betrayal of everything they'd been through.

"I'm just scared," she told him, whispering the truth.

That she'd lose him. And she could, now that the other woman was here.

He cupped her face in his hands, almost hurting her, his eyes watching her reaction.

"What could you be scared of, hmm?"

"I'm scared of her. For us—"

He covered her mouth with his, kissing her as he pulled the gown off her shoulders. She helped him undress her, shimmying out of her underwear, unzipping his pants even as she listened to the party-goers just outside the doors. Sometimes she wondered why she always rushed.

He looked deep into her eyes, keeping them connected. "Are you still worried?"

She couldn't close her eyes, just stared into his. "I love you, Daniel."

He dug his fingers into her thighs hard enough to leave marks. "I asked if you're still worried?"

She could see she'd made him angry. He wanted her to be nice to Holly Fairfield.

Do it, she told herself, as angry as Daniel now. *It's just a stupid game.*

Only, it wasn't. It was her life. A life she'd already screwed up.

Sometimes she couldn't say what scared her most. That Daniel would leave her…or that he wouldn't.

But Daniel had always been stronger than her, his need somehow more necessary.

"Whatever you want, Daniel."

Always.

3

Holly didn't consider herself prone to high drama. She tended to be too sensible, a pragmatist at heart. That's why she loved architecture's marriage of form and function.

Even her divorce had gone smoothly enough, basically because she'd rolled over and played dead for Drew…except for that one night with the margaritas when she'd asked Harris about the possible expense of a hit man.

But that searing anger couldn't last. Within a week, it had burned itself out. After watching her father die, walking in on Drew with another woman just didn't seem worth the emotion.

But tonight was different. Walking home alone, suddenly she felt as if she were living one of those women-in-peril movies.

Directly behind her she heard a sound. Was someone following her?

When she'd skipped out of the party, she'd jumped feet first into righteous San Francisco fog, the only thing on her mind leaving Cutty House and its mystery men far behind. It was less than five blocks to the apartment where she and Harris were staying, and, having already lived in Seattle, another vertically challenged city, she preferred hiking in heels to a heart-in-her-throat taxi ride any day. Nob Hill loomed 338 feet above sea level. The drivers here must hand out complimentary parachutes with each ride. It was probably part of a local traffic ordinance, like wearing seat belts.

Only, now she was clutching the collar of her trench coat as the echo of footsteps sounded behind her. She wasn't quite talking out loud, but her lips moved to the words, telling herself she was crossing the heart of Nob Hill, the castle keep to Chinatown and the financial district below. Here was prime real estate that still bore the names of the railroad barons and Comstock millionaires. Crocker, Stanford, Hopkins and Flood. Safe as houses, right?

As if she hadn't read about muggings on the streets of San Francisco. Hadn't there even been a television series set here, the streets were so famous for crime?

Just an hour ago, sending Harris ahead hadn't seemed like a risky proposition. The cold air would clear her head; the walk up the streets would get the blood flowing.

Instead, the mist conjured images of humanlike shadows, following, following. Ominous footsteps sounded too close.

Cue the foghorn. *There.* Baleful and haunting.

She didn't look back. She refused to give in to that prickling at the back of her neck. An active imagination was her only problem.

Not much farther...

Then came that terrible moment when she gave in to her fears and started to speed up...only to have the footsteps behind her keep pace. Town houses and apartments in a mishmash of architectural styles bullied the sidewalks for space, standing shoulder to shoulder. Like trees in a too-dense forest, each had its own hidey-hole of light and dark.

She broke into a run, no longer worried about how foolish she might look or the pinch of the Jimmy Choos.

The footsteps behind kept pace.

Oops. Not paranoia after all.

An arm reached out, hooking around her stomach. She felt herself propelled, her momentum carrying her around the corner. She realized he hadn't pushed her up against the wall; she'd backed up all on her own against the misshapen clinker bricks.

"I have exactly twenty-three dollars, a really neat Revlon lipstick called Silken Magenta and a half-empty tin of Altoids."

She didn't mention the shoes, for which she'd paid a small fortune.

"You missed your block."

She blinked her eyes open, realizing she'd screwed them shut. The light of a passing car spotlighted Ryan.

Ryans, Ryans, everywhere.

"I what?"

"You're lost," he told her.

"No," she said, waking up. "The apartment is right over…"

But even as she said it, she realized she didn't recognize the street.

He turned her around, pointed. "Turn left at the corner. Straight ahead. First building on your left after you cross Washington."

And when she looked at him like a child who'd just seen a man pull a gold coin out of her ear, he added, "Daniel's old place."

"Oh."

He knew the family. He knew Daniel. He wasn't plotting pillage and plunder.

"The fog," he said. "It confuses things."

She felt suddenly very silly.

"I thought you were chasing me," she said, as if she'd known all along where she was headed, wondering if the excuse didn't make her sound even more foolish. "I thought you were a mugger or something," she added for good measure.

He stepped back, tucking his hands into the pockets of his trousers, looking like an entirely different man than the one who'd cornered her in the ballroom. She wondered how he could do that, go from menacing to mild. Wondered which was the better act.

"You should get going," he told her.

"Right." She turned, took two steps…a few more…then pivoted back. "Right."

He'd implied he wasn't following her. He was merely being a gentleman, making sure she was safe. Just pointing the way down the yellow brick road, Dorothy.

Right.

Wasn't it just like a man to make a woman feel stupid when it was obviously his fault that she was acting the fool?

"Back there, at Cutty House…" she insisted. "All that talk about wanting to look at me and telling me to be quiet. What was that about?"

He shrugged. "I'm sorry. I was wrong. I made a mistake."

She shook her head. "More, please."

But apparently, he wasn't one for details. "I was leaving and I saw you walking home alone. And by the way, that's not a good idea."

"Because some strange man might follow me?"

He gave his first genuine smile of the night, and it was a dilly, one hundred percent bad boy caught in the act.

But just as suddenly, warm and fuzzy went poof. "Why would I follow you?" he asked. "I know exactly where you live." He hadn't meant to sound comforting.

Maybe it was the creepy mist, or the moody lighting from the bay window above shining down on them, but she saw something there, in his face. *Not Mr. Nice Guy, after all.*

"You better go," he said.

"Yes." She stepped back. "Thanks."

She could have bitten her tongue. Thanks for not mugging me—so fortunate you held the line at near heart attack.

She started walking fast, faster still, debating who she should be angry at, Ryan or herself. Behind her, she heard the familiar *clink, clink—clink, clink* as a car crossed the cable car tracks just ahead on Washington. But she didn't hear him following her.

Which didn't mean he wasn't there. Pins and needles still danced up and down her spine.

She found the landmarks she'd missed, the now familiar Foo dogs keeping guard over the apartment cattycorner, the Italian restaurant tucked into the building across the street. She crept past the courtyard gate and slipped down the garden path, taking the steps up to her apartment two at a time. Her hands shaking, she tried her key in the oak door twice. When she dropped the keys, she gave up altogether and had Harris buzz her in.

She was trying to catch her breath. When she reached the third-floor landing, her brother opened the door.

"About time—"

The lecture died on his lips. Instead, he followed her into the apartment where she tossed her coat on a

metal sculpture that doubled as a hat rack, kicked off
the shoes in the foyer and made for the living room.
She didn't even try to hide what she was doing as she
knelt on the leather couch and pried open the blinds.

She could see Washington Street from the window,
maybe even a bit of Taylor below.

"What happened tonight?" Harris asked.

"Nothing," she whispered, careful to keep her
voice down.

As if Ryan could hear her. As if he might be down
there right now, watching her fingers shaking against
the blinds.

In San Francisco, the fog came early and lifted late.
She wasn't familiar with the local nomenclature, but
she figured it was like the Inuit and snow. They had
a million words for the stuff. Tonight, she could see
the lights from the Transamerica Pyramid filtered
through the lens of fog. Smoky tendrils crept along the
street as Holly searched for strange men in leather
jackets.

"Okay, I'll bite," Harris said in the same whisper,
leaning over her to peer through the blinds. "Why the
007 act?"

"It's a beautiful night," she said. "I'm enjoying the
view."

The funky building just across the street with its
improbable balconies and columns—was there someone standing in the arched entry? Or maybe up ahead,
under the awning? By the tree?

Harris dropped onto the couch. He picked up a bowl
brimming with cereal from the kidney-shaped coffee
table and tucked in. "There's something, all right,"
he said around a mouthful. "And by the way, Danny
boy? Mr. Flash and Cash? Please tell me that even
you, oh naive one, finally hear the alarm bells?"

"It's a job, Spiderman, not an episode of *Alias*... and I should listen to a man who comes home from a gourmet bash to eat Cap'n Crunch. Did I mention it was a really nice paying job?"

"Come on, Hol. He paraded you around like you were some head of state. Meet my architect. Please. You want to tell me the last time someone threw a party for you before the job? Kinda makes you question things, like I've been doing ever since Danny made his appearance, all David Copperfield-like."

She turned away from the window, dropping her hold on the blinds. Harris was pushing her buttons. And there was an extremely annoying possibility that her brother could be right.

"He wants people talking about Cutty House long before the doors open," she explained, finding an argument or two up her sleeve. "It's a strategy known to work. And he read about me in *Architectural Digest*. I have a wonderful résumé."

"And he's damn lucky to have you." Harris put down the cereal. "It's just a little hard to believe some dweeb like Daniel East figured that out."

"Maybe that's how it happens. Someone like Daniel, ready to take a chance."

He didn't say anything, but she recognized that deadpan expression.

"I'm going to do this, Harris," she told him, putting the kibosh on her own misgivings. "And when I'm done, I'll write my own ticket as an architect. No more relying on other people like Drew. Do you get that? Freedom. The American way."

"I keep forgetting I'm supposed to be the cheerleader here," he said. He stood and stretched his six-foot-some frame, then grabbed the cereal bowl and headed into the kitchen. "I'll work on it. Really. Good night, Hol."

But at the hallway he stopped, not near ready to throw in the towel. Her brother tended to treat her like a piece of Murano glass, delicate and precious—most likely making up for his own risky lifestyle by riding herd on Holly. And it had only gotten worse since he'd joined the ranks of the unemployed. Now that he had all this extra time and energy, where else should he focus it but on her?

He wanted her safe...he needed her happy. What he didn't get, in typical male fashion, was that Holly wanted the same—for him. And Cutty House might just get them there.

From the hall, he gave her a to-be-continued look. "Hol, do me a favor. Just keep your eyes open, okay?"

She managed a short salute. "Always."

After Harris left, she turned off the lights. She knelt back on the couch and peered through the blinds again, careful that no one below should catch her snooping. But there was only a man walking his dog navigating the street below.

She didn't know what she'd expected—for Ryan to step out from the shadows and give her a thumbs-up.

Yeah, it's me. Your friendly neighborhood stalker.

Still, it was a long time before she left her window perch and headed for the evening's next struggle, a decent night's sleep.

Ryan wondered what she would do if he just stepped out and waved hello.

Really freak her out....

As if he hadn't already.

He waited, knowing she couldn't see him there

across the street, standing under the awning. She hadn't fooled him by turning off the lights. She was still watching from the window. Scared.

"You'd better be scared, sweetheart."

All night, he'd felt out of control. A lot of things felt out of control tonight. Like Daniel pulling the strings with his gig at Cutty House. All week long Ryan had had this running debate going in his head that the invitation was bullshit. There was no way he'd show. But good ol' Dan had dangled the carrot of a reunion, knowing Ryan would want to bridge the chasm of the past. *Twelve long years...*

And now, he was standing outside Daniel's old apartment, falling into the nightmare of the past, wondering if tomorrow morning he'd find the cops knocking on his door. *You tipped your hand....*

God, how the hell had Dan found her?

Ryan stepped out to walk alongside a man and his dog. He used them as cover, slipping out to Taylor Street and turning the corner to hike it uphill. He gave the guy a casual "hey," just to let him know he wasn't a serial killer. If she was watching, she wouldn't see him from this angle.

Earlier that evening, taking Daniel up on his invitation had seemed like a fine idea. Slide on back to the old place, let them all know that, hey, there were no hard feelings. Go with God, Daniel.

And then he'd walked into that room. He'd seen her.

And followed her, and cornered her.

A couple of times in the ballroom, watching her walk around, his hands had started shaking.

Only after she'd started that nonstop talking of hers, acting like some sitcom character, a bundle of nerves, had she broken the spell. Staring at her—her face so animated and curiously kind—he'd had these second thoughts.

She doesn't know anything. She's walked into a trap.

It was up to him to tell her the truth. Warn her. *Save her, Ryan.*

Save her? As if he could....

By the time he reached his car, he was sweating. The night was cold, but his fears were white-hot. He wasn't sure what Daniel was up to. He wasn't sure what any of them had going. But it wasn't good. Not with Holly Fairfield in the picture.

He started the engine, then pulled the Aston Martin into traffic. He headed for the bridge and home, his head all mixed up with these images.

Forget it. Forget every bit of it.

It was one of those gray nights the city was famous for, late enough that traffic was light. When he reached the Golden Gate, the two bridge towers had vanished behind a wall of fog, making the trip over the water look like a magic act, as if the car glided on nothing but a ribbon of concrete.

Daniel had it all now. Cutty House. Vanessa and Samuel in his pocket. Everything he'd ever wanted, ripe for the taking. It had to be enough, even for Daniel.

It was a good story, Ryan thought, heading for home. If only he could get himself to believe it.

4

Holly watched her brother dump the last of the Chex cereal into his bowl. He was sitting at the kitchen counter of what was to be—courtesy of Daniel and her dream job—their new home away from home, a pied-à-terre near the pinnacle of Nob Hill. Having mixed three types of cereal into his bowl, Harris sat reading the morning paper, spoon in hand.

"What is it with you and cereal?" she asked, pouring cream into her coffee.

He flipped open the paper and slid the pages across the counter to Holly. Recently remodeled, the room still had that paint-and-polish "new kitchen" smell. Buffed concrete counters, Gaggenau cooktop and stainless steel gleamed everywhere. Holly might not cook, but she could still appreciate the aesthetics.

"Here," he said, pointing out the pertinent section with his spoon, a gossip column penned by the improbably named Gigi La Plume. The accompanying photograph showed a praying mantis of a woman with large eyes and an upside-down triangle for a face.

"The society pages," she said. "I'm impressed."

"Only for you, Hol."

It wasn't the lead story, but the column covered some serious real estate. Even as her stomach took a roller-coaster dip, she had to admire the hook.

Black Sheep Or Fatted Calf?

Tuesday night's gala at ye olde Cutty House served up more than champagne and foie gras. And judging from Ryan Cutty's reception, San Francisco's fav bachelor-with-a-past (yes, we're still bleating about THAT *cause scandaleux*— baa! baa! baad!), had his served decidedly cold. Could a Cutty House revival have the black sheep of the clan hoping for the fatted calf? Those in the know seem to think this restaurateur-turned-vintner might just find himself crying over his sour grapes.

She folded the newspaper neatly and returned to her coffee, waiting for Harris to say the obvious.

Her brother obliged. "And the plot thickens. I think this is the part where I say, 'I told you so.'"

She focused hard on the coffee, pretending her heart wasn't doing a fair imitation of the Running Man. Last night, Ryan Cutty—the black sheep—had followed the family's new architect home.

Harris tapped the paper. "If I were you, I might be asking Danny a question or two."

"Hmm."

She was mulling over the particulars of the evening, trying to interpret Ryan's actions in context with this new information. The confrontation in the ballroom. Ryan cornering her on the street. The way he'd focused on her, following her home. If this was about business, why not just talk to Daniel? Or his mother and father, the silent partners in Cutty's new opening-to-be?

Unless Ryan thought he could somehow scare her off, sabotage the project.

"Okay," he said. "I'll bite. Why, Hol? Why not ask Dan a couple of questions?"

Because I might not like the answers.

But she told him, "It's all family stuff. It doesn't have anything to do with me." And when he didn't look convinced, she continued. "You know that expression, people who live in glass houses? Daniel didn't pry into my past." She turned away from the counter, taking her coffee to the sink. "Bankruptcy isn't exactly a strong suit for an architect. Maybe I'm just giving him the same courtesy."

"So we're still going with the beggars can't be choosers theme to life?"

"You have your point of view, Spiderman. I have mine. Only, from where I'm standing, mine includes a million-dollar view of the Bay." She gestured past the open kitchen to the living room beyond.

Everything in the place was state-of-the-art and custom-built. Blond ash cabinetry and hardwood floors, hi-tech lighting. The twentieth-century furnishings added both beauty and pragmatism to the apartment's décor. And last, but not least, that view of the Bay Bridge threading over the water where the sun rose over the hills of the East Bay and gilded the postcard-perfect image.

She pressed her point. "We have a beautiful rent-free place in a wonderful city, with an exciting job that will finally let me unfurl my wings. Why can't it just be our good fortune?"

She stepped around the custom counter and sat down on the stool next to her brother, honing in. "I know. Life has been this big struggle. That was us, always busting our butts, working harder than the next guy for half as much, beating the odds. Does that mean we're doomed to struggle for the rest of our lives? Why *can't* it be easy?" she added, on a roll, liking the sound of the tune she was playing. "So the job fell into our laps. So what? Why can't it—just this once—be our lucky day, Spiderman?"

But she could see a few "what ifs" on the tip of her brother's tongue, even if she wasn't as good as Harris at the mind reading.

Only, he surprised her, answering with a smile that changed the mood in the room. "And speaking of good fortune," he said, "I have an announcement. Your good-for-nothing leech of a brother—drum roll please—has a job."

"Really? Omigod, that's wonderful—"

"I'm tending bar at this new place on Polk," he said before she could finish.

Harris had worked for a firm in Denver that specialized in rain-forest pharmaceuticals. He was a bioprospector, a modern-day Indiana Jones who traveled from South America to Southeast Asia searching for plants and poisons that could provide future medical breakthroughs. That's how he'd gotten the nickname Spiderman: A spider poison he'd isolated promised to be the company's cash cow. Only, he'd been canned when he'd caused too many problems, fighting corporate America and the way it bulldozed native rights in the patent process.

"Okay," she said, trying to hide her dismay. Bartender. Yeah, that's why he'd needed that tricky Ph.D., to make a mean margarita. "That's wonderful."

He patted her cheek. "Atta girl."

She was still fighting her shock as she shadowed him across the kitchen. Harris rinsed his cereal bowl, taking his time, giving her a moment to let it all sink in. Holly only stared at the water streaming from the gooseneck faucet, needing that mental kick in the shin. *Say something!*

"I open tonight. Wanna come by?" he asked. "Give me your seal of approval? All you can drink. On the house."

Holly came up behind him and gave him a hug. She knew how painful this must be for him, to retreat. Harris had always been the fighter in the family, a man who didn't let much stand in his way. It hurt to see him suddenly roll over and play dead.

She told herself he was just licking his wounds after the fiasco of his job dispute. Goodness knows what the company had threatened. He knew all of their secrets, after all. He might still be contractually obligated by some onerous noncompetition clause. Eventually he'd go back to the work he loved. He had to.

She craned her neck to smile up at him, her brother, significantly taller than her five-feet-two. "Do I get to dance on the table if I drink too much?"

"I might even join you."

It was a new beginning for both of them. Why rain on his parade? Why not give Harris the same consideration she expected—blind trust. Let him believe the fantasy that he could be happy with the simple life. What did she know?

Getting her keys, she kept telling herself not to worry so much. Everything would work out in the end. It was like she'd told Harris: Why should life always be a struggle? Why couldn't it be easy just this once?

But she kept thinking about last night, the strange vibes, the story in the paper. And the thought that her brother was nearly always right.

Some things were too good to be true.

Too good to be true.

Those words gave a nice little rhythm to her walk that morning, a percussion beat playing counterpoint to the clang of the cable-car bell and the throb of the underground cables. She'd grabbed a cup of coffee at the Shaky Grounds Café, enjoying the fleeting sunshine of the late morning as she took on the popcorn hills.

Her tour book tucked safely in her purse, she imagined cresting a summit to swan dive into the Bay below. Multicolored condos and townhouses added to the illusion, climbing the steep streets like terraced gardens.

She even found this sign: Prevent Runaways. Curb Wheels. Park in Gear. Set Brake.

Runaways—as good a theme as any for the morning. The article in the paper alluded to some sort of family imbroglio. The fact that Ryan Cutty seemed intent on hunting her down added a rather cryptic note. She knew from experience that family-run businesses could be tricky, and Cutty House was now entering its third generation.

Given the task ahead, the last thing Holly needed was a rogue player thrown into the mix. All morning she'd been trying to sell herself on the adventure of "Cutty House, the Dream Job," fending off Harris's fears of "Cutty House, the Nightmare."

Two hours later, the nightmare ran with the opening credits.

"I was thinking of exposed pipes."

In true form, Daniel played the master of ceremonies, imagining the impossible—a nineteenth-century Beaux-Arts building converted into warehouse chic.

"Painted in primary colors," he continued. "Very George Pompidou Center. Steel and glass and brightly colored ducts."

She'd met with Daniel just after lunch. Like a lamb to the slaughter, she trailed behind as he detailed his plans for each room of the mansion. The tour—and her shock—dead-ended in the ballroom, which was destined to become Club East, the dance studio portion of his new place-to-be-seen.

He wanted to compete with trendy SoMa, San Francisco's party central, the dance club district south of Market Street. How he'd managed the variances for the plans filed by the previous architect with the planning department, and evaded historical review, was still a mystery—though Daniel had mentioned that "It's who you know, darling."

Right, until someone reported you to the local historical society. She'd seen permits revoked and contractors ordered to cease and desist. Basically, Daniel was asking her to put her license on the line, something she wasn't about to do. But how was she to accomplish Daniel's blue-sky ideas without crossing the line? So far, the morning's only piece of good news was that Cutty House had never been designated a historical landmark.

And then there was Daniel's punch-out-the-walls theory of renovation. He wanted to take advantage of the view. A window to the world, he called it.

"It's like they'll be dancing on air," he finished, his face flushed.

Which they probably would be in a few months, she thought. The glass couldn't act as a shear wall. The whole thing would go bust at the slightest San Francisco trembler.

She felt like Jonah staring into the mouth of the whale.

Daniel turned to look at her, at long last catching on to her silence.

"You're not saying much."

The Druid used to refer to any client as the "user."

She'd always considered that an unfortunate term, but Daniel gave new meaning to the word.

He smiled. "I think someone's a little scared."

He crossed the room, arms outstretched, all comfort. Today he wore leather pants the same creamy color as his suede shirt. Half rimmed glasses perched on his handsome nose. With his highlighted hair, he was a study in butterscotch, looking good enough to eat. But then, he had a tall lanky build that would probably show off a potato sack, and the heavenly face of a Hugh Grant.

"It's part of the reason I chose you for the project, Holly," he whispered in her ear. "You have a reputation for not holding back."

"Daniel, right now I'm holding back."

"All right. I'm asking too much. The impossible. So keep me grounded."

He watched her with earnest brown eyes. He seemed so sincere.

"And then, make it happen," he added with a grin.

She managed a tight smile and hid her fear. She told herself it was early in the game. She might pull a rabbit out of a hat.

"I'll see what I can do."

"Shazaam," he said, making like the magician he thought her to be.

"Any more surprises?" she asked, hanging on to that smile for all she was worth.

"Count on it."

He glanced at his watch, something flashy and expensive that her pedestrian self wouldn't recognize. She knew what was coming from practice. Daniel East didn't stand still for long.

"I have to catch this guy about this thing," he told her, already halfway to the door.

"Don't let me keep you."

And then she was alone with the beast.

She walked around the ballroom, listening to her footsteps on the wood floor. After a while the sound morphed into the cadence of the theme music from *Jaws*. Ba-dum, ba-dum...

Last night, the ballroom had been a funhouse of shadows, the perfect stage for Mr. Ryan Cutty, worrisome man of mystery. But today, the light had transformed yesterday's haunted house into a treasure. Despite her misgivings, there was a part of her that couldn't be afraid, as if she craved this sort of challenge. Making dreams come true could be very seductive.

She placed a hand on a plaster column. She couldn't imagine a sledgehammer having a go at these. The floorboards ran the length of the room, alternating light and dark, reminding Holly of the striped sateen walking gowns that might have crowded the streets of Nob Hill in Victorian times. A bay window provided the room's only view, its rose velvet banquette now threadbare and faded from years of sun exposure.

A music shell opened to the left, the place where Ryan had performed his disappearing act. The space was large enough to house a grand piano or a string quartet. Enormous mirrors mimicked arched doorways down the length of the room, flanked by pilasters and columns. Lavish plaster work—reeded and egg-and-dart moldings, rosettes and medallions—dazzled throughout.

Don't fall in love, she told herself. Remember Daniel's grand plan. Exposed pipes...steel and glass. Shock value.

"Oi," she said.

"Does he want you to hang the world's biggest disco ball from the ceiling?"

Holly hadn't heard anyone coming up behind her. She turned and, seeing Emma Wright, the chef from last night, braced herself.

Only, today Emma's expression was openly friendly. She was wearing a simple white cotton T-shirt and jeans that hung low on her hips, exposing a healthy amount of skin. She had Doc Martens on her feet, a far cry from last night's tortured fare. She'd tucked her strawberry-blond hair into a ponytail and wore little or no makeup. Above the left corner of her lip, a small silver stud pierced the skin.

Emma smiled, looking suddenly like a wise pixie with her spray of freckles. "That's Daniel. Everything has to be grand, over the top. Make a scandal," she said, the perfect mimic. "He once asked me to make a rice pudding soufflé. And the Boba bar? Puleeze." Emma stuck out her tongue.

"You see things differently?" Holly asked, hoping to keep the receptive mood moving along.

Emma sighed, all drama. "He keeps forgetting about the clientele this place attracts. It's Nob Hill, not SoMa. You can't change that overnight. Let's try this again." She held out her hand. "My name's Emma. And I owe you an apology for my fabulous imitation of Super Bitch last night."

Holly shook her hand gladly, holding back her sigh of relief. "Holly Fairfield, and there's no need to apologize. I think openings make everyone a little tense. The expectations."

Emma stepped around Holly and took a seat on the banquette under the bay window. She shook her head. "I'm at my worst whenever the family is around—not that it's any excuse."

Holly made a sound of sympathy, but she was thinking about what her brother had said that morning. *I
might be asking Danny a question or two.*

"Have you known the family long?" Don't pry—
don't ask.

"Forever," Emma said. "My dad used to be the
cook here, before he decided that he preferred alcohol
to a paying job." She gave that same quirky smile, as
if she'd said the line a million times. As if it didn't
hurt. "They sort of adopted me."

She stood, then walked around the room. She tucked
her hands into the back pockets of her jeans, looking
all of eighteen.

"But I didn't get all the real family crap. You have
to be a blood relative for that, thank God."

Questions, questions, questions. There were a million of them on the tip of Holly's tongue.

"Well," Holly said. "You wouldn't be up for a
drink later? I mean, I really would be interested in
getting your ideas for the dining room. And my
brother just started working at this new place on Polk.
I promised I'd show."

Holly held her breath.

"Sure," Emma said, without hesitation. "Why
not?"

"We can meet just outside, at the gate," she said,
nailing her down. "Five o'clock?"

"I'll be there."

"Great. See you then."

Heading back to the office space she'd been given
upstairs, Emma walking alongside, Holly told herself
she really was after ideas for the dining room. She
wasn't the least bit interested in family gossip. Whatever threat Ryan Cutty represented, she'd deal with it.

Still, leaving the ballroom, she felt a familiar tingling at her neck. She shivered.

Emma gave her a look. "What?"

"Nothing," Holly answered, glancing over her shoulder, wondering how long she'd keep checking the shadows for dark and dangerous men.

5

It didn't take much to pry the story out of Emma. And boy, was it ever a doozy.

"That was so in-your-face last night. Ryan showing up," Emma said. "I mean…kapow! Just strut right in and say, 'Hey.' Like it hasn't been twelve years? He's lucky they didn't call the cops."

Emma and Holly sat on the bamboo bar stools of the Bali Bistro, the restaurant where Harris worked as Top Kahuna behind the rail. Nestled in a nondescript condominium complex on Polk, the restaurant specialized in East meets West cuisine, and judging from the palm fronds and Tiki torches, the place took particular glee in its garage-sale chic Polynesian decor.

"No way was he invited," Emma added. "Trust me."

"So I figured," Holly said, pretending to admire a wall covered with hand-painted ukuleles and guitars. Her chest had gone all tight and her fingers tingled. Was this a panic attack?

"How's your drink?" Emma asked.

Both women stared down at the ceramic Tiki head emitting smoke. A festive umbrella sprouted from the top alongside a slice of pineapple stabbed through the heart and sandwiched between two cherries. A fragrant pineapple-coconut blend, the drink probably contained enough rum to take down a man twice her size.

Emma, who had not left it up to Harris's discretion as Holly had—*Surprise me, Spiderman*—drank beer from a demure glass sporting nothing but frost.

Looking at Holly, Emma raised a brow as if to ask, *well?*

"Potent," Holly answered.

Emma's smile deepened. Despite the rocky introduction, the East Side Café's chef had proven a delight. A charming combination of humor and intelligence, Emma was a no-nonsense gal, the kind Holly had learned to appreciate.

Emma sipped from her beer. "They wrote about Ryan in the paper this morning. The prodigal son returns or something. I bet Daniel got a kick out of that. It's publicity, anyway. Ryan was supposed to run the place. Cutty House, I mean. He's their only child and all, Vanessa and Samuel's. But that was before."

Emma turned on the bamboo stool. Her smile said it all. *I have a secret.*

"Before?"

It was all the prompting Emma needed. "Before he murdered his fiancée," she said.

Emma popped another wasabi pea into her mouth. She'd picked them out of the rice cracker mix and set them on her cocktail napkin all in a row. She'd been eating them, one by one, as she told the story.

Holly stared at the napkin and at the peas lined up. *Murder?*

"He got away with it, too," Emma said. "No jail time or anything because they couldn't find enough evidence." Another pea disappeared. "The whole O.J. thing all over again. It kinda makes you sick how often they get away with it."

He followed you home, no one the wiser.

"Of course, he could just be whacked. You know, psycho or something—"

Better still.

"But I think there was justice in the end, 'cause he lost everything. The girl, the money. He totally flipped after that."

Holly listened like a dedicated fan of the soap opera *Cutty House.* Forgotten was any pretense of asking about the dining room or the kitchen design or the drink bubbling and smoking on the bar before her.

"I think he was even institutionalized," Emma continued, on a roll. "Now he works at some vineyard in Napa. Lives on a boat. A total loser worker bee. Imagine. I mean, he has all these fancy degrees from a hotshot school. Thank God Samuel and Vanessa have Daniel."

Holly stabbed the two colorful straws into her drink, trying to put it together in her head. At worst, she was being stalked by a killer. At best, she'd been directed home by a man who had a giant grudge against her employer...the employer she was helping to take over a family institution that bore Ryan Cutty's name.

Ryan was supposed to run the place...before he murdered his fiancée.

"Here's your brother."

Emma waved Harris over. She'd related the story to Holly like an urban legend. Everybody knew, nothing to it. Just like the paper said this morning, it was old news. *Baa baa baad!*

Now Holly was trying to figure out how to keep the overprotective Harris from ever finding out.

"Hey." Harris glanced down at Holly's untouched drink, disappointed. "The great Tiki gods will take umbrage."

She could whisk Emma away, quickly, quietly…before the chef's sweet looks lured her brother into conversation.

Oh, and by the way, your sister is working for the family of an ax murderer. Did she mention that?

"How are you doing?" Harris asked, glancing at Emma's beer.

"This is great, thanks."

"I was trying to get Emma's ideas on the dining room for the new restaurant." Holly made it sound as if they were all business here. *We're very busy, Spiderman. Move on.* And when he didn't take the hint, "She's the chef for the East Side Café so it's very important that I get her input on both the space planning and the aesthetics of my proposed designs."

Choose a topic. Any topic. Preferably one far removed from Ryan Cutty and his colorful past.

"No kidding," Harris said. He leaned over, elbows on the bar, smiling that wicked grin nature seemed able to give only to the men in her family. "Funny, you don't look like a chef."

Emma returned the look. "Funny, you look exactly like a bartender."

"I meant it as a compliment." Harris never lost his smile.

Emma pushed her glass away. "So did I." She winked. "I gotta book. See ya," she said to Holly. "Thanks for the drink," she told Harris.

Disaster averted, Holly breathed again.

"She's cute."

Scratch that. "Harris, of all the girls in all the gin joints, are you actually going to hit on the future chef at my new job?"

His eyes never left Emma's cute backside displayed

to perfection in low-cut jeans as she worked her way past the tables. "Wouldn't dream of it. I'm all about class, Hol. You know that."

Getting in that last word, Harris slipped away to tend to a customer. All sorts of alarm bells fired off in Holly's head. It had been a long time for Harris. Maybe too long. And Emma was cuter than a bug in a rug and had enough attitude to catch even her brother's world-weary attentions.

Not that Holly believed she could hide the truth from Harris forever. He'd find those skeletons in the Cutty closet sooner or later—probably from Holly herself in some torrid confession. She'd never been very good at keeping secrets from him.

She took another stab at the drink, remembering Ryan standing in the shadows, the lights from the car spotlighting his face. He didn't look like someone who'd been institutionalized. Or like a crazed killer.

But, suddenly, her very practical mind shut down and her imagination took over.

He murdered his fiancée...

"You going to drink that or wait until it tells your fortune?"

She looked up from the smoking Tiki. "Harris, do me a favor. Call me a cab."

He gave her a look.

"It's been a long day," she said, picking up her bag. "I'm tired."

Her cell phone chimed the "Hokey Pokey" when Emma reached the lobby. She flipped the phone open, anticipating the call.

"Talk to me," she said playfully. She knew who it was.

"Were you nice?"

"I was so nice," she said, dropping into one of the lobby chairs where she wouldn't be seen or heard if Little Bo Peep Holly decided to follow her out. "I deserve...presents. Expensive jewelry, perhaps."

"Are you friends?"

"Only the best of."

She wasn't going to mention their conversation about Ryan. Daniel wouldn't appreciate the humor in it. That wasn't part of his Big Plan. If Emma put the fear of God into sweet Holly Fairfield, she might just go and run off scared.

If only it could be that easy, Emma thought.

She slipped lower into the chair with a smile. Holly's brown eyes had practically popped out of her head with the story. *Murder and mayhem, oh my!* Daniel would be pissed if he ever found out.

"So what do I get for being nice?" she asked coyly. She watched from her hiding place as, indeed, Holly Fairfield skipped past to navigate the revolving doors, clueless as ever.

"Tonight. When I get home," came the voice through the phone. "Don't fall asleep waiting. I'll make it worth your while."

"Promises, promises."

"I love you, baby."

"I know," she said, hanging up.

She dropped her head back against the chair, wishing she'd finished her beer at the bar, needing the buzz. But up there, she'd wanted to keep her wits about her. She couldn't afford to make any mistakes.

Only, now there was this letdown, as if she needed to hear Daniel's voice to keep going.

Keep to the plan.

The weight of what lay ahead settled on her chest along with her doubts. Suddenly, bringing up that stuff about Ryan didn't seem so funny. What had she been trying to prove, playing with fire?

She thought about those witches in Salem, how they had stones put on top of them until they were slowly crushed. She shut her eyes, trying to fill her lungs, needing to shove off that weight. But when she remembered Holly and their conversation in the bar, she only felt more stones piling on.

She didn't want to think about the past. She needed to concentrate on Daniel. He was everything to her, the be-all and end-all of her existence. He had to be.

But Daniel wouldn't be home for another three hours.

Emma stood, trying to shake off her fears as she paced around the lobby. She felt as if she was made of raw nerve endings, completely exposed. She needed Daniel right there in front of her, breathing life into his plans.

She should just go home to her empty condo. She could call Dan, leave him a message that she didn't feel up to coming over. Maybe try out that new recipe for the restaurant and forget all about his stupid ideas. But then she'd be alone with her thoughts—with her fears.

"Screw it."

She could feel her heart thumping as she headed back to the bar. She remembered that saying: Never return to the scene of the crime. Daniel would have a cow if he ever found out…which was maybe why she was going back.

In the elevator on the way up, she wondered if there wasn't something wrong with her. Maybe she wanted to get caught. She was sick and tired of her secrets. But suddenly she was walking into the restaurant, and it was too late for retreat.

Looking big and handsome in his Hawaiian shirt, Holly's brother saw her right away. She glanced around, making a show of searching the tables before she made her way to the bar. Over the years, she'd learned how to hide things. She knew what people wanted to hear, wanted to believe.

I can do this. I can pull it off.

Holly's brother was standing over her in no time, a grin on his face. She pressed her fingers against the counter to make her hands stop shaking.

"Hey," he said.

"Did your sister leave already? My plans for the night just fell through. I was hoping to catch her. She said something about dinner?"

She knew she was pushing it, lying about dinner. She felt the rush of it, maybe even liked the feeling.

"Sorry," he said. "You just missed her."

He kept his smile, but there was a hint of something else. He wasn't as trusting as his sister.

Careful. He won't be so easy.

He poured the beer she'd been drinking earlier, placed the glass in front of her like a magician.

"Tada!" she said as if it were a performance. She toasted him. "Thanks."

She took a drink. He was still watching her, cautious but definitely interested. She put the glass down. "Is the food here any good?"

"Yeah. Sure. I'll get you a menu."

She watched him grab a menu from somewhere behind the bar. *What are you doing, Emma?* But when he handed her the menu, she took it and smiled.

"Checking out the competition?" he asked.

She leaned in close and whispered, "Would you throw me out if I said yes?"

"I don't know. First day on the job? Hard to have that kind of loyalty."

"I can't help myself," she said. "Food is my passion. If they have something new here, I want to know about it."

It was as good an excuse as any, and he looked as if he needed a reason.

"The ribs," he said. "If you like ribs, they're pretty good. A lot of people order them. Hawaiian barbecue."

She shut the menu and handed it back. "Ribs it is."

He took the menu and picked up her beer. "There's a table free over there. I'll serve you myself."

"Thanks," she said, turning to get off the bar stool, still shaking a little. "Can you take a break? Maybe join me?"

He seemed to think about it. To a guy like Harris, he was sure to interpret the conversation as just another come-on. One of many, by the looks of him.

"Please?" She gave it her best shot. "Let me pump you for information."

"Give me fifteen minutes," he said, guiding her to the table. He pulled out her chair and placed the beer in front of her. "When I bring you the ribs, I'll take my break."

She watched him walk away. After a few seconds, she could breathe again, not so nervous anymore.

Daniel wouldn't like it. But then, Daniel was a dreamer. What did he really know about Holly? Not nearly enough. Over dinner, she could ask all the questions Dan wouldn't because he was so damn sure of himself. As if his scheme with Holly couldn't blow up in his face.

She picked up the beer, feeling better. She told herself she'd done the right thing by staying. She was just being smart. For Daniel's sake. She was keeping him safe...even if it was from himself.

6

Ryan watched Holly spill out the revolving door onto the sidewalk. There was a taxi waiting in front of the condominium complex. A doorman stood at the ready, beckoning.

Only, she didn't get inside the cab right away. She perched on the curb, clutching the jacket collar of her sensible gray suit, hugging her bag and purse. Peering over the car, she searched the street.

She'd been doing it all day—stopping to look over her shoulder.

Under the halo of light from the street lamp, he imagined he could see her face despite the fog. She'd be plenty worried. Worried about him.

In his infinite patience for a tip, the doorman waited for his cue. She looked tiny beside him. It wasn't the first time Ryan noticed how small she was, almost insubstantial, like maybe even that oversized bag might be too much for her. He couldn't remember Nina ever looking small. She'd been five feet ten inches with an equestrian's posture, and enough attitude to crowd a room.

He kept to the shadows as the taxi sped past, Holly Fairfield now safely inside.

He jammed his hands into the pockets of his jacket, walking uphill. She was probably going back to the apartment. With traffic, he might even beat her there.

He stopped, thinking about the last twenty-four hours. Jesus. Was he really going to do this?

If he followed her, if he let this thing get out of control, there was no way of knowing if he could come back from all that. Not again. Which was exactly why Daniel had brought her here. To screw with his head.

Ryan started walking up the hill again. Last night, he'd dreamed of Nina. How long had it been since he'd had the dream? Five years maybe? Ten? Then, out of the blue, his head hits the pillow and he's there, every detail just the same. The party at his mother's house. Watching Nina fall apart, screaming her venom. Him, screaming right back at her. *That's a fucking lie. You're lying!* Trying to catch her. Trying to stop her.

After the dream, he hadn't gotten much sleep. He'd come back over the bridge before dawn, watching the light paint the hills as the fog spilled into the Bay behind him like a giant wave machine set on slow motion. Long before Holly had walked to work, he'd been waiting at the corner for her. The fog made it easy to follow unnoticed.

He put his head down against the wind and headed for Dan's place. After tonight, he'd be done. No more driving into the city. He'd make himself stop.

Just once more.

He reached the street in fifteen minutes, but he figured she was already inside. He stood under the awning across Washington where she couldn't see him. There was an Italian place right on the corner. Venticello. And an old-time grocer just down the block, a nice place run by a Greek. The night was young, but the foot traffic seemed notably absent. As if maybe the locals had gotten the word: Strange man loitering. Guard your children and pets.

The wind kicked up the fog, turning everything gray and out of focus. The film-noir effect made him feel as if he'd stepped out of time. Like maybe this didn't count somehow, him standing here acting crazy.

Tomorrow he'd go back to being Mr. Normal. He'd never lay eyes on her again, swear to God.

Daniel's building used clinker brick on the first floor, then switched to stucco and wood, making the top two floors look half-timbered. And there was a courtyard. There weren't many of those in the neighborhood.

The lights on the third floor were out, but he figured she was keeping vigil at the window. Last night, he'd known exactly when she'd given up for the night, had felt it like a switch turning off inside his chest.

He'd leave before the brother got off work. *That's right, set a limit to the lunacy.* Come morning, he'd get back to business at the vineyard. He had a million things to do. If he kept busy, he'd keep sane.

He leaned against the brick, waiting. It wasn't so bad, coming here this one last time. It didn't mean anything. Only, he'd been saying the same thing all day. Just a little longer…

Harris considered that he had a God-given talent, like some weird sixth sense, a hypersensitivity of a sort. He discovered it in grade school, when his mother told him she'd be right back from the grocery store with a loaf of bread and he knew he'd never see her again.

Even then, he could put certain things together— the way his mother wouldn't meet his eyes when she talked, that a mother wouldn't leave her first grader and his toddler sister alone in the house if she was up to any good. He was just a kid, but he'd known she was lying.

He could always tell when someone was lying. It made romance a real drag because when a woman lied he tended to hold it against her. Like Emma here, sitting across the table enjoying her ribs. She was lying through her pearly white teeth.

"Mmm," she said, wiping her mouth with the napkin. "Good."

People who lied had a tendency to do that. Fill in the silence. Emma hadn't stopped talking since he'd sat down.

"Glad you like them."

"Is that allowed?" she asked as he took a sip of his beer. "Drinking on the job?"

"I thought it was part of the job description. Maybe I should check?"

She laughed. A nervous laugh. Or maybe there'd been so much cloak-and-dagger in his life that he'd begun to suspect everyone. But he had a good radar for this sort of thing, and the gig with Daniel East had stunk from day one.

"Do you like it?" she asked. "Bartending?"

"I live for it. I left the Evil Kingdom of Corporate America determined only to do good in the world," he said, reciting the old line.

"And that would be?"

"To pour drinks and serve as supertherapist to the masses. At no charge…all tips appreciated, of course."

His antennae were telling him that Emma here was in on whatever Danny-boy had going. That's why she'd come back, to pump him for information about his sister. Not that he'd been very obliging. No such luck for the chef. In fact, he had a couple of questions of his own.

"That guy last night," he said. "The one who barged in and made such a ruckus at the party. Who was he?"

"No one important," she told him.

He nodded, going with it. That's why she'd spent half an hour haranguing Holly with the soap opera of the man's life?

He hadn't been listening so much as keeping his ears open to the conversation between the two women. But as soon as the name Ryan Cutty came up, he'd paid attention. Ryan Cutty. The guy in the gossip column. Mr. Black Sheep himself.

He smiled, seeing that when she raised her glass to drink Emma's hands shook. It was a shame really. A nice girl like her involved with Daniel East.

"Well, I'm back to work," he said, getting to his feet. "Let me know if you need anything else."

She wiggled her fingers in goodbye, but he could tell she was only too happy to see his backside, that she was sorry she'd asked him to join her.

He walked away, whistling to himself. He nodded to the other bartender. It was a slow night, no biggie that he'd taken his break early.

Holly thought Harris had lost his job because he'd been fighting corporate America, working on the side of good as he helped the little guy. Problem was, she didn't know the particulars of how he'd gotten there, what he'd done along the way to his change of heart. By the time he'd destroyed his career, Harris couldn't wait to join the ranks of the unemployed.

But those assignments had allowed him to hone certain skills, skills that were coming in handy here in beautiful San Francisco, where his sister had chosen

to start her brave new life. Lucky for her, Harris was
on the job.

Not two minutes after he left the table, Emma was
heading out the door. She'd practically left tread
marks.

Apparently, the ribs hadn't agreed with her.

Emma shut the door and collapsed against the wall
of Daniel's Pacific Heights apartment, catching her
breath. She'd run most of the way here.

That's it, girl. Outrun the fear.

She'd made a mistake. A terrible mistake.

"Hey." Daniel stepped out from the kitchen, surprising her. She hadn't expected him to be home.

"Where have you been?" he asked.

She stood there looking like someone who had
something to hide. Which she did.

*I was out ruining all your careful plans. What do
you say, Daniel? Do you still love me?*

"I asked you where you were?"

And now he was jealous.

"You said three hours," she reminded him. "I decided to stay for dinner at that new place where Holly
and I had drinks. Try it out."

She dropped her keys onto an anonymous sculpture
of a hand resting, palm up, on the Louis XV occasional table—one of the few pieces she liked. Everything else in the apartment had names attached—the
Kevin Walz steel lamp, the Dennis King dining table.
She'd decorated her apartment with primitive masks,
Oaxacan wood sculptures and colorful arts and crafts
from South America, liking the humor and lively colors. Daniel's furniture needed labels. He could point
to any little piece and say, "Look at my Kem Weber
chair, my custom-designed Marco sofa."

"The Bali Bistro, it's called." In the kitchen, she poured herself a glass of chardonnay from the bottle he'd opened. She couldn't stop her hands from shaking. "By the way, their ribs suck."

"Ribs." Daniel made a face.

Nothing so pedestrian as ribs could be part of the menu at the East Side Café. Daniel wanted only the new, the innovative, while Emma hated all his nouvelle cuisine hoopla. She preferred ethnic, what Daniel termed "food for the unwashed masses."

"I wouldn't have bothered if I'd known you'd be home so soon," she said, wishing now she'd never gone back to the bar. "Have you been waiting long?"

"Ages."

He came up behind her, kissing her neck. Daniel was jealous for only a minute, basically because he knew that she loved him. And why would she cheat on the great Daniel East, anyway? "You did good tonight."

Making friends with the enemy.

"Don't," she said, pushing past Daniel when he started to raise the hem of her T-shirt. "I'm not in the mood." Not in the mood to hear his chortling plans. Too often Daniel sounded like a twelve-year-old boy with a new toy.

But it wasn't Daniel who'd screwed up tonight, she reminded herself. She dropped onto the couch and drank her wine. She felt as if she were teetering on the edge of some stupid confession. *Get a grip.*

She sunk back against the cushions as if she could disappear there, tucking her feet under her, clutching the wineglass. Daniel lived on the tenth floor. On a clear day, she could look east along Pacific Avenue all the way to the Bay Bridge and Berkeley.

Daniel preferred the view north. He'd stand at the

window, ignoring the magnificent blue of the Bay to stare toward Sausalito where his nemesis lived. He took particular glee in that fact that Ryan had been driven from the city he once loved. Daniel alone remained to take up the baton of familial responsibilities, King of the Hill.

Dammit, why couldn't she get her hands to stop shaking? What had she done that was so bad, anyway? She'd eaten some ribs, maybe flirted a little with Holly's brother. So what?

"I thought I was going to be nice to you?" Daniel asked softly.

He was standing in the doorway, wearing one of his favorite outfits, a mini-herringbone tan suit and a custom-made tank top to match. He'd ditched the jacket but still wore the Dolce and Gabbana lizard-skin boots. The outfit had cost a small fortune and made a stark contrast to Harris's Hawaiian shirt with its hula dancers.

The comparison didn't stop there. Daniel was tall and fashionably slim with defined muscles and narrow hips that barely caught the waistband of his trousers. The sharp angles continued in his face, drawing attention to his mouth, full and sensuous. And his eyes. There was always a sort of hunger in those brown eyes.

By the looks of it, Harris didn't skip meals and didn't stress about it, either. But if she had to hazard a guess, she imagined that while Daniel looked good in clothes, Harris would look even better out of them.

Daniel prompted, "Baby?"

She shook her head, startled by her thoughts. "Nothing."

She couldn't tell Daniel that she was afraid of a bartender who asked too many questions. For all his smiles and affable banter, Harris Fairfield looked like a man who knew she had secrets.

She'd thought he'd be like his sister, all sweet and easy.

"Does it ever get to you?" she surprised herself by asking. "What we're doing with Holly?"

Daniel watched, turning the etched-crystal glass in his hand. The muscle in his jaw pulsed. This was the part he hated. Her doubts.

"I'm just getting what I'm due," he said gently.

"And a little more." But she could see he didn't want to hear it. Daniel always resented any hint of reality in his life. Another contrast between the two men. Daniel put on a show, making a woman feel important with his avid looks and beguiling smiles. Tonight, Harris appeared just as busy, only he'd been looking past her flirtatious manner to discover what lay beyond.

She shivered on the couch. She couldn't believe the guy had her this freaked out. He was just a stupid bartender, she told herself.

"Hey," Daniel said, stepping into the room. "It's me. What gives?"

She could see Daniel was worried. And maybe he should be.

She couldn't remember a time before Daniel. They'd been kitchen brats together. Later, when she was ten, she'd fallen in love, mooning over the handsome waiter who never failed to bring her presents— ribbons for her hair, a necklace made of candy. When she'd been fourteen and in trouble, it was Daniel she'd run to for help.

She'd started sleeping with him when she was fifteen. Daniel had been twenty-three. Since then, he'd been her one and only.

Out of habit, she patted the couch beside her. "Sit." She didn't want to see that look on his face. She couldn't stand to see him hurt or upset. All these years, they'd kept each other's secrets…and had a few of their own.

She leaned her head against his shoulder. "Tell me what happens next."

Above all, she needed Daniel to be happy.

TROMPE L'OEIL

7

Inspiration struck at two in the morning.

Holly had been going over the problem most of the night until her head felt a bit like a Rubik's Cube, twisting this way and that, hoping the next turn might make all the colors line up. Daniel had hired her to create a postmodern jewel out of a Beaux-Arts treasure. He wanted notorious—shocking—and she needed context. The house itself had given her that.

The key was to keep the soul of Cutty House while realizing Daniel's vision. But incorporating Daniel's out-there ideas—Japanese accents, *Star Wars* redux laser show—was no easy task.

She'd fallen asleep on the floor, her face plastered to the as-built plans, using Daniel's "what if?" as a distraction against the trickier topic of Ryan Cutty. When she'd jolted awake, she thought the cable cars were on parade. Just down the street, they steamrolled into the Cable Car Barn like a herd of mechanical elephants turning in for the night.

It wasn't the cable cars making the ruckus, but Harris stabbing his key into the door. Bleary-eyed, she studied her brother wearing a shirt that practically screamed Aloooha!

The realization struck like a bolt straight out of the big blue. The fundamental she'd learned from her first architecture class was so obvious it hurt. *Context is everything.*

Harris stood just over six feet, towering a near foot over Holly. He had strong masculine features to her wide-eyed gamine looks. When he smiled, it meant trouble, while the same gesture on Holly came off as delicate and unsure. But no one ever failed to guess they were brother and sister. They looked alike. A variation on a theme.

Sitting on the floor next to the coffee table overrun by plans as if a can of snakes had exploded, she must have had some look on her face. Harris struck a pose, arms outstretched as if to ask, "What?"

But the lightbulb had flipped on with enough clarity that even the smallest rogue doubt had scurried off to find shelter. What Cutty House needed was a reinterpretation of the Beaux-Arts theme, updated dramatically to cause Daniel's necessary sensation.

It could be done, she realized. It could be fantastically done.

Her imagination on fire, she'd spent the whole of the day and part of that night doing quick sketches. The ideas came fluidly, naturally. The energy felt pure and right and cosmic.

What she proposed was revolutionary. Truly, her finest hour as an architect. By God, she'd done it! She'd pulled a rabbit out of the proverbial hat.

So, of course, Daniel hated it.

At his suggestion, they met the next day at a lovely sidewalk café, public humiliation always being the best sort. Seated across the table, Daniel gifted her with a smile as he handed back her sketches.

"Now see, I'm actually surprised," he told her. "I never thought for a minute you could disappoint me."

Like a chameleon, he'd composed a new look, dark-

ening his roots to make a more dramatic contrast with
the blond highlights. He wore white jeans and a leather
two-button blazer over a gray-and-white cotton shirt
with a paisley design that most likely cost a fortune.
Holly had on the same sensible A-line black skirt
she'd worn on a previous occasion, though she'd updated it with a white tuxedo shirt she'd bought at
Macy's.

Daniel craved pizzazz; she searched for substance.
Of course, he would find her ideas drab. She could
well imagine how the last architect might have gotten
in over his head. Daniel was a bit impossible. To tame
his ideas to fit the feel and structure of Cutty House
and its surroundings was the most difficult task she'd
set for herself as an artist. Today, she'd practically
skipped here believing she'd nailed it.

"This calls for a celebration," he said, signaling the
waitress for the check.

"That I've utterly failed calls for a celebration?"

"Absolutely." His grin lit up the sidewalk. "It's
time we give you another test drive, little girl."

Her high continued its searing crash and burn.
"Why don't I like the sound of that?"

Daniel wore sunglasses, adding that special movie-
star touch. She watched as a tourist or two actually
whiplashed around, wondering if they'd just passed
"someone," Daniel having the look of a man destined
for greatness or infamy or both.

"PR, baby," he told her, putting down the tiny ex-
presso cup. "As easy as it gets. A party. A little champagne. Lots of razzle-dazzle."

"That's the part I don't like. I did mention that I
don't do PR? I'm sure it was in the small print in my
contract, right beneath embarrassingly shy."

"Nah," he said, not the least discouraged. He

leaned over the miniature table. His hand caressed her cheek, the gesture walking a tightrope between intimate and avuncular. "You're up for this. Trust me."

"Not much for hearing 'no,' are you?" she asked.

"All part of the package. Beautiful and talented. Who could resist you?"

"Are you talking about me? Have you heard my small talk? Barely grunts and groans," she said in a rush. "And I talk with my mouth full. Very vulgar."

Another evening of mingling with society's elite, people whose eyes would constantly roam the room for more important fare as she listened to conversations about their most recent remodel. She'd stopped counting how many times people mistook her for an interior decorator.

Another evening of wondering if Ryan Cutty might once again part the river of the crowd.

This morning, she'd shoved aside the covers and stared at the ceiling, weighed down by a strange feeling of loss. Slipping out of bed, she'd tried to put her finger on this new doom and gloom when the realization struck. She'd walked to the window with the eerie knowledge that this time he wouldn't be waiting outside, wrapped in fog.

That's how Harris found her, kneeling on the couch, craning her neck to take in every corner of the street below. He'd asked what she was up to, and she'd jumped half out of her skin. She must have looked like a fish, her mouth opening and closing without making a sound.

"Well," her brother had said. "I'll find out the truth soon enough."

And now she appeared just as transparent to Daniel. She stood, putting away her sketches, her eyes avoiding his, wondering if she should tell him what she really thought.

I'm scared of your house. I'm consumed by thoughts of your cousin. And you, my man, are a fool not to see the beauty of my ideas.

"I suggest we put the razzle-dazzle on hold," she said instead. "That's not my method. Why be premature and celebrate at the cost of our credibility later? You have no idea what lies ahead or what we might find under the plaster molding—"

Daniel's hand covered hers on the table. He waited until she looked up, giving him her full attention.

"I don't much care for excuses, even little white ones," he told her. "Holly, darling, I'm not worried about a setback. I've seen your work, so I won't push for results now. Just tell me that tonight you'll be there on my arm."

"Daniel," she said firmly. "I need sleep, not dinner and dancing."

"I'll pick you up at eight o'clock."

"Daniel—"

"Let me explain *my* method." He dropped a roll of bills on the table and picked up her portfolio, steering her down the street at a bit of a clip. *Move aside, folks. Man on a mission.* "In this city, people make things happen. People invest. People show up on opening night. People write about my restaurant in newspapers and magazines. Do you understand now about my method?"

Another party, she thought dismally, stopping beside him at the street corner.

"Perfectly," she told him.

He winked, handing over her portfolio case. "Eight it is, then."

She watched Daniel strut away. He truly was a beautiful man. And a fool.

"It could have been brilliant," she said out loud of her plans, not that Daniel would ever hear her. Or care even if he had.

Walking in the bleary light of noon, she reminded herself of what she'd told her brother. This was a dream job, and she was more than up for the task. *Pull yourself up by your bootstraps, girl. God helps those who help themselves. A stitch in time saves...oh, whatever.*

She'd take them all on—the house, the boss, the man. And that strange emptiness? The idea that Ryan was no longer there, if he'd ever been? She'd get over that, as well.

All the truly great houses in Pacific Heights had names—the Haas-Lilienthal House, Wormser-Coleman, the Spreckels Mansion. Many were wedding presents, like the Italianate mansion on Vallejo, an ex-sailor's gift to his son. And William Haas had deeded the house on Franklin street, now known as Bransten House, to his daughter, Florine, upon the occasion of her marriage to Edward Bransten of MJB Coffee fame.

Vanessa Cutty, née Moore, had grown up in a house with a name. The only child of Annabelle and Foster Moore of the Moore's auction house—known in its heyday as the "Sotheby's of the West"—Vanessa received Moore Manor, a lovely Queen Anne Victorian, as a present from her father upon her marriage to Samuel Cutty. At the time, Foster Moore hadn't approved of his daughter's choice. Being a man who could tangentially trace his bloodlines back to the railroad barons, he considered the Cuttys well beneath his daughter's pedigree. And there was Samuel to consider, who Foster believed too handsome, too spoiled and too stupid.

Of course, Daddy had been right on all counts, but Vanessa convinced her father that he was being old-fashioned. She wanted Samuel, and in the end that proved enough for Foster.

Moore Manor stood a stone's throw from the famed corner of California and Franklin, considered by many as the gateway to San Francisco's elite in Pacific Heights. Since the accident that had wiped out that toxin, Nina, from their lives, Vanessa's one and only child had made it a point to avoid the old homestead. This morning Ryan waited in the vestibule.

Vanessa prepared to receive his visit in the conservatory, arranging Madeleine cookies on a china plate with her favorite Blue Willow pattern. Attached to the house, the room was where she greeted her most important guests. It was the only place free of Samuel; she kept the key. With glass to the ceiling and temperature control, here she could coax life from even the most recalcitrant of plants. Like Vanessa, some of the orchids in the room had pedigrees going back a hundred years.

"Hello, Mother."

Ryan stood at the door. Somehow, she didn't remember him being so tall; his shoulders so broad. *Just like his father.* She thought the blue cambric shirt set off his eyes nicely.

Today, she wore pink, a color she favored. The pantsuit was something most women would choose for an afternoon of shopping at Nieman Marcus but Vanessa might just as well wear gardening. She watched him as if confused. Standing there, she felt like a bird. Insubstantial, ready to take flight.

She'd felt much the same at the party for that architect. *Like standing on the edge of a cliff, looking down.* She'd watched her son storm the room to face off with his cousin, unsure of how to stop their collision course. Ryan had his father's good looks but he had Vanessa's temper. She hadn't known what to expect with Daniel's little surprise package standing beside them and that wretched La Plume woman waiting, her poison pen at the ready.

"Thank you for coming," she told Ryan, sounding cold and distant and disapproving.

Is this the best you can do? she scolded herself.

She stepped down the path circling like a yellow brick road toward Ryan. Coming nearer, she held her arms outstretched. But her welcome was too much. Ryan kept his hands at his side as she embraced him. Still, she didn't let go, holding him even tighter.

When slowly he raised his arms, she imagined the action came out of memory more than desire. The last twelve years he'd managed the obligatory phone calls, even the occasional lunch. But this tender moment had caught him off guard.

He'd made it clear—she'd chased him away by her lack of faith and he wasn't about to forgive her. She would have done the same. But now she felt more than ever this need to reach him, to make amends.

"I know what you must be thinking," she whispered. "I don't know what to tell you. Daniel claims she's nothing but a talented architect—"

He placed her at arms' length, the expression on his face so clearly filled with disappointment.

Taking her cue, she stepped back. Because she knew better. Everything, even confession, had its time and place.

"Please." She gestured toward the rattan chair and

the waiting coffee service. After the slightest hesitation, Ryan preceded her down the garden path.

She told herself she'd earned her banishment from his life. When the police arrived at her door investigating that girl's death, she had seen only her boy's guilty face, how easily he'd gone with them, almost knowing, expecting the charges. She'd known then that he'd killed her. Foolishly she'd interpreted the act as a betrayal. She couldn't imagine him being so weak of character. *My son, capable of murder?*

Only later, here in her conservatory tending her orchids, did she have her revelation. She'd been cutting off diseased leaves, sterilizing her blade between cuts, not wanting the black rot that infected a few plants to spread, when the thought struck. To cut off a diseased limb—to take action while the other sheep in the family watched Nina destroy them—wasn't an act of cowardice, at all. Perhaps it had been an act of courage.

Of course, she'd never spoken to Ryan about the matter. She'd done her work behind the scenes, calling an important friend to urge the district attorney to drop the charges. The autopsy showed Nina had been under the influence of both alcohol and prescription drugs, the combination alone providing a sufficient basis for the accident. Why torture Ryan by this endless scrutiny?

She'd never put into words what she'd come to believe, that Nina, that black rot, had been cut from their lives.

She'd lost him after that, because she'd been too schooled in the art of right and wrong to act herself. She'd left it up to Ryan to rid them of Nina.

No wonder he hates me.

She stepped over to the coffee service, one of many artifacts handed down through generations of uppity

ancestors. It was all she had left really, these gems
from the past. That and her righteous anger. Everything else had been sacrificed to Samuel's appetites.

"Coffee?" she asked. "I know you're not much for
tea."

He stood watching, his eyes so much like his father's that it hurt. "Somehow I thought this would go
differently."

She ignored the coffee and sat down on the rattan
chair. "All right. Let's skip the chitchat." She gave
him an assessing look, feeling that Moore control taking hold.

"When did you lose your backbone, Ryan?" Her
temper flared again, because he'd disappeared from
her life and she couldn't quite accept his lack of forgiveness. The wound was there, fresh and painful,
every day of her life. "You let Daniel take everything.
You didn't stay. You didn't fight. What else was I to
do but give him control of Cutty House?"

He granted a smile, on common ground now. "I
never said he wasn't the right man for the job."

He stepped over to a spray of exquisite blue vandas,
reminding her of all the times she'd brought him here,
reciting the origin and genealogy of each plant. *Don't
touch, darling. The oils from your skin will turn the
petals brown.*

How carefully she'd cultivated his life, taking Ryan
to cotillion and supper club, sending himself off to his
sailing lessons and Marshall's Academy. Eventually
he'd earned a berth at Stanford. Only to watch Gil and
Samuel with their chortling plans—*uniting our two
kingdoms!*—destroy everything by forcing Nina on her
boy.

"You'll let Daniel take it, then?" she challenged.
"Without a fight? Cutty House is your birthright."

"So you've told me once or twice."

It had been a litany during his youth. How many times had she told him? *You're the last of the Cuttys, Ryan.*

"I love it when you try to manipulate me," he said with a smile.

"Not that I've ever succeeded." She tucked one leg beneath the other. "But just to let you know the old bird hasn't lost her touch, let me update you on the state of affairs here." Fully in gear now, she continued. "Your father has become an alcoholic, not that you seem the least bit interested. And Daniel, of all people, is the only man I can count on."

"Poor Mother."

She raised her chin. "God knows I need him to come through. And he will. With a little help."

"From Holly Fairfield?"

"She seems competent enough. You should read the press Daniel has on her. It was reassuring—"

"Daniel didn't hire her to rebuild Cutty House."

"So you think she's some tawdry publicity ploy? So what, if it works," she said, calming her own misgivings. Vanessa had never had much faith in Daniella's boy. She believed in blood showing through. Daniel's was tainted. "And how can you know Daniel's intentions?" Meaning, he hadn't bothered to be part of the picture for some time.

"I think you're taking a big risk, trusting his judgment."

"As if you've given me a choice?" With a little acid to her voice, she added, "How is Gil? Is he still needy and pitiful and sad?"

"All of the above," he told her, not budging.

She stood and slipped her hand into his, a change

in tactics. "Your father needs you just as much. If you want pathetic, take a look at him."

"But then, Gil didn't try to put me in jail."

"He thought you would run away. It would have made everything so much worse. You were young and reckless and he wanted to help. With the proper advice, you would have made it through the crisis. You know how you were back then. How could you not expect your father to think you would run away?"

"Quite honestly, it wasn't Dad I was counting on."

"I listened to Samuel, my husband," she said, defending herself. He wouldn't know about the calls she'd made on his behalf. And what had she done really but swept the trash under the carpet, leaving the stench in the air?

"I made a mistake," she said, trying to appease. "There. I said it. Please. Stop punishing me—"

"Don't. Just, don't."

She caught his longing glance for the exit. She tried to preempt him. "You're right. I'll tell Daniel to get rid of her." Was that feverish voice really hers? "He can find someone else to finish the renovation."

And why not? Holly Fairfield had been an unpleasant surprise, to say the least. All along, she'd thought she could control Daniel. But now this?

"Of course, she's upset you. How could she not? I should never have agreed to it. But you know Daniel. His hopes and his dreams."

"And long may they reign," he said, still looking at the door.

Vanessa squeezed his hand, anchoring him. "I've lost the gallery. I've lost your father. I may soon lose Cutty House if Daniel isn't up to the task. Don't let me lose you, as well. I couldn't bear it."

But the moment of high drama was over as easily as it began, at least for Ryan.

"You haven't lost me, Mother. You know where to find me," he said gently. "But I just can't be a part of this. Maybe I never could. Maybe it should have been Daniel all along."

She was shaking her head, genuine tears coming to her eyes. She wanted to tell him, I have missed you so. But he wouldn't know how to react to her show of emotion. She'd never been that sort of mother. Why make him bear the weight of it now?

She stepped back, transforming into the matriarch, a woman more familiar to them both. "Please tell Gil he's wasting his time sending his silly invitations to his parties." She raised her chin, anger so much easier an emotion. "He stole what is mine—he made you choose. I won't be going anywhere near his vineyard."

Ryan gave a tired sigh. "It wasn't Gil who sent the invitations. I'll call you next week," he said, leaning down to give her a peck on the cheek, finally getting the job done and heading for the door.

Leaving her once again alone.

8

Emma kept her father alive in her kitchen. With every recipe, she could conjure bittersweet memories of her childhood. She still remembered making her first dish on the cast-iron range original to the kitchen at Cutty House. She'd been so small, she'd had to climb on a stool to see inside the pot where her father cooked red beans and rice. From her father, Emma learned to cook with color and shapes.

Humming softly, she lay the shrimp atop boats made from corn husk shells dusted with cayenne powder. Alongside, she placed a dollop of the golden *maza* for *tamale dulce*. When he wasn't cooking or falling-down drunk, Carlos Wright liked to play his guitar, making music an integral part of her memories. She could hear that music now inside her head as she dribbled the brilliant red roasted pepper sauce over the shrimp grilled and basted with *mojo*. She studied her creation. Not bad.

But not what Daniel would want in his kitchen.

"Think squab consommé and seared swordfish in quivering *gelée*," she told herself.

She glanced at the clock over the stove. Daniel would be home any minute. He'd expect a report.

Under Daniel's instructions, she'd spent the afternoon dragging Holly through spas and boutiques for her makeover. She'd felt like a dirtbag the whole time, knowing that what she was doing was twisted, Daniel at his scheming best. But it was what he wanted, to transform Holly for tonight's party.

Even worse, Emma found she'd enjoyed herself trying on the clothes, laughing along with Holly. More than once, she'd had to remind herself that Holly was the enemy.

At least Holly's brother wouldn't make the party tonight. She'd made sure to ask, too scared not to. She couldn't shake the feeling that she'd made a big mistake by going back to the bar the other night.

She heard the front door open and glanced down at the food with a sigh. She'd have to hurry and get ready; she didn't want to make Daniel late.

She listened to Daniel bouncing around the apartment as she wrapped the shrimp dish in wax paper and boxed it for later. They'd been off lately. More and more, she'd been spending time at her place alone, Beth, her roommate, having taken off for a much-needed vacation.

She wished she could do that sometimes, just run away.

Her relationship with Daniel had always had its ups and downs. You couldn't be with a guy like him and not expect the occasional disappointment. She'd even left him a couple of times, wondering if their love was cursed and could never be the fairy tale they pretended.

But Daniel always managed to find her, convincing her to believe just one more time. She'd tried to explain it to Holly earlier, why she stayed.

"Daniel's not so bad. He's worked at Cutty House all his life, you know…while they shipped Ryan off to all those fancy schools. Ryan never wanted anything to do with the restaurant business. He was way above all that. But every summer, there was Daniel, working his tail off, while Ryan sailed off into the sunset, Mr. Rich and Spoiled, getting his wanderlust fix. Kinda hard to watch, you know? How unfair it was.''

And it had been unfair. Sure, the business belonged to Ryan's father. Daniel's mom had stuck her foot in it, getting pregnant when she was really young. She was supposed to get married, but it didn't go so well for her. When it all fell apart, Daniel had come to live with Samuel and Vanessa.

Years later, Daniel's mom had gotten her act together, going off to have a real family. She'd left Daniel here, at Cutty House, like some afterthought. Samuel's hired help.

Despite the long odds, Daniel had pushed himself, going to school, paying for everything. He'd even gotten some sort of degree in finance, though not a fancy one like Ryan at Stanford. That's why he was taking over now, because he'd proven himself to Vanessa.

The story always had the desired effect. Emma could see Holly's expression change to one of sympathy as she told it.

''That's why he likes to give people a second chance,'' she'd told Holly, sealing it, because she knew Holly's company had gone belly-up. Emma even believed what she'd said. Most times, anyway.

''How did it go today?''

She turned toward the door and found Daniel positively glowing as he stepped into the kitchen. She smiled to herself. No kiss. No ''Hey, how are you?'' Just Daniel and his agenda.

Maybe that's why everything was going wrong between them. She and Daniel didn't see this Holly thing the same way. She knew it was wrong, while Daniel just kept on, full speed ahead. Lately, she'd even had the rogue thought of taking off again. *Just leave him.*

But having chosen this path, she was stuck. Even if she had made her choice on a dark and scary night when she was all of fourteen, she would still have to pay. She couldn't just run from her past.

She put the shrimp away in the refrigerator and turned around, giving Daniel what he wanted, a big thumbs-up. But it worried her. Tonight, when Holly walked through the door—who would Daniel see?

"Operation Beautiful Swan, complete," she said.

He snatched her up and kissed her, too keyed up to even notice when she didn't kiss him back.

But after a minute, he cupped her face in his hands. "What's up? You're not still worried about me and Holly?"

"It's not just that—"

"Come on, baby. I love *you*. Remember?"

At times like this, she could almost convince herself. This one moment, he was all hers. Her hero again. Protector and guide, just like before. And it didn't matter that their love was based on some horrible lie. That was then, this is now.

"You worry too much," he told her, smiling. "Tonight will be a piece of cake. You'll see, Ems. There's nothing to worry about."

The problem was, she couldn't quite convince herself. More and more, her faith just fizzled out. Like now. *You worry too much.* As if it was all so easy, trying to destroy people's lives. *A piece of cake...*

Easy for him to say.

Holly stared into the mirror. She had no idea how long she'd been standing there, looking at herself, mystified by what a little makeup and new clothes could accomplish. Reflected back at her in the mirror was another woman altogether.

The stylist at the salon had cut her hair into one of those messy bobs, an updated Audrey Hepburn look with bangs. The cut made her eyes look bigger, turning her into even more the ingenue.

And the clothes… She'd picked them out with Emma as advisor. The outfit was exquisite and simple, like nothing she'd ever worn. Flowing black trousers, a white halter top with a ruffle that came up to frame her face and a plunging neckline that made her plenty nervous. The salesgirl had explained how Holly could use double-sided tape to keep things from crossing over into an NC-17 rating.

"Yikes," she said to the lady in the mirror.

After Holly had left Daniel at the café, her ego checked at the door, Emma had shown up at Holly's office—surprise!—declaring herself the Fairy Godmother to those persecuted by Daniel, the Wicked Warlock of the East.

"Enjoy every minute of it, dahling," Emma drawled during their impromptu facials at this outrageous spa they'd found. "It's all on Daniel's expense account."

Emma explained that Daniel felt bad. He'd been too hard on Holly, dissing all her hard work. She shouldn't give up. How many times had he trashed a prized recipe before Emma figured out the rules? It's Dan's way or the highway.

And the party tonight? He wasn't so much demanding that Holly show up as needing her there. And boy, would he make it up to her. She might even have fun, Emma told her with a wry smile. The trip to the spa and stylist, and the shopping spree—that was only the warm-up act.

By the time Emma was through, they'd done the whole *Pretty Woman* thing, complete with a wardrobe that left Holly breathless by the cost and daring of their choices. At first, she'd vowed to pay back every cent, keeping a strict tally of each expense. But some time after she bought the Manolo Blahnik shoes on Emma's insistence—"Daniel will love these!"—she thought maybe Daniel deserved a couple of hits to his credit card.

They ended up laughing over a cup of coffee at the snotty expression Emma had gotten from one boutique owner. With her torn jeans and pierced lip, Emma wasn't the kind of client they were used to fawning over.

"It's seductive, isn't it?"

Holly turned around. She'd been so caught up in the fantasy in the mirror that she hadn't heard Harris, who was standing in the hall just outside her bedroom door.

"The outfit?" she asked. She'd been afraid it was too much.

"All the goodies, Holly. The clothes, the job." He gestured at the posh surroundings. "This apartment."

She could see that her brother was warming up. She braced herself, turning away from the mirror, trying not to look guilty as charged.

"I've been there, sis," he told her from the doorway. "Finally, getting the goodies. Where we came from, all this would be too much to pass up. But I wonder, what's the price? In my experience, there's always a price."

"I'm trying to do a job here, Harris."

"Right." He gave the outfit another look, his silence saying it all. Like it would ever be part of her job to dress like this.

He looked so disappointed, it actually hurt.

"You're not normally the one to take the easy way. But kiddo, did you ever grab for this one with both hands."

"Easy?" She thought about her meeting with Daniel today, how he'd shot down every idea. "Let me bring you in on a little secret, Harris. I am terrified here. I'm supposed to renovate what amounts to a historical treasure and I'm working for a crazy man. Daniel has no idea what he wants, but it certainly isn't anything I'm coming up with. I don't sleep so well these days, if you haven't noticed."

"Which is exactly my point. You're working for a crazy man. You said it, not me. So why keep at it? Why not just say we made a mistake and get on home?"

"Because we didn't make a mistake! *I* didn't make a mistake. Is it really so hard for you?" she asked, confronting him with the truth. "That for once, I'm the one bailing us out?"

"I don't need bailing out." He shook his head. "No way. Don't do this for me."

"All right. Agreed. God forbid that you should let me help you. Harris, all those years…it was always you. I mean, how old were you when Mom walked out? Seven, maybe? And Dad working two jobs, until he realized you were so damn good at taking care of me that even he bailed."

"I did what I had to do. You don't have to be here, Hol, looking like that. You don't have to do any of this."

"Well, maybe I do," she told him, raising her voice to match his. "Did you ever think that maybe I need this?" She was breathing fast. She couldn't remember the last time she'd argued with Harris. Over Drew, probably, when Harris had tried to convince her not to marry the jerk.

"For once, Harris, please…let *me* be the knight in shining armor."

He got this fierce look, no longer the sweetheart of a brother she knew him to be. His dark eyes never failed to intimidate when he stared at someone like that.

"So you've dug in your heels, have you? All right." He nodded, stepping back from the door. "We'll do it your way. But not alone. Just give me a sec."

She ran out into the hall, shouting, "Who said you were invited?"

"Just try and stop me." He slammed into his room, taking his bad temper out on the door.

She smiled, not necessarily averse to Harris tagging along. But she yelled, "Just don't cause any trouble."

For good measure.

9

Harris had seen a couple of wild places in his life, but this joint might crack his top-ten list.

Buried in the heart of SoMa, the Samba, Samba! club had its own little Carnival going. Conga lines snaked past the dance floor and half-dressed models wearing feathered headdresses and G-strings to make Vegas blush pranced up and down a catwalk to chest-thumping techno music. A full bar awaited at each end of the warehouse-cum-dance club. At each bar, a video of the models strutting their stuff appeared on giant screens on opposing walls, so you didn't have to crane your neck to get a look-see.

The crowd, too, was a kick in the pants. Vamping lollipop women wearing not much of anything hung on the arms of Dow Jones suits. A bare-assed boy was being led around by a dog collar, while another man wore only tinfoil, complete with antennae. And a drag queen dressed to look like a wedding cake, with an enormous wig topping the layers, caught Harris staring and said with a wink, "The higher the hair, the closer to God!"

The place was hopping all right. Still, he didn't have any trouble finding her.

The way Harris saw things, it was long past time to get off his keester. Sure, Holly wanted to play the knight in shining armor, and any other time he'd be happy to give her a big brother thumbs-up. But Harris knew too well about that kind of motivation, knew how a person might look the other way, thanking their lucky stars for supposed good fortune, forgetting that the goodies always came with a price tag attached.

His sister's fairy tale had a big bad wolf by the name of Daniel East tacked on. The way Danny was throwing money around, he was either an idiot or he was doing something illegal. Harris figured it was the latter.

But the story wasn't coming from the man himself. Nah, old Daniel wasn't giving any hints. Which meant Harris had to pick on someone else.

"Emma," he whispered, coming up behind her.

She had on this white strappy dress cut real low in the back so that you knew she wasn't wearing a damn thing underneath. The pearly silk looked like it was hanging on for dear life. Really, it surprised him that the dress didn't just fall right off when she turned around to see him.

Her eyes got all wide. In this light, they looked an even deeper green. "Your sister told me you weren't coming." An accusation.

Harris smiled. No need to read between the lines.

"And here I thought you'd be happy to see me." He knew she was scared. That's the kind of thing he could get from people—the easy emotions like fear and hate.

"Holly told me you were working tonight," she said, losing the edge to her voice, a little more in control.

He took a drink of his beer. "What? And miss this?"

He gestured to where Daniel escorted his sister past the gauntlet of the city's rich and mighty. Danny was on a high, introducing Holly to those willing to plunk down money for tonight's charity du jour.

He turned back to Emma. She'd pulled her hair into a tight knot at the base of her elegant neck and wore a tiny diamond stud where she'd pierced her lip, like a beauty mark meant to attract attention to a damn fine feature. The dress, too, was pretty distracting. For an instant, he wondered which lucky guy she'd dressed for. For a second, he wished it was him.

"Nice dress" was all he could muster, like a kid on a first date.

"Are you going to stand there and stare at my tits all night?"

She'd said it to be shocking, and it worked. He raised his eyes to her face.

"Well, don't I feel like an idiot." But he couldn't wipe the grin off his face.

"I've got to go."

She made to step around him, but he stopped her. He'd meant to come on easy, make like the good guy. *Trust me, babe. Tell me all your secrets.* Now he'd blown it. He was usually better at this sort of thing.

"I was hoping you'd introduce me around," he said.

"I don't know any of these people. This is Dan's gig. I'm just the hired help."

"Really? I hope he pays well."

She gave him a look, catching his tone. "Meaning?"

"Oh, I don't know. The way you keep looking at him and my sister…" He gave a shrug. "I thought he should make it worth your while, that's all."

She crossed her arms over her chest so that the nearly transparent material pressed against her skin, making his eyes wander again, making him think she'd done it on purpose. She was drinking one of those froufrou drinks. She must have really been watching him close, because she knew the minute he stopped staring at her breasts and noticed the drink.

"It's called a Platinum Blonde." She toasted him and took a healthy sip. "And how am I looking at Dan and your sister?"

"How to put this delicately? My sister isn't moving in on your territory."

"No shit? And I'm suppose to listen to a punk-ass jerk like you about Dan?"

"You get a kick out of that? Shocking people?"

"Is it working?"

"Better than you want."

She had these clear green eyes. And man, could they show hurt. Which was a problem because Harris had a soft spot for damsels in distress. It had gotten him in a world of trouble long before tonight.

You'd think a man could learn a lesson, buckle down, get the job done. But not Harris. No siree. Right then and there, he could feel himself slipping, seeing her point of view.

"Hey. I'm sorry. Okay?"

She gave him a real smile this time, the kind that comes from somewhere deep inside a person. Watching him, she drained the glass and whispered, "Thanks," as she walked past...but not before he saw her tears.

"Wait a minute. Hey, wait!"

Emma was a tiny thing, making a nice job of cutting through the crowd, while he had to fight his way past, making elbow contact with the Mighty Wedding Cake, who looked like he could take Harris in a smackdown any day.

She'd already grabbed her wrap from the cloakroom by the time he reached her.

"Look, you don't strike me as the shrinking violet type," he said, coming up alongside her. "I'm sorry if I offended you. I was just trying to figure something out."

The tears were long gone, replaced by a hard look of suspicion. "Like?"

"Like if you'd want to have a drink with me. Or if there's already a prior commitment."

The words came from his heart, which shocked him. It had been a long time for him, precisely because he'd discovered his ability to make mistakes. He thought he might be making one now.

"Okay," she said, keeping those surprises coming. "But not here. There's a bar. It isn't far, but we're taking a taxi because I can't walk in these stupid heels."

He opened the door for her. "I like a woman who takes charge."

He waited there, with the door open, wondering where this could possibly be going, telling himself to be careful. It wouldn't be the first time he'd blown something over a pretty face.

But the worst part was seeing her turn around and case the room before she stepped past, getting in that last glance at Daniel hanging on Holly's every word.

The guy didn't see her. Didn't catch her dramatic exit with another man. Didn't even know when she left.

Emma thought she could make it all right again. Satisfy his curiosity, make him go away. She'd been too scared just to let him stay curious. So the last thing she'd expected was to be sitting here enjoying herself.

The club scene still thrived in San Francisco despite the dotcom bomb. Emma liked the Red Room. Small, dark and boozy, the place had an edge. It was easy to get lost here. A person could just slip on down the leather banquette, megamartini in hand.

Tonight, the alcohol steadied her nerves. And something else. Sitting on the edge of the stool, the grunge bar blessedly free of slumming yupsters and AMWs (actress-model-whatever), she found herself flirting with Harris.

The alcohol made it okay to do that. And Harris. That smile of his. He wasn't half bad with the banter, either. Looking at him through the blur of her drink, she could almost forget the sight of Daniel drooling over Holly.

"Don't drink so fast." He stopped her hand as she raised the martini glass. "It makes me think you're in a hurry."

"Maybe that's not such a bad idea," she told him. But again, she was flirting, saying it with a smile.

"Pain in the ass, am I?"

She leaned forward as if giving him a serious looking over. Dark hair, melt-you-down brown eyes. Tonight he'd dressed in a white guayabera shirt that somehow managed to scream straight boy when it wouldn't on most men.

"You're not too bad for an old guy," she told him, playing it up.

He grinned. "You into that, then? The old guy thing?" he asked, knowing that Daniel was even older than him.

"You don't know what you're talking about," she said, feeling the mood slip. She stabbed the olive inside the martini glass with her toothpick. She told herself she wasn't trying to make Daniel jealous by leav-

ing the party with Holly's brother. Just because he'd
fallen all over Holly the minute he laid eyes on her
didn't mean Emma needed to worry.

Just because it hurt like hell to watch him eat her
up with his eyes didn't make it okay for Emma to get
drunk and find some other man to make her feel special.

She poked the olive again. "Don't date dinosaurs,"
she told him, focusing her anger on the olive, trying
not to slur her words. "Very uncool."

"Why do I suddenly feel like checking my pockets
for a Sen-sen?"

"A what?"

"Right." That smile again. "Dinosaur status confirmed."

Daniel had explained how tonight with Holly was
just business. *A little joke on Ryan, okay? The shit
deserves it.* But the way Holly had looked made everything go fuzzy in Emma's head. It was kind of
spooky, like looking into the past and seeing everything in vivid Technicolor.

"I hate parties," she said. Hated watching Holly all
dressed up, feeling guilty and furious at the same time
to see Daniel's arm permanently attached to Holly's
waist. "Parties make me nervous."

"That explains it."

He lifted her hand in his. Her fingers were shaking.

She stared at her hand, so much smaller and whiter
than his. She glanced up, saying, "It could be the company."

"Don't I wish."

Taking her hand away, she said, "What makes you
so sure?"

He looked as if he wasn't going to answer, but said,

"Right now, sitting there, killing that olive, I'm betting it's not me you're thinking about."

With a final blow to Mr. Olive, she dropped the lot into the glass. "This conversation is getting boring."

"Is it? I'll try harder. Will you go out with me tomorrow night?"

Inside her chest, her heart did a swan dive. He'd surprised her again, putting her off balance, because she wanted to say yes in the worst way.

It would be for all the wrong reasons, she told herself. Because she was mad at Daniel. Because she was thinking too much about the past. Because of Holly Fairfield.

He's her brother, for God's sake.

If she wanted to teach Daniel a lesson, she couldn't have picked a worse choice. Or a better one.

"Why is it," she asked, "that the minute a guy thinks you're not interested, he immediately needs you to be?"

"Wow." He sat back on the bar stool. "Usually, my crash and burn takes more than—" he made a show of looking at his watch "—thirty-eight seconds."

He had a talent for disarming people with humor, something she found hard to trust. Or resist.

She picked up the drink again, the alcohol making her willing to take a chance. "Change of subject." She really liked his smile and tried to drum up one of her own. "Why a bartender?"

"Why a chef?"

She shook her finger at him. "I asked first."

"Because it's easy." The quick comeback. "And I needed that for a while."

"So. What was it before, rocket scientist?"

He smiled, as if he liked the sound of that. "You never know."

He wasn't going to say, which only made her more curious. *Something to hide…*

"Come on," she coaxed. "You can tell me the truth."

"Is that what you want?" he asked. "Honesty?"

She blinked. Just like that, he'd switched everything around again. They'd been laughing, having fun, then, whammo, he's trying to pry some confession out of her. What was he, some sort of spy? Grilling her like this?

She stood, the room suddenly swimming. She'd come here to show Daniel, make him jealous. *Well, you showed him, didn't you?*

"I gotta go."

He stopped her, grabbing her hand. "I said the wrong thing. I do that sometimes. But I have a good learning curve. I can keep it light. Don't leave. Not yet."

How long had it been since a man had sounded that desperate for her? How utterly seductive to hear that emotion in his voice.

"No, I…I have an early morning tomorrow," she said, pulling away.

But even running for the door, she knew it was too late. The way he'd looked at her, how he'd made her feel—it was like she'd tripped a switch in her head, getting it. The reason she'd gone back to the bar the other night, wanting to talk to Harris, why she'd left the party with him just now…

All along, she'd been telling herself it was for Daniel's sake. She was watching his back, just like he'd done for her when she was a kid.

But they weren't kids anymore. What she was feeling right now had nothing to do with Daniel. He wasn't even in the picture. And maybe that scared her most of all.

10

In a way, Holly was relieved to see him again. He was standing just outside the club, the first person she saw when she stepped out the door, ready to call it a night. He'd obviously been waiting for her, wasn't bothering to hide. She hadn't seen him inside, but she thought she'd sensed him there. She'd felt that funny tingling at the back of her neck again.

Tonight he could give Daniel a run for his money with the fashion sense. Saffron shirt, three-button dark charcoal suit, hair in stylish disarray. She tried not to be intimidated, walking right up to him, heels clicking on the cement as her heart sped up to another beat.

She'd spent all night watching the frenetic crowd at the club, anticipating that tap on the shoulder, disappointed when it never came. Half the time, Daniel had called her on it—Holly, baby, you still with me?—knowing she wasn't paying attention.

"I'm glad you're here. Really." She laughed, the sound coming out like a release. "It was driving me crazy, that waiting." She took a breath, settling. "Now we can get this over with." Because she knew there was something there, something they needed to settle.

"What do you suggest?" he asked almost lazily.

"You said you're not following me," she blurted

out. "But I know you are—I mean you were. And it actually surprised me when you stopped. And then, I knew that you hadn't, because tonight I felt you there, at the club."

He covered her mouth with his hand.

She took his hand away. "The thing with the talking again. Maybe you could explain your aversion to speech?" And when he played the statue, she nodded as if she understood, as if anything about this man came close to making sense.

She considered all the possible angles, but nothing seemed to explain that first time at Cutty House and the look on his face when he'd seen her. What could it mean to have a man stare at her with that much longing? And the question she wanted most to ask: Why me?

Only, she wasn't getting her answers. Not tonight, anyway.

"All righty, then." She gave him a salute, going for the better part of valor as she turned and strutted down the street, swinging her purse from its chain.

Then she pivoted around, coming back at him, because the man was beginning to haunt her. It was as if he knew some secret about her but wasn't telling.

"Look—" She stabbed a finger to his chest. *Oh, I'm a scary little thing, aren't I?* Giving him what for. "I don't claim to be good at this sort of thing, confrontations, but if there's a problem—"

He grabbed her hand and whispered, "There's a problem. But here's the thing. I'm wondering if you know what it is. Are you in on it with Daniel or is he just using you?"

Like that made any sense? But in a way it did, mirroring her brother's fears that there was something behind Daniel's generosity. *Too good to be true.*

She tugged her hand free, but she didn't move away. She thought about what Emma had told her. Ryan could be unstable. The way he followed her around, he most likely was. Still, she stayed where she was, looking up at him, evaluating. She might not have Harris's talent for reading people, but she just couldn't see violence in him. And that connection she felt? She couldn't admit she had that with a killer.

She hugged the expensive wrap closer. She tried to focus on her words, going for a different tactic. *I show you mine—you show me yours....*

"I know certain things," she said, being purposely vague. "At first, I thought, why me? But I pieced it together," she said, not wanting to add, *I know about that poor woman, your fiancée.*

"Cutty House." She raised her chin. "You don't want the restaurant to succeed," she guessed, throwing out the most likely motive. "Not with Daniel at the helm. And somehow, you believe I might be part of that success."

"Why did you let him dress you like that?" he asked.

It had been a long night, wearing dangerously high heels, and now this? The man made her head spin. "Suddenly, haute couture is a crime?"

"You make it sound as if you don't know what's going on, but you cut your hair, you wore his clothes. I hate it, by the way. Your hair. The clothes."

That prickling at the back of her neck was doing a rumba. "Again," she told him crisply, "I speak English. Very well, actually. But I don't get you."

"The charity tonight. Daniel knew I'd be here. That's why he brought you, showing you off. To me."

As if she were Daniel's own Helen of Troy?

But Ryan only stepped closer, sending up rocket flares as he violated all sorts of personal space. "God, if you don't know…"

Looking up at him, she thought of all the things she did know—the car accident, the murder inquiry. And the things she didn't know: Why exactly Daniel had hired her. For the first time, she allowed the possibility that she was a tad underqualified and significantly overpaid.

She whispered, "All right. Fill me in."

Ryan rocked back, needing the distance to take in the whole picture of her, checking her out, head to foot. He smiled and shook his head. Whatever he'd been about to tell her, she could see he was backing off.

"I think I've come to like Daniel's game," he said. "Maybe that was Dan's idea all along. Why the hell not?" He said it as if coming to a decision. "He went to a lot of trouble to find you."

"Is that a question?"

He smiled. "Not for you."

"I have a job to do," she said, going on the offense. "That's why I'm here. You can't stop me."

"No?" It was very much a question.

Somewhere, in the back of her mind, this little voice was screaming: *You're standing alone with a possible killer!* Only, she didn't want the conversation to end. Didn't want to spend the next week looking over her shoulder wondering when he might show.

Ryan had a different idea. He jogged out into the street and hailed a cab. She thought he was leaving.

She wanted to shout something provocative to stop him, something that would make him stay and explain. *You think you look hot in those clothes, but…okay, you do.*

But when the cab pulled over, he surprised her by holding the door open and waiting there beside the car. She didn't see any option but to take him up on his genteel offer.

Slipping inside, she remembered what Harris had told her. *Seduced by all the goodies.* She considered the worst-case scenario, that the attentions of a handsome and mysterious man might just be the biggest goody of them all. The crime of the lonely.

"So now I just run away again?" she asked, looking up at him. "How many times do we do this?"

He gave the cab driver directions to her apartment and smiled. "As many as it takes."

Shutting the door, he sent her on her way.

Half an hour later, Holly sat on the couch with her back to the window, the living-room lights off and a glass of red wine at the ready on the coffee table before her.

She was remembering her trip to the grocery store that morning. She'd been standing in line buying orange juice and sourdough bread—a San Francisco favorite—when her eyes happened upon the caption of a popular fitness magazine. *Get Bulge-free Knees!* (In only 20 minutes a day.) She remembered wondering, *Now I have to worry about my knees?*

In front of her on the conveyor belt, a six-pack of beer had ambled toward the cashier as the man ahead of her asked for Marlboros, "hard pack, please." She remembered some smart-aleck remark popping in her head like: What was beer without cigarettes, after all? Breakfast of champions.

Only later, inside the dark and empty apartment, she'd thought the man had the right idea. Why not self-medicate? With that brilliant idea in hand, she'd headed for the kitchen and opened a nice California Merlot. She'd set the glass untouched on the coffee table like a work of art.

She'd eventually run out of random thoughts, like the man and his beer, trying to forget about the Ryans and Daniels of the world. But it was a bit like that joke when someone tells you not to think about pink elephants, so that, of course, absolutely nothing else but comes to mind.

She ticked off in her head what might be signs of a mental breakdown. Being overwhelmed by the little things? Fears that you can't cope? Imagining people are following you so that you spend hours looking over your shoulder or staring out a window into the dark?

But he was out there. She knew he was.

In a second, she'd kicked off the heels, was up on her knees staring into the murky white night through a crack in the blinds. As if she might actually see Ryan down there? As if she'd somehow acquired X-ray vision? *Stop checking the window and turn on the lights, foolish woman.*

Right before he'd hailed the taxi, sending her on her way, he'd been about to tell her something.

"This is completely insane."

She snapped on the table lamp beside her, then dove across the couch and turned on its mate.

"There," she told the sudden brightness.

She picked up the wine. She put on her shoes and

tapped her foot. She put down the wine and took off the shoes. Then, inching down the couch, she crept toward the window blinds for another assault.

It was like a presence. He was out there, waiting.

He murdered his fiancée and got away with it... probably because he was crazy or something... pretty sure he was institutionalized.

At least, that was Emma's story.

"I suppose if I want to imagine someone following me," she told herself, "it should probably be a crazed murderer." No sense in holding back.

Dropping the blinds, she lay on the couch and stared up at the ceiling. She should probably get something to eat, raise the blood sugar, bring the imagination down a notch.

Only, she couldn't move. She felt pinned to that couch, at the same time exhausted and wound too tight. She thought about the article in the paper, knowing she'd entered some sort of family battlefield. And tonight, what had Ryan said to her? Something about Daniel's game?

Pawn to queen's four...

The image fit. The ice queen and the drunken king. Daniel and Harris, the two knights. And the castle, Cutty House.

Only, she didn't know the rules to this game, didn't even know its possible dangers. Harris thought she should walk away, just put another notch on the belt of failure and move on.

But to what? She'd never get another chance like this. Drew had taken care of that.

Questions, questions. And the clock long past the witching hour. She left the couch and slipped on her heels, thinking about her blood sugar again. But before she reached the kitchen, she did an about-face and raced for the door, grabbing her coat on the way out.

He wasn't there...only she didn't plan to spend the next hour worrying about the possibility. At least, that's the story she told herself as she ran down the stairs before she could come to her senses and turn back.

11

It was a terrible thing to be standing in front of an alleged murderer when it was really dark and deserted outside and you'd forgotten to bring a handy weapon, or a cell phone, or Batman and Commissioner Gordon.

A backup plan would have been nice.

But she'd misinterpreted the situation. Despite all the Sturm und Drang a girl could shake a stick at, she'd needed to face her fears. The idea that Ryan was stalking her was like the monster under the bed. She had to throw back the covers and look for herself. Emma's tale of mayhem could have started, "Once upon a time..." for all the good it had done Holly.

But darned if he wasn't standing right in front of her still dressed in his Armani best, the night and the fog making mischief all too possible.

He'd been across the street, using an awning for camouflage. She'd run right into his arms, as if she was trying to be convenient. The fog, again. He even smiled as he set her to rights, making everything that much worse because he was happy to see her.

"Holly Fairfield," he whispered down to her. "Aren't you a surprise."

The wind kicked up, turning the fog into a fine white mist swirling like a snowstorm. She'd swear he'd combed his hair with his fingers, it was such a worried mess, and she imagined his blue eyes had a strange focus. He was so close she could smell mint on his breath. A polite stalker, this guy, with minty-fresh breath.

He took a step toward her, she took a step back. Whistle a tune, and they could make their own dance movie.

"I should march right back up those stairs and call the police." Realizing her mistake, she added, "Instead of just announcing that I plan to call the police. Dear God, I really hope you're not dangerous."

"I'm glad you came," he said, picking up where they'd left off. *Cha, cha, cha...* "I would have gone up eventually. You're right. We're both tired of waiting."

"Waiting?" She still wasn't clear about the rules of their game.

"You need to know about Nina."

Every once in a while in life came these moments. Some were good, some, not so good. But they were always memorable. Right then, in that instant, Holly knew she'd never forget this moment.

She'd remember the fog, like a cloud closing in, the sound of the cable cars rumbling into their barn on Washington behind her, the throb of the compressor, the high-pitched squeal of brakes. The way he said the name *Nina,* sad and excited at the same time.

And Ryan standing before her. She'd remember him, and the anticipation in his eyes, most of all.

"Buckle up," he said. "I think you're in for a hell of a shock."

He grabbed her hand. She resisted the urge to pull away. *Don't antagonize...*

And suddenly, they were off.

He dragged her through the narrow streets, an impromptu Mr. Toad's Wild Ride, San Francisco style.

The two flat blocks of Taylor, almost at the pinnacle of Nob Hill, showed corridor views of the financial district through snatches of fog, as if they both might swan dive into the hazy metropolis of lights below. The Disneyland theme continued as they passed Huntington Park, the mist heavy there, and cornered Grace Cathedral, the bells chiming like Notre Dame.

"Cutty House," he shouted, confirming what she'd suspected was their destination.

She kept wondering when she should start screaming her fool head off, but she couldn't find the breath. She was panting too hard. *Geez, he must work out.* Long before she was ready, Cutty House loomed ahead, abandoned for the night, its Beaux-Arts splendor shrouded in mist. The house appeared to be lying in wait behind its wrought-iron gates, crouched like a beast in the shadow of the Cathedral Apartments next door.

He didn't need a key. He knew all the building's secrets, after all, finding a service entrance that just needed a jiggle of the knob, a lift and a push to open the door. He held out his hand for her, this time inviting her to follow. When she hesitated, thinking that walking into that dark house might take a leap of faith even she couldn't muster, he asked, "You want to know the truth?"

Only, she wasn't fast enough for Ryan. He snatched her hand, making her do the Slinky thing, whiplashing her ahead.

She imagined this had been his playground as a child, these dusty, untended halls. When he was old enough, he'd probably worked for his father guiding guests up the stairs while reciting the evening's specials. He didn't need lights to find the room they entered on the third floor, all dark and straight out of a

Hitchcock film. Even before he switched on the Tiffany lamp, she saw linens covering furniture and paintings, the white sheets glowing with reflected light coming from the room's only window.

Finally she found her voice. "Don't do this," she said, sounding all too meek. She tried to think of a good reason. *I'll scream. I'll kick you in the shins.*

"It's only a remodel, for God's sake," she said.

He didn't pay her the least attention, making his way past the shrouded obstacles. "They took her down."

They'd entered some sort of storage room. Ryan was busy navigating the furniture, dragging out what appeared to be a large painting covered with a drop cloth. There were several in the room, remnants of what was rumored to be a grand collection. Ryan leaned the portrait against the wall so that the light from the floor lamp would shine directly on whatever lay beneath.

"But I know all their secrets," he said, standing next to the painting. "It didn't take long to find her."

He pulled off the cloth. Holly was standing at such an angle that she couldn't see what he'd unveiled—and wasn't sure she wanted to. She kept her eyes on Ryan instead.

He's watching for my reaction…

She stepped closer but kept her eyes averted. He'd brought her here to look at a painting?

She took a few more steps. *Get it over with…then he'll let you go home.* She thought about the design sketches Daniel had turned down that afternoon, thought about his impossible dreams for Cutty House, the New Generation. She could be finishing that wine right now, her feet tucked away warm in her bunny slippers, worrying over another bout of financial ruin instead of this.

She realized she was afraid to look at the painting, as if he might show her something horrible, like those photographs they used to take of the dead in Victorian times. They were trying to capture the essence of loved ones who had crossed over before they were buried and lost forever. Holly had seen one in a book, a dead woman posed in her Sunday best.

"Look at her," he said. "Or do you already know?"

She thought about what she did know, his question triggering a memory. A possibility came to light, like a clue overlooked but suddenly recalled. Or maybe she'd picked up Harris's trick for reading body language. Ryan stood beside the portrait, almost hesitating, as if he, too, were afraid to look.

He murdered his fiancée....

That first night, in the ballroom, she could have sworn she'd heard him call out a woman's name. And just now, outside the apartment, what had he told her?

You need to know about...

"Nina," she said, guessing the subject of the portrait, her eyes rising to focus there—but not seeing what she expected to at all.

"Is this a joke?" she asked.

Because it was a painting of Holly.

Only, the woman in the portrait wore an elegant black gown Holly didn't own, accessorized with pearl earrings and a necklace Holly had never seen. She had chestnut hair cut in the same classic bob, a high-maintenance style Holly hadn't worn before today, blow dryers and irons not being part of her beauty arsenal.

The angle of the chin gave off a challenge Holly

could swear she'd never pull off. And the woman's expression belied her younger years, a girl captured in the transition to womanhood. The exotic brown eyes, too, appeared all-knowing even in the stillness of the painting. But the mouth, the shape of the face... *My face.*

On the gold plaque at the base of the frame appeared a name. "Nina," she repeated, reading the inscription on the plaque.

"Do you understand now?" he asked. "Why Daniel brought you here?"

Of course.

She thought she'd said the words out loud, the pieces coming together like the north-seeking pole on a compass. "Of course."

Nina's tragic death. Ryan's fall from grace. Daniel taking over the family business.

And Ryan, that first day when he'd seen her at Cutty House, following her ever since. Completely obsessed.

"I look like Nina." She looked up from the painting, at Ryan. "The woman you killed."

She saw the shock of her words on his face. She supposed it mirrored a bit of what she felt. *Touché, Holly.*

"They do say that, don't they. That I killed her," he said, admitting nothing. "That I ran her off the road."

But Holly's attention was back on the painting. "My hair, the clothes."

"He dressed you to look like her."

As if the resemblance weren't strong enough already? "You were engaged," she said, remembering the story. Emma, gleeful over cocktails: *They say he killed his fiancée.* And today, the fun they had choosing new clothes. *Come on, Holly, it's on Daniel. Try this one.* Turning her into someone else.

She felt bombarded, as if the information were scrolling past on a computer screen and she was trying to catch a word here or there to make sense of things.

Now she had her answer. Now she knew why Ryan watched her like a man possessed.

"Daniel went to a lot of trouble." She tried to imagine what it would be like for Ryan, seeing her. "He must hate you very much."

"And then some," he answered.

It was all she'd needed to say. Whatever was driving him seemed to collapse and slip away. He dropped the cloth, covering the portrait.

This time, he didn't try to stop her when she walked away.

Vanessa cinched the silk wrapper tight around her waist and slipped her toes into the satin mules. They were perfectly silly shoes for a woman her age, pink with fur trim—as if anyone cared if she looked elegant at this hour. She could hear Samuel's voice all the way down the hall. *The library, then.*

"Why can't I fucking come over! I paid for the damn place, didn't I?" Screaming like a child.

She followed the sound of his voice, knowing what she'd find. He'd have a whiskey in one hand, the cell phone in the other.

"God help me, sometimes I think...don't hang up on me!"

She pressed her palm to the heavy oak, the door already slightly ajar. She pushed until she could glimpse inside, inching open Pandora's box. *He can't hurt me anymore. I know what he's become.*

She watched Samuel pace before the fireplace,

slashing his free arm through the air, the rhythm of it emphasizing a word here and there as a sliver of whiskey hugged the bottom of his glass. He still wore his tuxedo; the bow tie hung limp like spaghetti.

The library had been her father's favorite room, its fireplace a masterpiece in marble and carved mahogany. Her grandfather had imported the piece from Italy, wanting only the best for his home. The sad thought came that the room deserved better than what she'd given, taking on Samuel.

"I'm not threatening you. I just need to see you." He had his back to the door, his temper now reduced to a needy whisper. "I'm here alone with the old bat, for God's sake. It's so fucking depressing, all these damn parties she drags me to."

They'd been at a charity function for the local Cancer Society. She'd left early, embarrassed by the looks of sympathy from friends as they took in Samuel's fall from grace. She'd gone straight to bed; Samuel, straight to the bar.

Of course, he was having an affair. For a moment, she actually wondered who might want him. Probably someone young and in need of money.

"I thought I'd see you tonight." The fight had left him altogether. She thought he sounded very much like a boy denied his favorite toy.

She'd read a book once about marriage, a little novelette no bigger than her hand, the kind they tucked away at the cash register for last-minute gifts. There was a passage she'd never forget, written by a young newlywed: *The most important decision I will ever make is who I choose to be my husband.*

She remembered the day she'd bought that palm-sized book. There'd been a party. Gil and Samuel were at the height of their conspiracy to bring Cutty House and the vineyard together. They planned to start a chain of restaurants that featured Gil's wines on the menu. Patrons could also purchase wines in the gift shop to take home.

That night she'd drunk too much and made a pass at Gil. She'd wept in his arms that she'd chosen the wrong man. How gently he'd rejected her, making her hate him all the more. Gil, who would never cheat on his beloved Marta.

She pushed the door open. Samuel turned, looking furtively over his shoulder. He had the puffy eyes of a drunk and the soft mouth of a man done in by his vices. Seeing her standing there, he dropped his whiskey. The glass shattered on the marble tiles of the hearth. Shards of crystal and ice scattered across the parquet.

"It's the old bat," she told him. "She'd like a word with you, if you don't mind?"

"I've made a mess," he whispered into the phone, his bloodhound eyes still on his wife. "I'll call you back."

He stood frozen, a tableau of guilt. She remembered the first time she'd met Samuel. He'd reminded her of those marble statues she'd seen while touring Greece with her parents. Every part of him was chiseled perfection. He'd been enormously popular in high school, the quarterback on the football team. Of course, every girl wanted him. Him and Gil.

"What do you want?" he asked, crossing the room for a fresh glass, ignoring the mess on the floor. It was someone else's job to pick up after him.

"I want to speak to you about the architect Daniel hired. I think we might need to do something about her. Ryan came by today. He was very upset. I just wanted your opinion."

"My opinion? That's a laugh."

But she ignored him, telling herself she had a noble cause. To protect Ryan. "I spoke to Daniel. He thinks she might help," she said, trying somehow to reach him. "The resemblance. Nina's ghost rising to save Cutty House and all. But I'm worried about what that kind of publicity might do to Ryan."

"For God's sake, Van," he said, turning on her. "He's not coming back, even if you dangle some look-alike before his eyes. He doesn't belong to you anymore, or haven't you figured that out?" He toasted her with the whiskey. "Ryan has Gil to look after, remember?" He took a drink, smiling at the joke. "But you can't help yourself, can you? Dreaming that he'll come sniffing after your little architect when she's not the real thing. Not even close. And just like Daniel, love—" raising the glass again "—she'll disappoint."

At times like this, she could understand what Ryan had done. That woman, Nina, she'd become just too painful to bear.

"When you run out of money," she said, the venom slipping out, "that woman will leave you, Samuel."

"Is that a threat?" He smiled. "I'm surprised you'd even bother at this point."

He came to stand before her, his eyes bloodshot, his nose flowering red with broken blood vessels. Years of disappointments had distorted his chiseled perfection.

He told her, "You don't know what you're talking about. You never did."

Samuel pushed past her, looking so smug. A man with a secret. She stared at the hearth and the broken glass.

"You've made a mess, Samuel," she said, feeling cold and used up.

Of everything.

He wanted to call her again. Desperately. But he settled on his friend, Macallan, of single malt fame.

"Shh," Samuel told the whiskey glass. "Mustn't tell."

He crept into Ryan's old room and crawled up on the bed, careful not to spill. So the old bat had overheard. Not that it mattered, he told himself. She didn't know the truth, no one did. *Just you wait, Van.* Samuel Cutty could still give them what for.

He fell back on the pillows, trying to catch his breath, the job of lying down almost too much for him these days. Vanessa, that controlling bitch. She'd long given up on him, but there was still Ryan to manipulate. The architect was just another angle to suck him back into the fold. Oh, maybe it started as Daniel's idea, sure. But Samuel knew his wife. Van couldn't help herself. She'd see a chance and she'd take it.

As for Holly Fairfield, he'd let Daniel and Ryan fight over her. He had the real thing now and that's all that mattered. That in the end, she'd chosen him.

She'll leave you. As if Van knew anything.

He devoured the Scotch. Vanessa didn't understand. She thought he was just a drunk. That he hadn't accomplished anything other than to ruin his business, steal her money and run off their son.

"She never believed in me," he told the ceiling.

None of them had. Foster, damn him, always bitching about money. Holding back. Making him beg. Even his own father had waited to die before giving him control of the business.

Only Gil ever had faith. "Good old Gil." And how had he repaid his friend?

"Don't think about that," he told himself, shutting his eyes as if he could block out the memory. "Don't think, don't think, don't think."

He reached for the phone, suddenly itching to call her again. But, no. She'd never let him come over, not after the fight they'd had. He'd better wait. Tomorrow morning, he'd call. Or maybe he'd just show up, a dozen roses in hand. Two dozen bloodred roses.

He yawned, his hand still wrapped around the empty glass. He could feel himself slipping into that lovely oblivion. *Mr. Macallan, I thank you.* He kicked off his shoes.

So Van wanted his opinion about the architect? Well, she might be right; the girl was going to be a problem. *Might have to do something.* He yawned again, reaching to set the glass on the bedside table. Missing. He watched the tumbler roll across the carpet.

Drifting into a hazy sleep, he blinked at the glass, looking forward to making yet another mess.

12

The summer of his eleventh birthday, Ryan built a sailboat with his grandfather. That had been something, him and Foster working on that clinker-built dinghy. Seven feet, six inches. Big red sail. And when they'd taken it out, aiming the flat pram bow in the direction of Alcatraz, nothing had ever felt that good again.

Foster died the following summer. Heart attack. But Ryan had always wondered if it wasn't his father who'd finally done Foster in. The way they fought about the business. Foster never could let go, and Vanessa was always talking him into giving Samuel another chance.

If Ryan had been a normal kid, maybe he would have made a different promise to his grandfather at the hospital. Watching Foster struggle for breath, machines clicking and beeping along with the soft whir of oxygen from the plastic mask, he might have told Foster that he'd make good on everything his father ruined, the expected vow.

Instead, he'd told his grandfather he'd build another sailboat. A schooner this time, with tropical hardwoods and copper rivets. Even at twelve, he'd figured it was the story he'd want to hear facing the same odds. *Just imagine, Grandpa….* He'd sail around the world, sending postcards home from exotic ports of call. Even halfway to heaven, he thought Foster understood because he'd smiled, giving Ryan's hand a squeeze.

The night Nina died, Ryan knew he'd never make good on that promise. Only by then, he'd figured he didn't owe anybody anything. Except Gil. Because he'd killed his daughter, he'd always owe Gil.

That's what he was thinking racing down Highway One in the Aston Martin. What it might do to Gil if Ryan kept this up, flying off the same road that had killed his daughter.

They dressed her up like a doll. They cut her hair so that she'd look like Nina.

When he'd seen her standing next to Daniel at the club, he couldn't breathe. It hadn't gotten any better up close. Like they'd taken Holly to one of those celebrity artists who could make anyone look like Madonna or Gwyneth Paltrow. Only, they'd been holding a photograph of Nina, telling Holly, *hold still....*

He pushed the gas pedal, shifted and heard the engine roar. He told himself: Just a little farther.

When she opened her mouth, she wasn't anything like Nina. Holly Fairfield talked faster than anyone he knew, as if afraid he'd cut her off if she didn't just spill it out in one breath. And he had, covering her mouth, liking the feel of her lips against his hand, too much. The whole thing was making him a little crazy, bringing back ghosts he'd thought long dead.

He hit the brakes and dove into the next curve, fishtailing out. Gravel flew out from under the wheel. Just ahead a mile or so, Nina had sailed over the embankment. Not so foggy tonight. Twelve years ago, he'd been chasing her taillights.

He could almost see her just ahead, those red lights weaving in and out of the mist, teasing him.

Hurry up! Catch me!

Ryan spun the car to a stop, the tires squealing as he hung on to the steering wheel, his foot smashed against the brake. He managed to keep control, the car doing a one-eighty so that it faced the wrong direction.

He sat with his hands shaking on the steering wheel, breathing hard. He cut the engine.

This was what Daniel wanted. He'd planted the seeds of the nightmare, was waiting for them to grow, hoping they'd bear fruit. If Ryan drove off that cliff, drenched in sweat and guilt, Daniel would win.

Ryan smiled, catching his breath. "Sorry, Dan. I can't give you that satisfaction. Not tonight."

Two minutes later, Ryan turned on the engine and headed for home.

She'd been at the computer a good half hour—the wine bottle now half empty and Holly unfortunately sober—when her brother walked through the door. She gave him a look of utter frustration and pointed to the computer screen.

"I've tried most of the papers and a couple of search engines, Google, Yahoo, whatever," she said, hopelessly lost on the Internet. Again the finger pointed at the laptop in accusation. "Zip, zero, *nada*. And I know it's in there." She slapped her hand on the table.

Harris shooed her aside and took her chair. She tapped on the screen where she'd written the name she'd seen engraved on the plaque, Nina Travers, and poured herself another glass of wine. "Old stuff. At least ten years back. A car accident or something. I want anything you can find on her."

Her brother's fingers flew over the keyboard. She read over his shoulder. "Flipper.com?"

"It's a search engine I use that can access the Deep Web." And when she gave him a look, he explained. "The spiders on most search engines only crawl around the surface web. Any major content sites, like the Library of Congress, are hidden in an invisible web, the Deep Web. Thing is, that's where you find the high quality stuff. The invisible web is about 500 times bigger."

In an instant, he had a newspaper article front and center on the screen. No slouch on the uptake, he zeroed in on Nina's photograph, clicking to enlarge the frame.

"Well, hell," he said, a master of understatement as he pushed away from the computer.

"Print out the article," she said.

The photograph looked like a high-school graduation picture, all diffused lighting and muted background. Even in black and white, the resemblance was strange and disturbing.

She could hear the printer humming to life. She remembered what her brother said: All quality stuff.

He lost everything. The girl, the money. He totally flipped after that. Emma telling the story, setting Holly up. She wondered now if Emma had exaggerated a little, giving the facts her own special spin.

They say I ran her off the road. It was the only thing Ryan had admitted.

"Holly?" Harris was picking up the articles as they spilled out, holding them up so she could read.

The headlines: *Community Mourns...Candlelight Vigil On Highway One...Fiancée Questioned In Death.*

She looked away. "I'll read it later."

Maybe it was all those pages spitting out of the printer. Maybe with the story at her fingertips, that fire to know every detail had all but burned out. Maybe it was something else.

She sipped the wine, wondering what it would take to get some sleep tonight, deciding it wasn't so important. It wasn't as if she had to have a sharp mind come morning for work.

She stepped closer, staring at the photograph still on the screen. She reached out to touch it. Nina looked all of eighteen.

Her brother held up more pages, a prosecutor waving Exhibit A. "We leave now, right? No more second-guessing. We're on the same page, you and me?"

She nodded, transfixed by Nina's smile. "I never smile like that. As if I own the world."

Harris came to stand beside her. "You smile twice as big, given the right circumstances. None of which we are currently living. Leave the sick bastards to their games, Hol. This has nothing to do with you and everything to do with them. I know these people. They think the world owes them. In the end, they'll tear each other apart over a dog bone."

She squeezed her brother's shoulder. "Nice of you not to say 'I told you so.' Not that I don't deserve it."

"It's not what I wanted." Rushing in, filling the silence, he added, "I'll get my job back. I'm good at eating crow. Done it plenty of times. You have me, Hol. We have each other."

He was quiet then, as if he knew he'd said enough. They both stared at the woman on the screen.

A picture speaks a thousand words.

This one said too much.

13

Not so long ago, Holly remembered feeling as if she held the world in the palm of her hand. Hubris, the Greeks called it. The past years had chipped away at that intoxicating confidence. And she'd missed it—those lovely highs of success. Hard to believe she could find herself here, back to square one.

The room was on the third floor. In the light of day, creepy transformed into old and musty. Holly found Nina's portrait propped against the wall, right where Ryan had left her.

It wasn't even difficult to lift off the sheet and look. She wanted to see her face again, give more definition to the memory. *Not a dream, after all.*

The morning after, the articles Harris had printed out lay unread on her nightstand back home. Even after a second cup of coffee, she hadn't wanted to explore those details. Plenty of time to know the ugly truth later, she figured. And how much would the newspapers really know? They could surmise and conjecture the heck out of the story and never touch on what it was about Nina that drove the men of Cutty House.

"You wanted to see me?"

She turned to find Daniel in the doorway. He didn't even act surprised. He sauntered in, owning the room as he slipped off his sunglasses and flashed a smile.

She'd asked to meet here not for the drama but because she'd been half afraid she'd slink away without
this evidence, giving some lame excuse about why she
needed to leave. A big part of her wanted to avoid this
confrontation with Daniel, take the easy way out. *I'm
homesick…Harris has this great job offer…sorry,
gotta book.*

But she'd signed a contract. She needed the job to
end with Daniel admitting what he'd done.

Holly focused on the painting, saying in a voice that
didn't sound so much like hers, "I'd always heard that
everyone has a double somewhere. And then there are
those celebrity look-alike segments on TV."

She could hear Daniel walking up behind her. He
came to a stop alongside, staring at the painting of
Nina Travers.

He took her hand in his as if to comfort her. She
jerked away, appalled.

"The hair is a little different." She had to say something, even something silly. "A little shorter. I really
fought Emma there. It had to touch my shoulders, I
told her. I was very firm. And the eyes. I don't know
if I've ever had that expression."

"Don't leave me," he said.

"You brought me here to impersonate a dead
woman."

"That's not how—"

"How is it, then, Daniel?" she asked, turning on
him. "How is it that I suddenly have this wonderful
job for which I am clearly not qualified—but, surprise!
I look exactly like your cousin's dead fiancée?"

"Okay. At first. Yes, I saw your photograph. I saw
how much you looked like Nina. I wanted—"

"I know what you wanted, Daniel. But here's a

news flash. I'm just an architect. I can't bring back the dead.''

"I can't do this without you, Holly. Please don't leave me.''

She closed her eyes. She hated the pleading, hated even more his choice of words. He gave so much away.

"My name is Holly Fairfield. I am an architect. A damn fine one. What you need is an actress. Or maybe a psychic.''

"No," he said, his hand on her shoulder, keeping her there. "I need you. And it has nothing to do with Nina.''

"Oh, I understand that much," she said, pushing his hand away. "It has to do with Ryan. Some weird competition that you have with your cousin.''

"I don't give a shit about Ryan.''

She slapped him hard across the face. She had never hit anyone in her life. She was trying desperately not to cry.

All that interest she'd seen in Ryan's eyes. The softness in his voice, his touch.

"You dressed me up to look like her, you piece of shit.''

"I deserve that.''

"And so much more.''

"Holly, those plans you showed me." He was talking fast, stepping in front of her to get in that last plea. "I've been thinking about them, talking to Emma. I don't know why I didn't see it before. Emma says I'm pigheaded, yeah? But I think your ideas are the way to go. Everything you want, exactly how you want it. You call the shots. Your way. No more interference.''

She looked back at him, shocked. "Oh, you're good.''

"Listen to me." He had an edge to his voice now. For the first time, she felt she was seeing the real man. "What if I did think it was some stupid sign, you looking like Nina? Good karma for Cutty House. Or maybe you're right, maybe I did want to mess with Ryan's head a little. Does it really matter how I found you or why I brought you here? Tell me you've ever done anything like those plans?" He was giving it all he had. "I saw it in your eyes, Holly. The pride. Cutty House brought that out in you."

She stepped around him, trying not to listen as she headed for the door, but he caught up with her, swinging her back around.

"You can save my house. And that, my dear, is the only revenge I want."

"I don't believe you."

"Then believe in your talent. Give me a month. That's all. One little month. And I swear you can walk away from the whole deal and I'll pay off the contract. But I'm betting you won't leave. This is right, you coming here. For whatever reason, I found you. It's right, and you know it."

"I feel like I'm doing business with the devil." She hadn't meant to say it out loud.

"I'm not the devil. But I will tell you he's here. Ryan. Okay, I messed up. No more stupid games, Holly. Scout's honor. I can protect you from him. I swear."

"Like you protected Nina?" Something else she hadn't meant to say.

"I wasn't part of that. I didn't know how bad things had gotten between them." He scrubbed his face with his hands. "I can't even say the bastard did it, though we all suspected he ran her off the road. Look, not a lot of people know this, but the autopsy—" He turned away, actually pulling off a look of reluctance. "Let's just say they were engaged, but Ryan wasn't stepping up to the plate while Nina had her reasons to speed things up."

But she wasn't listening to his version. "And who keeps me safe from you?"

He shook his head. "You have the wrong guy. I only want Cutty House. Give her back to me. I know you can."

She stared at him for a good long while. "Well, for once, you may have spoken the truth."

She walked past him, into the hall.

"What are you going to do?" he called after her.

"Damned if I know."

At day's end, she still didn't know.

Holly sat perched on the couch, taking in the sacrilege of the previous architect's ideas juxtaposed with her design sketches. Left to his own devices, Daniel would destroy Cutty House, historical context be damned.

Was it simply ego, then? Coming here, thinking she could take on a project of this magnitude on her own? Before Drew, she'd never experienced defeat. She'd passed all nine parts of the architectural exam the first time out. She'd been recruited by one of the top firms in the Pacific Northwest, licensed to practice in both Washington and California. Within a year, she'd been in charge of her first big project, a terminal at SeaTac airport, a huge commercial enterprise—every architect's definition of "you've arrived!" That kind of success could be intoxicating.

And all of it vanished in a wisp of smoke when she started sleeping with one of the firm's partners, Drew Manticore.

She remembered one day in particular. Evelyn, a woman on the rise who'd made no bones about her competition with Holly, had met up with her in the ladies' room. Evelyn had been fixing her lipstick in front of the mirror as Holly washed her hands.

"What you're doing with Manticore? Career suicide." She'd dropped the lipstick in her purse with a smile. "Just a thought."

Not that Holly had listened. Next thing she knew, the big projects dried up. She was assigned to basic type 5 jobs. Drew convinced her to leave the firm with him. *I can't stand how they're treating you. All because of me!* That conviction.

She'd been married and knee-deep in their new firm when she discovered the truth, that Drew had been pushed out of the company, leaving not for her sake but because he had to. Something about discrepancies in his expense account. *I'm not a numbers man, sweetie.* The understatement of the year.

But Drew always had his explanations. Jealous bastards, all of them. Of course he'd been set up. *That's how they do it, honey. They grab your nuts and squeeze.* And he still knew the right people, could get the jobs.

At twenty-nine, Holly had been newly married and opening her own firm. Daniel found her three years later, divorced, her name suddenly the kiss of death in architecture circles, thanks to Drew.

So was it all about ego, then, wanting to stay? A phoenix rising from the ashes. To say she could do this and all other considerations be damned. Or was there something else persuading her. Someone else? *Ryan.*

When she'd seen Nina's painting, there'd been confusion. And fear, too. But there'd also been disappointment that the interest she'd seen in Ryan's eyes had not been for her.

A woman who hadn't had sex in three years followed around by a man with Ryan's intoxicating persistence. Could she really be so silly?

"You always did like a good show," she told herself.

"Holly?"

She looked up from the plans to see her brother standing at the door. She hadn't heard him come in, wasn't expecting him. And now, he was looking at her hunched over the as-built drawings of Cutty House, reading her thoughts.

"No way," he said, crossing the room toward her. "No...freaking...way."

"I just thought—"

"Did you even read those newspaper articles? Let me give you the *Reader's Digest* version. Young man about town, all of nineteen, offs his possibly pregnant girlfriend, running her off the road. They'd had a fight, him calling off the wedding, and both of them drunk and driving, maybe even playing a little game of chicken that got out of hand. Who knows? Only, the charges don't stick."

He sat down beside her on the couch, on a roll. "But the guy's family pushes him out, see? Getting rid of the dross, possibly because they know something the cops don't. Not that they're turning in their own, but he has to pay a price. So, no more Cutty House for Ryan."

"That was twelve years ago."

"And isn't it interesting that they brought you here twelve years later because, hell, they're all over that. It's in the past. Must be just an amazing coincidence that Danny boy hired the dead girl's long-lost twin."

Harris wrestled in between her and the plans. He waved his hand in front of her eyes.

"Holly, what the hell is this about? They lied to you. That's enough, right? Daniel brought you here to play some sick joke on that Ryan guy."

She shook her head. "He said he'd let me do it my way. That he wouldn't interfere. He said only I could save Cutty House, and looking at these plans, I think he may be right."

"So you're a genius and this project will prove it. But is it worth your life?"

"How did we go from a sick joke to murder?"

"I have to draw you a diagram? Daniel wants to goad Ryan into a repeat performance, put the bastard in jail like he should have the first time around. Not that big a leap, I'm thinking."

"Don't you think you're being overdramatic?"

"Listen to you, Miss calm, cool and stupidly blind!"

"I look like Nina Travers," she said, raising her voice, suddenly only too happy for a good fight. "So what? That doesn't mean I can't do the job."

"Don't get all ambitious on me now, Hol. It's not worth it. Trust me on that. Look, I've been a jerk. Showing up on your doorstep like some loser, letting you take care of me. But I'm ready now, okay? I've licked my wounds and I'm ready to go back. Get a real job. We'll go home and you'll hunt up some other project."

She shook her head. "Not like this one."

"Exactly like this one. Only, there's no dead woman in the picture. You see the upside, I'm sure."

"Don't push me, Harris. You're going to push me right into staying."

He stood up, backing away as if he couldn't believe

what he was hearing. She could see he wanted to yell at her, but screaming wasn't his style. But neither was circling the room, shoving his hand through his hair, the pent-up frustration practically steaming from his ears. He wanted so badly to protect her.

"You know it's crazy," he said. "Better yet? You know it's wrong."

"I just can't promise anything right now, okay? You need to let me think about this a little longer."

That look again. But she took it, right in the chin.

He nodded. "You think about it real hard, kiddo. I'll be here to help you pack when you get it straight in your head. But I can't sit around and listen to this crap. I can't let you just…oh, screw it!"

Before he could say anything worse, he slammed out the door, angrier than she'd ever seen him.

She glanced at the wrinkled plans spread out over the coffee table. She remembered how happy she'd been when she'd first gotten the idea for the sketches. She'd felt brave and strong and clever.

How could Harris not understand why she wanted to stay? *He* got a kick out of trekking to places where you had to take malaria pills and five different vaccinations just to hit port. To countries where they had things euphemistically referred to as "the sleeping sickness."

How could he not understand his sister wanting to take a few chances?

I'll get a real job…you'll hunt up some other project.

Sure. No problem. Why hadn't she thought of that?

Because she knew better. She didn't even care if it was all about ego. So what? There were too few opportunities for architects in her position and she'd already wasted her fair share on Drew.

Which left her with the option of making a phone call. Surprisingly enough, he was listed.

His machine picked up. She waited for the tone. "We need to talk, Ryan." She ticked off her cell phone number. "Where should we meet?"

14

Harris pounded on the door, not seeing this as a polite doorbell moment. Not with him pressing off his toes, watching the knob, adrenaline pumping. He'd trained for just this sort of thing, a mission of sorts. The instant the door cracked open, he shoved it hard.

He'd wanted it to be Daniel. God, he'd needed the bastard to be there right in front of him.

"Where is he?" he asked Emma.

"Daniel?"

"No, Santa Claus." His sarcastic best. "Where is he?"

He could see that he'd scared her and he did feel a little crazy, coming here like this. But if he couldn't make Holly see reason, he'd make sure someone else pulled the plug on this job.

"He's not here," Emma said softly.

He looked around the empty living room. It was the kind of place he'd expect from Danny boy. Berber carpet, white leather furniture, shelves covered with expensive designer gizmos that screamed *look at me!* All the books were big and glossy and unread. Like the man, the room was all polish, no substance.

"You're living with him," he said.

It was obvious. He'd come to Daniel's apartment, but, honestly, he'd half expected to find her there.

"No," she said. "I have my own place. I...I spend a lot of time here."

"No, really?"

He dropped down onto the couch, shoving aside a couple of dainty pillows. "So what the hell is going on? I assume you know about this phony job of Dan's." He patted the cushion beside him. "Tell me a story."

"I don't know what you mean."

"The truth, Emma. A distant concept, I'm sure. But here I am, asking just the same, using the manners my papa taught me. Why'd you bring my sister here to play Nina Redux? Come on, darling. I know you're in on it, so why don't you share?"

She didn't come anywhere near him. He could tell she was scared. Her pupils were dilated, her breath all short and shallow. And maybe something else. He could sense the tension between them.

"It's not what you think. The first architect was such a disaster. Everything was going so badly. Then Dan saw Holly's picture in a magazine. He thought it was some kind of sign."

Harris made a rude noise. "Try another one, Mother Goose."

"Look, I tried to talk him out of it. I was worried it was another one of his crazy ideas. Like maybe he really believed it was Nina coming back from the dead, something weird like that. But when Daniel saw her photograph in that design magazine, saw how much she looked like Nina, he thought the job was going badly because he was meant to find Holly. He isn't always so professional about these things."

"No shit, Sherlock."

"He takes a lot of risks. Sometimes for silly reasons." She shrugged. "Like the way a woman looks."

He could always tell when someone was lying.
Strangely enough, Emma, here, was telling the truth.

"I knew the first architect he hired was a moron,"
she said. "A friend of a friend. Someone Daniel could
control, who would do things his way. I thought Holly
would be his disaster number two. But she wasn't.
Isn't. She's good."

"She's more than good. And she doesn't deserve
any of this crap."

"It's a wonderful opportunity for her."

"To impersonate a dead woman?"

"I told you, it wouldn't be like that."

He'd never moved so fast in his life, rising to loom
over her, grabbing her by both arms so that he practically lifted her off the ground. He was pretty sure he
was hurting her, not that little Emma would let on.

"What would it be like, hmm?" he asked. "I've
read the stories. Rich kid runs fiancée off the road,
pretty much bringing an end to his storybook existence
so that, suddenly, he's no longer the golden boy of the
Cutty clan."

She tried to push him away, but he kept his grip.
He knew how to intimidate. He'd had lessons from the
best.

"Let me guess at some of the details you might
have left out about this wonderful opportunity you're
giving Holly," he said. "There might be some bad
blood between the cousins? Something involving
Nina? Now, Danny boy brings along my sister, waving
the red flag."

"You're wrong."

"What if the story ends the same?" he said, giving
her a good shake. "What if Danny's little joke turns
into murder?"

"Nina's death was an accident. They didn't prove Ryan had anything to do with—"

"It's enough for me that she's dead." He pressed her harder. "This job is over."

"Holly is free to leave any time she wants."

"But she won't, so you make sure she doesn't have the option. You persuade Danny to find himself another architect."

Somehow, Emma, that tiny little thing, broke his grip. She pushed him on the chest hard enough that he lost his balance, actually stumbling back a step.

"You think I haven't tried?" she asked. She pushed him again. "You think I haven't said it was crazy from the first?"

Suddenly, it was Emma taking him on, that excitement in her eyes shining ever brighter.

"But Holly," she told him, "she's not what I expected. She's not some lamebrain idea of Dan's."

She licked her lips, sensing how dangerously close he was to losing control, but still wanting to have her say. "She could do it. She could save us."

"Us?"

"Daniel. The family. Holly could make everything good again. Save us from Nina's curse. You must have guessed I didn't want her here. Sure, I was jealous. Maybe I still am. But then I started thinking that she should stay."

She was talking as if everything she was saying was a revelation, even to her. Standing there, she was coming up with this incredible bullshit, all of a sudden seeing his sister as some sort of lucky find. Only, nothing she said made the slightest bit of sense. It didn't have anything to do with what he knew.

But instead of pulling away, she just kept coming, whispering up to his face. "At first, I didn't like her.

But who couldn't like Holly, right? She's all about heart next to Daniel's illusions. He's been spinning his wheels for so long and finally, through some fluke, he's hit on something good. Your sister. Okay, I got left out. I got my feelings hurt. So what? I can get over that. And if something comes out of this, something that could finally prove Daniel to his family, then it's worth it.''

She watched him, pleading with her eyes. And something else, something more.

"I know it sounds crazy," she said, "but don't take that away from him. I can't.''

She slipped her hand into his. Almost of their own volition, his fingers laced with hers.

"What the hell are you doing?'' But he knew. He knew.

Emma made it a simple thing, easing her mouth against his. Not that he needed coaxing. Half the reason he'd come was right there in his arms. Yeah, he'd wanted her. From the first.

They started on the couch but quickly moved to the floor. They couldn't get their clothes off fast enough. Emma didn't want to wait, but he did. He wanted to see her. Every bit. Her breasts, her hands, the shape of her everywhere.

She was tiny. A slight woman with all the necessary curves, a work of art under those jeans and T-shirt. He'd gotten a glimpse with the dress last night and she didn't disappoint.

Emma wasn't his first round at this sort of thing. That was part of his problem. He ran too hot sometimes, didn't stop to ask the right questions. Instead, he'd just go forward full throttle so that, here he was again, making a mistake.

She made these soft noises against his mouth, as if

she'd never been touched like this, as if she might just burn up right there in his arms if he stroked her here…if he moved slightly and pressed there.

And when he finally came inside her, her legs wrapped around his hips, her mouth on his, he knew he'd never done anything that felt so right and so wrong at the same time.

The storm was over as quickly as it started. They lay in a tangle on the floor. He was the first to move, standing to gather up his clothes.

When he'd finished dressing, her eyes locked on his. It wasn't hard to see what she was feeling. He was good at this sort of thing, after all.

She turned over, exposing the exquisite curve of her back to him.

He could tell the exact moment she began to cry. He wanted to say he was sorry, knew he should say something before he left. But he didn't. He didn't say a damn thing. He figured, between the two of them, they'd told enough lies.

Holly almost missed the exit, Alexander, immediately after crossing the Golden Gate Bridge.

The road curved sharply to the right, winding down to where Richardson Bay fed into San Francisco Bay. By day, Holly's tour book painted Sausalito as an Italian hill town. Bungalows and cottages clung to the steep hills above the yacht harbor sheltering sleek ocean-going vessels, day sailors and even a Chinese junk or two. Fab shops, galleries and restaurants crowded along Bridgeway, a gathering place for tourists delighting in the quaintness of the maritime village, while ferry passengers snapped picturesque views from the deck of dayliners. She remembered one passage in the tour book: *The port city was meant to be seen from the water.*

Ryan lived on a boat, a houseboat. The "floating homes" sat all in a row, eclectic as all get-out. Painted every hue imaginable, including purple and puce, they were moored in the waterfront area known as Waldo Point Harbor at Gate 5 Road. To any architect, his house was a miracle on water. Two stories high, wood cladding, steel-framed windows. With an enormous flagpole marking the entrance gangway and his neighbor a handshake away, it was truly a man's house.

Inside, the masculine theme continued with worn leather couches and an overstuffed reading chair. Dishes in the sink. Newspapers and magazines scattered over every flat surface, along with charts that appeared to measure rainfall and moisture. And books. Lots of those. On a surprising number of subjects.

She remembered what Emma had told her. While Daniel slaved every summer at Cutty House, Ryan, ever the playboy, would sail off into the sunset.

"Looks like he's still living the dream," she said to herself.

"Living what?"

He'd come up behind her on the deck, a platform hanging above the water so that nothing but a guardrail stood between her and the glassy blackness below. He held out the beer he'd offered when she'd first come aboard. She took the Corona and held tight to the bottle.

When she'd driven down the curving landscape, house lights dotting the hillside, she'd thought the view beyond romantic. Here was this tiny fairy-tale town, a Portofino of sorts, sporting views of the San Francisco cityscape and jobbing sailboats with crystal lights glowing atop masts.

She wondered just how crazy it was to come here. Would her fairy tale setting turn into a nightmare? That unstoppable curiosity of hers was at work again, risking all. *When he looks at me, does he see her? Does he see Nina?*

Asking all the wrong questions.

"Nice place." She took a sip of the beer.

He made some noncommittal noise. She saw that he wasn't drinking and she felt suddenly out of sorts with her beer. She still had a headache from last night's wine.

He waited, obviously letting her do the talking.

Most women would find him incredibly attractive. Dark, thick hair with just a hint of curl, eyes an incredible blue, he was the kind of man you'd expect to see on the cover of a book or a movie poster. A much younger version of Ryan had made a couple of the papers Harris had printed out. She'd halfheartedly flipped through the articles on the nightstand, even read through one, but she didn't feel any better prepared.

She turned to face him. "I am not," she said, "the reincarnation of Nina Travers."

"That much I figured out."

He said it rather mildly, disappointing her with his reaction. Even now, she supposed she lacked drama.

She took a drink from the Corona and gazed out over the painted rail. She could see what Ryan had called the "Anchor Outs," funky houseboats anchored in the middle of Richardson Bay, in complete violation of every code on the books but tolerated by the locals. When she'd first stepped onto the deck, she'd said they were beautiful. Ryan assured her that, by day, most were shanties.

"Why didn't you just tell me?" she asked, wondering what else the light of day might reveal. "Why the whole stalker routine? I could have called the police. I could have made it ugly."

"I wanted to see your face when you saw the painting."

"And what would that tell you? That I was scared? That I was stupid?"

His eyes met hers. "I wanted to know if you were in on it."

Of course, she thought. What else? He'd been watching her reaction, trying to figure out where she fit: victim or cohort.

"I suppose, from your point of view, I could be," she said. "An actress brought here to drive you over the edge."

And into murder, as Harris implied.

"Well." She toasted him with the beer she didn't want. *I should go home, walk out now.* "I'm not. Again, just an architect looking to do her job."

She could hear a dinner party from the boat next to his. She imagined life just a few feet away, so normal. She wondered if Ryan had ever tasted that kind of ordinary. If someone could really get beyond his tragic past.

"How horrible," she said, giving in to her sympathy out loud. "Daniel springing me on you."

"If it helps," he said, "for a while there, I did think I was losing my mind."

"What does it say about me that it does help?" she asked with a smile. Because he was right, there was a tiny part of her that wanted retribution. He'd followed her; he'd scared her. It was nice to know it worked both ways. "Okay," she said, bringing them back to the business at hand. "Now what? You want me to go away, I assume."

"If only."

And wasn't that the problem, she thought. These lovely hints of something else between them...how well she responded to the possibility.

"Meaning?" she asked, pushing a little.

That smile again. How many times had those looks opened doors, she wondered.

"Meaning," he said, "if only I weren't such an ass."

Oblique at best, but she thought she understood. How else could she have sensed him there in the dark watching her if not for that strong connection between them?

Only, his feelings seemed firmly rooted in the past, having a true *raison d'être* in Nina, while Holly had fallen for the same tired story. He was a hottie; she was lonely.

"You should be careful," he told her.

"Funny. That's exactly what Daniel said."

"Which makes things complicated for you. Who should you believe?"

"Maybe I believe you both."

"Sorry," he told her. "You have to pick sides on this one."

She wished he wasn't so attractive. Why were the bad ones always so good-looking? Was it some bizarre rule of DNA, like being left-handed? Drew had been good-looking. What if Ryan became just another chapter of Holly's Folly—Bad Taste in Men, Part II.

"When you look at me, do you see her? Nina?"

It was a gutsy move, just putting the question out there. Ryan didn't even hesitate, coming closer to cut off the light from the dock and stand over her. He brushed back her bangs, exposing her face, making her catch her breath. He had gentle hands, with calluses. They were a working man's hands.

Standing there in the moonlight, the air damp, music streaming over the water, she wanted so badly for that look in his eyes to be all hers.

"Here's what I think," he told her. "I think you were right a minute ago. You should go home."

She opened her eyes, for a moment confused. She hadn't realized she'd closed them, that she'd been leaning toward him ever so slightly.

"Right." Her back hit the rail as she stepped away, feeling clumsier than ever. "Of course." Get your breath, girl.

He wanted her to go home. To Seattle.

"Daniel asked me to stay and finish the job." She lifted her chin, thinking of that woman in the portrait. "He told me to take my time and think about it. Not to be hasty. As an incentive, he'll pay out the contract if I stay for a month."

"If you stay the month, you'll stay for the job."

"That, I assume, is what Daniel believes. But I could fool you all. I could just run off with my money, laughing all the way."

"No." He watched her, looking for clues, but not the way Harris did with his hocus-pocus act. With Ryan it was something personal between them, something that made the air sizzle and pop as if there were too much static electricity buzzing around.

"You're hooked," he said. "You want to stay. You want to bring Cutty House back to life. Even Daniel can figure that much out. But here's my humble opinion on the subject. You should get the hell out. Yesterday wouldn't be soon enough."

"Because you don't want Cutty House to succeed?" She crossed her arms, still holding on to that

Corona, needing to turn the tables on him. "Emma said you were working in Napa. How did she put it?" She wanted to get the words just right. "A total loser worker bee?"

"That's Emma. She only knows how to see Daniel's side of things."

"Oh, Emma was very informative. She told me you got away with murder. She even mentioned the possibility that you had been institutionalized."

Ryan took a beat and then started to laugh. It was a rich sound, his laughter, very deep, so that he had to take a moment to compose himself. When he did, he smiled, a nice smile, one she could learn to like.

"So now I'm a killer and a lunatic? Or maybe the two always go hand in hand? Poor Holly."

He stepped closer. With the rail behind her, there was nothing for her to do but hold her ground.

He picked up a piece of her hair and twirled it around his fingers absently. "You want me to tell you it's safe. That I'm not some demented psychopath following you around, ready to do you in. Go figure." His hand came to rest against her mouth, his thumb gently caressing her bottom lip. "Maybe it's better that you stay scared. Maybe you'll be more careful that way."

"I'm not a bit scared," she said, digging up a little bravado of her own.

Ryan dropped his hand. "If you've made up your mind, why did you come here?"

She gave him back the beer and pulled the strap of her purse over her shoulder, trying for a businesslike exit, at least.

"I suppose I wanted to see your face when I told you." She liked the sound of it, using his own words against him. "I thought I would know then if Emma was telling the truth."

She walked back toward the sliding glass door leading to the kitchen. She told him, "Don't worry. I'll show myself out."

Ryan heard the front door close behind her and her heels on the gangway back to shore.

Everything she'd felt, her outrage and desire, had been clearly on display. She didn't bother to hide a thing. Or maybe she couldn't.

He'd wanted to kiss her. When she'd leaned forward and closed her eyes like that, it had been damned hard not to.

Imagine, still able to strike up such a sweet little moment. Since the day he'd met Nina, there hadn't been many of those.

He looked down at the beer, smiling to himself. "She makes a hell of an exit."

Inside, the phone rang. He put down the bottle and slipped into the kitchen. When he picked up, he could hear the static of a cell phone and the distant sound of traffic on the other end.

"Leave her the hell alone!"

The line went dead. Ryan stared at the handset. The caller had been talking about Holly.

Someone had followed her here. They knew his number.

He released the breath he'd been holding and hung up the receiver. He hadn't recognized the voice.

Ryan stepped back outside. He picked up Holly's beer bottle from where he'd left it on the round glass-topped table. He took a drink, thinking. Could the caller have been her brother? A concerned sibling watching someone he loved take a misstep? Or something more sinister? The voice had sounded distant and harsh, as if the caller were trying to disguise it. *Some- one I know?*

He stared out over the water. Imagine, a long time ago, he'd dreamed of sailing away. Now, the only boat he had was solidly anchored to shore.

He told himself to be careful. Her coming here to- night…all those hours he'd spent following her around… Holly Fairfield was dangerously close to be- coming an obsession.

And apparently, she wasn't his alone.

15

One of the real gifts of architecture—what Holly loved most about her craft—was the ability it gave her to create order on paper. With her drafting board and drawing leads, she had total control. It was an illusion, and a wonderful contrast to the chaos life offered.

Only, tonight she wasn't in her office hovering over pristine drafting sheets and irregular curves, with a protractor at hand. She was driving into the city, back from Ryan's house—the last place she should have gone. Chaos was taking over, choking out reason.

In keeping with the spirit of the evening, she drove her rental not back to her apartment, but to the next "last place" she should visit: Cutty House itself.

She used the same door as Ryan. A magic jiggle of the knob, a good push with her shoulder, and she was in, hiking the stairs, finding a light switch here and there to guide her.

Back to her chess game. She'd certainly lost a knight in Daniel East. The Queen across the board no longer bore Vanessa Cutty's face, but Nina's. And now her castle looked about to fall. Everyone was settling back, waiting for Holly to make her next move.

She dragged the painting up against the couch and pulled back the curtains so that only moonlight shone like a spotlight. Very atmospheric.

The eyes seemed the most different. A bit knowing.

A little hard. Holly was staring at a painting of a young woman who had most certainly led a privileged life. Why was she so world-weary?

"What happened to you, Nina?" she whispered.

The article in the paper implied more than a tragic accident. The police report said something about an argument. The paper cited "unnamed sources" at the coroner's office, intimating that she'd been pregnant. Was that a motive for murder?

People quarreled. They got into cars angry, had accidents and were killed.

Or was she just making excuses? Everyone else seemed only too ready to point the finger.

She smiled to herself, wondering if that weren't part of the problem, her penchant for the underdog. She was a Sonics fan, after all.

She stepped around the portrait, her eyes still very much on Nina. "Big deal, I look like a dead woman. So what?" she told the painting.

Bravado, the last stand when reason runs thin.

She pulled up a chair and sat down. Well, she'd never been one for reasonable. Reasonable wouldn't have brought her here, full of dreams. She'd hoped the trip tonight out to his boat would clarify a thing or two. But there she'd been closing her eyes, lifting her face for the fairy prince's kiss. Dreaming again.

She remembered Harris asking her once: Don't you ever want to be the one who picks? At the time, she hadn't known what he meant, so he'd explained.

"Even in high school, you were always waiting around for someone to pick you. For a dance or a date. And Drew. Honestly, the guy just wore you down. Talked you into the business—the marriage. Don't you ever want to be the one who picks, Hol? Just see someone you want and go for it? To say, that's him, that's mine.''

And when she'd mentioned Harris's own track record, he'd answered with a smile. ''Well, there you go. That's why we're so miserable at love. We never get to pick.''

She told herself she hadn't picked Ryan. That's not what this was about. But if she left, he'd be what she missed. Him and Cutty House.

Behind her, she heard a door open. She turned around, startled. ''Hello?''

Creaking floorboards just outside in the hall.

Her first thought—the sounds of an old house settling. But there was a rhythm to the noise. Footsteps?

Ryan. He'd followed her again.

''Ryan?'' she called out.

A change in tempo, the staccato beat of running, bringing with it a frisson of fear.

''Is that you, Ryan?''

Well, it had to be. Who else did she have stalking her these days?

Anger seemed a futile emotion, but it came just the same. She thought they'd gotten past this sort of thing, that he understood his beef was with Daniel and not her.

''Ryan?'' She jumped to her feet. ''For goodness sake, this is ridiculous,'' she said, talking to herself as she walked to the door.

The sound of footsteps again. This time, farther down the hall.

She opened the door and took off, hoping to catch him, refusing to be frightened. She should give him a piece of her mind, that's what she should do. He was acting all of twelve, forcing her to chase him down.

But when she reached the end of the hall, she realized she'd entered yet another section of the house. The place looked long abandoned. An exaggerated mustiness filled the air, the smell of a house unattended. Not much light, either. Just the bare bulb she'd flicked on down the hall when she'd come upstairs. She looked down at the floorboards, scuffed and worn. She could see light shining up between the cracks in the floor from below. Not a good sign.

A fine sheen of dust covered the boards. She knelt down for a better look, seeing the faint outline of footprints.

Up ahead, a curtain fluttered as if a door had just opened. She felt a breeze, the hair rising at the back of her neck as a woman's voice whispered, "Nina."

Holly rose to her feet, her breath catching, turning toward the sound of the woman's voice. Not Ryan, then. It was someone else. Someone playing tricks, having a little fun.

"Whoever you are, I'm not scared." A complete lie. "I'm not giving up." Closer to the truth.

She was right about the door. Just ahead, it stood ajar so that a slight breeze trembled into the hall from the room beyond. She crept inside the room, stepping carefully on the floorboards. There wasn't much light, but the place appeared empty, without so much as a stick of furniture.

"All right. Whoever you are, you've had your fun."

And then she saw the windowpane, the writing there. The room was empty, but someone had been inside, all right. On the window, flushed with moonlight, words were written across the glass.

She walked more purposely now, drawn to what appeared to be a message of sorts. Quick jagged letters written in a hurry. The words stood out in brilliant scarlet as if done in lipstick.

Go Home!

She stepped back, her heart jumping to her throat. She didn't know what to think. The attack felt too personal. Someone had lured her here with the intent of her seeing this message. She took another step back, shaking her head.

And felt the floor give way.

There was a sharp *crack!* as she fell, screaming. She twisted around to break her fall, but her wrist collapsed with her weight, her cheek hitting the ground hard. Her ankle felt on fire, caught in the floorboards, pain shooting up to her knee. When she got her breath to look, she realized she was on her side, her arm pinned beneath her and her foot punched through the floor.

She heard more creaking just outside the door.

"Oh, God."

She lay perfectly still, like one of those skaters trapped on cracking ice. She tried to catch her breath, tried not to faint. She had this Stephen King image stuck in her head of the house coming to life, attacking her.

"Not the house," she told herself. "Not the house."

But someone.

Someone who wanted to hurt her. To scare her. Someone who wanted her gone.

Harris stared at the drawings on the coffee table. What had Holly called them? Idea sketches? He was smoking a cigarette. He'd quit five years ago but today was a special occasion.

He'd always admired his sister's talent, how she could create such beauty in her head. She could see inside a dead thing and give it life, while Harris knew only how to destroy.

He stubbed out the cigarette on a small plate, then stood to rinse it in the sink. Hell, he might even use air freshener, though he doubted he'd fool his sister.

He stood over the sink, suddenly fascinated by the sight of water gurgling down the drain. In the Southern hemisphere, the water would swirl in the opposite direction, counterclockwise. Coriolis Force. He'd had a friend try to convince him the damn thing was a myth, but every time he'd tried it, the effect had worked like a charm. Not that there'd been a lot of sinks in the jungle.

He turned off the water. He shouldn't have left Emma like that. Shouldn't have gone there in the first place.

He didn't know who the enemy was, couldn't imagine how to protect his sister. And after tonight—going to Daniel's like that—there was a distinct possibility that he had made everything much worse.

He heard the key first, then saw the door open. Too late for the air freshener.

Watching his sister, he noticed right away that something was wrong. She was walking stiffly. Limping? She turned to face him, stepping into the light.

"Ah, Jesus," he said.

Her pants were torn at the knee, the skin underneath red and raw. There was a cut on her cheek and she was holding her wrist.

"Don't fuss," she said, stepping around him. "I was just a klutz."

He followed her into the kitchen, watched as she took ice from the freezer with one hand and dropped it into a plastic sandwich bag. She hobbled over to a chair and put the ice on her cheek, then seemed to think better of it and put the bag on her wrist.

He picked up the other hand. Tiny cuts covered the skin across the knuckles. She'd broken a couple of nails.

"Go ahead," she told him, shoving the hand closer. "Take a good look. Put me under a microscope if it makes you happy."

"Holly?"

"You drive me crazy sometimes, Harris," she snapped at him. "I swear you do."

She sat up suddenly and sniffed the air. Just as quickly, she slid back into the chair, depleted of all her fight. "And now you're smoking again?"

He was staring at the cut on her knee. His heart started doing this funny rhythm thing. It wasn't good, this thing.

"I am absolutely fine," she told him.

"I can see that," he said, motioning to her face, her leg.

She rolled her eyes. "I went to Cutty House. There's a portrait of Nina in one of the rooms upstairs. The floorboards are old and, apparently, not so safe. One gave way and I fell. I twisted my knee and hurt my wrist." She lifted her chin, giving him a look that said, *satisfied?*

He'd had a girlfriend in college who'd accused him of loving his sister too much. He thought it was a strange thing to say at the time, but she'd gone on to explain that his sister was cramping his style. All those phone calls home and trips out to check on Holly? Maybe he didn't have enough time and attention for both his sister and a girlfriend, she'd suggested, which pretty much marked the end of their relationship.

Ever since he was seven, he'd known Holly belonged to him. Not as a responsibility. No way. But as a gift. His mother had given her to him the day she'd walked out for bread and never came back. *Take care of Holly…she'll need you.* Holly was the only family he had.

"Other than feeling quite stupid—" her voice had gone soft, catching on to the fact that he was dying a little inside "—I really am fine."

"See," he told her, making a bad attempt at humor. "I'm right. That house is going to kill you."

"Ba, da, duuum!" she said, providing the dramatic music.

He looked at her for a moment. Her face was flushed. She was trying to hide something…and, as usual, doing a damn poor job of it.

"You're going to stay," he said.

Maybe he'd known all along that she couldn't resist. She'd come here in fear, but, knowing his sister, she wasn't going to leave that way.

"A month," she told him. "After that, I reevaluate."

The nail in the coffin.

He stood, going back into the kitchen. He'd seen some kind of medical kit in the cabinet over the microwave.

It was always so easy for Holly, Little Miss Optimistic. All the worry and pessimism fell to him. Like now. He had a really bad feeling about where they were headed.

When he knelt down beside her with the antiseptic, she steadied his hand.

"It really is going to be all right," she said.

Because she hadn't the slightest idea that her big brother had slept with Daniel's girlfriend. And that he'd liked it. Very much.

"You should see a doctor," he said, soaking a cotton ball, dabbing the cut. The medical kit had lots of bandages. There was even an elastic one for her wrist. "You might have sprained something."

"I'm in one piece, Spiderman. Safe and sound."

"Yeah," he said, cleaning the wound on her knee. "Sure thing."

"I can't believe you started smoking again. Smoking kills."

"Really? I haven't heard anything about it."

"I'm sorry," she told him. "I know you're worried. Now you want me to worry. So you started smoking?"

He tossed the cotton ball on the table, grabbed another one. "That's me. Mr. Even-Steven. World's got to have balance, Hol. You take your risks...I take mine."

"It's not funny. Tell me you'll quit again. Promise me."

"The day you finish this job, I quit."

"If that's the best you can do."

He looked up at his sister. Holly was golden, as good as they came. And someone was going to take advantage of that, sure as shit.

"Yeah, Hol. That's the best I can do, because you're making me a nervous wreck. Wait here a minute. I'll get you some aspirin."

When he came back with the pills and a glass of water, she said, "If you really want me to— I mean, if it's going to put that look on your face, we can leave."

But he shook his head. "I don't think it's up to me, Hol. And I don't care what you promise tonight." He sighed, glancing back at her sketches. "You're not walking away from this."

More's the pity, he thought, grabbing the bandage to start wrapping her wrist.

They were in a pretty big mess, he and Holly. She thought it was just a job, but Harris knew better. That sixth sense of his told him so. Now she'd come home looking like a train wreck. And he worried that, in the end, all he could do was keep an eye on her, and hand out the aspirin and bandages when it all fell apart.

COMPOSITION

16

The invitation appeared the next day. *You are invited to an exclusive fête at Viña Dorada....*

Holly stared at the card, a lovely watercolor of a wine bottle, grapes and a Spanish fan opened across a lace tablecloth. She half expected the invitation to disappear in her hand. *Poof!*

Ryan had invited her to the vineyard where he worked. The card promised flamenco music and sparkling wine. Ryan's signature at the bottom appeared under the words: *Please come.*

Just like that. A date.

It had been a morning of surprises. She'd woken to the sound of Daniel's voice on the phone: *I'm on pins and needles, love. Tell me I have something to celebrate?* Having confirmed that she would indeed be staying on, Daniel had been a busy boy.

By the time Holly rolled into work at Cutty House, his people were moving new furniture into her second-floor office. A desk with a computer stood by the window, a large printer and a drafting table just opposite, with hanging files and another table for viewing plans alongside. There was even a copy of *Sweets,* a catalogue she already had on disk offering tools of the trade, everything from nails to exotic historical moldings. The catalog was neatly laid out with a personal message from Daniel. *Have fun!*

And now this. Her fingers slipped over the burgundy ink on the envelope, her name written in elegant scroll letters. A lot of foot traffic had come through her office that morning. Holly herself had been in and out several times. She didn't know who had put the invitation on her desk or how she could have missed seeing it before now.

"Knock, knock?" It was Daniel, stopping by to pay a visit.

She looked up, doing her level best not to appear caught in some act of sabotage, Ryan's invitation clutched in her hand. Daniel had dressed in what for him passed as casual—jeans and a T-shirt, but with fancy boots and yet another leather jacket, this one brown. Today he wore contacts, not glasses. He took the invitation from her hand, not even bothering a glance at the card as he dropped it on the desk next to the *Sweets* catalog, the invitation landing face up for anyone to read.

"You won't regret giving me another chance," he said.

"In a month, you may not be thanking me."

"I'll take that bet."

He dropped one hand to her waist and pressed her up into his body, sweeping her around the room in a waltz—a rather bad one—as they bumped into the filing cabinet, a chair, the desk. He was singing at the top of his lungs and, surprisingly making her laugh.

That's how Emma found them. In each other's arms, laughing and dancing.

"Emma, darling," he said, still tripping around the crowded office. "A reprieve. She's staying."

As Holly two-stepped around the room, she glanced back at Emma. The other woman looked incredibly small, her arms wrapped around her waist as if in the act of holding herself together.

The expression on her face... For an instant, Holly saw something there. *She doesn't want me to stay.* The voice last night calling Nina's name had been a woman's voice.

"Stop," Holly told Daniel. "You're making me dizzy."

He made another sweeping turn to finish their dance in a dip. He kissed her mouth, just a peck.

When she winced, he pulled her up. "Wait a minute." He touched her cheek and some of the makeup she'd used to cover the bruise came off on his finger. "What's this?"

"I walked into a door last night. Which means," she said, stepping around him, thankful that her cheek was the only visible injury. She picked up the invitation and dropped it inside her handbag. "You're already working me too hard."

"Take the day off," he said, magnanimously.

"Wouldn't that be nice," she said. She glanced down at the quick sketches she'd left on the drafting table. She'd need at least a week to come up with some decent design drawings. Even if Daniel had promised to give her free rein, she wasn't a tyrant. She wanted his input.

"Friday," she said, patting her purse and the invitation inside. "I'll take some time off, then."

The energy radiated from him, he had so much. He grabbed Emma and danced around the room with her, pushing Holly playfully out of their way.

"She's going to stay," he sang at the top of his lungs. "She's going to stay."

With a smile, Holly took in their dance. Only the expression on Emma's face marred the picture.

Watching her, Holly wondered about Emma's state of mind. *Does she think I'm angry? Could she care less?* With Daniel, Holly had always held back a little. Emma had been a different story.

She dressed me up for Daniel; she fed me stories. Yes, Holly was disappointed. Deeply so. But did she really think Emma responsible for last night? *She has the run of Cutty House, knows its every secret, including where not to step.*

A sobering thought, she told herself. This morning, she'd taken the wrap off her wrist and found it didn't hurt. The knee was another story. She wasn't going to hold up for another dance.

Her smile in place, she decided it was time to get some air. "I'm certainly not going to get much done with you two bouncing around the room. Tah, tah." With a wave of her fingers, she left Daniel and Emma behind.

Outside, she winced again when she put on her sunglasses. Thankfully, Harris's prediction of a black eye hadn't come true. But there was a lingering soreness in her knee, enough that she thought she might take a walk, stretch it out a bit.

Just this morning, she'd set up chairs around the hole where her foot had fallen through the floor. She'd even managed to get a phone number for maintenance from one of the men Daniel had sent to bring up the furniture. The man had come and gone, confirming what she suspected, that the boards in that room were rotten. Termites, age, what have you. The whole floor needed to be replaced. He was surprised someone hadn't warned her about that section of the house. Surely the family knew it wasn't safe?

Holly picked up her pace, walking briskly down Taylor, testing the muscles in her sore knee. The message in lipstick had long since disappeared, the glass wiped clean. In the sunshine of late morning, it was difficult to believe the warning had ever been there.

Listening to choral practice at Grace Cathedral, she let the music drown out the memory, then stopped to watch the children laughing and playing at Huntington Park. She should just go sit on a bench, enjoy the fleeting sunshine and shove off that cloud in her head now wearing the name Emma.

Just now, in her office, Emma hadn't said a word. Not one.

A little girl with red hair danced across the grass, carefree and giggling with the joy of the day. Wishing she felt the same, Holly reached for the invitation in her purse, almost as if checking to see if it was still there.

Harris knew the exact moment she stepped into the bar. He couldn't miss her. Only a few diligent souls littered the room. He'd been watching the door all night, waiting for her to show.

She fought back a few palm fronds as her eyes scanned the room, looking so unsure of herself. She was wearing one of those T-shirts with spaghetti straps and jeans that dropped low on her hips, a uniform of sorts for Emma. She'd pulled her hair back into another ponytail. She looked all of eighteen.

When she saw him, her whole body tensed. *That's right,* he thought. *A time of reckoning.*

She sat down at the counter in front of him. He waited for her to do the talking, but she didn't seem so inclined. Instead, she pulled the bowl of mix front and center and started picking out the wasabi peas.

He gave it a minute before serving her the same beer she'd ordered that first night. *Fine by me.*

"And here we are." Not his best icebreaker, but maybe he wasn't feeling the mood tonight.

"I just thought I should do the responsible thing." She started lining up the peas on a napkin. Three, four, five… "Let you know I don't have AIDS or anything."

"Good to know." He wondered if she really planned to spend the entire conversation staring everywhere but at him. "I used to get tested where I worked, and as I haven't had sex since I left my job, there you have it. The all clear."

"So the fact that you were sex-starved excuses you but not me?"

"Funny, did I look like I needed an excuse?"

She glanced up. She couldn't hold his gaze, but ventured a smile. Progress.

"I give blood," she said. "Regularly. They test you then. And I'm on the pill. I've only slept with Daniel, anyway."

Harris knew she was twenty-six. She was telling him that, since she'd become sexually active, she'd slept with one man, a cretin who was currently her boss and basically controlled every aspect of her life.

"Why the smile?" she asked.

"I didn't know I was your 'take that' for old Daniel."

She picked up her beer, hiding her expression behind the drink. But he thought he caught another hint of a smile.

"Change of subject," she said, avoiding the topic altogether. She put down the glass. "Your old job. It sounds like some sort of government thing. That's where they test people for everything, right?"

"Now that you've had your way with me, you want

to know if I can hold down a steady job other than tending bar?''

But she didn't bite. ''You said you left the evil kingdom of corporate America.''

''Ah. So you were listening.''

''What's the big deal. Why can't you tell me? Were you some sort of spy?''

A spy. He smiled. ''Good guess.''

''You were a spy?''

''Now, would I admit it if I were?''

''But your sister knows. That's why she calls you Spiderman.''

He leaned in, putting an end to the mystery. But it had been fun. Harris Fairfield, superspy. ''I've never worked for the government.'' He picked up her beer. ''Come on.''

He took her to what he'd dubbed ''their'' table in the corner. He set her beer down and pulled out a chair for her. After a slight hesitation, she accepted the courtesy.

He straddled the chair across from hers. ''I used to work for a pharmaceutical company. They had research stations in the rainforest, harvesting plants, fungi, frogs—pretty much anything—trying to discover the next cure for cancer, arthritis or just a better wrinkle cream. My sister calls me Spiderman because I found this spider and the venom turned out to be pretty complicated stuff.'' He shrugged. ''There are lots of long words for what I did, none of them particularly interesting.''

''Wow. All that education must come in handy working at a bar.''

He laughed. ''I told you, I am a changed man. A supershrink to the masses. Anything you want to confess?''

"That I'm sorry it happened?"

He shook his head. "I'm not."

"Look, I know you're acting all tough because you're a guy. But I saw your face when you left. You were sorry."

He helped himself to a drink of her beer. "I shouldn't have left you like that."

She took the beer from him, sipping from the glass before putting it down, giving them both a minute. "I think what happened caught us off guard." She looked up, holding his gaze for the first time. "And maybe I *was* mad. About your sister and Daniel, I mean. Only, not in the way you think. Ever since she came on the scene, I started wondering how much I could actually help Daniel. Make a tastier éclair, sure? But Holly's going to do way more." She puffed out her cheeks, blowing out a quick breath. "So…okay…I needed a little consoling."

He had this flash, a picture of their naked bodies, both of them acting as if they couldn't get enough. Consoling? That's not how he would have described the night. Just the same, he thought he'd pass along some good news. It was the least he could do.

"Holly isn't going to sleep with her boss." His sister didn't repeat her mistakes.

"You have no idea what Holly will do for Daniel."

"What have you done for him?" He recognized that tone.

She glanced up, all cool green eyes. "You're not a very good spy if you need me to tell you that."

"Hence, maybe why I was fired. And for the record? I never said I was a spy." He took another sip of her beer, then pushed it back toward her. *Your turn.* "As for the tastier éclair? Sounds pretty promising as a contribution to mankind. Me, I'm working on something I call Tiger's Blood. Some Malibu rum, a little Charmbourg for color. I'm just not sure about the cranberry juice. It's good for the color, but not so much for the taste."

"Pomegranate," she suggested. "More exotic."

"And how long do you think we can keep up the inconsequential banter?"

She was staring at the table, maybe wishing she still had those peas to count. She dropped her head, blowing out another breath. "I don't even know why I came."

He grabbed her hand when she made to stand, keeping her there at the table. "Because we had sex. And, I'm fishing here, but it wasn't half bad. Maybe even worth a repeat performance?" It's what he'd been thinking about ever since he'd left her.

He could see the same emotions he felt on her face: guilt, need. Like the song said: *words that go together well.*

But suddenly, she jerked back, the intimate moment vanishing as she focused somewhere behind him. He watched her pop to her feet like a jack-in-the-box so that the chair almost tipped over.

"I have to go." She began making her way to the exit—to where Daniel East waited. But Danny boy wasn't watching Emma. He had eyes for only Harris.

He wondered how much Daniel had guessed from seeing them together just now. He half thought he should walk over, make sure Emma was going to be all right. But they disappeared out the door before he had a chance.

You have no idea what Holly will do for Daniel.
She'd sounded so trapped.

Daniel East had some sort of hold on her. And Harris was betting it wasn't about the sex.

"Good job, Spiderman," he said to himself, picking up her beer, ready to dump it behind the bar. "Way to screw the pooch."

17

Emma stumbled across the room. Daniel pushed her again so that she lost her footing, crash-landing on the couch. She'd never seen him this angry.

"What the hell were you doing with her brother?"

She'd known it was going to be bad. He'd been so quiet on the drive over. It wasn't like Daniel to be quiet.

"You were following me?" Trying to turn the tables, throwing out her own accusations.

"You haven't let me touch you in days. Of course I was following you. And wasn't I in for a surprise."

"You're the one who told me to make friends."

"With Holly. Not her brother."

"It's pretty much the same thing, or haven't you noticed?" She sat up on the couch, making herself less vulnerable. "Daniel, don't be a dumbass. I met Harris when Holly and I went out for a drink, remember? You're making a big deal out of nothing."

She was a good liar, a talent she'd perfected with Daniel at the helm. And Daniel wasn't the most perceptive man on earth.

He came to stand over her, his intimidating best. "There's a lot at stake here, sweetheart. I can't afford to blow this with a little impromptu thinking on your part."

"Stupid me. How could I forget priority number

one, your precious Cutty House? Oh, and rubbing Ryan's nose in it—that most of all. Don't worry, hon," she said, pushing some buttons of her own. "You know me. I won't step out of line or forget my status."

"From where I was standing, you were forgetting a lot. So I'm asking you again. What were you doing with her fucking brother?"

"Wow. Is that real emotion in your voice?" She leaned forward, taking him on. "Don't you mean am I fucking her brother? Go ahead, ask me. Am I fucking Holly's brother?"

She knew Daniel could get ugly, knew better than to push. She didn't recognize this angry woman throwing confessions in his face, waving the red flag in front of the bull.

"How did it feel to see me with him?" she asked. "Were you jealous? A little scared? Or did it just hurt your stupid pride? Did you think I'd leave you all alone after everything we've been through? Because those are my fears, Daniel. That you'll forget she's not Nina."

"Now who's being stupid?"

"The clothes, the hair, the makeup? Was it all for Ryan? Wasn't there just a little something in it for you? Trying to bring Nina back—"

"Don't give me that crap, Ems. You know why I need Holly."

"I know why you think you need her. But what if there's more to it?" she asked, voicing her biggest fear. *I helped her buy those clothes; I told her how to cut her hair. My fault.* She couldn't be responsible. Not again.

"All those years you let Nina use you, but you were never good enough for her, did you know that? Did you guess? You were, how should I put this? Recreational—or maybe it was comic relief?''

He jumped on the couch and grabbed a fistful of Emma's hair. But even when he yanked her head back, pulling her hair by the roots, she kept going. ''Ryan at least had some pride. He wouldn't do half the shit you did.''

Straddling her. ''Shut up!'' Pulling harder. ''Shut the fuck up!''

''It's the truth! It's always been the truth. You were never good enough for any of them. Your mother's ugly secret.''

He wrapped both hands around her neck and pressed. Emma tried to kick him off, to break the grip of his fingers, but he leaned his whole weight into her, pushing harder.

He's going to kill me....

Even as she struggled, a part of her wondered if it really mattered what happened to her. She and Daniel would always be linked by death. Maybe this is how it ends, she thought. This was how she'd finally stop hurting people.

She couldn't get air in her lungs. She could hear herself making gasping sounds deep in her throat. After a while, she stopped struggling, wondering if this was how it felt to die? How Nina had felt? Maybe she hadn't even been scared in the end, Emma thought, her hands falling away.

Daniel jerked his hands away. ''Oh, God!'' He rolled off the couch and knelt on the ground beside her. He helped her to sit up, rubbed her arms as she sucked in air.

''I can't believe— Did I hurt you? Emma?''

She pushed him away. She pressed her fists to her

face, not wanting to see him, fighting the desire to answer that plea in his voice.

"Emma, please. Jesus, tell me you're all right? I'm sorry, baby. God, I'm so sorry."

Listening to him, she knew that there was something wrong with her. Daniel had pressed the life out of her—even for a moment, lost control—and still she wanted to comfort him, had to fight the overwhelming need to tell him she was fine. As if she deserved no better.

She knew if she opened her eyes she'd see what she always saw—Daniel, horrified by what he'd done.

Dan sat beside her and turned her body in to his on the couch, holding her even as she pummeled her fists against his chest. She could feel him shaking against her, trembling.

"I'm so sorry. God, I'm sorry."

He just kept saying it, over and over. He'd never done anything to hurt her before. But she'd known there was violence there; she'd been afraid. That hate of his kept rising to the surface. Every time Daniel clawed and fought for what was his, there was no telling what the collateral damage might be.

When he started to cry, the coil inside her began to unwind, responding just the same. The entire episode felt like an old song they knew by heart. Daniel falling apart, Emma keeping him together.

"Shh," she said, giving in. "It's all right."

"I don't want to hurt you. Not you."

"Daniel, I won't betray you." That old familiar tune. "I would never betray you."

"I'm sorry. I'm sorry."

"I was trying to help," she said, making it up as she went along, sinking deeper into an alliance she could no longer control. "She's really close to her brother. You said to be her friend. Maybe it's not so bad if he likes me?''

"You know what she can do for us. I just want to get back what's mine. I can't blow this, Ems. I can't lose. I won't get another chance.''

She stroked his face, letting him talk.

"It's my last chance. You know it is. We both do.''

His last chance to succeed. To make things right. To put the past behind them.

And Nina, long dead and buried, was still pulling the strings.

As the story went, it was supposed to be a cheap vacation. Holly's father always told it like an apology. *I didn't make enough money—I wasn't enough for her.*

Holly had just turned three, Harris was maybe seven. They'd worn their bathing suits under their clothes and piled beach balls and buckets into the Buick, heading for Alki Beach, the "Birthplace of Seattle," a sudden burst of warm weather their inspiration. Their mother had packed a picnic basket full of food, a thermos and water. They wouldn't need to spend a dime.

Holly and Harris had been entrenched in the sand, water lapping at their feet, building what, from the perspective of first memories, remained their largest and best sandcastle ever. Harris did the real work, but he coached Holly to fill the buckets or clear the moat. They were a team. The sky, a stunning strip of blue, had lured a crowd away from the city. Turf wars ensued, until a big kid belly flopped on their castle, making Holly cry.

Taking one look at his sister, Harris jumped right on him, fists flying. He had the boy pinned in the sand when the kid grabbed a rock and beamed Harris right above the eye. Four stitches and three hundred dollars and change at the emergency room. No insurance.

Her father had been between jobs; they'd let him go at the private school where he'd been teaching. He was working part-time and tutoring on the side. Things were tight. They couldn't even afford a decent vacation.

The next year, their mother left them, presumably tired of waging the battle.

Whenever Holly saw a sandcastle, she remembered the story, a hazy memory given shape by years of her father's sullen retelling. In the late afternoon, with precious sunshine burnishing the sandstone walls of its keep, that's what Viña Dorada reminded her of: a dazzling castle.

The stone chateau overlooked the ribbons of vines garlanding the hills. A gurgling creek ran past lichen-covered stone walls, ancient gnarled olives and oaks melted into the surrounding forest. Beautiful people strolled in ridiculously high heels over the blue-green lawns marking the entrance to the Napa vineyard. Heck, even the air tasted better here.

Welcome to Viña Dorada.

She tucked the invitation into the silly little handbag she'd bought to match her dress and walked up the path to where the party was in full swing. Ivy and colorful flowering trumpet vines tangled over every surface, making the vineyard appear almost mystical.

Holly passed a rose arbor where a waiter offered her a glass of sparkling wine. She stepped onto the lawn, beginning to mingle, drawing attention with her off-the-shoulder blouse and slit skirt. She'd bought the ensemble with Emma, but the skirt's cascade of ruffles added a Latin flare that seemed just too perfect for an afternoon of flamenco music. Like any sensible woman, she'd resisted the urge to believe the clothes were cursed, despite whatever Emma's intentions might have been in coaxing Holly to buy them.

She'd pulled her hair back and wore just lipstick and mascara. Checking the mirror before she left, she thought she looked more like the Holly of old.

Tasting the wine, she searched the crowd for Ryan. A classical guitarist played as a woman, dressed in a flowing white gown laced with red ribbons, danced, clapping her hands, kicking her heels with the music. Holly thought it might not be so bad, acting as a loser worker bee here.

She kept to the shadows, listening to the guitar and rhythmic clapping, watching the dancing woman curve her body around as she flicked the tail of her dress with her foot. Holly told herself she needed to "out" some of those skeletons from the Cutty House closet. If she wanted her work to succeed, best to know what she was up against. That was the only reason she'd come—in these clothes, with her face flushed and her blood zinging, causing the occasional double take.

It's called playing with fire, girl.

Well, maybe.

After the incident with the floorboards, she'd spent hours evaluating. Despite her brother's facile prediction, it was no easy choice to stay. But once before someone in her life had driven her from what she loved. She wasn't about to fall into a pattern of running scared. She'd leave after a proper fight, and today she'd come to do battle. Which again didn't explain the clothes and her best perfume, or the flower she'd pinned in her hair.

At the center of the courtyard, a stone fountain of a stag watched over the gathering, white and pink lilies floating on the water at its feet. The act of not stepping on toes became a dance in itself until she found a safe haven beside an enormous fern.

She'd stay just long enough to see what Ryan had to say, she told herself. He'd invited her here, after all, an olive branch she'd be rude to refuse. She knew what lay behind his dark stares now; she was more than ready for him.

Across the courtyard, an older woman held court. Along with the dancer, she seemed another reference point. With her own audience gathered around, she still managed a nod to passersby. She had a warm smile and held her glass as she used her hands to tell a story. A neat trick that, Holly thought. The woman wore a dark burgundy dress to the floor that hugged her matronly curves. There was nothing of subterfuge about her; she was the picture of sophistication without the pomp.

The vintner's wife, Holly decided. No doubt, the heart of Viña Dorada.

And wouldn't it be nice to someday measure up half as well, Holly thought, drinking from her glass. To be confident that her beauty didn't come from the size of her hips or a wrinkle-free face.

The music swelled and the woman turned with her audience to watch the dancer. For an instant, her eyes caught Holly's across the way. Holly smiled.

But the woman didn't smile back. Instead, she dropped her glass, so that it shattered into a million pieces on the flagstones at her feet. A cry escaped her lips.

The music stopped. Everyone turned in Holly's direction. She turned, as well, searching behind her.

But they were staring at her. At Holly. The woman's hand rose, then dropped limp to her side as those around her stepped forward to shore her up. Even at this distance, Holly could read her lips as she whispered, *Nina.*

After that, the revelations came easily enough so that Holly knew that once again she'd been outmaneuvered, falling, despite all her care, into another trap.

Out of nowhere, Ryan appeared. He grabbed her arm, hustling her down a covered path. Holly could hear the murmur of guests as they passed, the champagne spilling from her glass. But Ryan seemed intent only on getting away. He dragged her along a walkway that hugged what appeared to be the back of the main building. Holly tried to keep up, almost losing her shoe.

Eventually they ducked into a small room, entering through a pair of French doors. It was a sitting room of sorts, sun-filled, with a sturdy round table bracketed by two chairs and a banquette by the window. His breath coming hard, Ryan pressed her against the door, tucking her out of sight.

"What the hell are you doing here?" he asked her.

She could still see that poor woman's face. She looked as if she'd seen a ghost.

She knew Nina.

"You invited me—"

"No way." He was shaking his head. "I would never invite you here."

He pushed her down onto the banquette. She could see he was terrified. Behind him the door opened. She heard the scrape of a cane as a man struggled inside.

"Gil." Ryan blocked the man's view of Holly. "It's not Nina."

"I want to see her, dammit!"

The man stepped around Ryan. The woman Holly

had seen in the courtyard followed, coming to stand beside him.

"She looks like Nina, Gil. That's all. It's not her."

But the man wasn't listening to Ryan. He inched forward, every step a struggle, reaching for Holly.

"Come on, Gil. Catch your breath."

He would have fallen if Ryan hadn't been there to hold him up. Holly saw there was something wrong with him. The right side of his face had fallen, as if paralyzed. A stroke, she thought.

The charity at the Samba, Samba! club. Daniel had insisted on her going. The party had been to benefit stroke victims.

Ryan telling her: *The charity tonight. Daniel knew I'd be here. That's why he brought you along. He's showing you off. To me.*

She could hear the woman speaking to Gil in a foreign language. Spanish, Holly thought. Ryan helped the older man turn for the door, the woman taking over so he could lean on her and his cane.

"No," the older man said. "It's not her." He stopped at the French doors to give Holly a final glance, appearing almost apologetic. "I'm sorry. I shouldn't have made a fuss."

He shuffled forward with the woman who was most certainly his wife, stopping just outside the doorway to rest. When Ryan tried to help, he gestured him off.

Holly heard him say, "See to our guest, Ryan. I think I've given her a fright," followed by a self-deprecating laugh. The woman spoke again in Spanish, this time to Ryan.

Holly watched as the couple disappeared outside, feeling incredibly numb. She could see Ryan standing at the door, so stiff he looked frozen in place.

"I'm sorry," she said. But if Ryan heard her, he

didn't turn around. She was speaking to his back. "I didn't know."

"You have to go now."

It was all he said before he, too, vanished, leaving the "guest" to fend for herself. Holly felt out of breath, almost stricken by what she'd pieced together.

She looks like Nina, Gil. That's all.

Apparently, it was enough.

It took her a good ten minutes to find her way out of the labyrinth halls, avoiding the courtyard and the crowd. At the entrance, there was a small table with a stack of glossy brochures and a little note card painted with the word *Welcome.* Inside the colorful pages of the brochure, the printed text told the tale of the vineyard's modest beginnings.

The Travers family opened Viña Dorada...

Nina's family. Her father...her mother.

She hadn't put it together. The name of the vineyard sounded Spanish, Travers did not. That Ryan worked for Nina's family seemed too incredible, given the fact that everyone blamed him for her death.

The disbelief on their faces. Disbelief and pain.

She was the bully now, stomping on their sandcastle, throwing the rock.

Driving out of the parking lot, she turned for the road heading home. Whoever had sent that invitation had planned their assault well, with incredible cunning and care.

She'd thought coming here was her move. But all along, she'd been nothing but the pawn.

18

Ryan turned the glass in his hand, painting the sides with the Syrah. Pale legs of red ran down, showing a nice consistency and weight. He'd used the wine thief to extract a pitcherful from the barrel for the staff. They got a kick out of tasting the vintage, guessing it would be his best. He nosed the wine and tasted. It wouldn't be much longer before they bottled.

Viña Dorada was primarily known for its sparkling wines made in the Spanish tradition. Expanding into other wines had been one of the first changes he'd made. In the United States, consumers bought sparkling wine primarily for weddings and New Year celebrations. Before Ryan took over, ninety percent of the product at Viña Dorada had sold in the month of December.

The reality was that they could only make so many changes in consumer habits through marketing. He'd explained to Gil and Marta that Viña Dorada needed to evolve. Now the label had a name outside of the sparkling wines where it once dominated and won medals at top competitions.

He put the glass down, flipping through a couple of messages on his desk. The lab again. He'd call tomorrow. He needed to keep a tab on the carbon dioxide levels. They might need to blow some nitrogen.

He realized he was moving things around the

desk—the glass, his papers, the phone—like one of those plastic puzzles where the trick was to slide the pieces around until the picture made sense.

You sent me an invitation.

Or maybe he was trying to rub out the picture altogether—Holly looking so dismayed and so hurt.

Ryan walked over to the window. The house sat atop a knoll like the castle keep it mimicked, looking over the hills of the vineyard. That's why he'd chosen this room for his office. The timeless view gave him perspective.

Inside his head, the plastic pieces shifted again. Twelve years after her death, he could still see Nina right there in front of him. Laughing at him. She always did enjoy a good laugh. He had this one memory of Nina laughing beside him in bed.

They'd broken into a house in Pacific Heights. The home belonged to one of his "godmothers," so he'd known the code to the alarm. Nina always thought it was hilarious how Vanessa had only one child to share with her many society friends, hence the multiple uncles and aunties.

The house had been empty, the occupants gone on vacation to Hawaii. With his help, Nina had broken the door to the wine vault. He'd been pretty far gone already from a night of partying or he never would have agreed to open the Lafite-Rothschild, 1982. The wine was worth about a thousand dollars a bottle and they both knew it. But that wasn't enough for Nina.

They'd been naked on the bed in the master bedroom, the wine almost gone. Nina had tried to give him some pills she'd found in the medicine cabinet. She was a year younger than Ryan, but she'd always been the more daring. It fascinated him, how she was willing to try anything. Fascinated and repelled.

He'd shaken his head, refusing her pills. He didn't like that loss of control that Nina seemed to crave. But she'd moved over him, straddling him, pressing her gift past his lips with her own.

I need you to be more alive than this. That's what she'd told him.

She'd had a beautiful wicked laugh. It was the thing he'd loved most about her.

Ryan turned away from his office window, the view now nearly done in by dusk. He thought that if Nina were here, she'd get a good laugh out of what was going on. And she'd like how twisted everything had become. Nina had always loved the spotlight.

You sent me an invitation.

He hadn't sent Holly a damn thing. But he thought he knew who had.

When he and Daniel were kids, Ryan had tried out this theory. He'd been really excited, absolutely certain Daniel would climb aboard once he heard. They could trade places, like that book, *The Prince and the Pauper.*

It made sense. He was tired of the burden of being the Cutty heir, tired of the "tremendous responsibility" his mother would tell him about every other minute. He had to dress right, go places he hated, get the best grades. He had to be perfect.

It's only you, Ryan. He remembered his mother telling him that. *Both Cutty and Moore are depending on you.*

He used to wonder about that. Why he was the only one. Why Daniel didn't count.

He'd never coveted the Cutty fortune, probably because it was constantly shoved in his face, while Daniel had the family business dangled teasingly out of his reach. Ryan grew up dreaming of making his own way, of being his own man. *My choice.* He'd needed the challenge, just like his grandfathers before him.

"I'll sail off and they'll never find me," he'd told Daniel, explaining the details of a ten-year-old's escape plan. "They'll need you then, see? There won't be anybody else."

Which was pretty much what had happened after Nina died.

He'd actually been relieved when Daniel took over Cutty House. It was like paying off a bad debt. *So sorry my dad was such an asshole. I never wanted any of it, really....* And Daniel had stepped up to the plate to take over and run the place. It was almost too perfect. At last, Daniel would get the recognition he deserved.

But Ryan should have known better, should have guessed it wouldn't be enough. Like Nina, Daniel needed more. And now it seemed he wanted Ryan gone altogether.

Ryan picked up the glass from the desk and once again swirled the wine to take in the aroma. Black currant, cedar and spice. In a way, the Syrah represented everything he'd learned the last ten years from Gil and the other vintners in Napa. The first two years had been tough. He'd been a wine maker, manager, nursemaid and surrogate son all at once.

But last fall, they'd had their best harvest ever. He'd successfully expanded their product base. Between functions like today's flamenco festivities and other entertainment, the boutique vineyard did a nice business and was getting ready to spread its wings and grow.

He'd been so caught up in the business of Viña Dorada that he'd convinced himself he could sit back and enjoy their success. Forget the past—let life take its course. The pattern of his days dictated by the vines...

Ryan left the wine on the desk and dug out his car keys. Let life take its course. Now didn't that sound perfect?

But then, platitudes usually did, he told himself, heading for the door.

As it turned out, he didn't have to go far to find her. She was waiting in the parking lot.

Surprise, surprise.

She walked up to him, looking so determined. Sometimes her face was a bit of a shock. He'd see her from afar and imagine Nina. But then she'd come closer, and it was like one of those kaleidoscopes shifting into another pattern altogether.

Like now. She was wearing clothes right out of Nina's closet, daring, sexy...but she'd put a gardenia in her hair. Nina never accessorized with anything that wasn't twenty-four-carat something. And the expression on Holly's face would never happen if she'd been Nina, a spoiled beautiful girl who just couldn't care that much.

"I was halfway to the city when I turned around," she said.

He noticed she barely reached his chin despite the heels. Nina could almost look him straight in the eye.

"I had this idea," she continued. "I was going to march right up to your door. But I've been standing here for the longest time, trying to find the courage."

"Then it's a good thing I came out."

She nodded, but somehow he knew it wasn't in response to anything he'd said. She had a speech going in her head and darned if she wasn't going to have her say.

"Someone is doing this. Setting us up," she said. "And I want it to stop. What happened earlier with Nina's parents—"

"I understand."

"No...no, you don't. You can't."

She began to pace, as if motion somehow helped. Another difference between her and Nina. Nina was like a cat, languid, never making an unnecessary move, always holding a reserve. Holly had energy to spare.

"I have this wonderful job." She stopped, catching his eye to make certain he was listening, as if she might have to fight to keep a man's attention. Nina just assumed she had the world at her feet.

"Only, the dream job is mine because I look like some poor dead woman, and that is so beyond weird that I still don't quite believe it."

Her eyes were dark enough that, in the low light, the pupils almost disappeared into the rim of brown. "Daniel said he thought it was some sort of sign that I looked like Nina. Good karma for Cutty House. He told me I was the only person who could save the project."

"And you believed him?"

"I drew some sketches, just quick design ideas to try and get Daniel to see a new vision for the place." She shook her head. "I've never done anything like those sketches. Cutty House just came to life for me. It was this amazing experience, a real rush." She looked up, meeting his gaze dead-on. "I'd had three really bad years and then, suddenly, everything was going to be okay. I was back on my game, doing the work I loved."

He could see all those hopes and dreams in her face, the energy of discovering that talent inside herself.

"Yes, I believed him," she admitted. "I wanted to. Cutty House just seemed to fit, the project and me."

"Like magic."

"I'm sure you think that's very arrogant. Look, I'm not channeling the spirit of Nina or anything. And I realize now you didn't send that invitation. And," she said with a tiny smile, "I can see you're not some loser worker bee here at the vineyard, either. I don't know what's going on—well, actually, maybe I do. But to send me here to scare these poor people? I just can't imagine that kind of malice."

There was apprehension in her eyes. At the same time, she held herself stiff and straight, as if trying to assert herself.

She'd never looked less like Nina.

"But I think…" she said, stepping closer, making that connection, the one that sizzled and popped inside his head, making him a little crazy because he'd never felt the charge of it before. Not with Nina or any other woman. "I think *you* can imagine people who would want to hurt them."

He took her arm, gently this time, steering her back to her car.

"Welcome to the family," he told her.

If SoMa was dance central for the city, North Beach turned out to be its breadbasket.

Ryan explained the neighborhood's history, beginning with the Barbary Coast and its whorehouses and gambling parlors. Even before the earthquake in 1906, Italians had migrated here to work as fishermen and factory laborers, giving birth to "Little Italy." The 1950s brought the Beatnik era, the 60s, Carol Doda baring her breasts at the Condor nightclub.

But things were changing here in the big city.

Trendy shops and restaurants replaced the mom-and-pop outfits. A martini might cost you ten dollars and dinner your firstborn. Still, Ryan liked the diversity, not to mention the food.

He took her to the Rose Pistola, with its fall colors, rich wood and leather upholstery. It featured an open kitchen, and the hostess made walk-in seating sound like the Second Coming. Something about no conventions in town. Ryan ordered the octopus. Holly, the prosciutto and figs.

She glanced at his beer. "An interesting choice for someone who works at a vineyard."

"The loser worker bee likes his brew."

She could feel herself flush. "I'm sorry I called you that."

"Don't worry. They weren't your words originally. Drinking wine is my job," he said. "It's seldom my entertainment. Now a good beer? That's refreshment."

"The article said you were drunk."

She could see she'd surprised him. She'd surprised herself, something she'd been doing a lot lately.

She still wasn't used to the way he looked at her. Of course, it was because of Nina. There would be this shift in his head every time he saw her. *Not Nina.*

He took his time to answer. "We'd both been drinking, yes."

"I don't think you killed her. You're not the type." She was going for the gold medal in provocative statements. "But an accident. And the drinking. Well, it happens like that sometimes, doesn't it?"

He gave her a look. "You know me that well?"

"Maybe I like to see the best in people."

"No. You take it a lot farther. You want to see the best in complete strangers."

"And here I thought the way you were following me, that we were getting close."

It was a joke, but neither of them laughed.

"Look, I saw you with her parents," she said, finding evidence to support her argument. That's usually how it happened for her unfortunately. First the gut reaction, then reason bubbling to the surface to back it up. "They don't hold you responsible."

He never broke eye contact. "I was nineteen. Nina was a year younger. We were engaged to be married." He spoke the short terse facts as if he had them memorized. She wasn't the first to ask him about that night, not by a long shot.

"Our parents were old friends," he continued, marching out the story. "Gil and my father met in sixth grade and hadn't separated since. The Travers' sparkling wines were practically a staple at Cutty House. Gil and Samuel wanted to expand. They were opening a string of restaurants, a marriage of the two businesses. So why not arrange another kind of marriage? A real one. Like in the old days. Nina was beautiful, adventurous. At the time, I didn't think it was such a bad idea."

"What happened?"

"What always happens when you sell yourself on someone else's dream. I woke up. They'd planned out the next fifty years and it scared the life out of me. Before she died, I told her I wanted to break things off. I didn't want to take over Cutty House or the vineyard."

He took a moment before he delivered the last devastating piece. "And I told her I didn't love her. That maybe I never had."

"You said all those things after getting drunk?"

"A condition that wasn't exactly out of character for me in those days."

"I gather Nina didn't take it well."

He got back to the octopus. "She had a few choice words for me. We fought. She took off in that damn sports car of hers. I tried to stop her."

"It was an accident," she said, seeing the truth in his eyes, relieved.

He seemed to think about it. "If you give a kid matches and a bottle of gasoline, then leave him to his own devices? I wonder."

"You think you're responsible?"

"I knew she was drunk. I was too much of a coward to tell her sober. Nina was volatile. I should have guessed something would happen."

"The newspaper said you were accused of running her off the road. There was a witness."

He glanced down at the plate. She could almost hear him sorting through the information. What to tell, what to hold back.

"Someone left a message with the police but didn't identify themselves," he said. "They never came forward. And the evidence found during the investigation didn't support the story."

"But why would someone lie?"

"Ask Daniel," he said simply.

Daniel, the answer at every turn.

"You think Daniel left me that invitation."

"As a matter of fact, yes. My mother would have received one. Right now, he's her boy wonder. It wouldn't be difficult for him to get it from her."

She shook her head. "But why? I mean, why hurt Nina's parents like that?"

"Because they are important to me."

And when she shook her head, finding it hard to

believe, he added, "After Nina died, Gil had a stroke. Marta pretty much shut down the vineyard. They were going to lose everything. I felt I owed it to them to step in and take over. To turn things around. That's where I've been the last twelve years. With Marta and Gil. You want to hurt me? I can't think of a better target."

She imagined what it must have been like. If he'd wanted to slip into the sunset on his boat as Emma claimed, he'd sure taken a wrong turn. Nina's death had pinned him down to the very things he'd tried to escape.

Still, it made her wonder. Were these the actions of a hero or a guilty man?

She shook her head. "I can't believe Daniel would set me up, not for this. There has to be something else, someone else."

"If he thought I got away with murder? Maybe he wants to make sure I get what I deserve—or maybe he just wants to make sure I don't get anything at all."

"No. That doesn't sound like Daniel."

He grabbed her hand from across the table. "And what would? You know him about as well as you know me, which is not at all. Who gave you that dress, Holly?"

"If I believed—"

"Those clothes," he continued. "That's the way Nina dressed. He's trying to make you into Nina, sending you here like a little present. Surprise! You're right, it doesn't make sense. But then, Daniel doesn't always follow the rules. You have no idea who you're dealing with."

"Yes. Yes, of course." Because everything he said sounded perfectly logical.

"I'm tired of watching you play along," he said,

releasing her hand, a different man in his anger. "You want my advice? Pack up and race on home. He's not the man you think he is and neither, by the way, am I."

She nodded, as if listening to every word, but at the same time hating how starry-eyed and naive he'd made her sound. *If the shoe fits...*

"Well, that certainly clears things up. Thank you." She slipped out from the table, leaving the appetizer untouched. She picked up the silly purse she'd bought with Emma, realizing how much she'd enjoyed that shopping trip, how fun it had been to become someone else. *Another trap.*

"What are you going to do?" he asked, rising to his feet.

She smiled. "Everyone keeps asking me that."

She walked out, digging through her purse for the valet ticket. Ryan was right behind her.

"I can't believe you'd be this stupid," he said. "You're staying. You're building his damn house. Even after what happened today?"

She didn't answer him, just kept on going. Why try and defend her choice?

"You want people to use you?" he asked, not giving up. "You want more episodes like today?"

"I'll be more careful." Of course, he wouldn't believe her. Who would, under the circumstances? "I'm on guard now, you see." The argument sounded weak even to her ears, but it was the only one she had.

They were standing outside, the valet looking nervous with their raised voices.

Ryan pulled her aside. "Trust me on this, you're not ready for what's coming."

"And still, it will be a refreshing change from unemployment."

"I haven't told you everything."

"That much I figured out."

"There's no reason for you to stay and more than enough reasons for you to leave."

With a glance back at the valet, Ryan grabbed her hand and guided her down the street. When they turned the corner, it was like that night in the alley. Suddenly, there was no one around to help if it all went wrong, which it most certainly would. But not in the way she'd feared that first night. What was happening between them now was totally different—and even more dangerous.

Because she was starting to think all sorts of crazy thoughts. That sometimes things happen for a reason. That what she was feeling now, staring up at him— practically in his arms—might be as good as any reason she could come up with.

"It's not as easy as you think to walk away," she told him, not talking about Cutty House anymore.

"It should be."

They'd been having an argument. He needed to make her listen to reason. Logic, the male cornerstone.

But suddenly, the energy between them changed. Ryan kept staring at her mouth. Holly raised up on her tiptoes.

He kissed her, his mouth opening over hers. He held her by her shoulders, bringing her closer. It was unexpected and passionate and more devastating than she could have ever planned. What's more, she kissed him back.

"If you're trying to scare me away," she said, "this is a really bad tactic, because I've been thinking about this for a very long time."

He didn't answer, just pushed her up against the wall and leaned over her, his two hands on the brick on each side of her face. Deepening the kiss, he whispered urgent words she couldn't quite understand as his hands stroked and eased. She didn't know how long the kiss lasted, a few seconds or forever. She just knew she didn't want him to stop.

Only, Ryan did, stepping away from her as if it were the hardest thing he'd ever done. He caught his breath, his hard blue eyes asking the question: What next?

She'd never been one for silence, comfortable or otherwise. There'd just been too much of it in her life. Harris, working all those hours. Her father relegating himself to the role of failure, a mere observer as his children struggled to keep the boat afloat.

"This isn't who I am," she said, breaking that tense silence. "I don't do crazy."

"If you stay, it will only get crazier. You're living the life of another woman. You're stepping into her shoes. Trust me, it's not a place you want to be."

But that wasn't what worried Holly. Right then, she focused on something much more trivial.

"Just now. That kiss?" she asked. "How do I know you weren't kissing Nina?"

"My point exactly."

She hated that he'd said it. She hated even more that he could look her in the eye, making himself seem strong when she thought he was only being weak.

Or did she have it wrong? Was she the weak link here, wanting him to give in to the fantasy she'd been building for them?

How do I know you weren't kissing Nina?

"Well," she said, stepping away. "I guess this is good night, then."

Now it was Holly putting distance between them, horrified that she'd compared herself to Nina in the first place. She walked to the restaurant just down the block. She handed the valet her ticket, trying to settle her breathing. She told herself not to look back. *Keep your eyes forward.*

When her rental drove up, she stepped inside, tip in hand. She didn't turn to look around, didn't search the sidewalk to see if he'd be there waiting.

When she drove away, she told herself to be careful. *Don't get distracted.* It was a busy street, after all. She only glanced in her rearview mirror the one time.

She saw him then, standing at the corner where she'd left him, watching her drive away as the fog circled and teased.

Watching the lights of North Beach slip past, she focused on the road. At the next stop, she took a breath. She touched her lips.

His kiss. A very bad move on his part. Because despite everything he'd told her, Holly was learning that, these days, she didn't always do what was sensible.

19

Emma didn't believe in regrets. Twelve years ago, she'd learned how to take that kind of emotion and bury it so deep, most times it couldn't even hurt. Like making love to Harris. She couldn't say it was something to repent.

But here she was, first thing in the morning, full of regret. Drowning in it. Because right now, more than anything, she didn't want to be lying next to Daniel in his bed.

Last night had opened some peculiar door inside her, allowing regret inside as Daniel coaxed her to stay. Not for sex, he assured her. And they hadn't made love. They'd just lain in bed, their clothes still on, Daniel holding her.

The fight had been their excuse. He'd hurt her. He didn't deserve her forgiveness. Certainly not her love. Not yet. He'd work on it. He'd earn her back. He'd done it before. Many times.

But all night that regret bloomed inside her, opening the door to others.

Emma slipped out from under the covers, trying not to wake Daniel. She didn't succeed. He grabbed her hand, reeling her back into the bed, his arm anchoring her there.

"Don't go," he whispered. "Stay." He kissed her neck. "Just a little longer."

She settled back against him, giving in.

You always give in.

She'd never thought of it like that before. Giving in. Whatever Daniel wanted, it just seemed right, a part of her. She couldn't remember a time in her life that she hadn't loved Daniel.

She used to dream that he would marry her. She remembered the first time: *Please, God. Let me marry him.* Remembered how handsome he'd looked in his pristine white apron over black slacks, white shirt and tie. All the others waiters hovered around him, the center of the kitchen like the old-fashioned stove. She'd thought even then she'd be the luckiest girl in the world if he'd have her.

"I have to go," she told him, her memories choking her with regret.

This time, he didn't to stop her. It surprised her a little that Daniel was capable of guilt, at least where she was concerned. In Daniel's book, everything else—Cutty House, the family—was owed him.

She showered and dressed quickly. Before she left, she sat beside him on the bed. He'd expect that. No use causing a scene, leaving without saying goodbye.

He huddled closer, the smile on his face letting her know he expected forgiveness.

"I've been thinking," he said.

"Hmm."

She didn't want to hear his plans, and she thought she should leave before she told him so to his face.

"You were right." He stroked her arm, sitting up in bed beside her. "It's a fine idea. You getting to know Holly's brother. Harris is his name, right?"

"Yes. Harris." She wondered how she could feel so dead inside and still sound normal.

He gave her hand a squeeze. "I won't be jealous

anymore. I promise.'' And then, more tentatively still,
''You understand?''

''I understand.'' That he'd found another use for
her.

''I don't love her,'' he whispered.

For a minute, she wasn't sure who he was talking
about. Nina…Holly…or possibly herself.

''I don't know if I ever did,'' he said.

Nina, then. ''Sure.''

''Don't say it like that,'' he chastised. ''Like you
don't believe me.''

She sighed. ''Daniel, she was pregnant with your
child.''

''Shh. I don't want to talk about it. Come back to
bed.''

But she gave him a quick kiss and stood. He followed her out, letting her know he felt bad enough to
make the effort. She knew all his secrets, after all.

At the door, he kissed her again. ''I'll see you at
the house, okay?''

That's what they called Cutty House. They'd called
it that since they were kids, pretending they would live
there someday like royalty.

She'd been part of his plans even then, she thought,
taking the elevator down to the ground floor. She and
Daniel against the world.

Only, it was all changing now, coming apart. And
she kept thinking about what they'd done by bringing
Holly here. Giving the past new life. How it couldn't
end well for anyone—even Daniel.

But Daniel wouldn't see it that way. He'd just keep
at it. Like this morning—*I won't be jealous anymore*—pushing her. He didn't know any better. He
just wanted…needed. Later, when it all went to shit,
then he'd think, *What was I thinking?*

By then, of course, it would be too late.

*   *   *

Emma found Harris waiting for her at the gates to
Cutty House. He stepped out of the shadows, looking
as if he hadn't slept. She imagined him waiting there
all night, a romantic notion not rooted in any sense of
reality, but a nice antidote to her morning with Daniel.
As if she could ever be that important to anyone.

But he was there. And he was waiting for her, making Emma hate herself even more for wanting him
there.

"You need a shave," she said.

"I wanted to make sure you were okay."

His eyes. He had the most beautiful eyes. Brown,
very mellow, but at the same time watching you with
this intensity.

"I would have gone to his place," he said. "Done
the whole knock down the door, high drama." He
shrugged. "But I thought I would make everything
worse."

She nodded. "Incredibly worse."

And then he did the strangest thing. He held out his
hand to her, still watching her with his lovely brown
eyes. And she found herself stepping forward, slipping
her hand into his hand as if it belonged there, for the
first time in her life desiring someone other than Daniel.

"Do you have time for a walk?" he asked.

She nodded, taking her first steps into another kind
of deception.

Holly slept in fits and starts, falling in and out of
the strange dream. She and Daniel were dancing in the
ballroom at Cutty House. They both wore masks, the
kind that just covered the eyes. Dressed to the nines,

they were the only two people in the room. A string quartet played from the music shell, and when the music stopped, she felt a hand on her shoulder turn her around. Suddenly Ryan stood before her. He smiled, as if about to cut in, but instead reached over and ripped off her mask.

"You're not Nina!"

She sat up straight in bed. *I'm not Nina.*

"I'm not Nina," she said, repeating the words out loud in the dark bedroom.

In the dream, she'd been wearing Nina's black gown from the portrait. She remembered Ryan's warning, that she was stepping into another woman's life.

Which was probably what had brought on the dream. Her fear that he was right. She was playing a part. Enjoying the clothes she bought with Emma, the posh apartment given by Daniel—and kissing Ryan, that most of all. The practical, hardworking Holly Fairfield had vanished. In her place was a woman taking risks—and liking it so very much.

Living the life of another woman.

"Arghh!" She covered her face with the pillow.

The picture didn't get any clearer walking to work in the chill early morning. Almost within reach of Cutty House, she saw the mansion looming, and stopped. The street ahead fell away like a roller coaster, as if the house resided at the edge of some dark precipice, reminding her of the passage from Poe's, "The House of Usher." *During the whole of a dull, dark and soundless day…a sense of insufferable gloom pervaded my spirit.*

A businesswoman, a briefcase swinging in hand, stepped around Holly, reminding her to move on. She prompted herself to put one foot in front of the other, knowing that, at times like these, life had to be reduced to its simplest components.

A few minutes later, she arrived on the second floor of Cutty House with her coffee in hand. As she backed into her office, she was giving herself The Talk: One day at a time, girl! She even felt a little better for those last few minutes of concentrated optimism. As she'd told Ryan, she was on guard now. Once everyone figured out who she was—*that's right. Not Nina. That architect woman. What did you say her name was?*—then everything would fall into place.

"I hope it's all right that I showed myself in."

The voice caught her off guard. If Holly had been a little less tired, she might have overreacted. Might have jumped right out of her practical walking shoes, instead of managing a fairly decent about-face to find Vanessa Cutty leafing through her design sketches.

"Please." Vanessa gestured toward Holly's desk. "Sit down." Like she owned the place. But then, of course, she did.

Holly slipped behind her desk and dropped the briefcase at her feet. She kept her coffee in hand, praying for the magic of caffeine to kick in. She had the idea that she was looking at her opposite number. Nine in the morning and Vanessa already looked as if she'd spent a productive day at the salon. She wore her shoulder-length hair perfectly coifed, a very chic take on the old-fashioned flip. The clothes were equally stylish, a python print pantsuit in a subtle tan-and-white. For the life of her, Holly couldn't remember what she was wearing under her trench coat—not a good sign.

Vanessa glanced at the drawings spread out on the drafting table. "These are lovely."

She could just as easily have used words like *cute,*

fun…interesting. Vanessa Cutty wasn't here about Holly's work.

Watching her cross the room, Holly wondered if she could ever achieve that kind of sophistication. At the same time, she remembered Marta Travers, how she gathered people around her by the warmth of her smile.

"There's a few things I think Daniel has, regrettably, kept from you, Holly," Vanessa said, taking off at a full gallop. "Let's start with his name, Daniel East. That's incorrect."

"I don't understand."

"Estes. His name—his father's name. Panamanian, I believe. Daniel excels at creating a fantasy, then making it come true."

Vanessa relayed the information with a complete lack of expression on her face. *Don't crack a smile, you'll get a wrinkle.* As if someone had overdone the Botox.

But then, Holly thought there might be more to it. *She doesn't like me—I'm part of that fantasy Daniel's creating.*

"His mother, my husband's older sister, ran off with the hired help," she said, confirming Emma's story. "Of course, my father-in-law and his wife never approved. As a result, they disowned her. She had Daniel less than a year later. Daniella. That was her name."

She made a face. Daniel's mother had named her son after herself—Vanessa didn't approve. As if she couldn't stretch her imagination beyond the obvious.

"I'm sure it was difficult for my sister-in-law. Especially since that fool man left them both. By the time Daniel was eight, Samuel, on my insistence, brought him to live with us. I tried to make him feel welcomed, part of the family, but you can imagine."

This time, her expression was as good as a prompt card. "Of course," Holly said, not really sure she *could* imagine. According to Emma, Daniel had been treated more or less like the hired help.

"I think you may have guessed that Daniel and Emma are an item," she said, almost reading Holly's mind that Emma might not be the most objective source. "Though they try to hide it. Emma's father was our chef for years. A fantastic cook when he wasn't falling-down drunk. Emma and Daniel have a lot in common. Only children of single parents. The struggle that binds. Daniel started working in the kitchen when he was ten. Emma spent a lot of time there because of her father."

Vanessa looked like she was just warming up. And boy, did she know how to keep an audience. *Give her a minute, enjoy the show.*

"If Nina hadn't died… It's impossible to know how much that horrible day changed our lives. But after her death, Ryan felt certain obligations to Nina's parents. Admirable, yes, but devastating for Cutty House."

Holly noted the careful wording. Devastating for Cutty House, but no mention of her own feelings. A mother's rejection. *Strictly business.*

"As you can see, Daniel has stepped in, something I appreciate more than I can say. He runs Cutty House." A delicate pause—a simple glance. "And now, it seems, he's hired you."

Holly could feel the caffeine kicking in. "Now he has both Cutty House and Nina. You think he's trying to take Ryan's place?"

Vanessa sighed. She liked the subtle approach. And here was Holly forcing her to be all crass and direct.

"He's certainly done his best to convince both my

husband and myself that you're here on merit and not on looks.'' She glanced back at the drawings, her expression not quite insulting. "But I do worry," she said. "Daniel...he's still working through his past. Cutty House means everything to him.'' She smiled. "Yes, you're right. I am afraid that on some level he's still competing with his cousin.''

"I've met Ryan. We've talked about Nina,'' she said, needing some defense in the face of Vanessa's assault.

"Of course you have. He saw you at the party. I assume he couldn't let it pass. But I think you should be careful just the same.''

She spoke the last words so softly, Holly wasn't sure she heard correctly the warning there at the end.

"Of Ryan?'' she asked.

The door opened. Daniel stepped inside. The look on his face when he glanced from Holly to Vanessa said he wasn't happy to see them.

"Auntie. What a surprise. Not warning off my best worker, I hope?''

Having done just that, Vanessa came around to give her nephew a peck on the cheek. "Don't be foolish, Daniel.''

After the door closed, Daniel shook his head, as if he didn't know what to make of his aunt.

"What is it, love?'' he asked. "What did Auntie say to upset you?''

"No,'' she said. "Not your aunt.''

"Who then?'' he asked, ready to put her mind at ease.

When Holly had thought of coming here, she hadn't intended to confront Daniel. She didn't trust him to tell her the truth, so why bother? But now she couldn't seem to hold back. At the same time, she hesitated, feeling push-me/pull-you forces at work.

Giving in, she said, "I went to Viña Dorada."

Daniel watched her as if looking for clues. She was careful not to give him any.

"How...unfortunate," he said.

"To say the least."

"Marta and Gil—"

"Of course, they saw me. I received an invitation to a party there. Presumably sent by Ryan...who now claims to know nothing about it."

"Of course." There was anger in his voice. "I'm surprised he didn't blame me."

He read the truth on her face.

"Ah," he said with a smile.

Daniel walked around the room. Even though she had a million questions, she waited. He ended up stopping where she was seated at her desk. He dropped to one knee, a gentleman asking for her hand, taking it when it wasn't offered.

"I didn't send that invitation, Holly." His expression was so earnest. "You know I didn't."

"Daniel. The clothes."

"Yes, I know how it looks."

"I came here on your request, not his. I buy a bunch of clothes that apparently make me look like Nina, then I receive an invitation to her parents' vineyard? You're telling me Ryan is the one pulling the strings?"

He stood. "I'm not saying anything of the sort. Look, I'll find out about the invitation, I swear. But you have to believe me, I wouldn't do anything to hurt Marta and Gil. They are good people."

"Who seem to believe in Ryan."

"A fatal flaw, I assure you, but don't we all have

one?'' He pulled her to her feet. ''All right. Maybe I have a blind spot when it comes to my cousin, but Holly—''

He cupped her face in his hands. Whatever his intentions, right now he wasn't making her feel warm and fuzzy. Rather the opposite.

''You know how much I need you. Can Ryan say the same? Don't you think it would be a tad convenient for him if you left me now? So that everything could come crashing down around my ears?''

He was talking about sabotage. That Ryan would want to scare her away and make sure there was no Cutty House revival with Daniel at the helm.

After a while, she nodded.

''That's my girl.'' He smiled. Only, he didn't let go. Instead, he stepped closer as if to tell her a secret, whispering in her ear, ''Now, don't freak.''

He kissed her.

And he didn't stop. He kept at it, as if he might somehow convince her, trying to deepen the kiss even as she struggled to push him away.

When he finally released her, he took a couple of steps back and dropped his arms. They both stared at each other. Holly could imagine the look on her face. Beyond shock.

''Clearly,'' he said, ''I should not have done that. But, Holly, I can't say I'm sorry—''

''If you finish that sentence,'' she said, ''I'll have to walk out on this project. Right now.''

He held his hands up in surrender. ''I said we'd do it your way.''

She turned for the door, shaken, realizing she had never even taken off her coat. She felt as if the world had turned upside down. *Living another woman's life.*

When she reached the door, she heard Daniel say,

"I know you believe him, whatever he's told you. Don't I know he can be so sincere. You go to his vineyard, you see him in his element, taking care of those poor people, Gil and Marta. So self-sacrificing in appearance."

She turned around. Daniel was standing with his arms crossed, looking very enigmatic.

"Remember this," he told her. "No matter what you think you know, the fact remains, he's already killed one woman he loved."

He said it with a smile, an expression that stayed with her as she made her way down the stairs. As if he'd just delivered the punch line at the end of a very bad joke.

This is what becomes of arrogance, Vanessa told herself. She stepped into her car, then turned on the engine as she slipped the seat belt across her lap. Arrogance had always been her weak point. Her father had blamed himself, claiming he'd bred that pride into her. *Because I could never say no to you, darling,* he'd told her. *And now you think no one ever will.*

Coming to see Holly had been the height of arrogance. What had she truly thought to accomplish, convincing herself that a little information could go a long way, hoping Miss Fairfield was shaken enough to listen.

Only, it was Vanessa who was shaken. *She looks so much like Nina.*

On the seat beside her, the cell phone in her bag began to ring. Jeffrey, no doubt. She was late for their meeting. Another strategy session for the AIDS benefit she was chairing with him. Vanessa ignored the sound, staring at the road ahead. Every week it was something—a dinner or some charity function. She was on everyone's list.

There used to be more. Lavish parties, smaller, more intimate gatherings at her home. She used to compare herself to those ladies in France during the age of Voltaire, having her own little salon where the city's intellectuals and artists could gather. The last few years, she'd cut back severely.

She slammed on her brakes, just missing the car in front of her, a blast of a horn her thanks. She hated driving in the city and avoided it like the plague. But she had a tight schedule today.

She closed her eyes, suddenly exhausted. The girl's resemblance to Nina drained her. And the resemblance didn't end with the mere physical. Holly Fairfield had ignored Vanessa's every word, just like Nina.

You really are some weird society freak.

Vanessa blinked, trying to bring the street back into focus, concentrating on the traffic ahead. The last thing she needed was a car accident. But that voice... The past sounding so clearly in her head.

Of course, Holly had brought it all back. Nina's vicious attack.

The phone again. Vanessa knew enough to pull over. Jeffrey wouldn't give up, and she found the sound incredibly distracting. She glanced at the number before she answered.

"So insistent, Jeffrey? I'm on my way, dear. Just start the meeting without me."

Ending the call, she sat double-parked. The phone call somehow seemed the height of irony.

"Still the society freak," she said out loud.

She remembered the day she'd first heard those words. She'd asked Nina to tea at the Ritz-Carlton, a fine establishment Vanessa thought worthy of their first outing together since Ryan and Nina had announced their engagement. Nina had sat through the meeting like a perfect lady. She'd had impeccable manners, seeming to hang on Vanessa's every word. *Someday, he might even go into politics, Nina. You'll have to be ready for that.*

She remembered how Nina had folded her napkin, as if getting ready to excuse herself politely from the table. Instead, she'd leaned over to tell Vanessa, "You really are some weird society freak," all the while keeping her lovely smile.

Vanessa had thought at first she'd misunderstood. Nina was only eighteen. To speak to her—to anyone—in such a crass manner. But the girl had only been warming up. "My dad told me about you and him. How he asked you to marry him. But he wasn't anybody then, so you got all hung up on Samuel. Dad said it was their only real fight, because he asked Samuel to back off and he wouldn't."

It was a startling transformation to watch. To hear that venom coming from the mouth of almost a child, realizing for the first time who she was dealing with.

"Daddy doesn't understand about women like you," she'd told Vanessa. "He thinks people are honest and good and follow their heart. But you follow a plan, don't you, Van? And now you want to make sure I'm on board."

"Don't hurt Ryan." A mother's reflex. "Not to get to me."

Nina had clucked her tongue, disapproving. "It's always about you, isn't it, Van? You know, I watch you sometimes. How you stare at my dad. You have this weird hungry look in your eyes. And you make up these lame excuses to touch him. Can I get you something to drink, Gil?" It was a fair imitation of

Vanessa. "You don't even realize how invisible you make my mom feel. I wonder if anyone ever made you feel invisible?" Again, the smile. "Coming on to a man in front of his family? That's so tacky."

Vanessa would always remember that tight feeling in her chest growing as she listened to Nina, as if a vise were closing around her heart. She hadn't even defended herself. She wondered what might have happened if she had? Would Nina have left them alone? Had it already been too late?

Up until that day, she'd thought the girl only a nuisance. Not quite good enough for Ryan, but they'd make do.

Vanessa took a deep breath, wondering if now— after everything they'd gone through—life wasn't coming full circle. Her little speech to Holly this morning had left out a few details. How after Nina's death and Gil's collapse, Samuel had taken on the restaurant's expansion alone, stopping only when Vanessa sought legal representation to cut off access to her trust fund after she realized what he was doing. *Throwing it all away.*

She reached to start the car, taking more deep breaths. She needed to push away the past. Needed to focus on the future. Or maybe just the traffic ahead. *Concentrate on getting into the next lane, making the turn.*

She had always thought she was like her father. Strong. Her mother had told her so many times how strong she was.

But her mother had raised just another woman like herself, so that, in the end, she'd been too late to save her husband.

And now she wondered if she was already too late to save her son.

20

Harris hadn't slept last night. He'd been too keyed up, worrying about Emma.

Lying in bed, he kept seeing Daniel at the entrance to the restaurant, kept thinking about Emma's retreat to the man's side, like some trained puppy fearing a scolding. Or worse.

Had the bastard hurt her? Would Harris read about Emma in the papers the next morning? Grisly details painted in Technicolor words on the front page of the local?

Two minutes into his spiral, he'd done a one-eighty. Emma was in on it. She had to be. And here he was, falling for her act, hook, line and sinker.

He was losing it, imagining conspiracies everywhere. Holly was probably right. There was nothing going on other than the usual family soap opera.

After work, he'd gone to Daniel's apartment. He'd stood outside the building, cigarette in hand, sucking in nicotine like an old friend until his hands shook with the drug. *Better than caffeine.* He'd had his mobile, kept playing with the idea of dialing in some complaint about a domestic disturbance to make the cops check things out.

Instead, he'd waited, finally heading home to knock back a couple of drinks, seesawing back and forth between worries for Emma and fears for his sister. Some-

time around five in the morning, he'd switched to coffee. An hour after that, he'd been standing outside
Cutty House, waiting for Emma to show.

When he'd finally seen her coming, he'd dropped
the cigarette and crushed it under the Nikes, waiting
for her to come to him. He'd already figured out where
he'd gone wrong. Going to Daniel's steaming mad, he
hadn't realized what he was getting them into, hadn't
prepared for that instant when he'd seen Emma and
wanted her so badly he couldn't worry about the cost.

And now, the damage was done because, walking
beside her holding hands, he didn't want to let go.

They'd been walking in this comfortable silence for
at least ten minutes. Every once in a while, Emma
would glance down at their hands locked together, as
if checking to make sure he was real.

She had these tiny hands, the fingers thin and flex-
ible. An artist's hands. He could imagine her making
some amazing things with those hands.

"I didn't know you smoked," she said, breaking
the silence.

"That makes two of us."

"This is going to end badly. You know it will."

She had such spunk in her voice. A woman who
liked getting to the point.

He gave her hand a squeeze. "I'm just glad to hear
it's started."

He'd been thinking that he was so used to a life of
intrigue, he didn't know how to stop lifting up rocks
and searching the dirt underneath. Even now, this
thing with Emma could be some weird form of sabotage. If Holly wouldn't leave the job, why not blow
it up in her face by sleeping with the boss's girl?
Emma was just another person he could use.

"I should get back," she said, stopping.

But he tugged her hand, bringing her along, not ready to let go. He wasn't sure what he could say to her, how to get her to trust him. *I know all about being on the wrong side, kid. You can tell me what you fear most.*

Because that's what he saw in her. Someone scared—someone trapped.

"Don't be in such a hurry," he said. He looked around. The air here was moist. *Like walking inside a cloud.* "At a guess, I'd say Danny boy sleeps in."

She stopped, this time yanking her hand free. "Look, I think you should know—"

But she didn't finish, didn't want to ruin the fragile camaraderie between them after all, which only made him smile.

"You don't have to say it," he told her.

"I think you should know," she said, struggling along just the same. "I did stay with Dan last night. I didn't say anything about what happened between us. I just said you were Holly's brother and I was making friends." She made this half gesture with her hand. "I can't do this. I can't…just leave him."

"Why not?" he surprised himself by asking. Talk about life's complications. *Bring it on.…*

She looked absolutely miserable, staring up at him. "We had sex, Harris. What could that possibly mean to you?"

"Actually, it meant a hell of a lot. But maybe I'm just nutty like that. Weird, huh? Sex means something."

She shook her head. "We had a fight, Harris. You weren't in love, you were mad."

"Does it really matter how something starts? It's how it ends that counts."

"This is so crazy." She pushed her fingers through

her hair and laughed. She wore it down this morning so that it just brushed her shoulders. "You don't think…you're not asking me to—"

"I'm not asking a damn thing," he said quietly. "I just want you to know that I want to pursue this. You and me."

"Just like that?" Now he could see she was angry. "One minute, you're accusing me of sabotaging your sister, now you want me to turn my back on the only family I've ever had?"

"Is that what he is? Family?"

"You can't understand. You don't know."

"I know that you smell like lavender. I know you cry when you make love. I know that you're in some kind of trouble, that you might be dragging my sister right in. And, surprisingly, I'm still here wondering if I can have another chance to hold you and kiss you. I think I know more than enough."

She stood there staring at him. Maybe no one had ever said those things to her, had never taken on that lock, stock and barrel relationship of hers with Daniel. Like she'd said at the bar, she'd never slept with any other man.

And there it was on her face, the potential.

She could leave Daniel. She could be with someone else. As if she'd never seen that desire inside herself. Tempted.

And scared, that most of all.

She backed away. "Leave me alone, Harris. Leave me the hell alone."

But before she could disappear into the fog, he called out, "In your pocket."

She stopped, not turning around. As he watched, she slipped her hand into the pocket of her jacket, finding the piece of paper he'd put there.

"My cell phone number," he said. "If you ever find yourself in trouble."

She started to walk faster, then run. But he was glad he'd given her the phone number. In his experience, people like Emma eventually needed an escape hatch.

Ryan watched his cousin step out of his Bentley, double-parked outside his building. Nice car. Just like the one J.Lo gave Ben. Even nicer digs. The old Victorians of Eastern Pacific Heights had long since given way to swank apartment buildings like Daniel's. His cousin owned the tenth floor, what he called "the cloud club." He'd told Ryan he found the reference in a book about San Francisco homes.

That was Daniel. Looking up his address, checking to see if it was good enough to make the book. It was probably why he'd moved out of the place on Nob Hill. Now that he was running the show, he needed something bigger, grander.

Daniel always did like the finer things. In that way, he reminded Ryan of his father. It was interesting, actually, how alike uncle and nephew were. When Daniel took over running Cutty House, everyone suddenly woke up to realize how much better the fit was, as if Dan were more Samuel's son than Ryan could ever be.

Catching sight of Ryan now, Daniel stopped in his tracks, frozen like some prey animal. Ryan could see that his cousin was doing some fast thinking. He figured he could help him out.

"Daniel," he said, walking over.

"I can't say it's a surprise, Ryan," he said. "I talked to Holly. She told me about the invitation to the vineyard—"

Ryan grabbed him by that fine linen shirt. "I know

what you're up to, Dan, though I can't say I understand why.''

Because it didn't make sense. Why risk everything just to mess with Ryan's head? Why put all those fine things Dan loved at risk?

Or maybe it made perfect sense. All those years Daniel had taken a back seat to Ryan, the golden boy, because, no matter what Daniel did, he'd always be the busboy's son. Ryan even heard his mother say it once: Blood tells. Or some bullshit like that.

But unlike his parents, Ryan didn't sell Daniel short. He figured once he pointed out a couple of mistakes, Daniel would see the light. Hence, his trip here. A planned moment of enlightenment.

He leaned in close, whispering to his cousin, ''It's all yours, Danny. Everything you ever wanted. Are you telling me you're willing to risk it? Your dreams for Cutty House? Just to take care of my miserable hide?''

''Is that what you think?'' Daniel, smiled from ear to ear. He pocketed his car keys as he stepped back, freeing up his hands. He was loving this, the confrontation. ''Ever heard the saying, kill two birds with one stone?''

''Now isn't that clever? Only, here's a thought. Holly gets fed up, doesn't stick around for the big show. You lose the girl and the house.''

''She'll stay. She doesn't have a choice.''

Which gave Ryan pause. *What does he know?* ''Everyone has a choice, Daniel. I think you're making some rather poor ones.''

Something on Daniel's face changed—his eyes narrowed, his nostrils flared. Just like that, the prey turned into the hunter. Ryan braced himself, knowing that whatever was coming, at least he'd be closer to the truth.

"Does her face haunt you?" Daniel asked, his voice barely above a whisper. "Does she visit you in your dreams still? Do you even remember her? I can just imagine what it feels like, to see her so close. Alive again."

Ryan felt each word drive into him like a bullet. *Does her face haunt you?* Dan was talking about Nina. The way he looked at Ryan—the venom in his voice.

A moment of enlightenment. Isn't that why he'd come? Only, here was Ryan making all the connections. *All the trouble Dan went to finding Holly, bringing her here...* This wasn't the simple reprisal Ryan had always assumed.

Nina and Dan?

He told himself maybe he'd known all along. The knowledge was just waiting for a moment like this, a trigger. Like those suppressed memories. He hadn't been ready to face the truth until now.

He's just like my father....

Ryan whispered, "Did you really love Nina that much?"

Daniel stepped back, giving himself room. At the same time, his fist swung around, aiming for Ryan's face. Ryan ducked. He punched Daniel in the gut. Again. Bringing him down.

Of course, Ryan thought, catching his breath. Everything always came back to Nina.

He thought he'd known the truth. All of it.

Jesus.

Daniel lay on the ground. He wiped the blood from the corner of his mouth where he'd bit his lip. They were gathering a crowd—the day's entertainment.

There weren't too many street brawls going down in
Pacific Heights that afternoon.

"It just might be worth it, Ryan," Daniel said, sitting up. "Damn if it just might."

Ryan knelt down, keeping a tight hold on his temper. He'd miscalculated, and there was no more room
for error.

"You never were very farsighted, Dan, but this is
just plain dumb," he said, still hoping for that enlightenment. "You think about what you have right now.
Cutty House. Samuel and Vanessa in the palm of your
hand. Everything you wanted ripe for the taking."

He stood, looking down at his cousin. "My advice?
Don't fuck it up."

But as he walked away, he heard his cousin yelling.

"You killed her, Ryan. You know you did."

21

Vanessa found her husband seated on Ryan's old bed, almost comatose with drink. With his shoulder slumped against the headboard, she thought he looked like a piece of baggage. A lump. He was so far gone, he didn't even see her standing in the doorway watching him.

Samuel called this room The Shrine: *Here once lived my son.* It was almost fifteen years since Ryan had lived there and Vanessa still hadn't moved or changed one item of furniture. The walnut headboard and plaid comforter, the shelves with sailing trophies and books. Everything was just as Ryan had left it before going to college.

Except Nina's photograph, the one in the Tiffany frame. Vanessa distinctly remembered putting it away in the bottom-most drawer of the bureau.

Now the photograph was back on the bedside table. Her husband was staring right at it.

She felt the blood rush to her face. Don't they make a fine couple, the drunk and his make-believe bride.

She felt herself collapse a little inside with the horrible thought. The last years had been wearing, making her wonder how long she could keep at it, playing "the good wife," the one left behind and taken advantage of. The good soldier, Samuel Cutty's wife. Another useless title like all the others she'd cultivated over the years: guest editor for the *Orchid Gazette,* president of the horticulture club, chairman of the local Cancer Society. The list went endlessly on.

You really are some weird society freak. Well, perhaps Nina had been right all along. It's all she had left. Her dignity, her courage—those had long since drained away.

Almost in slow motion, Samuel raised his hand in a half gesture, as if reaching to touch Nina's face. Watching, Vanessa felt a familiar rush of heat. *Wake up, Samuel!* She wanted to shake him, wanted to hit him with her fists to wake him up. *Look at me! Not her!*

Instead, she forced herself to see Samuel through something other than her disappointment. *Visualize. See if you can change your reality.* Isn't that what her husband did each day with his drink?

She closed her eyes. Opening night, the Opera House brilliantly lit. Samuel had worn a top hat and she a mink stole he'd bought her, their first appearance together as man and wife. That night, she'd felt an almost maddening exhilaration looking up at Samuel, so tall and handsome it made her heart ache. They'd attracted a crowd, the new crown prince and his bride. She'd looked over at her father, saw him give a wink of approval. *You see, Daddy? You see!*

She held tight to the memory and opened her eyes. Looking back into the room, she tried to fit the image like a overlay on the man sitting on the bed. Puffy eyes, red nose, yes, but he was still handsome. His hair, now completely silver, abundant and well-kept...the cleft in his chin and piercing blue eyes. A woman might still find him attractive.

A few years back, she'd read about alcoholism. *With support and treatment, many alcoholics can re-*

build their lives.... She had thought she could help him. She'd gone to meetings and sought counseling. But in the end, it was just another project. Like her orchids and charities. Something else to pour her soul into, to make her feel less empty.

That book about marriage? Was it possible for a person to pick the wrong fork in the road and run straight into ruin? One bad decision leading to forever?

What about doubling back to find a new path? Was she just being lazy, letting it all slip away? What if she worked harder, pushed harder?

Even now, she could feel that desire to change rise within her. The emotion warmed, rejuvenating her, so that she felt herself able to move inside the room toward her husband. The day she'd asked Daniel to take over Cutty House had been much the same. Something in her had screamed for a chance.

But there was fear, as well. Her meeting with Holly hadn't gone well. Daniel no longer seemed such an asset. And Nina. Watching her husband mooning over the girl's photograph, Vanessa now found that Nina seemed more terrifying and alive than ever.

In the end, she wasn't sure what forces urged her to sit next to Samuel, hesitating just an instant before she put her arms around him. She leaned her head against his shoulder, stroking his back as she sat beside him on the bed.

She knew Samuel was lost somewhere in his head. *Welcome to the world of drink.* But perhaps she could use this moment in her favor and reach out to a place where things could still be fluid instead of fixed.

"I want you to come back to me, Samuel."

Her duty as his wife. *The choices we make...*

"I can help you get through this," she coaxed. "Together, we can start over."

Did it really matter that he'd lost their money? They still had Cutty House—barely, but it was still viable. If she could get him back, make him even half the man he used to be. Together...

But Samuel didn't so much as break his gaze from the photograph. Slowly her memory of him, those days when she thought it might be her husband's political career she'd be planning, vanished back into the ether of the past. *How little you left me, Nina.*

All that potential lost, while she tried desperately not to see Nina smiling at them both—laughing at her.

Imagine, Daniel bringing Nina back to haunt them.

Vanessa didn't know how long she sat there. Minutes? An hour? She just knew her arms ached, and she was tired of being the only one carrying the burden. She dropped her hands, giving up.

"I'm having a party. At the house," she told Samuel, her voice sounding cold and full of instruction. "I need you to do something for me."

For the first time, he turned to look at her, her command bringing him back in a way that her warmth and forgiveness never could.

She told him what she needed.

"It's the least you can do," she said.

Her rage bubbled inside her almost as if part and parcel of the motion of rising to her feet. Like a child, she reached across Samuel for the photograph. She slammed it down on the nightstand. Heard the glass shattering beneath.

She didn't bother to wait for Samuel's reaction. Walking down the hall, she brushed away her tears, focusing on the day ahead. She had a benefit for the church to organize. Easter dinner for the homeless. A lot of calls to make.

She kept going over her schedule for the day, trying not to see Nina's face. Trying not to compare the memory of it with the image of the architect, Holly Fairfield. But she knew.

Just like Nina, Holly wasn't going away.

Work. It was as good an antidote as any for what ails a body.

That was Holly's thinking as she pored over design books, at one point even digging up old notes from a class she'd taken on the modern movement, trying to concentrate on the fundamentals of lines and symmetry.

The last few days she'd worked late into the night, fighting sleep, almost fearing the moment she might doze off over her drawings, stopping only after Harris would come home and shoo her off to bed.

The problem: She couldn't control her dreams. They were filled with images of Ryan. The strange sense that he needed her to stay, at the same time, pushing her away. Their kiss.

Come morning, she'd wake up and work even harder.

Eventually, the day came when she thought she was ready. Time to unveil her work. She'd dressed in her power suit and taken the designs into Daniel's office down the hall from hers at Cutty House. She'd held her breath as he flipped through the drawings.

As cheerleaders went, he wasn't bad.

He could go on a bit, sure, and at some point, Holly had to question his sincerity. But she chose instead to bask in the glory of words like, *genius* and *revolutionary*.

Daniel might not know it, but she was dead-on with her designs. She just might cause that "scandal" he coveted.

She was on her way back to her office after their little pep rally—*Go, Holly!*—ready to check over the as-built measurements. She'd been thinking about crawling up into the space created for the heating ducts, trying to see what treasure might reside with the original ceilings. She'd need a hard hat with a light.

Only, the minute she stepped into her office, she knew something was wrong. Out of place. She'd been working long hours here and at home over the last days. She thought she'd gained a certain hypersensitivity. Or maybe it was just healthy paranoia.

It took a moment for her to spot the problem. A nondescript file, thick with papers, sat in the middle of her desk where she couldn't miss it. She opened the folder, seeing that each packet of papers had been stapled at the corner. Someone had stuck a Post-it at the top like a label.

Interview of Ryan Foster Cutty...

The words blurred a little. She had to focus as she set aside the design drawings and picked up the package. She removed the Post-it, leafing through what looked like a transcript, the kind used in criminal investigations.

"Did you kill her?"

"No, of course not. Jesus. I can't believe this is happening. I can't believe she's gone."

"But it's your fault, right? That she's dead?"

"Yeah...maybe."

Ryan's words the night of the accident. His taped statement to the police. Someone had left it all here, conveniently on her desk.

She wasn't sure how long she sat reading through

the papers. There were several police reports. Even a copy of the autopsy. When someone stepped into her office after a cursory knock, the fear must have shown on her face. *Caught red-handed.*

"Holly, it's just me," Emma said, leaning against the office door.

Holly gathered up the papers strewn across the desk and stuffed them back into their folder. She placed the lot upside down at the corner of her desk. "Emma, you scared ten years off my life."

"Your door was open. I could see you sitting there." Emma shrugged, tentative in her welcome. "I thought I should come by and talk about what happened. You're probably still pretty mad. About the clothes, I mean."

The clothes? Holly had to make a mental shift, had to drag herself away from a dark and stormy night of twelve years ago.

The shopping trip—the clothes. Almost a week had passed, but Emma had finally found the courage to confess.

"Come in," she told Emma. "I won't bite. Not yet, anyway."

Emma looked a little relieved, seeing that Holly hadn't lost her sense of humor. "I feel like I've let you down," she said, "and I wanted to explain."

Emma, Daniel's cohort in Holly's transformation into Nina, had come for absolution.

"Is this when I wave my magic wand of forgiveness?" Holly asked.

"Only if you want to. Look, I know it was weird and so dumb. Honestly, you shouldn't even talk to me." Here, she smiled. "But the clothes were pretty cool. She wasn't like us, you know. She'd never just throw on some jeans and a T-shirt."

"Apparently." Not giving an inch.

"I just wanted to tell you not to worry. It won't happen again."

"Approaching an apology, but not quite there. Come on, now. You can do this."

"I am sorry." Emma shrugged. "That just sounds so lame, given the circumstances."

"Maybe that's what I don't understand," Holly said, thinking about what she'd read in the report. "The circumstances."

"Yeah, well." Emma looked up at the ceiling. Frowned. Finally, she looked back at Holly. "Listen. I thought Daniel was okay with this. That he wanted you here, looking like Nina, because you were some kind of lucky charm." She glanced over her shoulder, checking the door. It was closed.

She stepped over to the desk and sat down in the chair in front of Holly. "And I knew how much he wanted to mess with Ryan. I mean, that party was set up just so that Ryan would get this big creepy feeling when he met you. Because Daniel blames him for Nina's death."

Holly felt an enormous weight press down on her chest. Her eyes flicked over the folder stuffed with police reports and transcripts.

Daniel blamed Ryan for Nina's death? *Well, he's not alone.*

But Emma wasn't finished. "Daniel was pretty upset when he thought you might leave." She seemed to think about what she was going to say. "I told him you would stay, that you weren't like that. I told him you wouldn't just quit."

Again, Holly glanced at the folder on her desk. Those papers were a warning, a folder stuffed with innuendo and finger pointing as the investigation focused on Ryan as a killer. A gift from someone who wanted her long gone, probably the same person who had sent the invitation to the vineyard, whispering Nina's name in the hallways. *Go home!*

"But I think you should," Emma blurted out. "I think you should leave. Go home."

Go home! Just like the words on the window.

"I'm not leaving," Holly said.

She couldn't read Emma's reaction, but she imagined it had to be one of relief. She'd warned Holly well and good. Go home; keep safe. And if Holly was just too stubborn to listen, well, that wasn't Emma's problem, now, was it?

No, Holly wasn't leaving, wasn't allowing "unknown sources" to run her out of town. But she was asking questions. Like why Ryan had lied to her, telling her the evidence twelve years ago didn't support the theory that he'd run Nina off the road.

She sighed, picking up the folder and setting it carefully inside her desk drawer. Once she had her hands folded neatly back on her desk, she asked Emma, "Do you have a minute?"

Emma nodded, suddenly only too eager to please. Holly picked up her pen. "Why don't we talk about your ideas for the kitchen, then?"

22

Ryan stood outside, enjoying the breeze, waiting for his father to show. Out on the deck, he could feel the motion of the water beneath his feet. The tide here ranged from five to seven feet, the houseboats resting on a tidal flat so that sometimes he'd look down and see only mud. When the tide came in, the house would pull away from the bottom, rising gently. Smaller homes rocked noticeably during storms.

I can just imagine what it feels like, to see her so close. Alive again.

Good old Daniel. His cousin had always wanted to step into Ryan's shoes. Now it seemed he was content to live his nightmare.

You killed her, Ryan. You know you did.

And now Daniel had some big idea to punish him. Make Ryan pay for his high crimes. Because God knows a fucking lifetime of regrets wouldn't be enough.

Ryan stared up at the bruised night sky. Wispy clouds scudded across, but otherwise everything stood out brilliantly clear. Sausalito rested below the fog line. Tonight, a big dish of a moon waited above as city lights reflected off black water, shimmering with the wind.

One of Gil's many lessons came to mind. A little stress to the vines from drought wasn't so bad. Hardship could give a wine character later. But what if the drought became so severe that it killed? At the vineyard, they used drip irrigation. Ryan couldn't think of a similar fix for himself.

You killed her, Ryan. You know you did.

Well, maybe not in the way Daniel thought. But yes, he'd always accepted responsibility.

The day he'd told Gil that Nina was dead, that the accident was his fault, Gil had already had the stroke. He'd been unable to respond as Ryan had poured out the whole sorry story, too young and distraught to hold back.

I killed her, Gil. I swear I did. I told her she got pregnant on purpose, because she knew we were drifting apart. I said I didn't love her, that maybe I never had. We couldn't get married, even for the sake of a child. I was so stupid. I was stupid and mad and drunk.

Gil had reached out with his good hand and placed it on Ryan's, trying to comfort him. Even as he lay there, barely able to move, he'd done his best to tell Ryan he forgave him.

"Ryan."

He turned, crash-landing back into the present. His father had let himself in. Even now, he wandered across the deck.

Of course, he was drunk.

Samuel stumbled into a chair, stared at it as if the furniture somehow offended. *How did you get there?* He made his way to the rail, catching his breath, those last steps a hard journey. He'd called almost an hour ago, letting Ryan know he wanted to meet. Now, Samuel looked out over the water, biding his time.

"I could slip right in and disappear." He playacted the whole thing, even putting a leg over, almost losing his footing. "But then they might think you did me in."

"For my inheritance?" Ryan asked, not impressed.

"Well." He turned away from the water and laughed. "I see your point."

His father had made it clear when Ryan chose Viña Dorada over Cutty House that, once Ryan made his move against his family, there would be no coming back. Everything would go to Daniel.

As if that were some kind of a threat. As if he'd ever wanted any of it.

"Your mother is worried," he said, seeming to catch his breath, getting to the point of his visit. "She's afraid of what this woman might do to you. Seeing Nina all over again."

"I don't know, Dad." There was a wealth of sarcasm to his voice. "What's it done to you?"

It took him a moment to answer. They'd never talked about Nina, but Samuel knew exactly why his son had turned his back on his family and Cutty House.

He didn't look at Ryan as he spoke. "She's nothing like Nina. Nina can light up a room with her smile. She makes a man feel alive. Makes him do foolish things." His father gave a distracted smile. "And love every minute of it."

He was talking about Nina as if she were still alive. *She can…she makes.* Present tense. The amazing part was that it still pissed Ryan off, like it was yesterday and she was telling him the truth all over again. The part about his father…

Ryan's confession to Gil had left out a detail or two.

Nina, screaming at him. *It's not even your baby! You'll see. It will be me turning you out, Ryan. Once I tell your father the baby is his.*

He hadn't believed her. She'd been drunk and in a rage. He thought she was making it up, searching for the most painful blow she could deliver—and finding it. *That's right, Ryan. Your father fucked me!* How could he believe her? That either of them could cross that line?

Only, the next day, his father had been completely undone over Nina's death. When he turned Ryan in to the police, a few things came into focus.

Ryan stared at his father still leaning hard against the rail. He tried to feel something, then quickly shut off all emotion. If he let go, he wasn't sure where it might take him. Not some stupid street brawl like him and Daniel. There'd be so much more. His father might even be close to the truth, suggesting Ryan would want him sliding over that rail.

"You're right," he told Samuel. "Holly's nothing like Nina."

Everybody seemed to make that mistake. Daniel. Even Holly. Worried that maybe it was Nina he wanted in his arms, when nothing could be further from the truth. But he and his father knew.

"Which is why she shouldn't be here," he warned Samuel. "Shouldn't be part of our mess."

"Yes. I see your point. But I'm not sure what I can do to change the situation."

"Think of something," he threatened.

His father granted another distracted smile. His hands on the railing shook.

"Your mother and I haven't…well, there's a thing or two she hasn't forgiven. And she's very supportive of Daniel at this time. Daniel, of course, wants the girl to stay."

Ryan could see he'd have to make things a little clearer. He came over to stand in front of Samuel, making sure he had his father's attention. "Fix it. Or I will."

His father smiled, then licked his lips. "Is that a threat in your voice, my boy?"

"There's nothing wrong with your hearing."

Ryan stared into eyes a mirror of his own. They looked alike, everyone said it. But twelve years ago, his father hadn't been this old used-up man. He'd been strong, vibrant.

He could almost hear his mother again, worried about Samuel. As if Ryan should care. As if he could give a shit.

"All these years, I've kept your secret, old man. Don't make the mistake of believing I did it for you."

His father smiled wanly. "No, no. I imagine your efforts are all for Gil. He does seem rather delicate these days."

Ryan pressed into him, making his point. "Forget what you did to me. Forget even what you did to Nina." But Gil. Jesus, if Gil ever discovered the truth. "Yes, *Dad*," the word full of irony, "that's very much a threat you're hearing."

Samuel stared at him, surprised and almost delighted. "All right," he said, stepping back. "Let's do this your way, shall we? Your mother is throwing a party. She'll invite you, of course. And you'll decline, as always. But you should come. I insist. Your architect lady will be there. I think by then we'll have more to discuss."

His father pushed Ryan aside and walked to the door. Before leaving, he stared over the water. He seemed to be contemplating how tempting it might be. Just get the job done. Why the hell not? He was half-way there already.

"You come to your mother's party," Samuel said, "and I'll see what I can do."

After the door closed, Ryan whispered, "You do that."

He couldn't believe the depth of his rage, couldn't imagine how little was left of his control. Ever since Holly, it was as if he'd turned into this other man. For years he'd been setting the score straight, and now he was letting it slip through his fingers.

Get control.

Almost a week had passed since the last time he'd seen Holly, and not a night had gone by that he hadn't picked up the phone to call her.

He stood at the rail, hoping the breeze off the water might cool some of the heat. When his father had asked to come over, Ryan hadn't thought it was such a bad idea. The fact was, he'd had a thing or two he needed to discuss. Because Holly wasn't leaving town unless someone pulled the plug on the job at Cutty House.

Ryan glanced down at his hands. He'd balled them into fists at his sides. *She's nothing like Nina.*

"Damn straight."

Maybe Ryan had always known there was something wrong with Nina, something a little off. Maybe that's why he'd held back, calling off the wedding. Twelve years later, he still didn't understand why she'd done the things she had. What had she lacked in life? What made her need more?

He'd read this article about people who didn't make enough dopamine. They needed to take these weird risks in order to get their fix of the stuff, just to feel normal, and tended toward high risk sports or dangerous jobs. Thrill seekers.

Maybe that was Nina. Nothing counted but the next

thrill, the next fix. Or maybe it was just a young girl's mistake. Nina had liked extremes, never knowing when to call an end to the party.

His father and Nina. Dan and Nina.

Ryan pushed away the memories, a little surprised that he could still feel that much anger. He would have thought he'd have more forgiveness in him. She'd paid the ultimate price, after all.

Your mother is throwing a party...your architect lady will be there.

Walking back inside, he remembered another one of Gil's lessons about the vines. In the winter the vines lay dormant. It was an important time, Gil had told him, for the vines to rest and recuperate for the next season.

Ryan had a feeling they'd all been waiting...Daniel, his father, his mother. Even Cutty House, resting these past years.

But their dormant winter had come to an end. At long last, it was time to act.

Samuel Cutty staggered up the gangplank, his hands shaking as he gripped the rail. At the top, he caught his fine shoes on the last step and fell.

"Damn all." He'd ripped the knee of his trousers.

He gained his feet, trying to catch his breath. The meeting with Ryan. He wasn't so sure he'd carried it off.

He needed a drink. Badly.

By the time he reached the Jaguar, he dropped his keys in the parking lot in his haste to open the door. He flopped into the seat and searched for the flask he'd left on the floor. He drank down the Scotch.

When he felt some of the cold leave his bones, he punched up the number on the cell. He started the car.

"I'm just leaving. I told him about the party. Damned if I know if he'll show up."

He listened, drinking from the flask as he drove with his knee, getting courage.

"I can't guarantee shit. I did my best."

But the voice on the other end had no desire to hear his nay-saying.

"Bloody hell," he said, dropping the phone as he tried to hit the End button. Another long pull from the flask.

He knew he was a weak man. They all knew his weakness. His own father, his wife...Daniel and Ryan.

He thought about what he'd said to Ryan. *What if I just hoist my leg over the rail?* The problem was, he was too weak even for that.

He laughed, feeling the alcohol warm him. He knew it wouldn't last. He'd need more and soon. And he knew a place where he could go to get more. His haven. Yes, that's exactly what he needed tonight. He needed Nina.

He managed to get to her place in one piece. She'd be angry with him, just showing up. He almost laughed as he stumbled up the steps and pushed the buzzer.

"It's me," he whispered into the tiny speaker.

He was afraid she wouldn't let him up. She didn't always. It was touch and go with Nina these days. That was part of the thrill. You just never knew her mood.

But he had to remind himself that after all these years it was still him she loved. Not Ryan or Daniel. Only Samuel, the soggy old man.

He'd never been happier than when she buzzed him up.

When she opened the door, she frowned. "How

very naughty of you, Samuel," she said. "You should have called. I have half a mind to turn you away."

"Please," he begged her.

She didn't torture him too much, letting him in, taking him to her bed. It was getting more difficult now, age and alcohol catching up with him.

"Nina, I need you. They all want something from me. I can't keep up. They're pulling me apart."

"I know," she told him, guiding him alongside her naked body. "I'll help you. I'll make them go away."

He wasn't sure he'd be able to get an erection. These days, that mattered less and less. He just wanted to be here, in Nina's arms. "I think the baby would have loved me." *A second chance.*

"Why do you always bring up the baby? Dammit, Samuel, you give me the creeps sometimes, I swear you do."

"You're right. I'll stop."

He wasn't sure why he'd brought it up. Perhaps because the one child he'd managed hated him so much.

He studied her for a moment. She wasn't petite or fine-boned anymore. She didn't laugh like she used to. But she was still Nina in every way to him.

"You're right. It doesn't matter," he told her. "Because I have you."

Nina applied her mouth to the task. He could feel himself slip away into that alcoholic oblivion, a lovely black hole.

"I'm glad you're still alive," he told her. "They all wanted you, but you loved me best. For me, you stayed alive."

"Hush, now," she said. "You have me all to yourself, just like you always wanted."

"I didn't want you to die," he said, everything beginning to blur. "But we all die, don't we?"

He wasn't even sure she was listening...or that he was talking.

But death. It was coming. Tired and drunk and dreaming, sometimes death seemed the only sure thing.

23

Emma waited at the kitchen counter, her obligatory pit stop at Daniel's apartment coming to a close. Because she knew how to play by the rules—show up on time, listen like you're interested—these last days had passed without too much damage.

"You know the really amazing part? I *like* what she's doing," he told Emma, going on about his meeting earlier with Holly. He had his feet up on the chair opposite at the dining table, a glass of Merlot in hand. King of all he surveyed.

"At first, I thought it was all going to be so dull. But now she's added an odd column here and there, making things look kind of staggered but still balanced. She's using color to emphasize certain walls. And she has this amazing idea of taking the plaster work we tore down and creating a design to cover one of the walls. She's taken all that stuff from the past and made it into something fresh and new."

He couldn't be more delighted. He'd never hired Holly for her talents as an architect. Now, the complete revisionist, he was making it all sound so reasonable. Good thing he'd brought Holly on board, right? Now, she'd get what she wanted, as well, a chance to shine. Wasn't that what they all wanted? Him with the East Side Café. Emma with her cooking. Now, Holly and Cutty House. A win-win all around.

Maybe a conscience was like a muscle, Emma thought. If you didn't use it, it slipped away to vanish altogether.

She made a show of checking the clock on the microwave. "I have to go." As if she hadn't been counting the minutes.

She picked up the earthenware pot she'd placed on the counter, ready to make a quick exit. She'd told Daniel that she had to cover for Beth on a job.

"I thought Beth was out of town?" he asked, looking at his glass of Merlot and not at her.

"That's why she needs me to cover for her," she said, leaning down to give him a peck on the cheek, hoping to get off easy.

But no such luck. He grabbed her arm, keeping her there beside him. "I thought you said you were giving up the catering business. Working for me full-time."

She shrugged off his hand. She could feel her blood racing, the adrenaline rush of lying. "And I also said I would help when she needed me. She won't call often. Besides, what am I doing for you, really? Until the kitchen is up and running."

He used his lie-detector stare on her. But clearly, he didn't want to fight. Not now, with his triumph so fresh in his mind.

"You need to forgive me," he said, surprising her as he stumbled over the words. He stood. She could see he was fighting himself not to take her in his arms. "I'm worried about us."

"Daniel—"

He turned her to face him, focusing on the wrong thing. "Hey, we're forever, right? You still love me, you know you do. If you love me, you'll forgive me."

She thought about how, sometimes, things just go rotten inside. You think it's good because the fruit appears shiny and perfect on the outside, but you slice it open and find it's all rotten. Nothing there you can save.

"You know I forgive you," she said softly. And because she meant it, she could look at him and add, "I can't help myself."

At the entry, she grabbed her coat. She knew he was completely capable of following her in his current state of mind. She would have to be careful.

"How long are you going to keep punishing me, Emma?"

He was standing in the hall, watching her. She could feel herself trembling, surprisingly with anger. When she'd told Holly to go home, she thought it would be over. Only, Holly wasn't giving up. She wasn't leaving. And Emma hadn't had the courage to tell her everything. She'd held back that little bit, the important part—the truth. *My fault.*

"Have you ever stopped to think, Daniel," she said, "that I'm punishing myself?"

"Honey." He pulled her into his arms. "You scare me when you talk like that," he said, not looking scared at all.

"I've got to go."

"God. I can't believe…Emma."

He caught up with her just outside the elevator, pleading with his eyes. "I'll be waiting for you tonight, okay?"

"Right."

She managed to step inside the elevator and watched as the doors slowly closed like a curtain on his face. End of Act I.

On any given day, Chinatown teemed with its own life force. Past the ornate entrance gate to the neighborhood, colorful facades and balconies paraded down Grant Street. Fish markets, temples and herbalist shops crowded the avenues. Paved alleys worked like arteries filled with a constant flow of locals and tourist alike. It was an exotic, ambiguous place where pagoda roofs warded off evil spirits, and street signs in Chinese calligraphy heralded the message: You're not in Kansas anymore.

Emma lived in an alley between Washington and Jackson. She thought the most beautiful morning of the year was Chinese New Year. That's when she'd see elderly men carrying leafless branches of quince budding in pink to their apartments, the very thing she carried now.

She reached her apartment and arranged the branches in a ceramic vase. She thought it was a little crazy, what she was doing. But more likely tonight was a selfish act—Emma trying to grab a little bit of happiness before everything went to crap.

She'd spent a lot of time the last week thinking over that inevitable question, "What now?" The first time she'd seen Holly, she'd been afraid. Now those fears centered on Daniel and what he might do to Holly, Nina's clone. But she was just as scared for herself. Nina represented their hidden past, secrets that, once revealed, would change their lives forever. Emma's most of all.

Chinese New Year: the time to settle debts.

When Harris rang the doorbell an hour later, Emma thought she was ready. She opened the door to find him waiting with one hand behind his back. He had the most amazing eyes. The whole Svengali thing in spades.

He brought his hand forward, *tada!* He held a bouquet of wildflowers, the stems wrapped in a scarlet ribbon.

"They're beautiful," she said, smiling up at him. "Are you going to tell me they remind you of me? No pretenses, beautiful in their free form?"

"Well," he said taking off his coat. "Not now."

She laughed, showing him inside. "Welcome to my world."

"Whatever it is," he said, heading for the kitchen, "it smells amazing."

"Sit," she gestured to the bar stool at the counter. "Watch and learn, Grasshopper."

She'd poured them both a drink. He took a sip of the Agave liquor and nodded with approval. He smiled at the branches of pink in their vase where she'd tucked in the wildflowers.

"Quince?" he asked.

"I'm impressed."

He shrugged. "It's Chinese New Year."

"Even more impressed," she told him.

"I can see you're going to be easy."

"Just you wait and see, mister."

She loved the banter. As if they had every right to this moment. Just a boy giving a girl flowers because she'd cooked him dinner.

"So what are you making?" he asked, staring down at the spices she'd set out on the counter.

"It's already made, but I left out the magic, the last key ingredients. I'm trying to impress you, if you haven't guessed. You told me you worked with native botanicals. I imagined this crazy mad scientist laboratory."

"Yup. Had one of those."

"Test tubes everywhere."

"Floor to ceiling. Quite attractive in a Frankenstein

meets modern science sort of way. It was a real turn-on for the ladies. If I left off my Poindexter glasses.''

"Do you even wear glasses?"

He barely held back a grin. "No."

"And the lab?"

"I was more into fieldwork, actually."

He reached for a piece of the chocolate. She slapped his hand away.

"This is a very special sauce." She took the chocolate and the black chilies and began grinding the two together in her mortar. "One that will seduce you, then bind you to me forever."

"Turning me into your love slave?" He took a thoughtful sip of Agave, his eyes never leaving hers. "Okay, I'm in."

"A willing victim. Always a plus."

She loved his face. It was masculine in a way that Daniel's could never be because it had character. There was even a scar, right above his left eye, making part of his eyebrow grow wonky. She imagined that his mysterious fieldwork was responsible.

"So I'm probably pressing my luck asking, that scientific curiosity really blows at a time like this, but…inviting me here, cooking for me? What exactly changed your mind?"

But she just smiled, knowing that she wasn't ready to tell him the truth and he would see through the lie. "Don't make it so complicated, okay? Just enjoy."

He took a long drink of the liquor. "You know, I surprise myself. Because I don't really like that answer, and I just know I should."

She spooned up a taste of the Oaxacan molé sauce simmering in the pot with the chicken she'd cooked earlier.

"Stop talking. Eat."

He looked like he'd just tasted food fit for the gods. "One word. Wow."

She went back to the mortar. "This recipe contains twenty-three ingredients. Black and Mulato chilies. Sesame seeds and almonds. Even avocado leaves, which surprisingly taste like licorice. But the most important part...the critical ingredient," she said, finishing the paste in the mortar, then turning it toward him to see, "is the chocolate."

He smiled, looking only at her. "Magic."

She nodded. "The Mexican woman who taught me this recipe claimed to be a witch."

"You're not going to pluck out one of my chest hairs or anything like that?"

"Only if you ask nicely."

He smiled again, giving her a sexy look that was a complete turn-on. "Maybe later," he said.

She dropped a piece of clove into the mortar. "The Aztecs used to make this drink called *xocoatl*."

"Say that three times fast."

"It means 'bitter water.' The drink was associated with the goddess of fertility, *Xochiquetzal*. The Spanish sweetened it with sugar, to take away the bitterness, and kept the drink a secret for almost a hundred years."

She dipped her finger into the mixture and held it out for him. He nibbled on her finger, taking his time, making the gesture incredibly erotic.

"Did you know that chocolate contains over three hundred chemical compounds?" he said. "Stimulants that increase brain activity. I hear there's even a study that compares it to marijuana."

"Are you saying I'm trying to get you high?" She watched his mouth on her finger. He used his tongue, then sucked gently.

"Mission accomplished," he said.

"Are you mine forever, Harris?" she asked, seduced by that look.

He came around, stepping inside the kitchen. He turned her to face him. "Funny, I was about to ask you the same thing."

"I didn't invite you here to make love." But she was so very breathless when she said it. "Not necessarily, I mean."

"Too late to back out now."

He kissed her. It was the softest kiss she'd ever had. As if he was just teasing her, wanting her to beg. A butterfly kiss on the mouth that made her step up on her tiptoes, searching for more.

"The magic won't work if you don't eat the molé," she told him.

"You couldn't be more wrong."

He guided her back into the living room, stopping here and there for a touch, another taste. "What is it with us and couches?" he asked, taking her clothes off, pressing her down onto the cushions. Following her there.

They weren't in a hurry this time. They cherished each touch, every kiss, almost as if they both knew it could be their last. She thought she'd never done anything so intimate, making love to him while looking into his eyes, as if neither one of them wanted to miss a moment.

Afterward, she lay curled up alongside him on the floor, the comforter from the bed now covering them both. She could feel her heart racing in her chest. She heard herself whisper, "Harris?"

"Hmm?"

"Have you ever done something really wrong?"

He was brushing his fingers up and down her arm,

stroking her. She tried to remember when anyone had touched her so tenderly.

"I have, Emma," he said. "More times than I care to admit."

"This is one of those times," she said, taking the conversation in a different direction. "You and me."

"On so many levels, I can't even count."

She had this horrible feeling that he could see right into her soul to all the darkness there. She'd thought she could be strong. Tell him everything. She'd asked him here to do just that. *Tell him the truth!*

"Emma, are you in some kind of trouble?" he asked, whispering the words in her ear. "With Daniel, I mean?"

She pushed him over so that he lay on his back. She rested her head on his chest, pressing her cheek against him.

"Shh. You should have eaten my food. I can never keep you now." She was fighting back tears.

"What are you doing?" he asked.

"Listening to your heart."

I won't let Daniel hurt Holly, she vowed. But she knew it was a promise she couldn't keep.

"Emma, tell me what you're thinking?" he asked quietly.

"I'm thinking about fatal flaws."

"Really? What's yours?" And when she didn't answer, he said, "Okay. I'll start." He turned on his side to look at her. "You wanted to know about my old job? Those native botanicals? Some people call it bioprospecting. But there are other names. Not-so-nice ones. Biopiracy. Biocolonialism."

She sat up, looking at his face. She knew what he was telling her wasn't easy for him.

He swept back the hair from her eyes, slipping her

bangs behind her ear. "A company sends a guy like me into the jungle, someone who feels comfortable living in a different setting, maybe has a special ability to establish rapport with the natives—the shaman in particular. You have to have a kind of sixth sense out there. Know when to ask questions, know when to keep your mouth shut and just observe. If you gain their trust, they share their secrets."

"I bet you were good at it," she said.

But he didn't take it as a compliment. "Too good. You asked me if I was a spy, and maybe I was. I stole their secrets and handed them over to my company. The lawyers would file a patent on the whole damn thing. The tribe wouldn't see a dime."

She frowned. "Can you do that? Aren't there laws against that sort of thing?"

"Damn straight there are. And I guess I got tired of being on the wrong side of them."

He leaned up on his elbow, now face-to-face. "I quit. Everything. Then I showed up on Holly's doorstep, licking my wounds. I let my kid sister pick up the pieces, which is how we got here."

She could see that he thought he'd made some horrible confession. "But in the end, you did the right thing. Because you quit. You stopped taking advantage—"

He pressed his fingers over her mouth, stopping her. "But not before I almost got somebody killed. It was a close call. Scary close. So don't go thinking I'm one of the good guys, okay?"

She could see the tale haunted him. He'd come back wounded by his close call, but his story had an "almost" to it. Hers didn't.

She took his hand and pressed a kiss into his palm.

She lay back down and spooned her back against him, holding his arm around her.

"Your turn," he whispered.

Her turn to confess.

"Daniel," she told him. "He's my weakness."

"Then leave him," he said. "Leave him for me."

"And what if you're the same? Just another bad end?"

"But I'm on the side of good now, remember? You said so yourself."

"But maybe I'm not."

She curled up against him, putting an end to the conversation.

She didn't know how long they lay on the floor. She might have dozed off. She woke up to the motion of Harris slipping out from under the comforter. He dressed quickly, as if he'd figured out while they lay there in semisleep that she was the enemy, after all.

"Emma, help me understand. We can't keep—"

"Just go," she said.

After the door shut behind him, she lay on the floor, trying to shut out that final look of his, filled not with magic but with a very human disappointment.

Holly heard the key in the door. She barely had time to take the papers she'd been reading and slip them under the plans covering the coffee table before Harris walked in. He looked incredibly tired.

She hopped to her feet, a preemptive strike. "How about some coffee? It's decaf. One of those dessert kinds. Amaretto something. I was just going to make myself some."

She was busy with the coffee in the kitchen when Harris came in holding the transcript she'd hidden under the as-built plans.

She turned, hands on hips. "You had to dig through quite a bit of stuff to find those, you know. It's called snooping."

He glanced at the coffee. "Better add something with a kick."

She brought out the steaming cups, now laced with brandy, to the table. Her brother was flipping through the contents of the folder she'd brought home, reading the police reports and transcripts of taped interviews. If possible, he looked even more worried than when he'd first walked through the door.

"So," she said, putting down his cup. "Go ahead. I'm listening."

"To what?"

"I'm ready for the speech. 'Obviously, he killed her. It's time to get the hell out of Dodge, Hol. Before he comes after you.' All that stuff."

"I'm not saying it would be a bad idea. Where did you get this?" He held up one of the transcripts.

"A little birdie left it for me."

He nodded, needing no further elaboration. "Someone is trying to scare you off the project."

"Apparently."

"But, you, oh wise one, are not frightened."

She thought about that. "Not enough."

Harris stood. He left the stapled pages on the table and carried his cup into the kitchen. A few minutes later, she heard him heading for the hall.

"Where are you going?" she asked.

"To bed."

"You're not going to try and talk me out of this?"

He peered at her from the hallway entrance. Very few times in her life had she seen that expression on his face—complete and utter defeat.

"Talk you out of what, Hol?"

She watched her brother leave. For the first time in her life, she had that psychic experience that so charmed her brother.

Harris was leaving something out.

24

"The caves, I suppose, are as good a place as any for a man to hide."

Ryan turned to find Gil at the cave entrance. Ryan stood in front of a specially-built wooden rack, bottle necks down. The punt of the bottles, the dip in the glass bottom so important to sparkling wines, faced him. He was riddling by hand, a process that worked the yeast sediment toward the temporary crown cap by shaking and turning.

At the vineyard, most of the riddling was done by machine, but in a nod to tradition, Gil insisted Ryan keep a part of the *tirage* to do by hand. Ryan had been working his way through the rows with his vineyard manager, turning the bottles an eighth of a turn, two at a time, slipping them deeper into their wooden sleeves to create a steeper angle.

He stepped away from the rack, letting the other riddler finish the job. He'd been at the caves most of the morning. He wondered if Gil wasn't right. He'd come here to hide.

He glanced around the cave. "Apparently, not so good a hiding place, after all. For example—and don't take offense here—you found me."

"As in the tired old man?" When Gil smiled, only half his face responded. "It's long past time for you to hide things from me."

He stopped alongside Ryan, the cane almost a part of him these days. Ryan could tell Gil had something on his mind, and he was pretty sure he knew what was coming. He'd been a little surprised it had taken Gil this long.

"And speaking of which," Gil said, starting in, "I was going to give you more time, wait for you to bring up the subject, let you ask the questions. But then it occurred to me that you might think the same. That you were waiting for me to bring up the topic. Let Gil decide, that sort of thing."

"Well, sure," Ryan said, turning to look at his partner. "Because that's how we do things here. Let Gil decide."

Gil's response was a short grunt, because he and Ryan were known for their drawn-out battles. Gil, always talking about tradition, the spirit of the vines, his muse. Ryan pushing to update, technology and marketing numbers his allies. They could go on, raised voices and all.

Gil made a show of taking out one of the bottles and giving it a look. "So, why haven't we talked about this girl? You're seeing her, of course. The one who looks like my Nina."

"I see her, yes." Not bothering to explain any more than that.

"Who is she?"

Ryan thought about the past few days, about how many times he'd almost driven over to see Holly. He'd held back because he absolutely knew their meeting would end with him taking her into his arms, completing the bad circle of pushing her away, then coaxing her to stay. The idea of trying to talk some sense into her had become an issue of being damned if you do—and damned if you don't.

He gave Gil his best assessment. "Who is she? A clever trap."

"Ah. Well, now I'm even more intrigued." Gil lowered himself to the bench at the cave entrance. The cave was next to the tasting room, a later addition to the vineyard. Tours came through twice a day, three times a week. There were more benches just outside. He signaled for Ryan to join him.

"The resemblance is quite…startling," Gil said.

He remembered their kiss. "At first, yes."

Gil nodded. "Like wine, then. The subtle nuances that come from the soil and the weather can make a world of difference."

Clear green bottles lay stacked upon each other along the cave walls, making the room look like an enormous beehive. Ryan had come to like the image, thinking that the bottles housed the grape's nectar. After the disgorgement, when the plug of frozen sediment was removed and replaced by a dosage—a special syrup of brandy and sugar—the bottles were sealed again to finish the second fermentation process. The *methode champanois* was expensive but well worth the cost. It made the difference between a quality sparkling wine and a grocery-store brand.

He thought about what Gil had said. It was amazing how the little changes could make all the difference.

"How is Marta doing with all of this?" Ryan asked.

Gil waved his hand in dismissal. "I don't even know why you ask. That woman is steel. The Catalan blood. It's me that is the weak one," he said, indicating the ravages of the stroke.

"I should have told you about Holly," Ryan said. "I would have if I'd thought there was a chance she'd show up here unannounced."

Gil nodded. "Well, yes. But you see—" he patted

Ryan's shoulder "—the old man can take it. No worse for wear."

"Daniel hired her to renovate Cutty House."

"Of course, Daniel," Gil said, only too familiar with the family dynamics.

"She's an architect who specializes in making the old into something new. Daniel wants to erase any last sign of what was once the Cutty heritage. He's even calling the restaurant the East Side Café, with my parents surprisingly on board."

"And you?"

He shrugged. "I say let him. If he's gained my mother's support, he has mine, though I still can't imagine how he got her to come around."

"Perhaps it wasn't such a long trip for Vanessa."

"Meaning?"

"Your father. He's a good man, my friend for too many years. But I know his weakness. He should never have taken on that expansion by himself. When he lost the gallery, I can't even imagine how Vanessa reacted. Everything your grandfather created dwindled down to a small collection, but Cutty House was still hungry for more." He gave Ryan a look. "Maybe she's not so averse to letting Samuel feel the sting of his mistakes?"

But Ryan disagreed, thinking that his father couldn't feel a damn thing and his mother was smart enough to know it.

"My mother would never sabotage the business." Ryan shook his head, knowing how much she'd sacrificed. "She'd never betray the family."

"She betrayed you, didn't she?"

He thought about that. "I'm the one who walked out, Gil. She only handed Daniel the reins after she gave up on me and Dad. The way she sees it, Daniel is all she has left.''

''And the girl? Why bring her?''

''That's the interesting part.'' Holly, who could explode the past right in their faces.

Gil stood and patted Ryan's shoulder. ''Still keeping secrets. Such a lot of bother for an old man. Don't try to protect me so much. I have Marta for that.''

He walked a bit, then picked up one of the bottles from a rack.

''It's going to be a great year, Ryan. Maybe we'll even get one of ours on the White House's table, eh?''

''I'm working on it.''

He slid the bottle back into place, not looking at Ryan as he spoke. ''Nina was my shooting star. She lived her life so big, as if she knew she wasn't long for this world. Or perhaps it is the way she chose to live that took her from us,'' he said in the clear-eyed sentiment Ryan had come to expect from Gil.

He sighed. ''I knew my daughter, Ryan. I knew that she wasn't always…good. But she held my heart in her hands, Lord knows she did. She could do that to a man.''

''Don't I know.''

He nodded. ''What will you do about this architect, then?''

Ryan thought about the last week. The obsession…the kiss that only added heat. And the risks he and Holly were taking, playing with fire. That most of all.

''Step right into that trap, I suppose. Take the cheese,'' Ryan said. ''What else?''

Gil smiled. ''Spoken like a man grown.''

''Or a fool.''

But Gil shook his head. ''I used to worry about

you,'' he told Ryan. "How easily success came. Good grades, first in anything you tried. But I never saw passion. That desire to achieve is what a man needs so dearly to survive. Except, of course, when it came to your damned boats. You saved it all up for the sea.''

Ryan laughed. "A lot of good it did me.''

He regretted the words immediately, knowing how it must sound. "Gil, I didn't mean—''

He held up his hand, cutting Ryan off. "Yes,'' Gil acknowledged, "at first I felt guilty that I'd accepted your help. But Viña Dorada needed you and I was selfish enough to accept your sacrifice.''

Gil had required months to recover from his stroke, and years of physical therapy. Without Ryan to help him, Gil would have lost not just his daughter, but his family's heritage.

Gil shook his head. "I was overrun by guilt. I thought, here I am, manipulating your life, just as I did when your father and I threw you and Nina together. Sometimes, parents, we think we are like God, knowing what is best. It's not until later that we learn humility.''

But Ryan had heard enough. "Moved by the spirit of the vine, I see.''

Gil smiled. Ryan always brought up the spirit of the vine when Gil fell into philosophizing. "Ah, but there's a point to my rambling. I don't feel guilty anymore, Ryan. Viña Dorada and I did not take without giving something back. You haven't seen it yet, of course. You still want those open seas. But someday, you'll realize what you have here.''

"Maybe that day isn't as far off as you think.''

They both knew the truth. The vineyard had become a part of Ryan. The spirit Gil preached about had reached Ryan, as well. He'd started as a vineyard manager, then gone to school for his degree in Enology. He'd traveled abroad to other vineyards, and eventually became one of Viña Dorada's two wine makers as well as its chief operating officer.

Gil was looking outside, keeping that smile. "What was it that you told me she did? Made the old into something new? A bit of a miracle that, don't you think?" He nodded, liking the fit. "A little like wine making, the miracle of the grape and its transformation. Take the cheese, Ryan," he said. "You need passion. We all do, whether we want it to complicate our lives or not."

"The spirit is really working it today."

Gil winked. "You have no idea. By the way, that cheese of yours? She's waiting for you in the tasting room, probably wondering what's taken me so long to fetch you. Hopefully, Tony has poured her a few more of our fine vintages. Slowed her down a bit. She talks very fast, that one. But we did have a lovely time, the two of us. I like her, Ryan. So go and be nice."

Amazing, Ryan thought watching Gil shuffle off. Even with the paralysis, Gil still managed a smart-aleck grin.

Holly had done the full-on starlet-in-distress. She'd covered her hair with a scarf, and wore sunglasses big enough to hide half her face. She hadn't wanted to upset anyone with her resemblance to Nina.

She thought she might have pulled it off, too, waiting in the tasting room for Ryan to show, coming to Viña Dorada without disturbing the innocent.

But it was Gil who greeted her five minutes later at the tasting room's bar, insisting that she get rid of the "silly getup," that he wanted to take a good look.

"No need to be frightened of a beautiful woman,"

he'd said, with a half smile that managed despite the paralysis to charm.

Oh, they spent a cozy half hour together, Holly being grilled to see if she was good enough for his Ryan. Always with a smile and an anecdote as Gil poured the next libation. She learned how the vineyard belonged to his wife's family, hence the Spanish name. She listened to stories about Ryan growing up, always taking a polite sip of the offered wine, careful to keep her wits about her. In the end, he surprised her, giving Holly a thumbs-up before going off to find Ryan.

She'd been waiting a full twenty minutes now, her fingernails tapping on the bar as she turned the glass still full with something award-winning and delectable, the long name attached including words like *demi-sec* and *créme.*

"And here he is." This from Tony, who'd taken over as guide to the vine in Gil's absence.

Holly thought it was a bad sign, that hitch in her breath when she saw Ryan walking toward her. He made her think of the bubbles. *Mousse,* Gil had called them. Rising up inside her.

He sat on the stool next to hers. He'd rolled up his shirtsleeves and his hair looked a wreck, as if he'd spent a fair amount of time harassing it. He was tanned and fit and just as delectable as the *demi-sec* creamy thing she'd been drinking.

He picked up the huge sunglasses, then dropped them back on the counter. "These fool anybody?"

Sitting up straighter, she took the manila folder from her lap, presenting him with her reason for coming. "There was no screaming this time. I consider that progress."

She pulled the documents out of the folder and slid them across the bar to Ryan, leaving the folder on the counter. "By the way? You lied," she told him. "I'd like to know why."

He picked up the pages, started reading through them at a rate of speed she refused to believe possible. *Show-off.*

"Daniel told me you wouldn't quit the Cutty House job." His eyes never left the pages; he was still flipping past. "He said you didn't have a choice. I was wondering what he meant by that?"

She thought it was nice how he could multitask. Read and interrogate.

"I have no idea," she said, refusing to elaborate.

"So you do have a choice about quitting?" He finally put down the pages, giving her his full attention. "There's nothing he's holding over you?"

"Well, yes. It's a called a paycheck. Getting one every once in awhile is kind of nice. Even necessary, where I come from." She tapped one of the pages with her finger. "This passage here I find particularly interesting—"

He grabbed her hand. Their eyes met over the champagne glass. She could almost hear the bubbles rising, bursting.

"I know which passage interests you, Holly."

He didn't say her name very often. It always surprised her a little when he did. He managed to make it sound as if he liked it, as if her name were some strange new word rarely heard. Like *kumquat* or *absinthe*.

"You said the investigation didn't support the eyewitness account," she told him. "But that report clearly shows you—or someone—ran her off the road."

"And I have no explanation," he added with an

enigmatic smile. "None at all. So you need the money? That's why you're staying?"

"I need—want the project. It's challenging and creative work and, here's the really neat part, I'm going to be a roaring success."

"Write your own ticket afterwards?"

"That's the general idea."

"And Nina. All that stuff from the past doesn't bother you?"

She rolled her eyes. "Of course, it bothers me."

"But still worth the risk?"

"I don't agree with your characterization."

"What characterization? It's a risk...you're willing to take it."

"My commitment only lasts out the month. I'm sure with your background you understand the term breach of contract, which I don't intend to do. Breach my contract, that is."

"An arbitration panel wouldn't understand your situation?" Sarcasm. Loads of it. "Lured here under false pretenses?"

"But then Daniel can afford better lawyers, can't he?"

Not one to let the little things get past, he took a beat. "It sounds like you've been there before. The lawyer thing."

"My ex-husband. And believe me when I tell you, he had better lawyers."

He raised his brows, the smile on his lips suddenly pure mischief. "An ex-husband?"

"Yes, I know. I'm a fascinating girl. Who knew? But I came to talk about these," she said, once again pointing to the stapled pages.

He slid the reports back to Holly. "Now you have your proof. I lied. There it is in black and white."

"You have nothing to add?"

His expression shut down. "Why, no, counselor. As it happens, I don't."

She closed her eyes, counted to ten. "I'm sorry if I sound as if I'm accusing you of something. But I think I deserve an explanation."

He shook his head. "That's not what you want. Not even close to why you came here today. I almost did the same, you know. Tracked you down." She thought it might be the wine, how his voice suddenly sounded low and intimate. "I told myself I needed to set you straight about why staying was too dangerous. That you needed to listen to reason and go home. But somehow I knew it wouldn't end there."

He leaned closer, turning the papers so that she could easily read how well they condemned him. "You don't want an explanation, Holly. You want a damned miracle. And maybe I do, too."

There was no one else in the tasting room, Tony long since having made a timely exit. Ryan put his arm on the back of her stool, his minty breath again cool and sweet.

"Wouldn't it be nice if this all went away?" He said it like a story. *Once upon a time...* "We met under different circumstances. Maybe I hired you," he continued, weaving the fairy tale for them both. "To do something here at the vineyard. You look nothing like Nina. You have red hair and green eyes and you wear glasses. We get to talking, and I ask you out, and when we kiss, there's nothing more to it than this wonderful heat that tells us both we want more. No one else involved. No ghosts."

"And because it didn't happen that way—" she could feel this tightness in her chest, making it hard to talk "—it can't happen at all?"

"Well, now. Why don't you tell me?" He touched the report.

"Why is it that men always want the girl to do all the work?"

"Lazy bastards, every last one of us." His eyes never left hers. "Jesus, do you know what you're like? You don't give up. You just keep on coming. You're like running with the wind," he said.

"I don't know what that means."

"It means sailing with the wind at your back pushing you. I had this sloop, a thirty-foot Newport. One time, while running with the wind, I hit a perfect 10-knot high."

"Oh, that's me, all right," she said with a smile. "A perfect ten."

"Absolutely."

They were kidding around, but there was this crazy energy.

He sighed, giving in. "You still want that explanation?" And when she nodded, he said, "My mother. She knows a lot of important people. Most likely, she worked behind the scenes. No preliminary hearing and Ryan's off the hook. I was told there wasn't enough evidence to support the charges."

He stared at the report. Clearly the possibility that Nina's death hadn't been an accident wasn't good news for anyone.

"How did you get this?" he asked.

Exactly what Harris had wanted to know. "Someone left it on my desk."

He nodded. "Scare tactics," he said, obviously coming to the same conclusion as her brother. "Not that they seem to be working." He raised his brows. "Maybe just the opposite."

"I believe this is where I refer you to the earlier part of our conversation."

He tried not to smile, but couldn't quite manage it.

He picked up the champagne glass, turning it in his hand. "Did you like our specialty wine? A little softer effervescence, more fruit but not sweet. We leave it on the yeast for two years to give it more depth. At the time, Gil told me I was crazy. Now there's a chance this will be our first vintage to make a White House dinner."

She took the glass from him, drained it. She picked up the folder and papers along with her purse. She couldn't help a small sigh, looking at how beautiful he was.

"Sometimes crazy can be good," she said, leaving them both with that thought.

FLYING BUTTRESS

25

Take the flying buttress. Holly considered the device an architectural marvel. An inclined bar on an arch resting on top of a solid pier to carry the load of a roof or vault. Even the name had a certain ring. Flying…buttress.

Seeing one for the first time marked the launching point to her fascination with architecture. Notre Dame Cathedral, Paris. July 21, 1983. Everyone in her tour group focused on the gargoyles and the bells. All of that was pretty fantastic stuff, sure.

But for Holly, it was all about the flying buttress. Dozens of them lined up like good soldiers, holding up the miracle of it all. Making that fantastic inner space possible.

In life, she'd come to think of her stubborn spirit as a metaphorical flying buttress, something that kept it all in place, sharing the load, making sure she didn't collapse in on herself. Good times and bad.

But stubborn could also be bad. Stubborn could keep you places, refusing to give up. Just knocking your head against the proverbial wall until one day you woke up and wondered, *what was I thinking?*

She could have been somewhere else by now. She could have moved on, been doing something else. Instead, she was still knocking her head against that wall. These were her thoughts as she stood in the entrance hall of Moore Manor, cocktail in hand, staring at a model of her project.

Vanessa's party began fashionably at eight. Holly arrived unfashionably early to find a miniature of Cutty House front and center for all to see. It looked like a doll's house; you could see both inside and out. Newly minted, the structure was made of bristol board and based on the preliminary sketches she'd shown Daniel two weeks before.

Holly hadn't heard anything about it, of course, didn't even know he'd commissioned the thing. Looking at the model, she felt oddly exposed and a little off. *My designs. Used against me.*

She told herself it was ugly, even though technically she had to admit the model wasn't bad. Good enough to earn a trickle of oohs and aahs from the crowd moving past enjoying their second cocktail.

But the design was a shadow of her current ideas. So much had changed since she'd roughed out those sketches, plans that still developed as she added layers and nuance.

She'd never seen a preliminary design on display. Basically, it was unheard of. Preliminary designs were just that—preliminary.

For his part, Daniel watched her reaction from a safe distance. As she stared at him, he reminded her of a wolf. His eyes on hers, his muscles tensed, he was the hunter waiting for his prey to bolt.

Holly turned away, not wanting to give the image life, replacing the notion with something harmless: Daniel, the preening peacock whose worst crime was making her stand in heels, once again playing the part of Cutty House's architect on parade.

Emma stood beside her. She bit into a canapé.

"Too much salt," she quipped. She gave Holly a

pensive look, then wiped her hands on a cocktail napkin. "Congratulations. Daniel loves everything you've done."

"I just bet he does."

She followed Holly's gaze, found the target. "Has someone been a naughty boy?"

"Oh, you betcha."

Holly tilted her head toward Daniel, passing along the message that she was on her way over. Tonight he wore chunky-rimmed glasses and a dark gray suit jazzed up by the striped pattern of his shirt and tie. The combination reminded her of an eye exam: *Tell me when the objects line up....* As she walked toward him, he smiled like a man who didn't mind a little trouble.

Coming to a full stop before him, she said, "Daniel, a word." That flying buttress again.

She didn't actually rail into him once she had him alone. She thought she was quite professional, until the very end when she looked him dead in the eye and warned, "Don't you mess with my stuff again, bucko."

"Come on. It's beautiful."

"Not the point. And no. It's nowhere near my standards."

He peered over her shoulder at the model, as if confused by her anger. He'd hired the best, no doubt.

"Those were preliminary designs," she said, preempting his defense. "A lot has changed—"

"And this is just a preliminary party, babe. Relax, we are way off from opening night. And by then, who the hell is going to remember tonight? You think I invited reporters from some architectural magazine? These are my people," he said. "They're here for the champagne and the fashion and to try and guess who's screwing who.''

He came to stand behind her, gazing over her shoulder at the milling flock. "Look at them. They're feasting on gossip."

She caught a gaze here and there, watched as indeed whispers were exchanged.

He leaned in close, saying, "Want to give them something to talk about?"

She pushed him away. "Not funny."

But his lips crimped at the corners just the same. He took her hand and kissed the palm.

"Stick around. It only gets better. Smile," he said, turning her around, still keeping a grip on her hand. "We have an audience."

Toward the back. It wasn't difficult to find him. He tended to stand out in a crowd. Ryan was watching them from his post near the door. He was dressed in black, and his mood didn't appear any brighter. Not from that expression on his face as he stared at her and Daniel holding hands.

Their gazes met, held a minute. She felt pinned to the spot, targeted by that look...until Ryan turned and left.

"Suddenly, I see a new purpose to this party," she told Daniel, her heart racing. "What's the matter, Daniel, still worried he's the better man?"

"Don't be dense," he said, squeezing her fingers too tight. At the same time, he signaled to someone standing just a few feet away, his facile expression changing, the chameleon. "Gigi, so wonderful to see you here, darling. Come meet the woman of the moment, the artist in charge." He gave Holly a wink as he steered her front and center. "*Voilá*. My muse."

And he wasn't near done. The torture continued as

she was introduced to group after group, Daniel keeping a tight enough grip on her arm that he'd leave a bruise—one to match the blow she'd delivered to his ego. They gathered around Holly, making her the center of attention—which was a hard place to be when you were used to talking only to the walls. But courtesy of Daniel, she'd become the epicenter, the bull's-eye at the heart of it all.

In retrospect, she thought it must have been a charming opportunity, one difficult to resist for a reporter.

Wear her down…attack.

"Miss Fairfield? Any thoughts on your incredible resemblance to Nina Travers?"

The question came from Gigi, a woman with sharp eyes behind her Dolce and Gabanna glasses. The name clicked into place.

Gigi La Plume. The reporter.

Baa, baa, black sheep….

"Certainly, Nina Travers and her tragic loss provides one of the more colorful episodes in the history of Cutty House," the newspaper woman continued, taking Holly's look of shock as the green light. "But here you are, a perfect replica. Just like the model you commissioned. It's almost macabre, don't you think? The resemblance?"

She could see Gigi taking notes. Holly tried to imagine what would appear in print tomorrow. Double's Trouble, or some such nonsense. Holly stood speechless, stunned by the woman's characterization of Nina's death as a "colorful episode." Which was precisely why she'd said it. To shock.

"To tell you the truth," Holly said, keeping her voice surprisingly bland. "It's the first time I can honestly say I got a job because of my looks."

Everyone laughed, the tension lifting so that the crowd began to disperse, no longer interested in blood sports. But Gigi knew she'd scored a hit. Earlier, Holly had donned her camouflage, a nondescript suit she found buried at the back of her closet. She'd pinned her hair back. She thought she'd done a nice job of making herself invisible.

"You'll have to pardon Gigi," Daniel told her. "She loves to stir things up, then watch to see what scurries off."

"It's my job to be provocative," the woman said without apology. "The paper expects me to earn my keep."

"Gigi covered the original story," Daniel continued, "and managed somehow to turn our sad tale into the worst sort of melodrama."

Gigi smirked. "Daniel didn't always agree with what I put in print. I tried to be sensitive to the family, of course, but the public has a right to know."

"Bullshit," Daniel said, then blew her a kiss. "I only stayed friends with Gigi because she's such a fiend with that column of hers. Keep your enemies close, I say. And she came tonight only because she smelled a follow-up. Nobody who is anybody dares take a step in this town unless Gigi gives the say-so. We are all such sheep."

The woman preened under the compliment. "A sheep and a liar. But I love it, of course."

"Another drink, darling?" he asked.

"If you don't mind," she said.

Holly watched Daniel deftly turn the tide in his favor, while she felt as if she were falling deeper under water, chest tight, trying to catch her breath.

Until she couldn't. "Excuse me."

She squeezed past, searching for that air…and

something else. She couldn't help it. Her eyes scanned the room, looking for black hair and broad shoulders.

As if that would help. As if seeing him again would solve anything.

Her gaze slipped over the crowd just the same. *He saw me and left...the thing with him and Daniel has gone too far.*

But no. She found him, like a divining rod to water. He was standing across the room, pretending to listen to a portly man with a red face, a twentysomething blonde hanging on his arm looking bored and a little drunk.

Holly held her breath, wondering how to get the courage to just tell Ryan what she wanted. *Take me home, please.*

She could almost see the moment he realized how badly she wanted that escape. His shoulders relaxed just a bit; the fierce look in his eyes lost its edge. She saw him excuse himself from the conversation, watched the blonde's disappointment as Ryan walked away.

Holly waited for him, rooted to the spot. He took his time, answering a query here and there. She imagined the questions: *How's Gil? The vineyard? We don't see you enough.* His eyes stayed on hers as he made his way through the crowd.

"Don't tell me you're afraid," he said, stopping before her. "Not after your little Rambo act at the vineyard."

"I am as cowardly as they come."

"But then, I'm not the dangerous one."

"Really? I beg to differ. Last night I couldn't sleep thinking about you. Not a wink. That's not anything new, by the way. Did you know there are a hundred and fifty-three reasons why I shouldn't be attracted to you?''

"That many?" he said, giving it a smile.

"I took out one of my drafting pads and made a list. It was like counting sheep.''

"What would be a for instance?''

"I absolutely prefer blondes. I don't even like men with dark hair. And you're too pushy, of course. Nothing worse than a bossy man.''

"I think this is one of those times I stay wisely silent.''

She thought it was a little strange, talking like this with the crowd zinging around them, human pinballs bumping past. But then this thing between them—time and place had little to do with its progress.

"Here's another one," she told him. "Just because a man is a good kisser, doesn't mean he does anything else well in life.''

"You know what I think? I think those sound like the stupid excuses people come up with in the middle of the night to put on lists. Like the bogeyman under the bed. They don't matter. They don't even exist.''

"Well, how about this, then," she said, about to do the most foolish thing a woman could do with a man— confess. "At the vineyard, I said I couldn't leave because of my job at Cutty House. Only, it's so much more complicated. Harris, my brother, he told me my problem was I never get to pick. But now I think I have. And I'm not sure I care what brought us together in the first place. Even if it's something twisted, like being the mirror image of Nina. I only want to know how it ends, if that fairy tale you told me can possibly come true.''

He gave her glass to a passing waiter, taking her hand. "We'll just see who did the choosing here.''

He knew where they were going. Another mansion in the life of Ryan Cutty. Somewhere private. Somewhere safe. They were both game—they'd practically said as much.

The room where they ended up looked like a library. He pressed her up against the paneled walls. He cupped her face in his hands, taking in every inch.

"I've been having a hard time sleeping, too," he said, not bothering with long-winded explanations. "And when I close my eyes, this is what I see."

He kissed her. And why not? Hadn't they kissed a hundred times in her dreams? Lust was in the air; pheromones were flying. She couldn't touch him enough, couldn't get close enough. She was lifting his shirt, needing skin. He was doing the same.

But if Holly couldn't take a minute to catch her breath, Ryan didn't have that problem. He slipped back, easing her face up to his. The look he gave her was electric, as if this wonderful sign flashed above them: Meant to be!

She couldn't help it. "Okay, I'm going to sound like a commercial, but how can something that feels so good be wrong?"

He smiled, taking her breath away. "And here I was thinking the same thing."

Amazing. And it would have been, if she hadn't looked over his shoulder right then to see Daniel watching them from the door.

She dropped her hands, stepping back like a teenager caught in the act. Ryan tensed, turning to follow her gaze.

Daniel began to applaud as he stepped into the room. Seeing his expression, Holly wondered why he'd never been a suspect in Nina's death. Where had he been that night? Did he have an alibi? That desire to hurt was so clearly stamped on his face. She'd swear she'd never seen Ryan look like that.

"Well, bravo." He kept clapping, slowly walking toward them. "You finally did it. You resurrected Nina."

Ryan stepped in front of Holly. Slowly, the two men circled each other. Daniel's smile looked almost feral; Ryan infringing on his territory.

But Daniel, the coward, turned his attentions on the weaker game. Coming around Ryan, he reached out for Holly—only to have Ryan grab his arm and shove him aside.

Ryan stepped in front of Holly again. Daniel stared, clearly appalled as he saw Holly slip her hand into Ryan's.

"Oh, have you chosen the wrong man, little girl." He took a step back, giving her a pensive look. "All right. Have it your way, then."

She wasn't sure what he'd just threatened. The whole situation made the room spin. Especially when she watched Daniel leave, slamming the door behind him, and Ryan moved to follow.

She grabbed his arm. "Don't."

He shook his head. "Look, I don't believe in fairy tales, but if this is going to happen, if we even have a chance, there's a lot of business to take care of first. Understand?"

And then he kissed her, quick and hard.

She watched him take off after Daniel, suspecting she'd only make everything worse if she followed. She couldn't appreciate the undertones, wasn't even close to knowing the history between these two men. She was a simple girl who needed plans and instructions, a woman who'd always liked math and other things that added up.

But everything here was like some Greek tragedy. The stakes seemed equally high.

Good reasons to stay put, she told herself. Only, she found herself walking toward the door, with each step picking up her pace.

She was on a mission, but not by way of the crowd watching for her to continue the evening's entertainment. Instead, she ran down the hall toward the back of the house. The voice of reason warned that she was only throwing gas on the fire if she found Ryan and Daniel. But she hadn't shown much sense since she'd landed here at Club Cutty. Why start now?

She searched from room to room, wondering where Ryan and Daniel might have taken this thing between them. Not that she could stop them from a full-on brawl if it came to that. Still, she stepped into what looked like a parlor, her gaze taking in the room.

Only, it wasn't Ryan she found, but his father, a very drunk Samuel leaning against the hearth. Seeing her, he stumbled toward her. He looked like his son, except Samuel's face showed too much of what the last years had been like. Still, the resemblance was there in how he watched her now, in the urgent look in his eyes.

He barely kept to his feet. "Nina?" he said, a touch of awe in his voice.

Holly stepped back, caught by surprise. The way he'd called out Nina's name, he'd sounded as if he'd just left her, as if Nina was around the corner and he couldn't imagine how the minx had doubled back and followed him here.

"Nina. You came after all," he said, falling into her.

"I'm not Nina." She managed to push him away,

but he grabbed her again. "It's me, Mr. Cutty. Holly Fairfield."

"I told you to stay away, you naughty girl." He raised his finger to his lips. *Shhh.* Still keeping his grip. "They mustn't ever know about you."

She found herself fighting him, but he had the strength of his drunkenness. He pinned her to the wall, his heavy body flush against hers.

"Next time listen to me," he whispered, his breath hot on her cheek. "Vanessa has a temper, you know she does. If she catches us here, like this—"

When his mouth covered hers, she lost it. She slammed her foot into his shin, pushed him with both hands. Before he could grab her again, she slapped him.

"Leave her alone, Samuel. She's not who you think."

From the doorway, Vanessa Cutty spoke in the well-modulated voice of a woman speaking to a child. As if she'd said the same, many times.

Samuel rubbed a hand against the bright spot on his face where Holly had slapped him, looking accusingly at her.

"That's right. The other one. The one who pretends to be Nina."

Holly backed up. She looked from Vanessa to her husband. For a moment, the room blurred; she thought she might pass out. But then the whole place came into startling focus. Vanessa's eyes full of venom. Samuel's drunken smile.

Holly shook her head. She ran past Vanessa, not bothering to wait for an explanation, trying to forget that horrible kiss. Down the hall, she searched for the closest exit.

The way he'd touched her, his voice so intimate. *Samuel loved Nina?*

She pushed her way toward the front entrance, no longer worried about the crowd closing in. She heard someone call her name, saw Ryan heading toward her. In a silly scene from some romantic comedy, he chased after her, shouting for her to stop, caught in the bottleneck of bodies.

Speeding down the steps outside, she was Cinderella. She even thought she might leave behind the damn heels she was wearing before she twisted an ankle.

At the gate, a man dressed in a uniform, cap and dark glasses, approached her.

''Miss Fairfield?''

''Yes,'' she said, out of breath, feeling as if a mob with sickles and torches might be following close on her heels. She didn't want to talk to Ryan, didn't want to explain what had just happened.

''Your brother arranged for a car to take you home.''

She slipped into the Lincoln Town Car, catching her breath, happy to see the street disappear behind her. Thank God for Harris. She wanted to put as much distance as possible between her and what had happened, wanted to forget the smell of Samuel Cutty, the taste of him in her mouth.

He thought I was Nina.

''Please hurry.''

''Yes, ma'am.''

She wanted to cry. She wanted to scream. That scene with Ryan's father. Vanessa breaking in. *She's not who you think....* Suddenly, that chance Ryan had gone to fight for? She couldn't imagine it, couldn't see a way through this tragic mess.

Had they all fallen for Nina? And now, she—Nina resurrected—was she supposed to fill the void? She felt caught in this strange tangle she didn't understand. She didn't want to become someone else for Ryan or Daniel or some sorry old drunk.

But the more she thought about it, the more she wondered if that wasn't exactly what she'd done by staying despite every warning. Falling for the sparkle and pop of it all. And a beautiful man as the door prize, obsessive love for her already downloaded and functioning.

The car swerved. She bumped against the armrest, then toppled across the seat with the next turn. Sitting up, she looked through the tinted glass. It was difficult to make out the darkened streets, but she thought they were headed in the wrong direction.

"Excuse me." For the first time she realized that the driver had raised the partition. She pounded her hand against the barrier. "Hello?"

No response. Nothing.

She couldn't see much less talk to the driver, but she could feel the car picking up speed. She tried the door. Locked.

And her last cogent thought before panic struck: She was headed for the coast in a speeding car. Just like Nina the night she'd died.

26

It was happening again. Just like before.

Just like Nina.

Ryan followed the Lincoln speeding down the road. They'd taken Geary to the Great Highway, a straight stretch of road that ran parallel to the coast. In no time at all, they'd left the bay city behind, heading out of town.

He'd tried to stop her. Twelve years ago, he'd done just the same, screaming at Nina to listen. Not to do anything stupid.

But with Holly, he hadn't thought she was in any danger. Her driver hadn't even taken the same route out of town. He and Nina had blown through the Presidio, raced the lights at 19th.

No, he hadn't thought Holly was in danger. But when he'd seen her face as she'd run past, he'd sure as hell followed her. This thing with him and Daniel was eating her up. He'd wanted to comfort her, to tell her it was okay. Whatever it took, they'd work it out.

Daniel hadn't stuck around to confront Ryan, disappearing instead into the safety of the crowd. When Ryan caught up with him, he had Emma on his arm and was holding court with the reporter. He'd toasted Ryan, daring him with his smile to step up and make a scene. Ryan had been thinking the bastard couldn't hide forever when Holly had run past.

His biggest fear was that she was giving up, her endless optimism drained. The thought made him shove his way through the crush of bodies, trying to catch up. He realized he wouldn't know what to do if he'd extinguished that ball-of-fire personality. He didn't want to be the source of that incredible loss; he'd come to count on her tenacity.

When he couldn't reach her, a strange panic rose inside him. Outside, he saw her step inside a waiting Town Car. Determined to follow, he'd headed for his own car parked on the street. He hadn't wanted to wait and call her later when she reached the apartment. Wasn't sure she'd even take his calls, not by a long shot.

Only, at some point he realized he must have been acting out of instinct. Because now the Lincoln was heading toward Pacifica, setting off these alarm bells in his head. *Just like Nina.*

Ryan sped up, getting closer to the sedan despite the fog and road conditions. The fact was, a lot of things about the evening seemed eerily the same. The fight. Holly running out the door. All of it triggered something—a memory. Making him run after her. Making him scared.

When the Lincoln turned for Highway One, his fears went into overdrive.

Now the car ahead of him was starting to swerve, almost as if the driver were teasing him. *Catch me if you can!* He could see the rear lights weave in and out of the fog, the car dangerously close to the soft shoulder. Highway One coiled above a ragged coastline. During the day, the sedimentary rock twisted and warped into strange shapes. But in the fog, he saw nothing but the past.

Jesus, he couldn't let it happen. Not again.

He'd been drunk that night with Nina. *I don't love you anymore, Nina. Maybe I never did.* Hurtful words that only some teenager buoyed by alcohol would dream of saying. But now, he was stone-cold sober. He knew someone was playing a game, and he had no idea how far they'd take it. That smug grin on Daniel's face, as if he'd known all along what was coming next.

Ryan couldn't let him hurt Holly. *Not Holly.*

He pressed the gas pedal, coming closer, almost on the car's bumper. Suddenly, he could see her there, pounding on the rear window. Trapped.

The blood roared in his head. He kept his foot on the accelerator, wondering how to stop the car ahead without killing them both. He tried to imagine some maneuver to keep her safe. He couldn't allow fear. He needed to think about the next curve.

That night, Nina had wanted to scare him, fishtailing across the road. She'd probably thought it was some great joke. *Scare the crap out of him; make him pay.* She'd been that mad, that crazy and that drunk.

Sometimes, he believed she'd miscalculated. She hadn't meant to skirt so close to the edge, hadn't thought it would cost her life.

Other times, he'd think she'd been suicidal, only too happy to bring it all to an end. That he'd pushed her there with his anger. *My fault.*

But tonight, this was different. Staged, in a way that made his hands lock around the steering wheel. If he was going to stop the Lincoln, he had to make his move soon. They were coming up on the place where Nina had driven off the road. He knew the exact spot, knew it was close.

He punched the accelerator, swerved to the right, going around the outside. One of the wheels slipped off the paved road, making the steering wheel come to life in his hands as the dirt sucked at the car's tire. Ryan eased his foot off the gas, shifted gears, then floored it, trying again to swerve around the Town Car. If he could get ahead of the guy and slow him to a stop…

Right then, the sedan turned into him. *Bam!* Ryan fought the steering wheel, trying to keep on the road. *Shit.* He hit the brakes.

When he got control back, the Lincoln was long gone.

Nina had died near a place called Devil's Slide just ahead a mile or so. But he could swear he heard the scream of tires. He could almost smell rubber burning. *Too late!*

He drove the last mile like a crazed man. He found the car shrouded in fog parked on the dirt shoulder. He pulled over and ran to where the Lincoln waited underneath a windswept cypress. The night he'd found Nina, her Mercedes had slammed past the safety rail and rolled down a steep embankment. But tonight, the car just kissed the ledge. *See, Ryan? X marks the spot.*

Nina's car had been totaled, the driver's side window shattered where she'd hit her head. They'd had to bring in a winch just to get the damn car back on the road.

He couldn't open the door to the sedan, could barely even see inside with the dark and the tinted windows. But he knew that if Holly was inside, she wasn't moving.

Grabbing the sleeve of his jacket, he broke the driver's side window with his elbow, watched as the glass shattered under the blow. He tried not to remember Nina and her blood-drenched face when he'd found her. He reached in and opened the automatic lock.

Holly lay slumped in the leather seat. She'd been knocked unconscious.

He checked her pulse, scared to move her. "Come on, honey. You can do this for me. I promise to make it 154 reasons, just be okay."

He tried to be as gentle as possible as he helped her sit up. Her eyes flickered open. She had a gash on her head but seemed otherwise unhurt. She stared at him, the moon behind him shining in her eyes.

"Ryan?"

"You're okay, honey," he whispered, stroking her face. "You're going to be fine."

The fog felt like rain, the mist was that heavy. The world was barely visible, but he could see Holly. How beautiful she was. How much he wanted her. Like no one else in his life.

At the same time, he was thinking about what had just happened. Someone was playing a game, bringing her here, putting her on this joyride. He could feel the adrenaline taking over, making his hands shake as he helped her out of the car.

She gasped and coughed for air like a drowning victim. He held on to her, waiting for it to pass. Finally, she seemed to get her breath back. She wrapped her arms around him, disappearing into his embrace.

"The driver told me Harris sent him to take me home. Harris has been so worried about me. It sounded like something he would do."

She pulled away, looking at him. Whatever she was going to say next, he could almost see her punch the mental "Edit" button in her head. She must have seen how scared he was because she stopped talking altogether.

So he told her, trying to set her straight. "They're going to hurt you. To get to me."

"Ryan. Your family wouldn't—"

He kissed her, as if trying to prove it to both of them, leaving no doubt. This was wrong, this thing between them. Cursed. And it didn't matter that she was different or even the complete opposite of Nina.

She'd fallen into the trap he'd been trying to escape his whole life. And it was going to get her killed.

But Holly didn't seem to be on the same page. She stared at him in disbelief.

"How can you kiss me like that?" she asked, her voice barely above a whisper. "As if you want to hold me and push me away at the same time?"

Which was exactly right. How much he wanted her—how important it was that she stay away.

"Come on." He took her to his car and helped her inside. Once he had her seated, he folded his handkerchief and pressed it to where blood had begun to ooze at her temple.

"He slammed on the brakes. I hit my head. Against the window, I think." She was holding his hand so tight.

"You might need stitches. Or an X ray or something."

"I don't want to go to the hospital. I want to go home."

"Well," he said, reaching for the keys. "So much for the things we want."

Samuel stumbled into the room, his arm around Nina.

"I thought that woman was you."

"You were that drunk?"

"Aren't I always?" he said, laughing with her. "You should have seen Vanessa. My God, if she'd had a gun. I tell you darling, I'd be a dead man."

Nina made a dismissing sound, not the least afraid. But he stopped her, turning her to face him.

"I think she knows," he whispered.

"She doesn't," Nina said, dispelling his fears. "She can't." She guided him to the bed. "Not that I would care. If you loved me, you wouldn't keep your wife. And here you are, admitting that you kissed another woman."

"I thought she was you."

This time, perhaps because of the excitement, he was able to actually make love to Nina.

"Why do you stay with me?" he asked, stroking her hair.

She lay her head on his chest. "Because I love you best. Remember? Better than Ryan or Daniel. Don't I say it enough?"

He stopped to look at her, his breath caught in his throat. He could barely make out her features in the dark.

"I almost believed you that time," he whispered.

She kissed him gently. "Be quiet, Samuel. Be a good boy and just shut up."

27

You have to stop him. Next time, he might kill her.

Lieutenant Amy Garten replayed the message, a recorded phone call delivered in the wee hours to Homicide. She paid special attention to the voice—the inflection, the choice of words—comparing it to her memory of another time.

She sat at her desk, tapping her pen against the pad of paper where she'd been jotting notes. She remembered the case, basically because it had stuck in her craw over the years, leaving her with the impression that they'd never gotten it right. At the time, Ryan Cutty hadn't been that much older than her own son.

She shifted her gaze to the newspaper next to her notepad. She'd folded the page into a tight square, displaying the article. Now, twelve years later, another anonymous call resurrected Lieutenant Garten's misgivings about the death of Nina Travers, timed as it was with today's curious mention in the paper.

Cutty House Channeling The Past?

After years of financial floundering, the beleaguered Cutty clan may have finally found their golden goose. Architect extraordinaire Holly Fairfield has been hired to revise, reinvent and revive the old homestead. But is there a more sinister truth behind the family's flagging fortunes? Could there be a Cutty Curse? In a bizarre coincidence, sources whisper that Miss Fairfield—who bears an amazing resemblance to the late Nina Travers—almost lost her life in a car accident identical to the circumstances surrounding another tragic death in the Cutty history. Which begs the question: Is the Cutty's golden goose about to be cooked?

The article went on to discuss selected details about the investigation twelve years ago, making it sound like a bad soap opera. It was one of those stories easily resurrected in print, the public having a quenchless thirst for the tragedies of the rich and famous.

Lieutenant Garten took another stab at the recording, listening to the voice. She'd sent a copy to the lab for comparison, but she'd give odds they matched. A woman. Young. Had to be the same person. Only, this time, the source wasn't pointing the finger at Ryan Cutty.

Ryan Cutty didn't kill Nina, but someone thinks he should pay just the same. Someone close to the family. He wants to see Ryan suffer. That's why he's doing this. To get to Ryan.

Interestingly enough, Amy had arrived at a similar conclusion all those years back. Ryan Cutty hadn't killed Nina Travers, but someone wanted to make it look as if he had—hence the phone call to Homicide. Someone with a grudge. Someone who wanted to sprinkle a little tarnish on the Cutty reputation.

Still, a lot had happened since then. Cutty House was no longer one of those places synonymous with a visit to San Francisco, like the Golden Gate Bridge or Fisherman's Wharf. The family itself seemed to have fallen on hard times. Hadn't she read somewhere that they'd shut the place down? And now the paper mentioned some kind of curse?

. And Ryan Cutty, he'd moved on, right? No longer part of the family business, what was left of it, anyway.

Which might in itself be a pretty good motive to try and dig up some dirt from the past. If the Cutty clan was on the brink, why not give a little push? The events didn't need to be connected. A crime of opportunity.

You have to stop him. Next time, he might kill her.

"Well." Lieutenant Garten picked up her phone. "Not on my watch."

The next morning, Harris read the headline to Gigi's column: Cutty House Channeling The Past?

He didn't think much of it. The reporter could have done better. Watching his sister at the dining-room table, the articles he'd printed from the computer way back when covering every inch of surface area, he thought he could help with a follow-up. Something like: Enraged Brother Takes Out Cutty Sharks.

He shook his head. Man, he was tired.

Holly had gotten up early to start what Harris had christened "Project Nina." Her research began last night after she gave up on the idea of sleep. Harris had been in bed, the door open, listening to the sounds of the house as he stared at the ceiling. He'd been so in tune with Holly, he knew exactly when she'd gotten up, was actually relieved when he heard her pad barefoot down the hall to the kitchen. Tired of waiting for the other shoe to drop, he'd followed her out, thinking he could at least make the coffee.

She hadn't taken the painkillers they'd prescribed at the E.R. The pill was still sitting on her nightstand next to a glass of water.

Now, Harris poured her a fresh cup of coffee. He'd read the La Plume woman's article first thing. The reporter implied Holly was Nina risen from the dead to save the family heritage that had once been her destiny. The column gave details about Holly's accident. It amazed Harris that they already had the damn story in print when his sister had come home from the hospital just a few hours ago.

Harris had been at the apartment when Ryan showed up with Holly, a line of steri-strip bandages at her hairline. The guy had stayed silent standing next to her as Holly tried to explain what had happened, his expression practically begging Harris to point a righteous finger and shout, "Your fault!"

Luckily, Ryan hadn't stuck around. He hadn't done anything too stupid, either, like tell Harris to take care of Holly for him or kiss his sister goodbye—which might have forced Harris to take a swing at the guy. Seeing them together, Harris knew exactly why Holly had decided to ignore all his good advice and stay on to do battle. This wasn't about the house anymore.

He took a drink of coffee. The light streaming past the window announced a bright shiny day. *Another jolly holiday…*

"I know it's here." Back at the dining-room table, Holly threw her hands into the air. "The answer is here." She jabbed a finger at the pad where she'd been taking notes, comparing all the articles. "Nina. She's the answer."

Harris stared into his cup, wondering if there was

enough caffeine in the world to get him through this. He put down the coffee, came around and sat next to Holly.

"Hol, listen to me. What answers do you think you're going to find in that trash you're reading? Was Nina's death an accident or murder? Are you next? You already have your answers. Right here," he said, pointing to her heart. How many times did he have to say it? "Time to pack up. To go home."

She shook her head. Her eyes were so red he couldn't tell if she was tired or if she'd been up crying half the night.

"I can fix this, Harris. I know I can."

She was pleading with him and it hurt so much to listen. He remembered what Emma had said. *She can save us from Nina's curse.*

Which pissed him off even more. They were using her—Emma, Daniel, even this Ryan guy.

He couldn't understand how his sister had landed in this freak show called Cutty House. Him? Sure, he'd screwed up his life. He'd done the deed and paid for his sins. But how does a complete innocent like Holly end up knee-deep in this kind of crap? Just because she looked like some dead woman?

"You don't have to fix this, Hol," he told her. "Actually, you *can't* fix this."

She put down her pen. She looked terrible. Pale, with dark circles under her eyes. The steri-strips reminded him of how close he'd come to losing her.

"What else am I supposed to do?" she asked. "I can't just walk away."

"But here's the thing. You can. You should. Walk away, Holly. Run, in fact. Look, have you ever considered that Daniel planned last night?" Seeing a crack in her resolve, he tried to pry it open and shed some light. "A new angle for the East Side Café? The mysteries of the past repeat themselves, come one, come all?"

Seeing her shake her head, he took the next step. Pushing aside her coffee cup, he picked up her hand in his. He wasn't above a little pleading himself.

"Is this what you want, Holly? Someone just tried to kill you."

"No," she said, emphatic. "They wanted to scare me off. This isn't about me, Harris. It's about Ryan. Because they want to hurt him. Through me."

"Yeah, well, in the end, it's just about the same thing, right? Are you waiting for me to say it? To take charge and haul you out of here? Because I can. Hell, if that's what it's going to take, I'll be happy to."

But she didn't say anything, just dropped her gaze to look back at the articles and her notes. She'd written it out like some math problem. His sister needed to put the pieces together, turn them around in her head and make out their shape.

"You know what's right, here, Hol. You know what you have to do," he said, putting an exclamation point on the conversation.

"That's what Ryan wants. For me to leave. He said it was the sensible thing to do." But she was choking on the words.

"Hey. Sometimes, sensible is good," he told her.

She stood, taking another long look at the work she'd laid out on the table, using it like a Ouija board. "We go home." Saying what he wanted to hear.

She started gathering up the sheets of paper, fixing them into this nice neat pile. As if she'd made up her mind. Time to do the sensible thing.

It was one of those times Harris really hated being

able to read people. Hated the fact that despite his sister's promising words, he still couldn't catch his breath.

The candy dish crashed against the wall beside Daniel's head, just missing him.

"Jesus, Emma. Get a grip!"

"You almost killed her, Daniel!"

Emma flew at him, pounding him with her fists. Daniel grabbed her around her waist and swung her in a smackdown to the floor. They rolled across the living room, Daniel ending up on top.

"She was going to save us? Isn't that what you told me?" she said, screaming back his words to her. She couldn't believe they'd come here, full circle, to another place of death. "You begged me to help you!"

"It's okay, Emma." His voice had gone soft and sweet, but he still kept her pinned to the floor. "I know you're scared, but Holly is all right. Come on, Ems. We can make this work for us."

"Not this. No way."

Last night, Emma had been standing next to Daniel at the party when the reporter got the call. Someone at E.R. had tipped off the paper, and Gigi had been right on the story, cell phone in hand. When she'd asked Daniel for a comment on the bizarre coincidence of Holly's accident, Emma had heard every word, dying a little inside every time Daniel opened his mouth to answer the horrible reporter's questions. *My God, Gigi, it's like the past is repeating itself....*

"Give me a break here, Ems." He was looking at her with genuine surprise. "You really think I planned last night? Honey, you have to believe that wasn't me." Saying it with such sincerity. As if she'd be stupid enough to still believe him. "I would not put Holly on some crazy car ride like that. No way."

"Of course, you did it. You fuckhead!" She tried to put as much venom as she could in her voice. Tried to get him off her. "You told me you wanted to show them. Well, you showed them, all right. God, that I could be so stupid. This is all about Ryan and your chance to destroy him."

Emma hadn't slept last night, knowing what she had to do. At the same time she was so very afraid. After she'd read the morning paper, she'd come straight to Daniel's place, trying to plead with him to stop. But all she'd gotten out of him were these stupid denials.

She'd always known Nina's death burned inside him. That's why she'd been so scared to tell the truth those years back, only too happy to continue Daniel's fantasy that it was all Ryan's fault. But now this...

"You're not God, Daniel. Messing with people's lives—"

"I talked to her first thing this morning. She's absolutely fine."

"Listen to me, Daniel," she said. She wasn't helping Holly, losing it like this. She had to keep control. "For once in your selfish life, listen. If that car had gone over, her brother would be planning a funeral right now."

For an instant, she saw a spark of conscience in his eyes. She pushed a little harder. "It's gone far enough, right? Time to stop. To leave Ryan alone."

But it was the wrong thing to say. "Jesus, don't you get it?" Every speck of doubt vanished as he rose to his feet. "This wasn't me, Ems. This was Ryan. He killed Nina and now he's going to kill Holly."

"Who do you think you're talking to, Daniel?" She jumped to her feet, following him into the next room. "Ryan did this? When Holly has been your gig from the first? I can't think of a better way to screw with your cousin than to make him relive what was possibly the worst day of his life.''

He turned on her, his face in a tight smile, almost enjoying the moment. ''Well, here's another scenario for you, darling. Ryan makes sure my golden girl runs away scared. You don't think it was a little convenient, him being there to save the day? Like I could plan that?'' He shook his head. ''He did this. He kills my project and gets the girl. What could be more perfect?''

''Only, the whole business has you written all over it, Dan. Didn't I overhear your stamp of approval when you talked to that reporter? Ryan goes down and you get publicity for Cutty House. All wrapped up in a nice neat bow.''

''If he confesses—''

''For something he didn't do!''

''He's guilty—''

''Not of Nina's murder, Daniel. Not that.''

''What does it fucking matter what he really did?'' Screaming now, out of control. ''He deserves whatever is coming. He stole what was mine. Doesn't that mean a goddamn thing to you?''

She shook her head, seeing it all slip away. *My fault. All of this. All my fault.*

She threw her arms around him, hugging him, whispering feverishly, ''She's a trap, Dan. Nina has always been a trap. Let her go. Let Holly go. Do it for me, Daniel.'' She reached up, holding his face in her hands to keep his attention. ''We'll go off on our own. I've never asked you to choose, but I'm asking now. Leave this funeral past. Be with me.''

Because it's what she had to do. Like paying a debt. She couldn't have Harris. *All my fault.* She and Daniel deserved each other.

But Daniel only pushed her hands away. He wasn't going to choose her, she could see it in his eyes. Maybe she'd known all along. Maybe that's what Harris was all about. *You're on the wrong side....*

She stared at him, seeing that nothing was ever going to be the same. "You're doomed, Daniel. Maybe we both are. You just haven't figured it out yet."

She walked to the door, but Daniel wasn't giving her the last word.

"Do you remember what it was like for me?" he yelled at her. "My mother was one of them, dammit! But what was I? Their hired help. How many times did I see that bastard throw away what I wanted most? As if it were nothing? Because, hell, to him, it was nothing. He never had to beg for a thing in his life. Not like me."

"All this time," she said softly, "I thought he'd wronged you somehow. That if what we were doing— bringing Holly here to fix the past—hurt him, that was okay in some strange way. But now I see that all Ryan ever did was be born the only child of Samuel and Vanessa Cutty." She shook her head. "That's not a crime, Dan. You of all people should know better than to blame someone for the circumstances of their birth."

She walked out of the apartment. She was in the hallway when he grabbed her from behind, his fingers digging into her arm, a murderous gleam in his eyes as he jerked her around.

She stared up at him, defiant. "Are you going to hit me? Right here for all your ritzo neighbors to see? Big macho Daniel, on top again? Come on, Dan. Take a whack. You want the publicity, don't you?"

Hit me, dammit. She wanted to hurt on the outside as much as she hurt on the inside.

But Daniel took a step back, dropping her arm. She didn't bother to wait for his apology, never looking back even when he called her name.

You're on the wrong side.

That's what Harris had told her.

Only, he hadn't figured out that she'd always been on the wrong side. From the time she'd been ten years old and saw Daniel walk into the kitchen wearing his new waiter's uniform.

All those emotions, so powerful and dangerous. And Nina had known how to take advantage of it. She'd always known. Even now, dead all these years, Nina still had the last laugh.

28

Holly sat in Daniel's office, her legs crossed at the ankles. She was perched on the leather chair in front of his desk, listening to Daniel's version of the facts. She was thinking she should feel something, anything. But even the pain where she'd hit her head seemed muffled, as if the injury had happened weeks ago and what she felt was just a memory.

Daniel had come around to stand beside her, not wanting any barriers between them. Listening to him, she was struck by how different the story sounded coming from him. But then, everyone had their point of view, and now here was Daniel giving his. Only, Holly was having trouble remembering the words, wasn't paying strict attention.

She wondered if the wrapped-in-cotton sensation came from lack of sleep. Or the concussion, maybe? The doctors had given all these instructions. *If you feel faint or nauseated.* They'd given her pills. But the funny thing was, she didn't feel a thing.

"You still with me, Holly?" Daniel asked, catching on to her lack of affect.

"Of course."

She'd come to Cutty House to meet with Daniel one last time. It probably wasn't the smartest move. It's like Harris had told her after Daniel called her at the apartment asking to meet. *Do you really expect him to confess, Hol?*

But Daniel had insisted on one last chance to plead his case. You can't convict a man without at least hearing him out. That was Daniel's take on things.

He wanted to talk. Only, Holly had come to believe that, with a man like Daniel, words seemed more than useless. They were perhaps even a hindrance. She couldn't know if he was lying because, basically, everything about him was an act. *Welcome to the Daniel East show....*

"I can appreciate that in your mind I'm the chief suspect," he told her, looking only too sincere. A slight frown, a purse of the lips, a pregnant pause well rehearsed. "Now honey, you know I couldn't do that to you."

She tried to stop seeing everything he did as a production number, but he even had the blocking down. Walk earnestly downstage, turn to look back at the audience.

"Let's talk motive," he said, coming around to her again. "I hired you to save my ass. I need Cutty House to survive. And I can't get there from here without you, see? You think I'd put that at stake? Me? Greedy little Danny—"

She held up her hand, suddenly tired of playing the audience. *Let's skip the dog and pony show, shall we?* "The accident," she said. "The driver said my brother sent him."

"And I'm the only one who knows Harris is the magic word for you?" He clucked his tongue. "It doesn't take a rocket scientist to figure out you'd trust someone if they claimed your brother arranged for a car to take you home."

"An interesting choice of words, Daniel."

The driver's exact words: *Your brother arranged for a car to take you home.*

But his face gave nothing away. Standing there in his *GQ* best, the man was the picture of earnest. Holly shut her eyes, trying not to put a big check mark on Daniel. *Shake off the fog, Holly. Focus.*

"Whoever put me in that car knew about the party," she said, making her point. "That Ryan and I would both be there. That I might want to leave in a hurry."

"And I'm the best candidate? Was I even the reason you were, how did you put it, leaving in a hurry?" Bringing her back to Ryan, the shady character of this particular drama.

But Holly had her own theories. "Daniel, what about the article in the paper this morning?"

Finally, the lightbulb flashed on. He dropped her hands, stepping back, actually pulling off an expression of surprise.

"You think I set up the accident for publicity?" He took another step back, as if putting distance between himself and the accusation. "I admit to being a publicity whore, but even I stop at attempted murder. Look, when I saw you with Ryan, I let my emotions get away from me...." The words trailed off, silence his new friend. "I guess what I'm trying to say is, I never gave up on you, Holly. Even when the chips were down and your firm bankrupt. Don't you give up on me."

But she was shaking her head, not going down that garden path with Daniel. The truth was, she'd come here exactly to give up—on Daniel and just about everything else she'd been holding on to. She'd promised Harris that she'd tell Daniel she was leaving. *Giving in, giving up.*

Which made it kind of interesting that she hadn't even broached the subject yet, hadn't even suggested this might be the end. Instead, she'd let Daniel do all the talking.

"A lot is going on right now." She tripped over the words, knowing it was all wrong. *Time to throw in the towel, Holly.* "There's so much to think about."

So just say it, tell him you're leaving.

The words stuck in her throat.

"I understand," he said, sensing her weakness, using it now in his defense. "I just want you to be careful. After last night…well, things are getting a little more exciting than I'd like, okay?"

"I'll let you know what I decide," she said. It was the best she could do—a hint that she might not return.

Fifteen minutes later, she was in her office staring at the plans she'd drafted for Cutty House. Of course, she'd let her brother down, she hadn't gotten the job done. And still, there was this curious lack of emotion. She wasn't even worried about what would happen when she arrived back at the apartment to face the music. And she should be. She'd let Harris believe she'd come here to give notice. Knowing her brother, he'd be on the Internet pricing fares.

And there was no excuse. Not really. She *should* leave. Today. This minute. Cutty House wasn't a failure like the episode with Drew, letting him wrestle the business and marriage away from her because she'd been unwilling to fight. This wasn't a fight. Not anymore.

She had to leave those unanswered questions. All of it. Even Ryan, whom she was putting in danger by staying.

Harris was right.

You can't fix this, Hol.
Maybe no one could.

Harris hadn't expected Emma. He hadn't made any plans to confront her. It was like he'd told Holly that morning. Sometimes it's best just to walk away.

But there she was, waiting for him at the bar.

It was early lunch, with the place surprisingly doing a brisk business. He came over to sit beside her. It was almost interesting how he felt nothing, just all dead inside.

"I called the bar," she said. "They told me you were expected."

He nodded, never taking his eyes off her. She was this beautiful creature, Emma. Petite and blond, with green eyes that were judiciously avoiding his. Hard to imagine her being involved in what had happened to his sister. But that was a man for you, a walking, talking libido.

"I heard what happened to Holly." She really couldn't look at him, not a good sign. "I just wanted to say how sorry—"

"Here's how it's going to be, Emma. Last night some man told my sister I'd hired him to drive her home. She got in his car and was almost killed in some bizarre reenactment of Nina's death. Unfortunately, you had something to do with that. So tell me everything, or leave. Right now."

He was good with the ultimatums. Old tomatoes, Holly used to call them. *Don't throw your old tomatoes at me, Harris.*

Emma stared down at her hands on the bar. "It's not…it's not like that." She shook her head, fighting some internal battle. "It's not so simple." She spoke so softly, he could barely hear her.

He took her hand and squeezed a little. "Emma, listen to me."

She looked up, her eyes full of tears.

"It is incredibly simple," he said. "You tell the truth. I can't think of anything simpler than that."

He hadn't meant to sound as if he'd already branded her the enemy. But he'd known all along who she'd choose even before she looked away.

She slid off the stool and walked out of the bar. She never even glanced back. Not once.

He hadn't wanted it to be Emma. Anybody but her.

He slammed his hand on the counter. "Shit." And then harder, another time, so that it hurt. "Shit!"

Lieutenant Inspector Amy Garten did him the favor of calling before she left the station, giving him the heads up that she was coming out to the vineyard.

Ryan watched her get out of the car and look around. She'd aged well, the lieutenant. He understood she'd gone up in the ranks and was now the Chief of Homicide. As she walked toward him, he could see she'd maintained that professional edge you had to admire, even when you were sitting on the wrong side of a question from her. It must come in handy, he thought, when interrogating suspects.

That would be him, of course. The suspect.

She'd told him that someone had phoned in a tip about the accident last night. She had some information she thought might be of interest to him. She'd come to tell Ryan in person what she'd found.

Which meant she wanted to see his reaction, the guilty man's expression when faced with the facts.

"Long drive up," she said, starting in casually. "Pretty here. I should bring my husband sometime."

She smiled. "Beats the homicide detail any day of the week."

"Why don't we talk in my office," he said, making it easier for her.

Inside, he didn't know what to expect as he offered her a chair, then leaned up against his desk. Maybe a tape recorder slapped on the desk, a flash of her badge and his Miranda rights. Other than reporting the vehicle abandoned on the highway, neither he nor Holly had gotten around to talking to the police. But he figured with the story in the paper this morning, it was just a matter of time.

Interesting that he didn't feel the least bit worried about it. More like resigned, as if this would always be his life. Nina and the murder merry-go-round. A bad tape looping over and over.

But as it turned out there wasn't a tape recorder. Instead, the detective took out her card and placed it on the desk. Folding her hands in front of her, she told him, "I think you're being set up, Mr. Cutty. I pretty much reached the same conclusion the last time around."

He stared at her, caught off guard as she slid the card toward him. The lieutenant had this look. *Gotcha.* She pointed to his chair behind the desk. Picking up her card, he took a seat and waited to hear the rest.

"We found the abandoned Town Car. The vehicle was reported stolen this morning from a limo service. The car was tricked up with all the bells and whistles and then some. The perfect car for the job. Whoever did this was a real pro. He didn't leave a trace."

She leaned forward, making sure she had eye contact. "You have an enemy, Mr. Cutty," she told him. "Someone out there is trying to repeat the past, maybe revive the investigation for their own reasons. Whoever is playing these games is wasting my time and yours. Not to mention that they're dangerous.''

But Ryan was thinking about the report Holly had shown him in the tasting room; the information in that folder pointed the finger squarely at him. ''Why the change of heart, Lieutenant? If there was evidence that some other car forced Nina off the road, why are you so sure it wasn't me? Why did you drop the charges in the first place?''

Because, back then, continuing the investigation might have come up with another name. Someone other than Ryan. Someone who could hurt Holly now.

The lieutenant looked at him with mild surprise. ''We dropped the charges because there was no evidence that a car forced Nina Travers off that road.''

And when he shook his head, about to tell her he'd seen the report, she added, ''Here's what the crime scene investigation came up with, Mr. Cutty, a little something that wasn't released to the press or anyone outside of the investigation. Nina wasn't alone in that car. There was someone with her. And unless you could be in two places at once, that someone wasn't you.''

He could feel his heart kick up in his chest. ''I don't understand.''

''We found two sets of fingerprints on the steering wheel, among other things. The theory went that Nina fought someone for control of the car. Maybe it was an accident?'' She shrugged. ''Maybe the owner of those prints wanted the car to careen off the road with Nina still inside. We never identified the prints. Unless someone has a record, it's not always so easy.'' She let him fill in the blanks. ''But here's what we do know—those prints weren't yours.''

He was trying to make sense of what she'd just said,

trying to figure out how this theory that no one had talked about could exist. "I've never heard anything about this."

The lieutenant stood, looking as though she'd had her say. "Nina Travers was driving erratically. The conclusion my boss came to at the time—to tie a nice little bow on the case—was alcohol and Valium. And sure as heck she had enough in her system, as well as a few other goodies."

She gave him a moment to reflect so that he could put together in his head what she was leaving out. They couldn't pin Nina's death on him and they had no other suspects. And here was Nina with all this shit in her system. Why cloud up the picture with mystery prints they couldn't trace? Case closed.

"But now you're in charge," he said, rising to his feet.

She nodded. "You should know it is my firm belief that your fiancée was murdered, Mr. Cutty. There was someone in that car with Nina Travers. Maybe it's not too late to find out who."

She made her way to the door where she turned, as if she had just remembered something. But he'd known all along that she wasn't through.

"Mr. Cutty, in my line of work, we look for a little thing called motive. Someone wanted Nina Travers dead. And after this much time, I think you know more about why that might be than I'm ever going to find out on my own." Garten broke out her first genuine smile. "Who else would have a better reason to help me discover the truth than the man who almost took the blame? That's my little theory on these things. It works sometimes. Really."

She pointed to the card now back on his desk. "You know my number if you think of anything."

Ryan stared at the door. He felt nailed to the spot, couldn't move. He was trying to figure something out. That folder Holly had shown him—those reports he'd read. None of it gelled with what Garten had just told him.

There was someone in that car with Nina.

Last night, leaving Holly with her brother, he thought he knew what he was doing. Back to the status quo before Holly. He didn't believe in fairy tales, didn't believe that you could look across a crowded room and find love. That was Holly with her theories. How had she said it? *I think I picked you.* Well, he had to be realistic. He couldn't just welcome her with open arms into his nightmare.

And now this.

Only, before he could work it out in his head—the next step, the right direction—the office door opened again, slamming back in a violent motion. Gil stepped through.

"That was her," he said, red-faced and catching his breath. "The inspector from before. When Nina died."

Gil stumbled forward so that Ryan jumped to his feet to help him. Gil rested both hands on Ryan's desk, his eyes wide and wild as he looked up at Ryan.

"It's about Nina, isn't it?" Gil prompted him when Ryan stayed silent. "Something's happened."

He loved Gil like a father. For the last twelve years, the focus of his life had been here, trying to make it okay for Gil since he'd lost Nina. With all his heart, he'd wanted to keep Gil safe.

Only now, he wasn't so sure that he'd done the right thing. Working here, hiding here. Maybe it hadn't been all about Gil. Maybe he'd been the one who wanted to stay safe, escaping that Cutty legacy, just like he'd told Daniel. Only, he hadn't sailed off into the sunset. He'd come here, to Viña Dorada.

And now he felt at a crossroads. He was pushing Holly away, but again, he wasn't sure why.

What was he keeping them safe from? The truth?

"Sit down, Gil," he said, pulling the chair toward him, helping him to take a seat. "We have a lot to talk about."

29

Holly was thinking that life was full of surprises. Maybe she should get used to that and learn to expect the unexpected.

The last five years in particular had been a merry-go-round of "surprise!" One after the other, she ticked them off: Holly, hot new associate at a top firm sliding into a bankrupt marriage and business; über-provider Harris walking out on his job; Daniel coming to the rescue; Cutty House and Nina.

She thought she should get a handle on these little bombshells, not be so out of sync with those darned bolts out of the blue. But when Ryan came up behind her, there she was, almost dropping everything, her case, the plans she'd been carting home from Cutty House.

Taking the plans from her, he guided her to his car, not saying a word. He'd parked the Aston Martin at the curb, the motor still running as if he'd been waiting for just this, for Holly to come down the steps of Cutty House. *Surprise!*

She thought he'd given up. Last night at the hospital, he'd almost said as much with each look, every touch. Everything he'd done spelled it out clearly: The End.

Only, here she was buckling her seat belt as he shifted into gear, which brought her back to the idea that life was full of surprises. And some were actually good, like the possibility that a happy ending with Ryan could still be in the works. All that hope springing eternal.

"I had a visitor today," he told her. "It's been twelve years since I've had the pleasure of Lieutenant Garten's company. She's aged well, by the way."

She reached down, grabbing the armrest on the Aston Martin, trying not to distract him during his Mario Andretti routine as he screeched through an illegal turn, heading out of town.

"The Town Car? It was reported stolen," he continued in what passed for a calm voice. "No leads, of course. But here's the interesting part. She had this idea, the inspector. Brilliant, really. Get this. She doesn't think I killed Nina."

He shook his head, the marvel of it all. Then he glanced at Holly. "But she thinks someone did. Murder her, that is."

The next turn defied the law of physics. She made good use of the armrest, trying not to lean into the door.

Ryan continued, "Those papers from the investigation you gave me, the ones someone left like a present on your desk? They don't quite mesh with Garten's theory. In fact, they all but contradict what the lieutenant assures me is the real story. According to Garten, there wasn't any evidence that Nina was forced off the road by me or anyone else."

It didn't take her long to put it together. "Someone doctored the papers they left on my desk?"

He nodded, his eyes now straight ahead. "I kept wondering about that when I was reading the report. I mean, I was there that night, right? I would have seen if another car was around. But there wasn't another car—just me and Nina.''

She felt this enormous weight float off her chest, to be replaced by another. ''Someone wanted me to think you were guilty.''

''Not a stretch of the imagination, by any means. But there's this other thing Garten told me, something not released to the press or anyone not directly involved with the investigation. They found a second set of prints at the crime scene. The theory is that someone was in that car with Nina, someone who fought for control of the steering wheel.''

He steered the car so that the tires made an awful squealing sound, letting him know to concentrate. He didn't talk after that.

Holly sat back for the ride as she thought about this new revelation. *Someone was in that car with Nina...fought for control of the steering wheel.* The information basically exonerated Ryan, and might even douse that conflagration of guilt he'd been feeding all these years. Because if someone wanted Nina dead, Ryan had no part in that. The accident was no longer something he alone put into play.

She looked at Ryan, wondering how he must feel, and knew she could take a good guess. They'd been on this emotional merry-go-round together the last few weeks.

In the end, Holly thought she might be getting a hold on the surprise thing. Her heart didn't even speed up when Ryan took them back to Highway One, eventually pulling over at the site of Nina's accident. Or maybe it was all relative. When she thought about it, the blood pounding at her temples, she knew that the adrenaline rush just couldn't get much higher.

He pulled out the keys and slammed out of the car. She gave it a beat, then climbed out to follow him.

He was standing in the dim light of dusk, the wind in his hair, the clouds overhead burning with the sunset. A flock of seagulls caught the same fire, looking like so many sparks rising. Standing there, he could have been some romantic hero—Heathcliff on the moors. She took a moment just to watch him, knowing right then why she hadn't told Daniel it was time to throw in the towel.

When she stepped up beside him, she slipped her hand into his.

"I'm not afraid," she said.

He seemed to appreciate the comment. Closing his eyes, he released a deep breath, the sound of it coming out like a sigh.

"My whole life there's been someone pulling the strings. And I felt it, you know. I knew the strings were there. I just figured that was part of the deal, part of the family obligation. You're the last of the Cuttys, Ryan, so carry on. Even when they set up a marriage for me, I figured, why not?"

He shook his head, disbelieving. She felt as if she were back in the car, the wheels squealing on the next turn.

"I was thinking about what it might mean," he told her. "My whole life these people told me what to do, then I disappeared into the vineyard after Nina died, believing that maybe—even a little more than maybe—her dying was my fault. So I needed to step in and help Gil. And for the next twelve years, it was all about the vineyard for me."

"And then I show up," she said, finishing his line of reasoning. "Just another string being pulled." She turned to him. "That's what Harris believed from the first. He never trusted Daniel and all the good fortune that he was sending our way.''

She could see the anger in his eyes—and something else. An energy, a challenge. ''Your brother has good instincts.''

''You have no idea. The guy reads minds. Really. He could take his act on the road.''

He didn't touch her, almost as if he thought it might not be fair, that somehow he might tilt the scales in his favor and she'd make a bad choice.

Still not looking at her, he said, ''Holly, someone killed Nina that night, and they might want to hurt you because of me. Maybe this isn't over yet?''

Taking his face in her hands, she kissed him, cutting off further doubts. When she thought she'd made her point clear, she stepped back, glad to see that, this time, he wasn't looking anywhere but at her.

''Some things,'' she said, ''I get a say in, right?''

He nodded, touching her now, stroking her hair. ''Yeah, but be sure, Holly. Be very sure.''

''You know what's really interesting?'' she told him, again going with her instincts. ''I don't think I was ever anything but.''

He took her back to his place. He could tell it had been a long time for Holly. For him, too. Because he'd never made love with his heart before, he knew how important every minute could be and he slowed her down when she'd speed them up.

''Not yet,'' he said, when she started to unbutton his jeans. ''Lay down.'' Pressing her to the bed.

He felt as if he was in a trance. It was the only way he could make those voices in his head shut up— *you'll get her killed, too!* He managed to keep them to a dull roar, background noise, as they explored each other.

"Is it strange," she asked, "being with me?"

He shook his head, kissing her. "I was nineteen. We were just kids. This is different."

And it felt different. No one had ever looked at him with such luminous eyes, showing that much desire, not hiding a thing. And she smelled so good. He couldn't remember thinking that about any other woman. Her smell was driving him crazy.

"Did you know that most wines taste a little rough when you first bottle them?" He unbuttoned her blouse, then slipped it over her shoulders. The cuffs of the sleeves caught on her wrists. He used them to trap her hands behind her as he kissed her neck. "As they age, they lose some of their roughness." He placed a hand on her stomach, felt her tremble at the touch. "Some quickly, some take years."

"Are you trying to tell me that you hope I'll age well?"

He smiled and turned her so that she lay alongside him. "The better ones," he whispered in her ear, "always take longer."

"Oh."

Ryan took his time.

Eventually, they lay naked together on the bed facing each other. He brought her up on his lap, Holly's legs coming around his hips, putting Ryan deep inside her. Connected like that, they never stopped looking at each other, never closed their eyes. When he felt her release, he knew he'd found this moment of suspended time. Finally, a feeling of peace, as if he'd waited a lifetime to find her and at long last here she was. Like a magic trick. As if they'd marked each other in some way. *Mine at last.*

He whispered against her mouth, "Mine." The right one.

"Too late," she said, opening her mouth over his. "I picked you first."

They made love twice before they dropped back exhausted on the bed, with the sheets bunched around their legs. Eventually the breeze from the open window brought goose bumps and Ryan reached for the covers, Holly cuddling against him. He lay with one arm around her, staring up at the ceiling, all these ideas rushing through his head—his conversation with Gil, the revelations of the lieutenant and Holly most of all. He thought about how much he wanted her, like a man should want a woman—forever. He could see a house at the vineyard for them and the babies they'd share with Marta and Gil.

Holding her, her breath against his chest, it all seemed so perfect and complete.

But the shadows were still there. The fear. She didn't know everything. And he had to tell her.

"I think my father killed her," he whispered so he wouldn't wake her if she was asleep.

He felt her tense in his arms. *Awake then.*

"They were having an affair," he said, admitting the worst. "Nina was going to tell my mother."

She leaned up. He could see the questions in her eyes. But he cut off the doubts. "Nina was pregnant. She told me that night the baby was Samuel's. That he would leave Vanessa and they'd have the baby and she'd make sure he'd cut us all off."

Her eyes reminded him of the water outside, dark and shimmering with the moonlight. "You think it was Samuel in the car with her?"

"The fingerprints, yeah. They wouldn't have any reason to compare his to the ones they found. Not unless they knew about the affair, and I didn't volunteer the information. No way. I couldn't do that to Gil, not with him in the hospital holding on by a thread. Samuel didn't drink back then. He was…in control. A lot like Daniel, actually.''

He stroked her hair, liking the feel of it. She had amazing hair. Which went right along with all the other amazing things about her, like the fact that she'd never given up on the idea of being together, pushing this miracle of her into his arms.

''Nina was angry,'' she said after a while. ''She was going to use your family to hurt you because she was hurting.''

He nodded. ''Nina wouldn't have known about my mother and father. Samuel would never just walk out on Vanessa Moore. Even if he'd loved Nina, he lacks that kind of will. But I don't think he loved her. I think she was part of his weakness, his idea that he deserved her—like my grandfather's fortune. He took it in stride that it was his due. And if he lost it, so what? It was his, right? But Nina would be different. His best friend's daughter—his son's fiancée. Even my father could feel shame. And he'd be plenty worried about what would happen if word got out.''

She settled into the crook of his arm as if she were cold. They were chilling facts he was telling her, that someone could sleep with his son's future bride and then kill her.

''I think it was an accident,'' he said. ''Or maybe at the last minute he wanted her to die, because it would make everything easier if she were out of the picture. No one would ever know about them, about the baby. Hell, even if there was some kind of paternity test, what would it show? Things weren't so sophisticated back then. He's my father, after all. We share the same genes. After we fought, she had time to find him and tell him.''

''Could he really do something so horrible?'' she asked, the shock clear in her voice.

''Maybe. Since the day she died, he's been trying to kill himself. The drinking is why he lost the business and why my mother brought Daniel in to take over. Samuel just didn't care anymore.''

It was as if he'd opened the floodgates. He couldn't stop talking, just telling her everything. ''I was the one who found her in the car. She was behind the wheel, like a broken doll, no seat belt or air bag deployed. She hit her head on the driver's side window. The whole window had shattered. She was still alive, so I didn't move her. Just called 911.''

He'd never talked like this before, never had someone to share his dark secrets with, and it felt good. At the same time, he worried that she'd given in too easily, putting herself into the drama of his life without knowing what she was taking on. And still, he couldn't stop.

''The first time I saw you,'' he said, ''I was scared. I thought that, somehow, you showing up would bring it all back. That Gil would find out about Nina and my father. His daughter pregnant with his best friend's kid. He'd have another stroke and that would be the end of that.''

She met his gaze. ''Maybe you didn't give Gil enough credit. Maybe he's stronger now.''

''Funny you should say that. Those were Gil's exact words. We talked after the lieutenant showed up at the vineyard. He burst into my office demanding to know what the police wanted. For the first time, I knew I had to tell him. Not everything, not about my father— but that there were other men in her life. That someone might have wished her harm to keep their affair secret. And that the police were looking into that possibility.''

He blew out a breath remembering how calm Gil had been. Sad, but calm.

''He asked me if the baby was even mine. All this time I was trying to protect him, and he asked me right out. Didn't even blink.''

''What did you say?''

''The truth. That I didn't think so. That I was always careful, taking precautions. Because, even then, I wasn't sure about the marriage.''

''That must have been hard for him to hear.''

''God, yes. But I think he understood. He said it was the drugs. The autopsy showed alcohol and Valium, but that wasn't all she did. Not by a long shot. He knew she'd been having problems, but he couldn't seem to reach her. He thought things would change if she settled down, got married and had some children. But she never got that chance.''

He spooned her into him, kissed her neck and closed his eyes, just holding her for a second. He'd told Gil how sorry he was and how much he wished he could have set Nina back on the straight and narrow. In the end, Ryan had only added to the problem, taking her to parties, then making sure she got home all right. Enabling her.

''At first, I really loved that edge about her. I mean, we hadn't seen each other since we were kids. Then I come back from school and she's all grown up. Daring, and with this great spirit. She could take over a room. Only, it got to be too much. Out of control. Eventually, I just didn't want to play anymore, so I called it off. And then she got into that car.''

''You didn't kill her, Ryan.''

But he was shaking his head, not so sure she understood. "Even now, I wonder if it's okay, this thing between you and me. Or will it start all over again, the past repeating itself? That's why I pushed you away. I thought if I toed the line, you'd be safe—but I don't really believe that anymore. I don't know who's pulling the strings, I just know it's time to find out—and to stop them."

He'd left so much unsaid. The part about loving her. How he'd felt when he'd seen that car parked at the edge of the highway, knowing she was inside. That making love to her had felt like finding some missing half.

But he didn't know how to say that they should be together any better. She wasn't Nina, and he wasn't the kid who'd let Nina die. He was just a man who wanted Holly more than he should, more than was good for either of them. And he couldn't find the words to tell her.

"I'm not going anywhere," she whispered.

He smiled. And she thought it was only her brother who read minds?

The next morning, he woke up to find Holly dressed in one of his shirts—sexy as hell. She stood in front of his gas grill feeding what looked like strips of her architectural plans into the flames.

Watching her, it was still a shock, how he felt. As if his heart was going to burst just looking at her, he wanted her so much. But at the same time he kept waiting for the other shoe to drop. *What next?*

"Not one for sleeping in?" he asked from the sliding glass door.

She turned around and smiled. That smile was one of the things that always made her look so different from Nina.

He realized that there would come a day when he'd stop making the comparison, and that it would be all about Holly. In time, she wouldn't even look like Nina. They'd grow old together. Things would change. He found himself looking forward to the changes.

She gave him a kiss and turned in his arms so that they both faced the flames.

"I've always wanted to wear a guy's shirt with nothing underneath. They make it look so sexy in the movies."

He kissed her on the neck. "It is sex personified." He nodded over her shoulder at the grill. "What's this?"

"A ceremonial burning of my flying buttress."

He gave her a look. "Okay. I'll bite. Flying what?"

"My safety net," she explained. "If it ever really was that. Those are the plans for Cutty House. I had them with me when you picked me up yesterday."

"That seems like an awful lot of work going up in flames."

"It's only symbolic." She sighed, easing back into him. "Everything is on disk back at my office."

He thought about what that meant, that she was burning the plans. When she turned to look at him, he thought it was a little awe-inspiring, that he could feel so much without even touching her.

"I came out here this morning to think about why I stayed," she told him. "I didn't want to fail again. I mean, after the bankruptcy, I basically decided that all hope was lost. I'd made the sign of the cross over my career, you see. And then Daniel showed up."

"Your own personal fairy godmother."

He liked making her smile and he made a mental note to do it more often.

"Something like that, yes." She sighed, staring at

the flames. "And it was a wonderful opportunity. Only, it was never real."

They watched the fire silently. It was a little cool that morning. The water made the air moist. He put his arms around her, trying to keep her comfortable.

"Ryan? When was the last time you went sailing?"

He sighed, holding her close. "Twelve years ago, Holly. Never after that."

When the flames died into embers, she kissed him. Without saying another word, she took his hand and guided him back to bed. This time when they made love, it was Holly who whispered in his ear, "Mine."

"Ditto," he told her, starting all over again.

Ryan woke up an hour later, again to an empty bed. He thought it was strange how he was already used to her there beside him, as if he'd been holding the spot for her, saving her place. When he woke up and she wasn't there, their arms and legs tangled together, the bed felt empty and cold.

This time, he found her in the kitchen dialing the phone. Seeing him, she smiled but she didn't stop what she was doing.

He thought maybe she was calling her brother, letting him know that they were on their way over, giving him the heads up so Harris could be waiting with the shotgun at the door. Because, heck, it's not like the guy was going to feel all warm and fuzzy about Holly's decision to fight alongside her man.

Only, it turned out it wasn't her brother she was calling. Instead, he heard her say into the phone, "Daniel?"

She waited a moment, letting Daniel have his say

on the other end. Finally, her eyes never leaving Ryan's, she finished the call with the simplest of statements.

"I quit."

30

The world had become a very confusing place for Samuel Cutty. Guiding the steering wheel, he thought about how, lately, things would get all mixed up in his head, how he couldn't tell the difference anymore between the past and the present.

It had happened this morning with Vanessa, the perfect lady. She'd been screaming at him in a rage, crying and screaming until she'd dropped to the floor weeping. Just like that day with Nina.

She said she'd gotten a call. That she knew the truth. Screaming her threats.

"I swear to God, I'll kill you. I'll kill you both."

When she looked at him, her expression—the fit of rage—was so unlike his manicured wife. That was the confusing part. It made him think of the night of the accident and how Vanessa had screamed then, threatening him.

You've ruined me, Samuel. You and your lust. And you betrayed our child. Have you no shame?

He'd taken a minute to try and figure out what to say. To imagine that he was somehow hallucinating, so no response was needed. In the end, he'd denied everything. Just like before.

How could she know? Even with Vanessa standing

in front of him, screaming about Nina, he couldn't quite remember the where and when of it.

And now, she would ruin everything, the same way she'd done twelve years ago.

The first time he and Nina had made love, she'd come to him. It was a little shocking, an eighteen-year-old girl wanting him. A girl who was his best friend's daughter and his son's fiancée. Shocking and exciting.

Afterward, when he'd asked why, she'd said he was more mature than Ryan, that she'd wanted a real man. All along, it had been him, not Ryan.

Later, she'd tell him he was old and gross and she didn't want him to touch her. Didn't he understand she'd made a mistake that first time? *Don't you get it, you stupid old man? I was completely wasted. I thought you were Ryan!*

So he'd beg her. He'd buy her gifts. Whatever he had to do. Didn't she understand how much he loved her?

He still had to beg sometimes. Still had to buy her expensive presents.

He staggered up the steps to the apartment. She didn't tell him he was old anymore. She could be kind, even.

He remembered wanting to die when he found out about the accident. And even though Nina was alive, waiting for him up those stairs, he still wanted to die remembering that night. Wanted to drink until he was incoherent, get in his car and drive right off the cliff where he'd lost her, finishing what he'd started so many years ago.

But she hadn't died, right? She was here for him now. Today. That's why Vanessa had been in a rage this morning. *You've ruined me, Samuel. You and your lust.* Making him think of the past, confusing him.

He was still wondering about the strange juxtaposition—the past alongside the present—when Nina opened the door. She was dressed in shorts and a T-shirt, looking just as young as the day she died.

"Sammy. What a surprise. But I'm not ready for you, love. Come on in. I'll just be a minute."

A good day, then, he thought, shuffling inside. A day he wouldn't have to beg.

When Ryan and Holly drove up to her apartment, Daniel was already waiting outside.

He was resting against the hood of his Bentley, arms crossed, dressed casually in jeans and a T-shirt. Holly could see that his hair was still wet from a shower. She almost didn't recognize him; she'd never seen him wear anything without a designer label.

He'd snagged a good parking spot at the restaurant across the street. Only, the expression on his face was full of rage when he saw Ryan.

"Wait here," Ryan told her, double-parking.

Closing the door behind him, he jogged into the street toward his cousin. He never even glanced back; he'd spoken without thought. *Wait here.*

She would, of course, stay put and wait for him, the man, to take care of things while she kept out of harm's way. Let the boys work it out.

"Right," she said, climbing out of the car to follow.

By the time she reached them, Daniel was pacing on the sidewalk. He moved like a cat, back and forth, tense and revved up. This morning when she'd called Daniel, she hadn't been afraid. Suddenly, that changed.

"I quit?" He spoke to Holly, ignoring Ryan for the moment. "Imagine what I'm thinking when I hear that? What did I do wrong? How can I fix this? Running over here like an idiot to talk it out."

He stopped, staring Ryan down, making it clear that he didn't like the fact that he was the problem.

"But I can't do anything about this, can I, Holly?" he asked. "This isn't about me and what I did. This is about Ryan and what he's been whispering in your ear."

"I didn't bother to whisper." Ryan stepped between Daniel and Holly. "I told her straight out. You put Holly in that car, Dan. Were you getting even with me after all these years by making me relive some nightmare past? Maybe you were trying to send me over the edge? How does that work for you, because I think it's a nice fit."

He shoved Daniel hard in the chest, taking his cousin by surprise so that Daniel lost his footing, stumbling against the building behind him.

"What were you thinking?" Everything Ryan felt was right there in his face. "You almost killed her, you bastard."

"So now I'm the villain of the story." Daniel's voice sounded deadly. "So Wonder Boy here wins again. Every fucking time. You—*effortlessly*—win." He tried to circle around, but Ryan stopped him, keeping him from reaching Holly. "And you're just going to hand it to him? Is that it? Does he get to win again?"

His words brought all her suspicions into focus. Just as Ryan suspected, the car ride had been some twisted plan to bring Ryan down. After all these years, Daniel was still working through his fears that he was the lesser man.

"I'm treated like shit in this family." Daniel was practically screaming, out of control in a way she'd never seen. "And do you know when finally, *finally,* I get my due?" He wasn't waiting for an answer. "When Cutty House becomes a piece of crap. When it's all gone to shit and Ryan's moved on to his vineyard and his other successes, I get the phone call for help. Look, Daniel, it's all yours now, this piece of shit!"

But Ryan wasn't having any of it. "No one's denying you got a raw deal. But bringing Holly here, putting her in danger? You don't have that right."

"You bet your ass I have the right." He jabbed his finger in the air in front of Ryan's face. "I didn't put the woman I loved in a car to watch her destroy herself."

Somehow, Daniel got around Ryan—only to be grabbed from behind so that Ryan kept him from reaching Holly. But that fire was still in his eyes.

"Yeah, sure," Daniel said, talking only to Holly. "I admit it. The plan was to mess with Ryan. Resurrect Nina. Get him to fucking confess what he did to her. But then you went and turned everything around—" the wonder of it in his voice "—so that I wasn't so sure anymore." Suddenly, financial success was better revenge.

"I thought that maybe this time, with your help, I could win." He wasn't fighting Ryan anymore. "I could see it, Holly. You made me see how you were going to save Cutty House, put me on top, give me that win because I'd found you. Not him. Me, Daniel East. I came to the rescue." He whipped around, pushing Ryan with both hands. "And now he gets to destroy that, too?"

"Forget it, Daniel." Ryan stood his ground. "She's out of here."

"So you win? You get away with it?"

"Get away with what, Daniel?"

"Killing her, dammit. Taking Nina from me."

"I didn't kill Nina—"

"Fucking a, you didn't kill her! Of course, you killed her! You and your damn father. She told me everything, Ryan. How you pushed her away, saying you didn't love her," he screamed. "She was crying her eyes out that night, you son of a bitch. Only, I said she'd be fine, see? Because, hell, she had me. I asked her to marry me right then, that very night. And do you know what she did? She laughed. She laughed at me, because she didn't want anything to do with me. She wanted the money, Ryan. The Cutty prestige. And if you couldn't give it to her, your father would. But not me. No way. I wasn't even in the picture. I was just some idiot she balled when she had some free time from you and Daddy. I wasn't…in the line of succession."

Even Ryan took a step back, shocked. "Jesus, Dan."

"You let her get in that car! You let her die!"

And that would always be his crime in Daniel's eyes. Holly could see that it wasn't about direct responsibility. Nina was dead and someone had to pay— preferably the son of a bitch who'd been a thorn in Daniel's side his whole life long.

"And now you get her, too?" Daniel shook his

head. The way he looked at Holly froze the blood in her veins.

"No way, Ryan," he said, walking away, but the threat lingered there in the air. "No fucking way."

31

"Nina?"

Samuel looked down at his hands. The blood. It was everywhere. He hadn't known the human body could have so much blood.

"Nina, please." He couldn't lose her again. "I need you."

How could a man be so unfortunate? How could life be this unfair?

He had no idea how long he knelt there beside her. The whole tragic chain of events seemed like a blur. The fight, the gun going off. *A bad dream.*

"That's right. A dream. Wake up, baby."

But even drunk, he knew. Nina was dead.

He tried to remember the details. The police would want to know everything. But he couldn't get the information to stay put in his head. The images buzzed around, a jumble. Making sense of anything seemed just out of reach.

And the police… The thought panicked him. Could he really call them after all these years? Tell them the truth?

But what did he really have to hide? Was there anything left to save now? Did anything matter to him if Nina was dead?

Still, when he picked up the phone, it wasn't the police he called. The machine picked up. He couldn't imagine what to do. He didn't have the cell phone number.

"Ryan?" Maybe he was there, screening his calls. Or he'd check his messages. God, the blood. He was covered in it.

"I'm in trouble, Ryan. Help me."

Emma had come to believe she was cursed. It was simple, really. She'd been trying to avoid taking responsibility for the past, and the bad luck of it just followed her.

She'd come to think of Daniel as her own special curse, and the title had never fit better than when she found him sitting in the living room of her apartment, waiting for her to return from her morning coffee run.

"Daniel." It shouldn't have surprised her that he'd come; he had a key. So he'd shown up unexpectedly after a fight? Big deal.

Only, he was sitting on the couch, stiff and straight, and his eyes seemed lit up from the inside. He was opening and closing his hands into fists.

"You have to stop him," he said. "Next time, he might kill her."

Those had been her exact words when she'd called the police after she'd heard about Holly's accident. Hearing Daniel repeat that message destroyed any hope that his coming here was a simple thing.

"Ryan Cutty didn't kill Nina, but someone thinks he should pay. Someone close to the family," he continued, giving her a hard stare but keeping his smile. "He wants to see Ryan suffer. That's why he's doing this. To get to Ryan." He stood, seeming to tower over her. "Did I get it right, honey?"

She felt her pulse jack up as he walked toward her. She had this idea that she should run while she still had the chance. But there was this other thought: Take responsibility.

"Are you going to tell the cops I killed Nina?" he asked. "Hmm? Because that's the only way they'll get the idea, right? You calling them. Just like you did the night Nina died."

She didn't know why she just stood there. She couldn't seem to move. *Take responsibility!* Couldn't say a word.

"I bet you thought you were so clever, calling the cops," he told her. "Only, I thought it was a little strange, the lieutenant coming by to talk to me yesterday. I mean, twelve years is a long time to be asking questions about the hired help. Not that she let anything slip. Not Garten. But I could smell it on her. The suspicion. And you'd be surprised. With a little money and the right questions, you can get just about anybody to talk. It didn't take long to hit pay dirt."

Finding the dirt was Daniel's specialty. With his charisma, who would even suspect him? That smile, his laugh. They would want to help him. What could it hurt to take his money and pass along a little information?

"Emma," he said, circling closer, sensing that she might bolt. "I am deeply disappointed."

He lunged for her.

Emma ducked under his arms, but he grabbed her jacket, pulling her back by the hood. She slipped one arm free, the jacket sliding half off before she ripped it from his hands. He was standing between her and the door, no longer smiling. She skipped back, turned and raced down the hall behind her.

He was going to kill her. She was sure of it.

She reached the bathroom, shut the door and locked it. She slipped on the tile and toppled to the floor. Her

purse skidded to a stop against the bathtub, bursting
open. Scooting away from the entrance, she could see
the door bow in with each punch of his foot. *Bam!*
He'd break it down any second.

She covered her ears, the sound of the blows deaf-
ening.

On the floor in front of her, the contents of her purse
littered the tiles. She saw her cell phone, grabbed it
and punched in the number she'd memorized, her fingers shaking. *If you're ever in trouble.* She hit *Send*
as the door crashed open.

"Daniel, please—"

"I was trying to build something here. I was trying
to save this family!"

"You wouldn't stop." She tried not to cry, tried not
to be afraid. "You almost killed her with your stupid
stunt with the car."

"Killed her? Like I killed Nina? You have to stop
him—next time, he might kill her," he said in a high-
pitched voice. "Is that how we're playing this,
Emma?" He crouched down in front of her. "My
fault?"

"I couldn't get you to stop."

"Well, you've stopped me now, haven't you?" He
slapped her hard across the face. He grabbed her by
her arms and shook her. "What happened to the plan?
What happened to us, together, on top?"

"I'm sorry." She acted instinctively, trying to hug
him. To stop him. "I am so sorry. You're right, I
ruined—"

He pushed her away. "You're lying. And you're not
even good at it."

But suddenly, he fell back, losing his balance as if
struck by some realization. His eyes grew wide. "Jesus. That son of a bitch, Harris? Her brother?"

"No, Daniel."

"Jesus Christ." It was too much. The betrayal. "All of you. Nina…Holly."

He punched her hard, in the face.

"Every last one of you!"

But when he aimed to punch her again, she dove at him, tackling him. She scrambled over him, her legs tangling with his arms. She kicked her way free. She ripped off her jacket, threw it in his face as he ran after her.

In the hall he caught her by her hair, pulling her to the floor. He straddled her, his face a mask of hate. She knew this was the end. *Just like Nina.* Finally, she would get her due.

It was her last thought before he hit her, a crushing blow that made her head explode in pain before everything went black.

Ryan stepped on board the houseboat to find the phone ringing. He almost let it go, wanting to get back to Holly. He'd told her he had a few things to clear up at the vineyard and that she was to stay put. Her brother had given Ryan his assurances she'd do just that after he'd told Harris about their encounter with Daniel. Ryan wanted to get back to her as soon as possible. *Let the machine get it.*

But he had this feeling. It could be Holly. In trouble, trying to reach him.

He hurried over, feeling his pulse race, worried all over again because she wasn't standing right there in front of him to tell him she was okay. Maybe his cell phone wasn't working; maybe she'd lost the number. He picked up.

"Hello?"

"Ryan! Thank God. I've been calling and calling."

It was his father, sounding hysterical.

"What's the matter? What's going on?"

"It's Nina. Ryan, please. Help me. Nina is dead. I don't know what to do."

Ryan felt his knees buckle, dropping him to the couch. "Nina?"

"Please, Ryan. You have to help me. I really think she's dead this time."

It felt as if Ryan's heart stopped in his chest. He couldn't catch his breath. His father couldn't be talking about Nina. Nina was dead. She'd been dead twelve years.

Holly.

"Listen to me," he said. "What's happened to Holly?"

But Samuel just kept ranting about needing his help. That it was Nina who had died. He needed Ryan to come over.

"Where are you?" Ryan asked, thankful when his father managed an address. Pacific Heights. "Stay put. I'll be right there."

Racing to his car, his next call was on his cell to Holly. *You're too late. She's dead. He killed her—just like he killed Nina.*

But Holly picked up, her beautiful voice there on the other end, perfectly alive.

"Nothing's wrong," he told her, trying to calm down as he started the car and steered into the street. "Just don't go anywhere." And when she protested, telling him he didn't have to repeat those orders every five seconds, he said softly, "Yeah. I know. I'll be over soon. Okay?"

Nina is dead.

He remembered back to when his father had come on board to coax him to go to his mother's party. His father had talked about Nina in the present tense then, as if she were still alive. How strange he'd thought it sounded at the time.

Nina had been DOA at the hospital. There'd been a closed casket at the funeral. Because identification hadn't been an issue, there was no need to subject her family to the trauma of seeing her mangled body one last time.

He'd never actually seen the body, not after the paramedics took her away. But he couldn't believe she'd survived to somehow hide for twelve years. And have one last laugh on them all.

Nina is dead.

He picked up his phone again, punched in another number.

Whatever was going on, he believed one thing was true. His father wasn't hallucinating. Someone was dead.

32

Harris wanted to ignore the call, wanted to be pissed off enough that he could turn his back on Emma. He had Holly to think about, after all. Standing guard over his sister while Ryan got his act together had to be his first priority. That's what mattered to him, not Emma and her last-ditch call for help.

Only, he kept staring at her number displayed on his cell, knowing that he had given her his number for a reason—her escape hatch.

He punched Send, but it wasn't Emma whispering "hello" on the line. Instead, he heard her begging, arguing with Daniel, the fight between them going full steam. He figured she'd dropped the phone somewhere; their voices sounded distant and muffled. But Daniel's murderous rage came through loud and clear before the call cut out.

He's going to kill her. Which didn't give Harris much choice.

He left Holly at the apartment, taking the keys to her rental car, his sister assuring him that she'd spoken with Ryan and he was on his way over. He headed for Chinatown and Emma's apartment. At the same time, he called the cops to report a domestic disturbance at Daniel's place. He didn't know who would find them first, him or the police. He just knew he didn't have much time.

The whole trip there, he second-guessed himself. He should have sent the cops to Emma's, gone to Daniel's place himself. Coming up the stairwell, he started thinking Dan had her somewhere else altogether and he'd never get to her in time. *You guessed wrong!*

He hadn't expected Emma to be home, after all…hadn't expected to hear her screams for help out in the hall.

He kicked in the door, almost taking it off the hinges. He found her on the floor, her face a bloody mess, Daniel towering over her ready to give it another go.

Daniel turned, looking almost glassy-eyed at Harris, consumed by the job at hand. "What the hell?"

He never knew what hit him. Along with a few other talents, Harris knew how to incapacitate a man. Only, he didn't settle for making it easy. He had to admit it felt good, beating the crap out of the bastard.

He had Daniel on the living room floor, hog-tied with the guy's Gucci belt. He pushed him over with his foot, so that Daniel rolled onto his stomach, head down on the floor. It wouldn't do to have him choke on the blood oozing from his nose. Too bad about the stains on the carpet, though.

He found Emma still in the hallway. She'd made herself into a tiny ball, huddling there against the wall. He crouched down. He didn't know if he should touch her. She'd covered her face with her hands, as if she didn't want him to see her.

"Hey," he said, taking hands from her face. There was a cut on her cheek; the eye had pretty much swelled shut. Daniel had split her lip. The stud above her mouth had fallen out and she was bleeding enough that it dripped onto her shirt. *Shit.*

He helped her up, holding her so that she leaned on him. "Maybe we should get some ice on that?"

"I'm so sorry." She said it over and over as he guided her into the living room and helped her down onto the couch. "He found out I called the police."

"You're a piece of work, Emma." The guy was spitting mad, rabid in his hate. "After everything we've been through, are you going to tell him I killed Nina, too?" Daniel asked, his eyes bugging huge with rage. "Is that how this is going to play, Emma?"

"He killed Nina?" Harris asked.

"No." She shook her head, if possible, even more upset. "I did. I killed Nina."

The police arrived before Ryan, which he'd expected, having made the call. His father was sitting at the dining-room table covered in a blanket, talking to a police inspector. He stood the minute he saw Ryan.

There was blood everywhere. His father's hands were red with it.

Father looked at son. "She just came and killed her."

There was a body on the carpet, the face turned away from Ryan. Someone was taking photographs so that intermittent flashes lit up the room. He could see a dark stain like a halo where the woman's head lay against the plush carpet.

But it wasn't Nina lying there dead. The body was that of a different woman, someone he didn't recognize.

Even in the horror of the moment, he realized she didn't even look like Nina. She was shorter, blond and very young. Nina would have been thirty years old. The woman lying there couldn't be more than twenty.

But a wig had fallen off and lay next to her, and

her clothes were similar to what Nina would have worn. To his father, drunk and obsessed...yeah, maybe she looked like Nina.

"She killed her," his father said, still clearly in shock.

"Who killed her?" the inspector asked, seeing his chance.

"Vanessa." Samuel whispered the word like a dark secret. He turned to Ryan. "Your mother. I was leaving her, you see. We had a terrible argument. She said I would humiliate her, take what little dignity she had left. She must have followed me here. I didn't know."

Ryan caught his breath, his heart speeding up. "Mom did this?"

"She had a gun. Foster's gun, I think. She must have guessed that I was leaving her for Nina, that I couldn't wait anymore." He was crying now, so that the words hardly made sense. "I didn't even know she was here. One of the neighbors must have buzzed her in. There wasn't any warning. She just came through the door and killed her."

Ryan tried to imagine his mother hitting some wall inside herself, realizing that his father was living a fantasy of Nina reborn. How degrading it would be, finding Samuel with this new Nina. It would be the last straw in a long life of last straws, and the poor woman playing out their charade had been caught in the crossfire.

"I don't know how she found out—we were so careful. She said Nina needed to stay dead. And now, she'll kill the other one," his father said, touching Ryan's elbow.

Ryan felt the words jerk him awake from the horror around him. "The other one?"

His father nodded. "The one who looks like Nina. The architect. She'll kill her, too."

Holly stepped into Cutty House. "Hello?"

Something wasn't right. Holly had gotten the call to come here and she'd found the door open, but the place looked abandoned.

"Hello?"

The phone call had come after Harris's sudden departure. She'd thought it would be Daniel, calling to make more threats. She'd braced herself, planning to tell him just what he could do with himself, the rat.

But it hadn't been Daniel. Vanessa's voice had come over the line, telling Holly she needed her help. She wanted to meet here, at Cutty House. Even on the phone, she'd sounded desperate and afraid so that Holly had scribbled a quick note and left it on the kitchen table for Ryan. She'd practically run the whole way.

"Vanessa?"

"Upstairs."

Holly followed the sound of the voice and found Vanessa standing on the landing on the second floor. Holly waved, giving what she hoped was a reassuring smile, but Vanessa only glanced at her before continuing to the next floor.

Holly frowned. "Vanessa?" she called out, continuing to follow her up the stairs.

The lights were off, but she could see Ryan's mother climbing ahead of her. Every so often, Vanessa turned to look at Holly, as though checking to see if she was still there.

"Okay," Holly said, speeding up.

On the third floor, there was only one room with the light on—the room where she'd first seen Nina's portrait. Her heart hammered against her chest as she reached the door. Vanessa had sounded strange on the phone; Holly had rushed here, worried. Suddenly, she wished she hadn't been in such a hurry. She'd left her cell phone out in the car, plugged into the recharger.

Holly knocked, then pushed the door open, stepping into the room. ''Vanessa?''

She could see Vanessa had been a busy girl. The sheets that had once covered the furniture and paintings were now folded in a neat pile. She'd rearranged the furniture.

''I'm right here.'' Vanessa said, standing before a small painting on the far wall. ''Thank you for coming.''

Vanessa turned. For the first time Holly noticed that Vanessa had something in her hand. It took Holly a second to realize it was a gun.

''Why don't you have a seat?'' Vanessa gestured toward the fireplace where two wing-backed chairs waited by the hearth.

She spoke the words as if she were hosting another party. Holly felt the breath seize up inside her lungs. She'd never seen a gun this close, and never had one trained right on her.

''I don't understand,'' Holly said, staying put.

''I know. That's why I needed to talk to you. To explain everything. Please, sit down.''

Holly felt her heart leap to her throat. Vanessa's eyes were red and swollen. Holly could see she'd been crying.

''Vanessa?'' She stepped toward her....

Vanessa fired the gun so that the bullet whizzed past into the wall behind Holly. The woman seemed to rally, standing straighter.

"Sit…the fuck…down," she told Holly, pointing to the chair in front of the fireplace.

Holly did what she was told. She could see that Vanessa was shaking as she came to sit in the chair opposite her.

"I had a phone call this morning." She straightened her skirt and laid the gun across her lap. "Very early. It was Daniel." She shook her head, fighting some strong emotion. "He told me—"

The tight control snapped. She couldn't seem to choke out the words. She shook her head. "It's too late," she whimpered. "Too late." Making no sense at all.

Holly waited, her hands gripping the chair. "You said you needed my help? I'm here now. I want to help."

Vanessa put both hands on the gun, almost as if checking to see it was still there. "I did what I was supposed to do, you see. I gave everything up for my husband." She was talking to herself, almost as if Holly wasn't there. "That's what a wife does. He wanted his dream and I made sure my father paid for it. With his life, as it turned out."

Vanessa stared across the room at the paintings now hanging on the walls. She stopped when her gaze reached Nina's portrait.

"You look so much like her," she whispered. "That's the mistake I made."

"I'm not anything like Nina," Holly said, trying to assuage a mother's fears, hoping she understood. "I love him. With all my heart. I won't ever hurt him."

Vanessa looked at her, seeming to judge the truth of her words. Suddenly, she pressed her fist to her eyes, shaking her head. She took a deep breath, her hands returning to the gun on her lap. "I went to see

Ryan on his boat. We'd spoken earlier, but the meeting hadn't gone at all well. I wanted to talk to him again, to tell him that he couldn't just keep turning me away. I wanted him to understand what I was doing, putting Daniel in charge. I saw you walk out on the deck—''

She shook her head again, suddenly looking beyond all hope, then she raised her gaze to meet Holly's. "I watched you talking to him. I waited in the car. When you left, I followed you here, to Cutty House. I couldn't believe you would come here.''

Holly remembered that night, how she'd broken in using Ryan's special technique. A push at the door, the jiggle of the knob.

"Ryan showed me Nina's portrait," she told Vanessa, explaining. "I wanted to come back and see it for myself.''

"I didn't plan it. I was just so angry, seeing you here." Her lips twisted, trying to hold back the flood of emotion. "So I used lipstick." She spoke in a weeping rush. "Childish and stupid.''

Holly remembered the message scrawled on the window in red. *Go home!*

"I fell through the floor that night," Holly said.

"Childish and stupid." Vanessa spoke as if she couldn't believe she'd done such things. She took a deep breath, her hand once more settling on the gun. "And then I decided that I needed to be more clever.''

"You put the invitation on my desk," Holly said, piecing it together.

"I always thought Gil sent them, all those invitations for the vineyard functions. Salt on the wound. But Ryan told me quite recently, he'd sent them. My darling boy, trying to make a gesture. And I was so bitter, I never guessed. I would take scissors to them,'' she told Holly. "I'd cut them into these tiny, tiny pieces. But this one, I kept. Because by then, I knew Ryan had sent it. I forged his signature and dropped it on your desk. I wanted to hurt Gil. He took my son. He stole my happiness."

"You put those crime reports on my desk," Holly continued, seeing how the pieces fit.

Vanessa nodded, catching her breath. "I had a friend in the district attorney's office who helped me to get the charges dropped against Ryan. He gave me a copy of the file. I don't know why, but I kept everything. I doctored some of the pages to make it look like he was guilty. I wanted to scare you away, but I couldn't. You just wouldn't leave."

With every admission, Vanessa seemed to collapse a little more. Holly was half afraid of where her confessions might lead them. "That's all behind us now," she said, trying to think of some way to get the gun. "He'll forgive you. I know he will—"

"No. No, he can't. He won't. I drove him away a long time ago. And now, he'll never forgive me. Because I put you in that car ride at the party."

The admission stunned Holly. She thought it had been Daniel. She'd been so sure.

"I just wanted you to be scared," she told Holly. "I thought I was helping him, protecting him from you, another Nina. I thought you wouldn't stay after that, that you wouldn't want to play the ghost of Nina. And once the papers got hold of the story, Ryan would understand. He couldn't live in the past, repeating his mistakes."

"I'm not a mistake." Holly had to make her understand. "I'm not Nina Travers."

"You're right, of course," she said. "Isn't it ironic, how twisted life can be? I thought I was helping him," she repeated. "But I became the nightmare instead of you."

"Vanessa. You don't want to do this. Please. Give me the gun."

She whispered, "Too late." She spoke with a sadness that seemed to sink her deeper into the chair.

When she raised her head again, her eyes stayed on the gun and not Holly. "I just wanted you to understand, to tell Ryan. Nina came to me that night. She told me she was carrying Samuel's child and that he would…divorce me. She would take my place and they would raise their child. Oust me and Ryan both." She looked around. "I kept this place alive for him, and he was going to throw me out?"

"He couldn't do that," Holly said, trying now to keep her talking. Her best chance was that Ryan or Harris would come home, read the note on the kitchen table and come here looking for her.

"This…place…cost me *everything*." Her anger was coming through, the last word a cry of frustration. "Always losing money. More money, he'd say. Every time I turned around, he had his hand out."

Vanessa was staring at the gun, her fingers around the grip. Her words filled the room, crowding it with ghosts.

"If I'd had the courage," she told Holly, "I would have killed Nina then. That night. But I couldn't think that way in those days. After she died, I thought it was providence, God's hand at work. The girl was evil. She couldn't be allowed to hurt us anymore."

Slowly, she hunched over the gun, holding it against her stomach. Holly realized she was crying quietly so that, bent over the gun, she reminded Holly of those Japanese warriors preparing to commit hara-kiri.

"I thought she was dead," she said, the words

barely audible. "But then Daniel phoned this morning and I was so furious. I wasn't thinking clearly. What he told me— I thought, please, God, not again. I was going to put a stop to it, you see? I took the gun only to make Samuel understand. He couldn't keep doing this to me, couldn't keep hurting me."

Holly said, "Let me call Ryan. Please, he should be here."

"I can't let him see me like this." She brushed the tears from her eyes, catching her breath. "His mother." She held up the gun. "With his grandfather's gun."

She was pointing the gun at Holly. Realizing what she was doing, she immediately dropped her hand back into her lap. "No. Oh, dear, no. I didn't mean—"

Vanessa shook her head. She covered her mouth with her hand, pressing it there as if to keep all that emotion from spilling out. She stared at Holly, her eyes wide.

"I killed her," she said. "That poor woman. I saw her with him, and I saw Nina. I wanted it to be Nina. God help me, I wanted it to be her."

33

Harris stood in the hall of Emma's apartment, catching his breath. He'd locked Daniel in one of the bedrooms, but had refrained from calling the cops. There would be plenty of time for that later, after he had Emma settled. Not that there was much the police could do about what had happened here tonight. Domestic disturbance—his word against Daniel's. But hell, he'd give it a roll. Only now, he had this other thing on his mind: Emma, admitting she'd killed Nina.

He came back to Emma. She was seated on the couch, staring into space, one eye swollen shut. Her hand on her lap held a bag of frozen peas as if she didn't feel the cold. He knelt down in front of her, then picked up the peas he'd taken from the refrigerator earlier and put the bag against her cheek, holding it there.

"Do you want me to call someone?" he asked. "Maybe take you to a doctor?"

She shook her head, winced.

"Careful with that," he told her.

She gave a small smile. "Sure. Like I deserve any better?"

"Self-flagellation. I like that," he said, going with it. "Because you're some big deranged killer now." He touched her hand. "Come on, Emma. What were you? All of fourteen?"

She didn't take her eyes off him, clear-eyed in her confession. "I'm not a kid anymore, Harris. I grew up a long time ago. But I kept that secret. And I let Ryan take the blame."

She looked down at her hands, suddenly realizing Harris was holding the peas. She took the bag from him, held it to her cheek and eye.

She sighed, the sound coming from somewhere deep. "I would tell myself, it's not like he's in jail, Ems. They dropped the charges, right? And he seemed happy enough at the vineyard, helping Gil and Marta. Then other times I'd think I drove him away from his home and family. He was in exile and it was my fault because I didn't have the courage to just admit what had really happened that night."

She was holding on to the bag of peas for all she was worth. He'd made her take a couple of aspirins earlier, but he figured the real pain hadn't hit yet, that she was still in a state of shock.

"So tell me now," he said gently. "What really happened that night."

"Daniel—but not in the way you think," she said, again giving him a tired smile. "I had this...mad crush on him the whole time I was growing up. I used to follow him around when he was at work. He had no idea, of course. That's how I found out about him and Nina. That he was seeing her. That he was—in love. Though now I wonder if she wasn't just part of his great race to become Ryan. The competition thing. I was only fourteen, but I knew Nina was bad. For him...for anyone. Only, I had to make sure, you know? Gather my evidence so I could tell Daniel what a mistake he was making. So I started following her, too."

She dropped the bag of peas back in her lap, the effort of trying to get better just too much.

"The party was at Moore Manor," she continued. "My father still worked for the family and I was helping him. I overheard Nina arguing with Ryan. They were having a full-out screaming match in one of the parlors. That's when I found out she'd been sleeping with Ryan's father. I hadn't known about Samuel. She told Ryan she was pregnant. That the baby was his father's." She shrugged. "She'd told Daniel the baby was his."

"She was a real piece of work."

"That's what I thought," she said. She moved the peas to the cushion beside her and rubbed her hands together as if suddenly feeling cold. "I couldn't imagine her lying about the baby to Daniel, though later, after the autopsy, Daniel claimed the baby was his. At least, that's what he told me. At the time, I didn't want her to get away with it, using Daniel. So I made up my mind to confront her. She couldn't treat Daniel like that. He was fragile, and she was going to break him."

"You wanted to protect him?"

"You have no idea. It was all I could think about back then. I couldn't keep my father from drinking himself into the grave, but Daniel, I could help. Yeah, I wanted to make sure he was okay. So I waited by her car. I wanted to catch her before she left. But when I saw her, I wasn't so sure that was a good idea. She was crying real hard, like when you can't catch your breath. Crying and drunk, mascara running down her face like some badass clown. She took one look at me and told me to get in the car. When I hesitated, she said she was in a hurry."

"When did Ryan show up?"

"After we pulled out. He came running, screaming

for her not to be stupid. She was in no condition to drive. I hid down in the seat, afraid he'd see me. I wasn't really supposed to be there. I kept thinking how mad Daniel would be if he found out. That he wouldn't like me anymore.''

She pressed her hands together. Harris didn't need to read her body language to know she was telling the truth, reliving the nightmare that had brought her here, beaten up by the man she loved.

''We drove for a long time. At first, she was really upset. She said she'd done something terrible and that Ryan would never forgive her. The thing with Daniel, sure. That Ryan would forgive. Hell, the guy had practically begged her, he wanted a piece of her so bad. It hadn't been her idea. That's the way she talked, real crude. But Samuel. She was crying when she talked about him. How she knew Ryan would never forgive the thing with his father.''

''No kidding.''

But Emma looked up. ''She said it was a mistake, that she'd been drinking, completely out of it.'' Here she stopped, taking her time, dropping the bombshell. ''She told me she'd thought he was Ryan. They looked a lot alike back then. So it was just this terrible mistake. It was the first time I thought maybe she did love Ryan because she was that upset. Like she wished she could take it back, you know? But Samuel wouldn't let it go. He kept hounding her, just like Daniel, so that she was afraid he'd tell Ryan if she didn't just keep sleeping with him. And then she found out she was pregnant.''

''Jesus.''

She nodded. ''Yeah. She was in an awful mess. But I didn't see it that way. Not back then.''

''And Ryan? Where was he?''

"By now he was following us in his car, though it took him a bit to catch up. When she saw him in the rearview mirror, she really floored it, like they were street racing or something. I was scared, but I was determined, too. I wanted to have my say before it all came to an end. I told her what I thought of her, of what she was doing to Daniel. But she just laughed. And she wasn't crying anymore. Instead, she looked kind of excited by the racing and by the fact that Ryan had followed her. Like maybe he still cared?"

And there was Emma, Harris thought, all of fourteen and stuck in a car with a woman who was completely unbalanced, racing through the streets.

"How did the accident happen?" He didn't believe for one minute that Emma had killed Nina.

"She started talking to me, saying she'd seen me watching her with Daniel. She said all these horrible things about how when I grew some tits, maybe Daniel would ball me, too, and she could finally get him off her back. She said it like that. Trying to shock me. Doing a good job of it, too. Then she started swerving in and out of the lane. It was late, no traffic. But I was so scared. And Nina, she just fed off of that fear, laughing when I started screaming for her to stop."

"She lost control of the car?"

Emma shook her head. "I grabbed the wheel. I don't even know what I thought I could do. I just wanted her to stop. Whatever it took, I wanted it all to be over. I was so scared." She took a deep breath. "I jerked the wheel straight toward the edge and jumped out."

He came to sit beside her, taking her hand. "That's not murder, Emma. That's called survival."

But she was shaking her head. "I wanted her to stop." She looked straight at him, making sure he understood. "Not just the car, Harris. I wanted her to stop everything she was doing to the family."

And in that instant, at the age of fourteen, she'd made her choice.

He gave it a minute, letting the idea that she'd wanted Nina dead, or had convinced herself she did, sink in. "Ryan never saw you?"

She shook her head. "I must have blacked out. I just remember waking up on the ground, hidden by the fog. By then, Ryan had already pulled up. He was screaming Nina's name, climbing down the embankment to where the car had gone over the guardrail."

Harris tried to imagine what it must have been like for her, jumping from the car, blacking out. She'd woken up and realized what happened. And, of course, she'd run.

She could see what he was thinking. "Yeah, I ran away. It felt like forever before I managed a ride into town, hitchhiking. I went looking for Daniel. By then, he'd already heard about the accident, heard that Nina had died at the hospital. I was going to tell him the truth, but when I saw him, saw how upset he was, I knew I didn't want to be the one responsible for that much pain. So there I was, trying to admit what I'd done, trying to find the words. And when I couldn't, Daniel stepped in and pieced it together for me. The car going over, Ryan following us. He told me Ryan must have done it, forcing her off the road. He made me call the police and tell them just that."

Of course, she went along with it. Daniel would make sure of that.

"The next morning," she said, "I realized what I'd done. I went immediately to Daniel. I told him that he'd misunderstood. It was my fault. I fought Nina for the wheel. I caused the car to go over, not Ryan." She was shaking her head, the tears coming. "But he wouldn't listen. He kept saying I was wrong. And when I insisted, he completely freaked out. He told me that if he really believed I had killed Nina, he didn't know what he'd do."

"He was warning you not to mess up his story."

She nodded. "He had his own agenda by then. And when we started sleeping together, that was pretty much the end of that."

A way to control her, so she'd keep to the story. If you love me, you won't tell...

"I don't know when I started to think like Daniel," she told him. "That maybe Ryan leaving the family was his own doing. Nobody forced him, right? And when Vanessa asked Daniel to step in, take over the family business, I almost thought..."

"That you'd done the right thing by keeping quiet? Because it helped Daniel."

She looked at him, those eyes suddenly seeming too old for her sweet face. Come morning, she'd have one hell of a black eye. He'd already stopped the bleeding from the split lip. He picked up the peas and placed them back on her face, but she took his hand away.

"It's part of what kept me here," she said. "That awful secret we shared. I tried to get away a couple of times—starting the catering business with Beth—but Daniel always found me. Always brought me back."

"And now?" He squeezed her hand. "What do you want to do now? Do you want me to keep your secret?" Because he would, if that's the way she wanted to play it.

But Emma shook her head. Letting go of his hand, she stood and walked to the phone. She punched in a number.

The police, Harris figured, coming to stand beside her. It's what he would have done.

That one last step to redemption was always the hardest.

Vanessa stared at the gun in her hand. She was seated in one of the wing-backed chairs by the fire-place at Cutty House, but in her mind she was back at the apartment where she'd followed Samuel.

She could see that poor woman falling in slow motion, like some horrible movie, the wig blown off now, along with half the woman's face.

"Vanessa?"

Holly was kneeling beside her chair. She'd placed a hand on Vanessa's arm. Vanessa looked down at her, seeing Nina—not seeing Nina.

"That's where I made my mistake," she told Holly. "I wanted her to be Nina." Nina, who had stolen from her—her son, her husband. "I came only to threaten Samuel. But then I saw him with that woman."

She was looking at Holly. For the first time, she realized her eyes were wide and brown, nothing like Nina's, really.

"We had a fight that morning," she said, needing to document every step. "I knew he was having an affair." Of course, she'd known. But after Daniel's call, it had all seemed so much worse and hurtful. She'd felt in agony, remembering the past. "I found Foster's gun and I followed him. I was thinking, he can't do this to me. Not again." She shook her head in disbelief. "Then I saw the name N. Travers on the buzzer, on the nameplate."

That's how far Samuel had taken his fantasy. He'd put the girl in an apartment under Nina's name. He'd made her wear a wig.

"I couldn't catch my breath when I read that name. I had one of the neighbors buzz me in. A delivery, I said. They hadn't locked the door. In too much of a hurry, I suppose. I just stepped right in and found them together. And I killed her. I killed Nina.'' She looked at Holly, letting her know the horrible truth. "But it wasn't Nina.''

"Vanessa—''

The older woman stood, surprised when her feet actually held her up. She pushed her shoulders back, the matriarch once more. "I want you to tell Ryan. I want him to know the truth. And that's all I needed to say to you, really. I'm going to call the police now. I would appreciate it if you could leave.'' Suddenly she sounded so in control that she almost laughed.

In control? *I just killed someone!*

"I think I should stay,'' Holly said.

"Please, I need to do this on my own terms.''

But she could see that the girl suspected something. In the end, Vanessa had to push her out. On the landing, she pointed the gun at Holly, her hand shaking.

"You need to leave,'' she said. "Leave now.'' And then, some strange instinct taking over, she added, "Take care of my son.''

She watched Holly back away. She waited, hearing her feet running down the steps.

Vanessa knew she wouldn't have much time. She walked back into the room, shutting the door tight behind her. She knew what she had to do. She was ready. At the hearth, she took the gas key she'd found on the mantel earlier. She turned on the gas, but didn't light the flame. She wondered how long it would take.

She stepped over to the window, making sure it was shut. The fog wasn't too bad tonight. She could see

Holly running out of the house, across the lawn. Just then a car drove up. Ryan.

She watched as they ran into each other's arms. She wondered if it was possible that they could be happy together. She was starting to feel light-headed from the gas and knew it wouldn't be much longer.

Vanessa stepped in front of the portrait of Nina and raised the gun to her temple.

"You win, Nina," she said.

The first person Holly saw was Ryan, miraculously driving up as she punched his number into her cell phone. Her own little cavalry.

She dropped the phone onto the seat of the car and ran toward him. She flung her arms around him, holding tight.

"I went to the apartment first," he said. "I found the note."

"Ryan, your mother—"

"I know. I just left my father. She killed his mistress."

"I left her upstairs. She forced me to go. She wanted to be alone when she called the police to turn herself in. She had a gun."

"Christ, Holly. Are you all right?"

She nodded, stepping back. "She wasn't going to hurt me. She just wanted to tell me—"

And then she realized what it was that Vanessa Moore wanted to tell her. She glanced up at the house, seeing Ryan's mother there silhouetted in the window. *Take care of my son.*

"Oh, my God," she said. She pushed Ryan away. She started running for the house, Ryan running with her.

They hadn't even reached the gate when the house exploded, pushing them back into the night.

34

Emma sat directly across the glass from Daniel. She picked up the phone, the only method of communication in the county jail.

"I'm keeping a seat warm for you," he said into his handset, because today, it was Emma on the outside.

She'd been meeting with the district attorney about Nina's death. They weren't certain about the charges. The lawyer she'd hired was asking for negligent homicide. She'd been a minor, and it would be hard to prove she'd intended to kill Nina under the circumstances. Any jury would be sympathetic. And she was cooperating.

"You think you're so clever," he said, leaning toward the glass. "Putting me in here?"

She wondered what he saw when he looked at her. Did he see past the dark glasses to the black eye beneath? The swollen cheek and split lip?

"I talked to Holly," she said. "She told me something interesting, that you called Vanessa the morning she followed Samuel to that girl's apartment."

The smile on his face was fairly beaming with pride. "That's right. I did talk to her that day," he said, as if he'd just remembered.

"Vanessa didn't tell Holly why you'd called, but I think I know."

Because she knew Daniel, knew how he worked. He'd just found out that Holly was leaving with Ryan. She'd quit. He'd be sulking, wondering what to do, watching his dreams slip away.

She told him, "I think you knew about that woman Samuel was seeing. Maybe that's even how you got the idea to bring Holly on board when you saw her picture in that magazine. You knew how it was driving Samuel crazy, having Nina back in his life."

Yeah, she could see Daniel putting his plans for Ryan together. By then the renovation was going to shit. He'd realized that his dream of Cutty House being resurrected was just that—a dream. So why not get even? Why not find his own Nina to torment Ryan, just like Samuel.

"So you called Vanessa and let her know about the new Nina in her husband's life. Maybe you twisted it around a little, pushing her to that edge. The past repeating itself. You knew she was vulnerable. Isn't that the way you like to do things, Dan? Working behind the scenes?"

"Come on, honey. How could I possibly know that she would kill herself?" He leaned forward, whispering into the phone. "But wasn't it lovely that she did. Though, honestly, I was hoping she'd shoot Uncle Samuel and not the girl." He leaned back, a wicked smile on his face. "You see, darling, I'm not completely heartless."

For twelve years she'd loved this man. She wondered if it was possible to love and hate someone at the same time.

"When I get out of here, I'll find you," he told her. "You know that, don't you? You're not getting away from me."

But it was her turn to smile. It's what she'd planned,

her own form of penance. To be Daniel's new obsession. Now he'd leave Ryan and Holly alone.

"Somehow, Dan—" she put her palm against the glass, bidding him goodbye "—I'm not too worried about it."

She left, having had her say. Soon enough he'd be out of jail for assault and battery, the only charges that would stick. She knew he'd come after her then, because that's who Daniel was, a man who never faced up to what he'd done, never took responsibility. He'd be searching for the next person to blame, a pattern that wasn't changing.

But Emma, she was moving on.

Ryan walked through the rubble of what had once been Cutty House. It was one of those blinding bright days rare for the city. Holly stood back, giving him the time and space he might need.

The funeral service had been Monday. For Holly, the service had seemed surreal. The minister's eulogy and the many charity organizations who spoke of Vanessa presented the image of a woman very different from the one she'd come to know.

Ryan spoke, as well, but said little. He'd loved his mother. He would miss her.

There'd been no mention of murder or suicide. That wasn't the woman they wanted to remember.

In the last weeks he'd been responsible for taking care of all the arrangements concerning his family. His father had entered a rehabilitation home called Reflections. Interestingly enough, it had been Gil and Marta who helped Ryan through most of the difficult preparations. As Gil had said, Ryan sold him short. These days, he was a stronger man.

She'd been astonished to hear her brother confess

about his involvement with Emma. She'd been even more astounded to discover it had been a fourteen-year-old Emma who had taken that ride with Nina, eventually causing the accident that took her life. Now Emma was taking all the blame.

But Ryan saw things a little differently. He knew Nina had been out of control that night, going for one last high. And she'd taken it too far.

To Harris's great disappointment, Emma was leaving town. She'd pleaded guilty to negligent homicide, but the judge had granted a suspended sentence, citing "extraordinary circumstances." Case closed.

"Emma told me that, no matter what I thought now," Harris had said to Holly, "I couldn't forgive her for putting you in danger. And maybe she's right. It wouldn't have worked out between us."

So he was back at the bar. But she saw a new darkness in him, one she'd never seen before, not even when he'd shown up on her doorstep fired from his job.

He loved Emma. He'd wanted a chance to make it work. But he wasn't going after her. Not Harris. He'd let this chapter, like so many others in his life, simply close. Which made Holly terribly sad. She didn't think life should be about giving up, making do, trying desperately not to get hurt again.

Holly turned back to Ryan. She had her own fears, of course. What if one day the electric excitement that defined how they'd come together should fade. They'd been forced on this roller-coaster ride, but could it really end in love ever after? What would happen when Ryan discovered she didn't cook? That what she enjoyed most was watching a video with popcorn or a lazy day sleeping in? And she wrote everything down on these tiny pieces of paper that she always,

always lost. What would become of them once the adventure waned and the annoying habits of life were revealed?

She watched Ryan bend down and pick up something. She couldn't see what he held in his hand, but he tossed it aside soon enough. When he turned to look at her, he smiled—and she felt it all the way down to her toes.

Holly smiled back, suddenly getting a burst of that infallible intuition. Everything was going to be okay, because she couldn't imagine not loving this man more every day. Ryan had her heart and she had his.

Slowly, he came walking toward her, the sun streaming down on him. She tried to find some of the darkness she'd seen the first time they'd met—a man dressed in black, with an enigmatic expression that kept others at bay—but the shadows had all but disappeared.

She wondered if the same thing had happened to her, if somehow the last weeks had changed her to the point where it became a physical difference. How she held herself, the expression on her face. Just yesterday Harris had commented, "Uh-oh. Someone's in love."

She smiled, liking the idea that if she looked in the mirror she'd see some of what was so clear in Ryan's face when he looked at her.

"So," she told him, slipping her hand into his as he reached her. "What's next, bucko?"

He kept his eyes on the horizon. "You move in with me. In time, you get over your I-once-married-a-loser phobia and we get married, build a place at the vineyard."

Another interesting self-discovery. All this time, Ryan thought he'd been tied down to Viña Dorada, hiding there. But instead, he'd found something of his own, something he was proud of, and a place from which he no longer wanted to run away.

"I figure," he continued, "we should have at least three kids, but I'm open to debate on the actual number. Just not one." He was still staring at the horizon. "Too lonely."

She had to smile, thinking she'd been right with that intuition. "You know, when I asked, 'What's next?' I kind of meant, did you want to get some lunch? Maybe grab a couple of sandwiches and go to the park?"

"I know what you meant," he said, putting his arm around her.

He guided her back to the car, turning his back on what had once been Cutty House. At the curb, he held the door open for her, a gentleman to the last.

But Holly wasn't through with him. "You know what I really want?" she asked, strapping on her seat belt. This car was a little too sporty for her taste and the streets here weren't getting any straighter.

"I can't imagine."

She smiled, thinking about it. "I want to go sailing. What did you call it, running with the wind? Come on, buddy. You're taking me sailing."

He grinned, shifting into gear. "A woman after my own heart."

LAURIE BRETON

FINAL EXIT

Published 20th February 2004

M360

MEG O'BRIEN

Mary Beth has come a long way
from her troubled past...until she
finds herself in the middle of a
murder investigation.

SHADOW OF INNOCENCE

Somebody has a secret

Published 19th March 2004

Published 20th February 2004

CHRISTIANE
HEGGAN

DEADLY
INTENT

SILENCE
CAN BE
BOUGHT...
FOR A
PRICE

M358

Published 16th April 2004

M368

TERROR LURKS
IN THE DARKNESS
OF HER MEMORY. . .

SHARON SALA

OUT OF THE DARK

HE KNOWS

MORE THAN

ANY INNOCENT

MAN SHOULD

Gabriel Donner has awakened from a coma to discover he has lost his parents in a car accident…and
now he's afraid he is losing his sanity. Gabriel can't
stop hearing voices crying for help, and starts to
sleepwalk, with visions of a local serial killer. He
finds help with Laura Dane, a psychic and criminal
profiler. She's willing to lay her reputation on the
line for Gabriel…until she 'sees' Gabriel with his
hands closing around her neck.

SHARON
SALA

REUNION

MIRA®

Published 16th April 2004

Tess GERRITSEN

"Tess Gerritsen writes some of the smartest, most compelling thrillers around."
Bookreporter

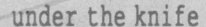

under the knife

Had she condemned her patient to die?
Or was it murder?

M361